A KINGDOM OF SALT AND STONE

LIV WEBSTER

A Kingdom of Salt and Stone

Cover design by @Designwithlaylaanddaniel

Editing by English Proper Editing Services

Interior Design and Formatting by Liv Webster

First Edition

Library of Congress Control Number: 2025920147

ISBN: 979-8-9998889-0-7 (Paperback)

ISBN: 979-8-999-8889-1-4 (Digital)

Independently published by Liv Webster

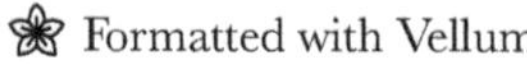

To anyone who has ever felt like anxiety ruled their life—this one is for you

CONTENT WARNINGS

This book contains heavy themes of mental health—such as but not limited to—anxiety, panic attacks, Post-traumatic Stress Disorder, trauma, Obsessive Compulsive Disorder, eating disorders, and mild suicidal ideation. In addition, this book includes graphic sexual content, gore, and curse words.

The Prilarean Empir

Livalafy Lake

Livalafy Lagoon

Warcrey River

Unclaimed Territory

The Kingdom of Mealioria

Marcilsa River

Southern Sea

CHAPTER ONE

"Do you think it hurts?" I asked, not waiting for a response before I captured a breath and let my body sink beneath the ocean's surface. Waves rippled over me, my weight levitating from the salt as the force of the sea flooded over my skin. I embraced the tranquility, allowing the liquid to cool my core and staying put until I had released all the life from my lungs.

When air was required, I breached back through the surface and slid my palms over my face, distributing the sea-salted water. "Being gifted by the gods," I clarified, noting the look of confusion on my sister's face.

Delani's eyes lit up in understanding. "I hardly think you need to worry about that." She flipped her hair out of her eyes, misting me with droplets that fluttered from her curls.

"You never know. I could get lucky," I said, though I knew that this *gift* was nothing to call lucky—at least not if you asked me.

"Maeve Willawood, you know damn well you won't get lucky. No one in our family has ever been gifted by the gods, what makes you think that you would be any different?" Delani shot back, half joking but half serious.

"Harsh." I flashed her an artificial frown.

She smirked. “I'm just saying.” Her shoulders shrugged, and I didn't deny that she was right.

I inhaled deeply, securing the air tightly within my chest before dipping under another passing wave. The chosen tended to follow through bloodlines, but not always. Even though it didn't come as a surprise, Delani was incredibly disappointed on her birthday two years ago to find that she wasn't gifted.

When my lungs began to burn, I reemerged, breathing in salty air as I wiped my dripping eyelashes. I took in another deep breath, blowing it out slowly and leaning back to float on the water's surface. The scents of the sea reached my nostrils with each inhale, reminding me how blessed I was to live so close to the coastline.

My family's village, Vicrallo, resided within the Kingdom of Caelestis and was just a short walk from the shore. For me, any time spent on the beach was enjoyable, but it was even more appreciated this time of year with the scorching heat of summer. Most days after I had finished my assignments at the village archives, I made my way here to revive myself in the ocean. It was the only place I ever felt truly serene.

I let my feet sink back down, mounting me into the thick, saturated sand. "Hypothetically, though, do you think it hurts?"

Delani swam towards me, paddling through the waves until she was close enough for me to make out the golden specks in her eyes, illuminated by the rays of the setting sun. She never failed to look beautiful, even now with her hair coated in sand, the strands twisted and matted against her neck. We mostly looked alike, apart from my curves and the streaks of sun-kissed blonde that had taken up permanent residence in my hair.

Our mother always told us how much we looked like our father. According to her, he was the reason behind our wavy, brown hair and lightly freckled cheeks. She claimed that he gave me his eyes—similar to Delani’s, aside from mine having flecks of green throughout.

“Yeah, Maeve, I would imagine a jewel that’s been burrowed inside of you ever since you were conceived would hurt when it tears through layers of nerve, muscle, and flesh," Delani retorted, sarcasm spilling from her plump lips.

Water flew as I splashed her in revulsion, scowling at her answer. "You're sick," I grimaced.

With a laugh, she ducked then waded away. I went after her, cutting through the waves to make my way back to the shore. The sand burned the delicate skin between my toes as my feet touched down on the earth. My wrinkled fingers twisted the seawater out of my hair, then I dropped to my knees to drink from my canteen.

My eyes drifted over the horizon, following the rise and fall of the waves. This piece of coastline has always been my favorite beach in Caelestis. The water was practically clear, and when the sun hit it just right, you could see the iridescent scales of fish that swam close to the shore. The ivory sand, coated in the disregarded homes of sea life, felt soft between my fingers as I picked up a pastel shell and rolled the shard between my fingers.

"Want to walk?" Delani asked from somewhere behind me.

I nodded my response, then scrambled to my feet and followed the footsteps she left in the sand.

We walked about halfway down the shore, stopping where the rocky area began. If you could make it past the boulders, the sand continued along the entire coast and surpassed the castle. I didn't dare lift my gaze upwards. If I did, I would see the very tip of a stone tower belonging to the focal point of our kingdom.

The castle, where King Aldous Hawthorne ruled, sat upon the highest peak in Caelestis, overlooking the wide range of terrain that our kingdom had to offer. From vast mountain ranges to deep, ever-green forests and beaches, the northern territory had it all. Good thing, too—most of us weren't allowed to leave the purview of the kingdom unless required by our profession or school. Of course there were some exceptions to the rule, but commoners rarely were granted them.

I poked at a starfish stuck to one of the boulders. One of its arms curled around my finger, its tiny suction cups gripping my skin. Despite my best efforts, when the sea star released me, my intrusive thoughts won and I raised my gaze.

My eyes rolled up the cliffside, responsible for taming the rampant surges of the tide from reaching the fortress. My vision locked onto the only portion of the castle that I could see from here, and the sight of the distant tower sent shivers scattering down my spine. An unwelcome feeling crackled within my bones as the stonework reminded me of the Jewel-Light Festival tomorrow.

Occurring at the midway point of the year, the Jewel-Light Meteor Shower was the kingdom's most anticipated event. I usually enjoyed attending the annual celebration of our gods and the gifted. This year, however, I dreaded witnessing the exquisite array of colored cosmos. There was more on my mind than simply stargazing.

In an attempt to distract myself from the angst swelling in my brain matter, I kicked a stone with my bare foot. It went flying through the air, landing with a splash in the ocean.

Delani glanced over at me—she knew me well enough to know that something was bothering me. "Why are you so sulky?" she asked, her attitude shining through in her tone.

I ignored her, taking one last glance at the castle before turning on my heel and starting back the way we came.

She trailed behind me. "Hello?"

"Why do you think?" I sighed. There was no way she had already forgotten about our conversation in the ocean.

She tapped a finger to her chin. "Hm. When was the last time you got laid?"

I scoffed. It *had* been a while. But that wasn't the problem.

"I know why," Delani said before I could speak. "You're worried that you will be gifted a *beautiful*, *shining* stone by the gods, and that you'll be forced to attend Caelestis Academy for two years. Which means that you're probably worrying about how you'll be mandated into a decade of soldier service and blah, blah, blah," she taunted.

I came to a halt in the sand and scowled at her.

A knowing smirk planted along her lips. "Am I right?"

She was, but I didn't give her the satisfaction of saying so.

"I know you've been dreading your birthday this year," she said softly, following behind me when I resumed walking.

Right again, but there was nothing she could say to change that. We've had this conversation before, and I always made my opinions very clear on how much I despised the idea of becoming another person for the king to control.

She called after me, "Oh, come on, Maeve. You're turning twenty-one tomorrow. Why aren't you excited?"

Because I was terrified that I would be one of the chosen.

If it weren't for the king's orders, I would have accepted being deemed worthy by the gods. But my soul longed for freedom, and the confines that came with being gifted struck no amount of desire in me.

It never used to be that way. Before the war, those gifted by the gods lived amongst the rest of the Caelestians as they pleased. Draemor, the southernmost kingdom of our continent and also the closest to us, has been our enemy for as far back as the manuscripts dated.

Two decades ago, the former King of Draemor greedily wanted to reign over some unclaimed territory by the eastern coast. A peaceful split of the land was never attempted before he tried to seize it. When Caelestis made efforts to stop him, claiming that the land should be left unscathed by mortals, he declared war over the terrain.

Caelestian soldiers were fairly scarce at the time of the war, and the lack of an army almost lost us our own land. Though outnumbered, our soldiers were ruthless, leading Caelestis to victory—but not without losing the vast majority of our troops. My father was one of the soldiers in this battle, losing his life to the blade of a Draemornian.

This war was one of the most horrific battles in Caelestis' history, and was the reason that the rules regarding the gifted changed. From the moment the war ceased, King Hawthorne made the executive order that anyone gifted by the gods must attend Caelestis Soldiers Academy. Following graduation from the course, the individual was to provide the kingdom with at least a decade of mandatory soldier service.

In my personal opinion, this was asinine, and not how the gods intended their gifts to be used. But I didn't make the rules.

I had no issue when it came to defending my kingdom. The fact that *my life* would no longer be in my control was what I couldn't stand the thought of.

Delani tapped her foot in the sand, waiting for me to admit that her claim was correct.

"What if by *some chance* the gods have deemed me worthy?" I asked, giving into the intensity of her stare.

Her dainty figure slid by my side, our shadows showcasing the difference in our body types. She weaved her fingers between mine as I turned my gaze to the horizon, immersing myself in the colors that painted the sky—the same hues that always appeared just before the sunset.

“If that happens, then you fight like hell to become one of the best damn soldiers the king has ever had.” She squeezed my hand tighter. “You wield whatever power you are gifted, finish your time at the academy, and your ten years of service.” She turned to face me. “*You stay alive.*”

I swallowed the lump that formed in my throat from those words. There were always a handful of students who struggled to properly wield their magic. Those few usually ended up dead before the end of their first year, never even making it to the armoring ceremony.

My eyes dipped from the sky and accidentally skimmed the tip of the tower again. Another burst of anxiety claimed me, but I shoved it away, focusing my attention on Delani.

She pushed her forehead against mine. “Then, you bring your ass right back home to Mom and me. I’ll bake your favorite biscuits, and you can tell me about all of the hot soldiers you had drooling over you,” she finished with a grin.

I let out a snort of laughter, then looked back to the nearly set sun.

Before long, the exhaustion of the day caught up to me. I settled myself down into the sand and dug a hole with my toes, burying my feet under the cool earth.

Delani sat down beside me and we watched the sky until the warmth of the sun faded, and the violet stained horizon deepened into a pigment of blue.

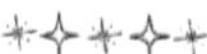

THE SUN GLISTENED THROUGH THE CLOTH OF MY CURTAINS, THE open crack of the window allowing for a mellow breeze to flow throughout the tight quarters of my room. I sat up in my bed, wiping the sleep from my eyes.

Daybreak indicated that the festival had already begun, and I groaned at the thought. Soon I would have no choice but to make the journey to the castle, where I would spend the entirety of my day including well into the evening hours.

The celebration would continue until the stars had stopped falling. The commencement ceremony would be held the following afternoon. There, the newly gifted would present themselves to King Hawthorne, damning themselves to fate.

Such bullshit.

I rolled my body away from the glaring sun—so bright and promising and not at all resembling how I felt about today. I'd been agonizing over this moment for months. If I am going to be screwed over by the gods, I'd know by the end of the day.

In all honesty, the whole process of being gifted baffled me. If I was deemed worthy, I wouldn't know until the precise second that I turned twenty-one, when the jewel that has resided within me since conception fully matured. The gemstone determined by whichever god chose me would break through my flesh, leaving my skin embellished with a glittering source of magic.

Nothing was more powerful and energetic than the forces of nature, and the gods used mortals to contain these forces in balance. Those who had access to a fragment of their divine power were seen as assistants to the deities. With every exertion of their magic, the chosen aided in controlling the chaos of the world.

Most of the gifted had worn their jewels for months now, but the powers held within would not be active until tonight. The meteor shower acted as a trigger, relinquishing the gods' hold on their magic. Only when the mosaic of jewel-toned stars tumbled from the heavens would the chosen feel the first sparks of their power. The transition was extraordinary to watch, but I had no desire to experience the event for myself.

Desperate to quiet the wandering chaos in my mind, I closed my eyes and begged my body to return to my dream state.

The attempt didn't last long.

Soon enough, my eyes were wide open again, gazing at the ceiling above me. My cheeks puffed out with angst-filled air as I glanced around my bedroom.

My family's home was small, to say the least. The floorboards creaked when stepped on, indicating the deterioration of the cabin. Some of the logs that built the walls had begun to rot, creating a musty smell that would waft throughout the house during the heat of summer. My bedchamber was snug, but despite its size, the space had been turned into a perfect depiction of myself. My writing and drawings coated the walls, some of them dated back to the moment I learned to hold a quill. Just enough light emitted from the single window, which I found myself grateful for in the evenings when rays of moonlight guided my hand as I wrote in my journal. Aside from the ocean, my room was my safe place.

Before my father died, we had lived in a larger, newer house closer to the coastline. I didn't remember it, though. I was barely a year old when he was killed. The only images I could paint of him were those described to me by my mother and Delani.

While lost in my state of nostalgia, I almost missed the sound of a soft knock hitting my door. I jolted upright, my quilt lying flat against my lap as Delani's head peered through the crack in the doorway.

"Psst. Are you awake?"

"Unfortunately."

"Happy Birthday!" she cheered, disturbing the peaceful silence of my room and pushing through the doorway.

"Thanks," I sulked, then pulled the quilt up and over my face, just for her to tear it off and glare at me.

Delani rolled her eyes as she flopped down beside me on the mattress. "Maeve, I know what you're thinking, and I *promise* that the odds of you being gifted are extremely unlikely. You aren't that special," she teased, then raised her voice even more before continuing. "So *please* just try to enjoy your birthday and Jewel-Light tonight."

I sighed through my nostrils and crossed my arms over my chest. "You say it as if it's such a ridiculous thing for me to be concerned about," I huffed.

"It kinda is."

"No, it's not."

"It is."

"I don't even want to go this year."

"Oh, please. Knock it off."

"I'm serious."

Delani rolled her eyes again. "You're just being stubborn. Get up and get dressed. I want to leave after lunch."

I didn't budge.

"Come on..." Her voice hummed as she begged. "It will be quite entertaining seeing which of the Fletcher boys makes an ass of himself this year."

Her comment pulled a chuckle free from my lungs. "He'll never live that down." I laughed. The oldest of the Fletcher boys, Cedric, had gotten so drunk that he stripped to his undergarments and jumped on top of one of the buffet tables. I was pretty sure he was banned from attending the festival this year after the display of meats and vegetables tumbled into the dirt.

"Gods no. I'll never let him. And remember how much fun we had last year?" Delani chimed.

"You mean how *drunk* we got?" I snorted. "That's the last time I let you make me a mixed drink."

"I'll have you know, that night was one of the last times I felt well rested. There's just something about waking up with sand caked to your skin and no recollection of how you ended up on the beach in the first place that's really fucking liberating."

A small smile formed on my lips. The memory brought back a

whole array of moments from last year's festival, and I sparked a *teeny* bit of excitement for the day. At the very least, I didn't need to worry until the evening. I wasn't sure of the exact time I was born, but I knew it wasn't during daylight, which meant that the hours leading up to the meteor shower could be spent carefree.

"Fine. But I'm not dressing up and I'm not drinking anything other than wine," I informed her, my face all too serious as I pointed a finger in her direction.

"Deal. Now get up."

Delani squeezed me into an awkward, horizontal hug, then rose from my mattress. She tore the quilt clean from my bed prior to leaving my room, just because she could.

As soon as the door clicked shut, the familiar feeling of anxiety came rushing back in. I forced myself to a sitting position, my hands gripping the edge of my mattress as I worked through the panic.

This feeling was all too normal for me. Usually when I felt this way, I would write in my journal. It may have been excessive, but I wrote down pretty much every detail of my life, ranging from the pleasures to the troubles. I had stacks of filled notebooks tucked away in my closet. Putting my thoughts down on paper helped to relieve the weight of them. Writing lessened the burden of life.

Unfortunately, there was no time for scribing. So I raked my fingers through the tangles of my hair, swiftly tying it into a loose braid that landed in the center of my back when completed. Reaching my arms over my head, I stretched before forcing myself to my feet.

I wondered if being gifted was actually as bad as I'd expected it to be. I wasn't keen on the idea of the next stage of my life being pre-planned for me, but surely Caelestis Academy wasn't as horrific as I imagined. After graduation, it was required that all soldiers lived on the castle grounds, stationed close-by in case they were called upon for service. But despite that, I would still be able to have a family if I wanted to—could still fall in love. As long as I stayed alive, it really wouldn't be so bad.

Right?

I had become good at using logic to talk myself out of things.

Though the tactics the gods used to decide who they deemed worthy were unknown, I *knew* that the odds of me being gifted were slim—that I was not deserving of such a blessing. Regardless of the logic, I couldn't shake the feeling that I still might be.

Swallowing the fear that threatened to tear me in half, I walked straight to my wardrobe and rummaged through the drawers. I slid a blouse over my head and wiggled my hips into my favorite pants, then stepped into a pair of boots to finish my outfit.

On the opposing wall hung my mirror, slightly crooked from the ripples of the wood. With a sharp inhale, I held my breath and stepped in front of it. My reflection tilted to the side while I studied the structure of my own face, noting the fullness of my cheeks that rounded out as I faked a smile.

"It's going to be fine," I assured myself, tucking a stray piece of hair behind my ear.

I released the breath I'd been holding, pushing the air through the barrier of my gritted teeth and kissing my anxiety away as I strode for the door.

CHAPTER TWO

I found myself regretting my outfit choice as soon as we arrived at the festival early that evening. Having put much more effort into their garments than I had, Delani and my mother looked as though they belonged at such a prestigious event. I, on the other hand, would have benefited from staying home.

I paused to take in the intricate design of the castle's architecture. The details of the pale stonework never failed to amaze me, no matter how many times I'd seen it. The fortress was genuinely breathtaking, its size incomprehensible. Pointed iron bars surrounded the main gate, standing high to prevent anyone from climbing over the fence. On top of the staircase that led to the main entryway, a few soldiers stood properly by the oak double doors. I didn't dare make eye contact with them—one glimpse of their drawn swords was enough to prevent me from doing so.

The grounds looked a little bit different each time I came to the castle, with a new array of flowers and shrubs for each season. To my left was the cliffside, lined by a cobblestone pathway that I knew would take me to the academy dormitories if I were to follow it.

In my opinion, the only benefit to attending the academy was living at the dormitories, which were stationed just feet away from a beautiful beach. I learned that information the hard way one year when I was younger. Delani and I had ventured off, only to be dragged back to the courtyard by a burly, female soldier.

Delani cleared her throat and then brushed by the soldiers, crossing the balcony to enter the party. She looked remarkable as she strutted into the event with poise. The silk of her sage gown flowed just past her knees, swaying with the motion of her hips. Her hair was pulled back into a tight bun, and though a few stray coils framed her face, the messiness of the hairstyle still made her appear put together.

I couldn't help but notice how a few wandering eyes followed her across the balcony.

The festivities always began in the courtyard, and this year was no different. We were greeted by the most elaborate decorations when we stepped onto the patio. I gazed in all directions, in complete awe of the presentation which somehow outdid the previous years.

Strings of twinkling lights hung from the trees surrounding the perimeter of the courtyard. The bulbs sparkled under the dimming sun as it phased into moonlight. The glimmer combined with the greenery, creating a tent-like framework for the party to occur in. Connecting the tops of the trees were rows of delicate white and pink flowers. The buds dangled from invisible strings, creating a partially transparent net that cascaded over the entirety of the courtyard. The flowers dribbled down, adding to the ambiance of the event as they spun in midair.

To the far right of the courtyard was a secluded area separated by hedges, which held within their bounds a statue of each god and goddess. The masonry was absolutely magnificent on its own, but better yet, each god was built from a large slab of the gemstone they represented. The figurines were spectacular to look at on any given day, but for the festival, they were garnished with exquisite displays of flowers and cloth.

Aside from the jaw-dropping decor, there was an irrational amount of food and wine almost everywhere I turned. Music played loudly throughout the courtyard and a smile broke through my lips at the sight of people waltzing together, chanting the melodies.

My admiration was ruined by my mother's abrupt notice of departure. "I have to go find Isobel Fletcher." Her voice broke through the tunes.

She took my hand in hers and I admired her beauty—so natural and elegant without even trying. Her forest green dress frilled out at the bottom, the color highlighting her fair skin while also emphasizing the dark curls of her hair. She looked nothing like Delani and I, and we often questioned while growing up if she was even our real mother. She always just laughed the idea off, telling us that we had overactive imaginations.

"I have something to discuss with her regarding the archives," she continued, taking Delani's fingertips in her free hand.

That was my mother. Always working. She was the top Archivist in Caelestis, responsible for maintaining the village records and history manuscripts.

Delani and I had been visiting the library since we were young, but only I stuck around long enough to assist my mother in her work. I enjoyed the quiet that the archives offered, and often used the space to write in. Delani, on the contrary, had no interest in manuscripts and quilling.

My mother pulled us into a deep hug, then stepped back, letting us go and directing her attention to just me.

"Happy Birthday, my star." Her red lips curved into a smile as she unfolded my palms and placed a small black pouch into my hands.

"You didn't have to get me any—"

She cut me off, "It's not every day that you turn twenty-one."

I smiled and accepted the gift, working my fingers to undo the knot of silver ribbon tying the pouch together. I peeled open the bag and pulled out a silver star pendant, dangling from a dainty chain. It shimmered when I held it up, swirling in tune with the wind.

"It's beautiful," I praised, marveling at the gift.

My mother took the chain from my hands. She brushed my hair to the side so that she could clasp it around my neck. She backed away when she finished, and I clutched the necklace against my chest.

"It's absolutely perfect. Thank you," I voiced my appreciation.

Though she smiled at me in acknowledgment, I could see the sadness in her eyes. My birthday was always difficult for her. The day was just another reminder of how I never knew my father.

She rubbed my shoulder for a moment before letting her hand slide off. Then she trailed away into the festival of lights, leaving Delani and I to our own devices.

I turned to my sister, and a devious look appeared on her face almost instantly. Her eyes lit up and she spun on her heel, directing me further into the gathering.

Sweet scents filled my nostrils as we passed by astounding buffets of sweets and plates of the freshest fruits. We came to a halt in front of one the tables—the amount of food on it being enough to feed my entire village for weeks.

Delani plucked some berries from the display and plopped one into her mouth. I took a handful, as well, savoring the tartness of the fruit as it coated my tastebuds.

I maneuvered to the table next door and swiped two goblets of wine from the surface. I passed one to Delani, then sipped on my own and familiarized myself with the space I'd be spending the rest of my birthday in.

I shouldn't have thought too hard about it, but my anxiety fought me once more. It blew through me like a gust of wind, the breeze whispering its doubts to me and scrambling my thoughts into disarray.

Though the air was flat, I still shivered.

"You are fine. Everything is going to be fine. You won't be gifted. Today is just like any other birthday," I breathed the affirmations into my glass, letting them tame the storm inside of me and settling on some peace in knowing that no matter what happened tonight, Delani would be by my side.

Never mind.

Delani's hand shot into the air, waving at someone across the courtyard. I followed my sister's gaze, making eye contact with one of her friends who gestured for her.

"I'll meet you by the statues in a few minutes," Delani informed me. She *clinked* her glass against mine before hurrying off to greet her friend.

Great. Just myself and my thoughts.

I picked a few more berries from the buffet and downed my goblet of wine, then swiped another glass before wandering off. I strolled through the courtyard leisurely, sipping on my drink and making small talk with familiar faces along the way. A few wished me a Happy Birthday, and I faked a smile as I thanked them.

My legs stopped moving when they stood before the eight statues of the gods and goddesses. I looked up and around, taking note of their size, which in return made me feel incredibly small.

The statues were varnished with various floral arrangements, the color of the buds representing the gemstone that the god or goddess cherished. Flowers hung around their shoulders, resting on top of a lustrous cloth draping, which would sparkle in the starlight as the sun set.

I turned in a circle, dropping the arm that held my glass to my side as I admired each statue. Hidden by some shrubs and other greenery, the statues and I were detached from the rest of the party.

My wandering came to an abrupt halt in front of the sculpture of Blythe, the Goddess of the Mind. Drawn to her glass-blue figure, I planted my feet firmly on the ground in front of her. My skin prickled as my fingertips slid up the stone, stopping to caress the cloth that hung from her shoulders. I ran the fabric through the gaps of my fingers, admiring the glossy sheen of silk that covered a good portion of the goddess' pure constellastone body.

Her sculpture must have taken the longest to craft, as the crystal was incredibly rare. I honestly doubted that the statue was made of constellastone at all, but the king claimed its truth.

The stone was only found at the crash site of fallen Jewel-Light meteors. Even then, it was a gamble on whether or not there would be any. The conditions had to be flawless for the stone to manifest from the remains of a dying star, and more often than not, the conditions were not optimal. Regardless, I couldn't fathom the amount of time needed to gather the amount of stone required to create something so detailed.

Blythe wore a floral crown of intertwined bluebells and white roses. The flowers cascaded along her neck and over the mounds of stone that implicated her breasts. They flowed down her crystalline torso, halting at her waist where her hair ended in a slight curl.

My skin continued to tingle as I examined the stone. The iridescent grains of the mineral twinkled under the light of the courtyard—sometimes appearing clear like a diamond, then blue, and then almost opalescent. The appearance of the constellastone varied so much that it was difficult to decipher exactly what color it actually was.

I wondered why the king even bothered to have her figure here. Blythe had never gifted a mortal her gemstone or the magic that accompanied it. I had always assumed this was due to the rarity of the gem, but wasn't positive.

All the same, the statue was a glorious piece of artwork that I found myself lost in the luminosity of. "Beautiful," I muttered under my breath when I at last pulled my hand away.

Wine flushed my skin as I resumed drinking, and minutes passed before I nearly jumped out of my skin in response to a smack of pressure on my ass. I spun around, my behind stinging. The racing of my heart eased as my eyes made contact with Delani and her beaming smile.

"I didn't strike you as a super spiritual girl, but if you need another moment to worship in private, I can come back later," she announced satirically, grinning from ear to ear.

My eyes raised to the heavens. "Oh, shut up." I crossed my arms and turned back to the statue.

A gust of wind blew the flower arrangement sideways, and a stray bluebell tumbled from the goddess. Delani bent down to pick it up, and her demeanor changed into one much more solemn as she tucked it behind her ear.

"I always hoped that if I were gifted by one of them, it would have been from her," she murmured, having a rare, vulnerable moment. Regardless of the years that had passed, she still hadn't fully accepted that she wasn't one of the chosen.

"Oh, please," I snorted. "If any god were to choose you, it would have been Emrys." Emrys was the God of Heat and Fire, whose magic fit Delani's personality quite well.

She bit back a laugh and tapped her finger on her chin, considering my comment. "Yeah. That makes the most sense." Then with a smirk, Delani turned from me, marching away from the statues without another word. She exited the courtyard all together and made no indication that I should follow.

I accompanied her, anyway.

THE SUN HAD FULLY COLLAPSED INTO THE HORIZON AND THE MOON gleamed, leaving streaks of silver light painted over the stonework of the castle.

People huddled into each other, waiting.

I stood at the front of the crowd, directly in line with the marbled staircase. My mother and Delani were on either side of me, silent as we anticipated the king's arrival. He was due to stride through the large double doors at any moment.

Bored, my eyes wandered, roaming over the king's head soldiers who stood in near perfect posture on the steps. There were ten of them, each holding a shield made of steel along with a blade sheathed against their thigh. They wore uniforms of leather, aside from the armor plate that protected their chests and shoulders, the metal crafted to match their shields.

Only one of the soldiers was female. The joyous look on her face made her an outlier, as the other soldiers stood expressionless. I scanned over the rest of them and refocused my sight on another soldier who grasped my attention almost immediately.

He stood highest on the staircase, and despite the elevation of his position, I could tell that he towered over the other soldiers. He presented himself properly—his arms crossed over his chest and spine straightened, both details helping to convey his dominating presence.

The man's hair was dark brown, almost black, and laid just behind his ears in a mess of delicate waves—maybe curls—the unkemptness of his locks made it hard to tell. And though the leather he wore left much up to imagination, I could make out the muscular physique hiding under his armor.

Wondering which god had gifted him, I bent my neck slightly, trying to get a look at his hands. They were concealed in a dark set of gloves, but based on appearance and demeanor alone, I guessed that he was gifted a sapphire gem by Thea, the Goddess of the Oceans and Water.

My eyes rolled up his body, then stopped at his face. It was then that I became all too aware of my gawking as my gaze collided with his.

Oh, come on.

My mouth drew into a tight line, and his lips fell slightly open—almost as if he was in shock that someone was watching him. He shouldn't have been, though. If he got a good look at himself in the mirror that morning, then he knew how breathtaking he was.

Though it wasn't for more than a few seconds, the intensity of the soldier's stare caused my breath to catch in my lungs.

Adrenaline fueled my motions and I whipped my head to the side, searching for *anything* to look at other than him. I explored my surroundings, but all I found was myself wishing that I hadn't looked away.

I fought the indisputable urge to turn back, but before I could make good on that intention, the castle doors peeled open over the balcony. Cheers poured from the people who swarmed the staircase—the same people who applauded as King Aldous Hawthorne appeared on the exterior of the fortress.

My mouth however, stayed closed. My hands stayed tucked by my sides. I would not applaud this man. He had done nothing worth recognition.

The king was middle-aged, obvious from the presence of his graying hair and goatee. His skin was tanned from the sun, hardly wrinkled despite his age. The crimson robe he wore was meant to represent Emrys, who gave him his magic. Big fucking mistake by the god if you asked me—the king let the power go to his head.

He finally raised his hands to silence everyone. The ruby rooted into his skin responded to the glare of the moonlight, shining with the movement of his hands. The voices quieted and King Hawthorne lowered his arms, then wasted no time as he began to speak.

"Greetings, my kingdom. Thank you for joining us tonight for the celebration of the annual Jewel-Star Meteor Shower—the most blessed evening of the year." His eyes grazed over the crowd before he continued. "Those who have come of age in the past year, and have received a sacred gemstone from the gods themselves, will soon spark with power as the activation of your blessing consumes you."

I had heard this same speech too many times to count, and could predict what he would say next. There was no need for me to pay attention.

Out of sheer boredom—

Fine.

Out of sheer boredom *and* curiosity, I let my focus drift back towards the soldier. While his attention was elsewhere, I examined his features, and gods…

He was undoubtedly the most handsome man I had ever seen.

The edge of his jaw was crisp—sharp, like the edge of an untainted knife. His chin was home to a small dimple, present from the way his teeth were noticeably clenched. I followed the line of his mandible, stopping my gaze on his lips. They were full, but not so much that they overpowered his other features. His dark brows laid arched over his eyes, which were the most beautiful shade of blue I'd ever seen. Even from this distance, I could make out the specks of navy that reside in his irises.

I was lost—completely immersed in his face until his sight coursed towards me and we mistakenly made eye contact. *Again.*

My heart leapt in panic and my gaze dropped to the ground. Although I couldn't know for certain, I sensed that the soldier was still watching me.

Ever so carefully I looked back towards the king, and when I did, I noticed that his eyes were the same hue as the soldier's. Both sets had an identical, mesmerizing effect. I elbowed Delani in the side. "Is that the king's son?" I pointed discreetly to the soldier, not daring to look back.

Her eyes followed my direction and her lips bent into a flirtatious grin. "I'm not sure. But he sure is *glorious* to look at isn't he?"

That he was.

"Soon a rainbow of stars will fall from the sky." King Hawthorne's voice boomed through the castle grounds, recapturing my focus. "Those who have found themselves with an unfamiliar bauble in their flesh will undergo a transition as the stars fall from the heavens. If this applies to you, I expect you to make your presence known at the Jewel-Light Ceremony tomorrow afternoon." He cleared his throat. "By now, you all are aware of the laws and ordinances that our kingdom must obey. Therefore, I know that the following information will come as no surprise to you."

This was the part of the king's annual oration that always made my skin crawl. I braced myself for his cruel words, the bite of them no less painful despite having heard them before.

"If it is found that you are gifted by the gods, and do not present yourself at the ceremony tomorrow, you can expect to be executed as soon as I am made aware of this betrayal to Caelestis."

Yup. There it was.

I shuddered.

King Hawthorne made a theatrical pause, building suspense before he concluded his speech. He wished everyone an evening of pleasure, then turned his back to his kingdom to step through the castle doors, closed behind him by the most exquisite man I had ever seen.

CHAPTER THREE

My mother never stayed to watch the meteor shower. *"I've seen it plenty of times before,"* she always said.

After the king concluded his speech, she gave Delani and me a lecture of our own, making us swear that there wouldn't be a repeat of last year. Of course we said what she wanted to hear, but as twilight got closer and my nerves got stronger, I couldn't make any promises.

After she left, Delani secured us some wine while I gathered a collection of sweets from one of the buffets. With my arms full of pastries and candied fruit, I followed Delani's lead as she directed us along the outskirts of the courtyard.

The lights from the festival still flickered around us despite no longer being under the tent made from magic. Our shoes left footprints in the plush grass we wandered through as we searched for the perfect spot to watch the meteor shower. We settled on a location—a grassy hillside with a view of the cliffside near the rear of the fortress. I dropped carefully to my knees, letting my snacks spill onto the grass. I was already too tipsy from the wine to care if they got a little dirt on them.

My legs kicked out from beneath me, allowing me to sit more

properly. I reached for the goblet of wine that Delani had set by my hip and savored the sweetness of the liquid as I gazed into the sky that darkened more and more by the second. Twilight was almost among us, and my fists clenched with the reminder that at any moment, my life could be forever changed. I wished that my mother knew the exact time of my birth. That information alone would have eased my nerves.

I looked around at the others sitting nearby on the lawn, observing who had shining jewels on their hands. The newly gifted looked excited, eager to finally access their magic. The others—the ones without magic—just looked drunk. Delani fell into that category.

We devoured most of our snacks, sipping on our goblets of wine when we finished the sweets. As soon as she finished her cup, Delani leaned back, slumping her body into the grass. Her eyes closed in relaxation. "Wake me when the shower starts," she mumbled, falling asleep as soon as the words left her lips.

I sighed heavily. Once again, I was left with just my brain for company. My thoughts drifted, pulling away from my fear to instead focus on the soldier from earlier.

As uncomfortable as it had been that he caught me staring, remembering the way he stared back sent shivers down my spine. His gaze was profound, as though I looked familiar to him but he couldn't quite figure out how. Though the likelihood of ever seeing him again was slim, the image of his face would certainly stay sealed in my memories forever.

The inky sky had no source of light aside from the crescent moon lingering in the atmosphere. No stars had appeared yet, but it wouldn't be long before the blank canvas was speckled with color.

Tension pooled from my breath as I blew it out, releasing the anguish I'd been holding on to all day. There were only a few hours left of my birthday, which meant that the odds of me being gifted were next to none.

That logic allowed me to finally relax. I laid down next to Delani and nestled my head into the crook of her arm. With my mind finally at rest, I found myself looking forward to watching the mosaic of stars as they put on the most magical show.

As if the heavens could sense my ease, a violent force of starlight painted a streak through the blank sky, blasting through the atmosphere at an incomprehensible speed. It created a straight bisect through the darkness, then vanished as soon as it had arrived. The meteor was one like I'd never seen before, and left me in complete awe.

I shot upright, looking side to side, wondering who else had noticed the star. But there was no indication that anyone saw the start of the meteor shower.

My neck burned as I strained it to watch the sky, my gaze not faltering as I waited for more stars to fall.

But none came.

I blinked a few times, just to make sure that the *star* I saw wasn't really something caught in my eye. But I was certain it was real.

It *looked* real.

I frowned. I'd seen enough shooting stars in my lifetime to know one when I saw one. Maybe I was just exhausted and hallucinating. Maybe I drank more than I realized—that was also a possibility.

"Happy Birthday to me. Here's your present—being fucking delusional," I mumbled under my breath.

Minutes passed without any implication that the meteor shower had actually begun. I had accepted the notion that I *was* in fact crazy, until someone a few yards from me gasped. My head darted in their direction, then up to the heavens where they pointed.

I saw the star as it passed, its emerald tail flowing steadily until the entirety of its existence was swallowed into the blackness. Shortly after, there was a ruby meteor. Then a yellow star, followed by a violet one.

Soon enough, the sky was clustered with vibrant jewel-toned stars, flashing sporadically as they tumbled through the atmosphere. Some stayed stationary while others flew in every direction, creating a prism of color that replaced the darkness of the night with a beautiful illustration from the gods.

I nudged Delani in an attempt to rouse her. She stirred, but did not wake. I tried once more per her request, but she had so much to drink that I doubted I'd be able to fulfill it.

The all too familiar feeling of unease returned with the true induction of the meteor shower. I focused on the immobile stars, allowing the idleness of them to grant me a sense of control amidst the hecticness of the sky.

I breathed deeply, watching the display of lights above me. My hands didn't ache yet, which was a good sign. If I were to be deemed worthy by the gods, my jewel would present itself on the back of my palm.

That logic, and the fact that my birthday was coming to a close, pushed my dread fully aside. I let out a belly laugh directed at myself. I shouldn't have been, but I was ashamed that I let fear ruin my birthday.

I laid back down with my sister and listened to the joy of the others around me as they gained use of their magic with each falling cosmo.

Gazing into the heavens, I began to count the colored stars. Before I could get to ten, I drifted off to sleep.

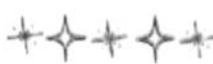

I WOKE UP TO A HORRIFIC POUNDING IN MY TEMPLE.

Putting pressure against my forehead, I sat up and leaned back on the heel of my free hand. I groaned, immediately regretting my decision to have that last goblet of wine. Delani was fast asleep, and the sky was still putting on its performance of dancing stars, so I must have not been asleep for too long.

Wait.

I did a double-take back to Delani. Where my head had been resting on her dress, was a blood soaked spot.

"What the—"

My hands pushed me off of the ground. I stood on wobbling knees, the pounding in my head increasing in line with my height. Upon further examination, I realized that it was not exactly my head that was aching—it was my face. Just under my right cheekbone, to be exact.

My arm quivered as I raised my hand to meet the puffed flesh under my eye, which burned to the touch. The skin felt warm—wet underneath the soles of my fingers. My eyes widened when I pulled my hand back into view, beads of fresh blood dripping from my fingertips.

Adrenaline coursed within me as I hastily repeated my inspection, this time noticing a group of raised bumps along the line of my cheek bone.

I froze as realization struck me.

This had to be a dream.

There was no way. *No fucking way.*

I must have still been asleep, because this wasn't possible. First and foremost, the gemstones of the gods *rarely* adorned one's body anywhere except for their hands. When they did, they usually were close by, like on a forearm or something.

Second of all—there was just *no fucking way.*

I scrambled around, collecting the few belongings I had with me and giving Delani one last glance before hurrying off, not knowing where I was going, but needing to move. I crept through the lawn, careful not to wake any of the others who had dozed off. Most were still awake, those gifted testing out their new magic. They really should have waited until they received some instruction on how to properly wield, but their foolishness wasn't my problem.

The air in my lungs thickened with each inhale, and I found the task of existing becoming difficult as panic lashed at me. "No, no, no," I grumbled in frustration, but couldn't stop the attack as hyperventilation swallowed my air.

I forced my shuddering legs to move faster, really needing to focus on the motions. I left the castle grounds and walked along the pathway that bordered the cliffside, my steps uneven from the shambles of cobblestone. I didn't care if one of the soldiers caught me leaving the festival. I had to move—had to sweat the panic out of my pores. More importantly, I had to find a damn mirror.

Tears started to flow, warm and salty against my cheeks. My face pulsated in sync with my heart and I could feel the blood mixing with my tears as it trickled down my skin. But I advanced forward, following the path until it revealed an open portion of the rocky cliffside, where I paused to peer over the ledge.

The drop only appeared to be a few feet. I could clearly hear the waves of the ocean crashing below, and despite the darkness of the night, I knew that I was just seconds away from a sandy shore.

I dropped down to a crouch and swung my legs over the ledge. The stones scraped my knuckles as I climbed down nature's wall, lowering myself, careful to get a firm grip on each rock before descending any further. I removed my boots as soon as I hit land, granting the sand permission to caress my feet. My toes kicked the grains as I maneuvered towards the ocean, the wet sand creating a plaster on my feet.

I came to a halt when I felt the sand being washed off by the sea. I focused on my breaths, inhaling and exhaling with the rhythm of the waves.

My breathing was already becoming easier—just being by the ocean calmed me. I got a handle on my leaking eyes, then gathered as much courage as I could before bending my neck to look down into the sea.

The jewel-toned stars mirrored off the surface, creating prismatic patterns that illuminated the water. I could see my reflection clearly thanks to the silver glow of the moon. I turned my head to the side, angling my face to get a look at the reason behind the ache.

I choked at what I saw.

Three shining gemstones, caked in dark crusted blood, peeking through the flesh that outlined my cheekbone.

I stood as still as a corpse. My body was in pure and devastating shock.

I wanted to cry, scream. I wanted to curse the gods for sentencing me to such a fate.

But I didn't do any of those things.

There was no point.

Nothing could change this.

The obligations the king had placed on the gifted had nothing to do with the gods. My fate was not their doing. It was not how the deities intended for their powers to be used.

The gods had no say in this imperative destiny. They wouldn't be able to save me.

It was hard to tell from the moonlight alone, but the jewels appeared to be pale blue. Or perhaps they were clear, like a diamond.

I blew out a wistful breath and traced my fingers over them again, familiarizing myself with the reason my life was about to drastically change.

"No..." My voice cracked in denial as my composure broke down.

My body crumbled into the sand, having no willpower left to keep upright. I stayed there until dawn rolled in and the sun reheated the air that had been chilled by the night. I grieved into the morning hours while preparing myself for the adjustments to my future that I would have to accept in mere hours.

Though I wanted to—more than anything in the world—there was no returning a gift from the gods.

CHAPTER FOUR

Only when the sky had been wiped clean from starlight and the sun had peaked did I make my way home. I sulked all the way to my room, only to find Delani nestled into *my* bed instead of her own.

I was glad that she made it home okay. I shouldn't have left her, but given the circumstances, she would understand.

As I crossed the floorboards towards my bed, I stopped to study my reflection in the mirror. My vision was still blurred from crying, and I had to work hard to focus on the jewels embedded in the fullness of my cheek.

I tilted my head every which way to get a really good look at my *gift*. The faint, bluish hue of the stones varied with the angle of my neck. Their strain was unclear in the ocean's reflection, but in this lighting, it was evident that I wore three diamonds in my flesh.

Damn.

It was already bad enough that my jewels had doomed me to a life of knighthood, let alone the fact that I wasn't even blessed by Thea. Her sapphire was accompanied by the power of water manipulation, which was quite fitting for my character. Though

Caius gave those gifted by him the power to manipulate snow and ice, which I supposed wasn't too far off.

I abandoned my reflection, resuming my journey to my bed and crawling in the sheets next to my sister. I soaked in the coziness of my own mattress, knowing that this moment would be the last of its kind for the years to come.

Lying flat on my back, I made myself comfortable and rested my hands on my stomach. I blew out a shuddered breath, my hands falling with my chest. The emptiness of the ceiling was greatly appreciated as I spent nearly an hour contemplating how I would say goodbye to my family before I left. What did you tell the most important people in your life, when you knew there was a possibility that those words would be the last you ever said to them? There was no question that training to become a soldier was brutal, and if I were to die—

There was no use in dwelling on maybes. I knew that, but I couldn't stop the thoughts as they possessed my brain.

Delani began to stir, but she still didn't wake. She rolled to her other side, then burrowed herself deeper into the sheets. She looked so peaceful, but she had no idea that she was about to be crushed.

I closed my eyes to stop them from watering. Saying that I would miss her hardly described it.

My sister. My best friend. After today, I wouldn't see her until the Jewel-Light Festival next year. And even then, I wouldn't be able to spend any time with her. I would be on duty, stuffed into a tight leather uniform in the dead heat of summer.

A single tear dribbled free from my eye. I hastily wiped it away as the familiar scent of vanilla and lavender filled my nostrils. I recognized my mother's perfume and turned my head to see her standing in my doorway.

She could see my cheek from where she stood—the look on her face made that much obvious. Her dark eyes sunk, but she flicked the corner of her lips up, trying to reassure me with her poor excuse of a smile.

I shuffled over as much as I could without waking Delani. The mattress was much too small for three people, but we found the room.

My mother rubbed her fingers through my hair as she had done ever since I was a child. The cloth of her shirt felt soft where my head rested on her. In the comfort of my mother's arms, I allowed all of my sadness to rush in.

I tried to speak—tried to explain, but choked on the words.

"Shh, my star. It's okay. I know," she assured me, the silkiness of her tone calming me.

Another tear slipped free. Then another. I gave up trying to stop them, letting the despair rain down my face. "I don't know what to do," I sniffled. "I don't know how to feel."

She kissed my forehead, her nails getting caught in the strands of my hair that she twirled between her fingers. "Feel it all," she said. "Feel sorrow that this journey was not in your plans, but feel excited that a new journey awaits you. Feel scared that you do not know what is to come, but feel blessed that the gods deemed you worthy. You were gifted for a reason—find it, use it." She kissed the top of my head again then repeated herself, "Feel it all."

I nodded into her, then wiped my nose with the back of my hand.

Our voices, though hushed, still woke Delani. Her eyes fluttered open and I angled my neck towards her. She took a few seconds to process being awake, but then her mouth dropped open.

"You were gifted?"

I nodded, and her expression turned serious.

"Why are they on your face? And why is there more than one?"

I shrugged, having no answers regarding either of those questions.

There were some exceptions to the location of one's jewel, but I had never heard of a jewel presenting on someone's face. Clearly, it was not impossible. The more confusing aspect of all of this was why I had *three*.

"At least one of those was meant for me. I'm sure of it," Delani joked, making light of the situation.

I forced a laugh.

Her eyes started to water and her smile drooped as the reality of the situation splintered her. "Dammit," she choked, pulling me into a sideways hug. "I'm going to miss you."

By mid-afternoon, I was back at the castle. Most of my morning was spent debating if I had diamonds or sapphires. I was still convinced that Caius was the one who gifted me, but Delani believed otherwise. Either way, we would know soon enough—the king's advisor was an expert on gemstone strains.

The more I thought about it, the less I cared what my jewels were, anyway. I didn't even want them.

I hadn't spoken a word since we arrived here, having already said my goodbyes back at home while packing whatever I could stuff into my rucksack. Looking back, I shouldn't have bothered. The bag was taken by a soldier the moment I stepped onto the castle grounds. The soldier went through everything I had packed, leaving me with hardly anything by the time he finished.

It was a good thing I left my journal at home. That would have made for an awkward encounter had he chosen to read it. I wanted to bring it, but figured I would be able to get my hands on some parchment here.

It was the king's orders that during your two years of academy, you were not to leave the castle grounds unless it was for battle. Contacting anyone outside of the grounds was forbidden, meaning I wouldn't even hear from my family until next year. He believed that having contact with the outside world caused too many distractions—that it could affect one's loyalty to the kingdom. The way I saw it though, these rules were just another way for him to control us. Apparently forcing the gifted into knighthood wasn't enough for the asshole.

This morning on the shore, I promised myself that I would do everything in my power to not crumble with fear over my fate. I planned to do as Delani said—fight like hell, wield my power, and stay alive. Emphasis on the *stay alive* portion. Some of the new students would die, and I didn't plan on being one of them.

Many of the decorations from Jewel-Light were still on display in the courtyard. The cascades of flowers—though wilting—still hung from the trees, the warm summer breeze scattering their petals throughout the patio. The buffet tables had been cleared out and replaced with rows of chairs, covering the patio aside from an aisle down the middle. The seats were pointed at a golden podium. It sat atop an elongated platform, where the freshly gifted twenty-one-year-olds would soon stand.

I wondered how many of us there were. Previous years had averaged around seventy-five new academy students. Based on the crowd, I had a feeling there were more this year.

The chairs filled rapidly as numerous Caelestians, gifted and not, arrived at the Jewel-Light Ceremony.

I inhaled purposefully, using the kiss of the sun to melt away the nerves in my chest. The air was sweltering, and the heated rays of the summer sky were sure to burn my skin if I sat outside for too long. A few wispy clouds loitered in the aqua sky, none of which were opaque enough to produce any shade over the courtyard. I brushed my hair over my shoulders, letting the sun-kissed strands tumble down my back. I used them as protection from the sun as it began to blister my skin, and found myself thankful that I chose to let my waves coil freely today.

Sighing, I looked to the left at my mother. I could tell she was proud of me, despite knowing that soon I'd no longer be standing by her side. Without looking at me, she took my hand in hers and squeezed it gently.

"I'm scared," I whispered to her, returning my gaze straight ahead.

"I know, my star. But there is nothing to be afraid of. The gods have blessed you with an amazing gift. It is an honor."

I bit back my scoff.

An honor.

I wasn't so sure about that.

My fingertips subconsciously twirled the pendant she gave me, the use of my nickname reminding me why the charm was so fitting. My mother had been calling me *her star* for as long as I could remember. I was unsure where the name came from, but I cherished it all the same.

My focus was redirected as heavy footsteps rocked the stone beneath my feet. I whipped my head around as the same ten soldiers who were present at the Jewel-Light Festival marched into the courtyard. The one who caught my eye last night led the rest of them as they filed down the middle of the chairs.

My eyes followed the soldier onto the golden platform. He wore the same uniform as last evening, and somehow the daylight made him look even more dashing. He situated himself then stood completely static while the others filled in next to him, copying his stance.

King Hawthorne bounded down the aisle after his head soldiers. He was followed by his advisor, and when the two of them took their position at the front of the crowd, the applause commenced in unison.

I shifted in my seat, twiddling my thumbs and preparing myself while the king settled himself at the podium, which came to life in the presence of someone behind it. The details carved into the furnishing were exquisite, a subtle representation of our gods and goddesses. The golden wood was home to a ring of colorful jewels, large enough to be seen by those in the furthest row of chairs.

As if he sent the crowd into a trance, the chatter quieted when the king raised his hands to propose silence. He cleared his throat before he spoke. "Greetings again, citizens of Caelestis. I sincerely hope you all enjoyed the festivities last night in honor of this year's Jewel-Light Meteor Shower."

I turned my gaze ever so slightly, still somewhat listening to the king's words, but diverting my attention to the soldier who continued to pique my interest. The heatwave today did not require him to wear gloves, so I was able to make out the diamond rooted into his hand.

My eyebrows raised. My assumption about his power was way

off, but Caius made a good choice by choosing the soldier. Not to mention that he and I shared the same jewel. *I think.*

The king's voice lifted, breaking my focus. "After today's ceremony has concluded, all of those blessed will be introduced to their dormitories to be briefed on what is expected from them in their coming years at Caelestis Academy."

He said a few more words, then took a step back, making space for his advisor to take his place at the podium.

The king's advisor was quite short—almost as though his growth had been stunted. His head bobbled just a few inches above the podium and his white beard skimmed the top of it. He wore glasses that were much too large for his face, blatant by the way he rebalanced the frames on the bridge of his nose.

Regardless of his size, the way he addressed the kingdom made it obvious that he was a figure of authority. "All of those who are newly gifted, please rise and make your way onto the platform." The advisor gestured to the empty area beside the soldiers.

My heart sank.

I was out of time.

Bodies jumped out of their chairs. The gifted rushed to the platform, practically pushing each other down to get a good position on the stage. I watched them, my legs plastered to my seat. My nerves stopped the blood flow to my brain, and I was physically unable to move a single muscle.

My eyes—the only part of my body I had control over at the moment—scanned back and forth over the platform. Most of the newly gifted already stood proudly before the rest of the kingdom. A few of them were sobbing, and though I didn't blame them, I personally wouldn't be caught dead crying in front of all of those people like that.

The king allowed his advisor to take complete control of the ceremony as he himself drifted into a chair near the podium. It wasn't by technicalities a throne, but it may as well have been with the luster of the seat.

This was ludicrous. All of it. Every single aspect of this fucking thing was absurd. The jewels in my skin were supposed to be a blessing—a *gift* from the gods. Not a possible death sentence.

The new Caelestis Academy students piled onto the platform, but I still refused.

Delani nudged me in the side. "You have to go up there, Maeve." Her eyes showcased her concern.

I nodded slowly. "I'm going," I said, but I still didn't rise.

I would go. I just needed a second.

"Then stand up," she whispered.

"I will," I snarled under my breath. My body and brain were at odds with each other, and I *just needed a damn second.*

My cheek twitched and my fingers jumped to apply pressure to the ache. Why couldn't my gems be presented on my hand like everyone else's? Then maybe I would have had a chance at hiding them. I could have worn a glove indefinitely…or cut my hand off.

I massaged the stones. No matter how hard I tried, I couldn't hide them.

Delani elbowed me again, harder this time. I turned to look at her face, caked with blatant fear.

"Maeve, if you don't go up there—"

She didn't finish her sentence. She didn't need to. I knew what would happen if I didn't get my ass up there soon.

I bit my lip as I looked back at the platform. I contemplated for a brief moment if being killed was really a worse fate than the one I was about to walk into. In all honesty, I wasn't sure. But I knew for Delani and my mother, watching my execution would destroy them.

This would just be twelve years of my life. Not my whole life. As long as I survived.

I forced my body out of my seat, my gaze drifting towards a certain soldier as I stood. Oddly enough, he was staring at me with the same expression as Delani.

My brow lifted, and he noticed. But as soon as I rose to my full height, his attention dispersed.

That's fucking weird.

Before I could think too hard about that encounter, my mother grabbed me by the shoulders. She forcefully turned my body, angling me towards the aisle. My feet dragged in the dirt as she directed me to the edge of our row, pushing me out and leaving me on display for peering eyes.

Too many eyes.

"Go, Maeve. *Please.*" My mother's voice was a warning. Her hands dropped, then she turned from me and didn't look back. Not even for a second.

Her motives were not ill intended, but the sudden disregard for me caused a hole to burn through my heart.

Delani granted me a soft grin, then turned her attention from me as well, copying my mother's apathy. My eyes watered as I watched them ignore me, but I refused to let any tears fall.

They knew how to play this game and win. They'd been battling with my anxiety for just as long as I had.

I drew a deep breath. *I had to do this.* There were no other options. Aside from death, which I had already ruled out.

Whatever courage had been burrowing inside of me broke loose, and I started forwards towards the platform. My whole body shook, but it continued moving.

Just like my family, I didn't look back.

CHAPTER FIVE

Every year I was surprised to discover which gods found the most mortals worthy. A few years ago, only one man was chosen by the God of Light and Darkness, Jesper. He was given a topaz gemstone, along with the ability to manipulate shadows and create blinding light at will. The year before that, the goddess Sloane did not select anyone to give an emerald jewel to. That came as a surprise, because the Goddess of Nature usually gifted a large number.

I followed instructions and lined up in my row, giving my peers a quick glance and noting a lot of sapphire stones this year. Interesting. Wished I was one of them.

Once we were all stationed in our assigned groups, the king's advisor—whose name I learned was Lucan—began to hustle up and down each row. One by one, each new student gave Lucan their name, followed by the god or goddess who had chosen them. Lucan confirmed the details, then announced them to the crowd of Caelestians watching intently. In between each student, he took a moment to document the data on some parchment for the academy's census.

Because I was one of the last on the platform, I was consequently in the last group. At least an hour passed before the advisor made it to my section.

"Name?" Lucan asked the first in my row.

"Anora Faintree," a young woman replied.

"State your jewel."

"Amethyst."

Lucan peered at her hand through the lenses of his glasses, and nodded with confirmation of the violet stone in her flesh.

He straightened his posture. "Anora Faintree. Gifted by the Goddess of Health and Healing, Eloise. Presented with the ability to heal those injured." Lucan's voice bellowed through the courtyard.

Anora beamed as she waved to the crowd, her gemstone on full display to the kingdom who cheered for her. It was going to be awkward when it was my turn and I had no gemstone on my hand to flaunt.

Once the excitement died down, Lucan cleared his throat, and moved on to the next in my row. My fists clenched as he got closer and closer to me.

The student right before me was gifted by the God of the Weather, Zenith. His onyx stone did not reflect light as well as the other jewels, but it sparkled all the same as he shook his wrist when announced to the kingdom.

When the crowd quieted, Lucan moved on. He didn't look up from his parchment as he stopped in front of me and my chest constricted as he spoke. "Name?"

"Maeve Willawood," I reported.

Lucan scribbled down my name without so much as glancing at me. "State your jewel."

I bit my tongue, stopping myself from giving an incorrect answer. I *thought* that my jewels were diamonds, but I also wasn't confident that they weren't just really pale sapphires.

I shuffled uncomfortably. This really shouldn't have been so hard to figure out.

Lucan cleared his throat, and there was no warmth in his tone when he repeated, "State your jewel."

My body temperature rose as I noticed the others in my row

watching me hesitate. My cheeks flushed in response to their steady gazes. I diverted any attention wasted on them and used all of my focus to form words.

"Um, I am not quite sure, sir." My voice quaked in a whisper.

Lucan sighed, rolling his beady eyes away from his parchment to look at me. He squinted at my hands, searching for my jewel, but obviously not finding it.

Brows furrowed, he raised his eyes to my face, narrowing them as he silently judged my ignorance. He looked as though he was going to speak—probably to ask why I was even up here—but his mouth clenched shut when he settled on the location of my gemstones.

"Unbelievable," he muttered under his breath. The king's advisor reached a hand out, brushing a finger over my cheek without asking. Just as he did, a cloud parted in the sky, and the inescapable blaze of the sun beamed down onto us. A glimmer of green light bounced off of the emerald in his hand, partially blinding me as the rays were absorbed by my irises. I turned my neck to avoid the glare and Lucan tilted his head to follow, giving himself a better look at my jewels. He studied them for what felt like forever.

My vision scurried around the students next to me, who wore similar expressions of awe at the location of my jewels. Then without a word, Lucan returned his hands to himself and walked off.

I followed him with my eyes as he scurried to the throne, his compact legs carrying him faster than I'd expected. He immediately began to prattle to King Hawthorne, whose hands were crossed as he absorbed the given information.

My body was completely still as I watched them discuss me. The only movement I allowed for was the rise and fall of my chest. Tension built inside of me as minutes passed of their attention flipping between themselves and me. My stomach rolled over, and I had to look away to avoid gagging all over the stage.

Without notice, Lucan reappeared. His expression was much too serious for my liking, and a rush of panic forced my insides to clench again. My nails drew blood as they cut into my palms, the pain distracting me from my worsening nausea.

"What's going on?" My voice shook, but I forced the words out regardless. I needed answers, but Lucan deprived me of that request.

"Please follow me," he said, not giving me a chance to counter before he pivoted and marched back to the king.

I could hardly feel my legs, but I did as he instructed, following closely behind the small man. Students whispered as we passed by their rows before coming to a halt in front of the king. Peering to the sides of my shoulders, I noticed how all ten of his head soldiers glared at me, not even trying to disguise their shock.

A pair of deep blue eyes glimmered in my peripheral vision, but I disregarded the soldier's gaze. The king rose from his seat, pushing off of the arm rests and moving so close to my face that I could feel his breath on my skin.

King Hawthorne muttered to himself as he inspected my jewels carefully, his focus steady. I flinched at the unexpected touch as he, too, put his hands on me. He stroked the pad of his thumb over my cheekbone, and my jaw clenched in response.

"Unbelievable," he described my jewels with the same word as his advisor had. He pulled away from my personal space and crossed his arms over his chest, his position of power making me feel so small. "Maeve, you said your name was?" he asked for clarification.

I swallowed the pit in my stomach and nodded.

"My dear, are you aware of the rarity of the stones that embellish your skin?"

"Apparently not," I murmured, sounding more sarcastic than I had meant to.

The king's forehead creased, but he did not retaliate against my tone.

I cleared my throat and sputtered out a real answer. "I know it's strange that my jewels are on my face, and even more odd that I have three. But I really don't understand why everyone is looking at me as though I am cursed."

As the words left my lips, a spark of concern pricked my skin. *Something was not right.* I should have considered the possibility that maybe I was an anomaly—a defect. Why didn't I question that more? My situation was entirely too unique. Unheard of.

I clamped my fists closed and forced myself to internalize that worry for the time being.

King Hawthorne chuckled, grinning in such a way that should have brought me peace, but instead did the opposite. "No, Maeve Willawood. You are far from cursed," he countered my claim.

My forehead creased and I shook my head. "Then I don't understand, I—"

"You are not cursed," Lucan chimed in.

"You are the most blessed of them all."

WHILE EVERYONE ELSE WAS GETTING ONE LAST CHANCE TO SAY goodbye to their loved ones, I was whisked away into the throne room as soon as the ceremony finished with one of the head soldiers escorting me. Lucan followed behind us, his petite legs suffering to try and keep up with the soldier's pace.

Lucan never even announced my name or gemstone to the crowd. He just stated that my gift was *of unknown sorts*, then rushed through the rest of the students. I couldn't have cared less—there was enough attention on me, anyway. Giving the crowd a name to work with would have just added to that.

The look illustrated on Delani's face when I was ushered off the stage would be eternally branded into my mind. I couldn't accurately describe the expression. It was something of utter horror. Panic. I was unable to get a good look at my mother, but was sure she had the same expression.

I was just as conflicted as they must have been, and I hated that I had no way of telling them what had happened to me. At least I wouldn't have to see their faces if I was on my way to be killed.

I sauntered along behind the soldier, who had not said a word since he took me away from the ceremony. He brought me inside through the main entryway, then steered me through the twisted, winding hallways of the castle, all the way to the throne room. I was instantly taken aback by the magnificent beauty of the space.

The walls must have been at least twenty feet tall, and were coated in detailed paneling. Every other panel was engraved with intricate floral designs painted in gold, while the ones in between were a deep shade of green. The drop ceilings were carved from oak, and in the middle of the channeled gridwork hung a glittering chandelier, lit with hundreds of finger-sized candlesticks.

I dropped my head in admiration of the floor I walked upon. The luxurious oak boards were arranged into a herringbone pattern, and were so shiny that I feared stepping on them would ruin their luster.

The most incredible attribute of the room, however, was the throne. It sat atop a velvet dais, raised a few feet off the ground by a short staircase. Crafted from the same oak as the ceiling, though stained a slightly deeper shade, the throne housed carvings of constellations. The illustrations decorated the sides of the chair, along with jewels placed randomly throughout the wood grains.

"Wait here," the soldier spoke at last, showing me to a much less impressive chair before exiting the room.

I sat down and tried to get comfortable, even though my half empty rucksack prevented me from leaning back and my mind stopped me from relaxing. I wasn't sure what to expect. I had no indication of what the king meant when he said that I was *the most blessed of them all.* I assumed that was a good thing? But again, I had no idea.

I blew out a sharp breath.

If I die today, I swear to the gods—

Lucan sat down in the chair next to me, his legs barely touching the wood below him. His hands were folded in his lap, placed on top of the parchment he had written on during the ceremony. His eyes squinted over to me, his gaze roaming over my body while he muttered to himself.

Weird.

The silence was obliterating, and I couldn't take being stuck inside my own head any longer.

"What the hell is going on?" I blurted out, granting myself a wide-eyed look from the king's advisor.

Lucan became aware that he was ogling at me, and his face softened. He rose from his seat then bent down in front of my chair, performing a quick check of the room before speaking to me in a hushed tone. "The stones you wear on your face are rare enough simply by their number and location." His head shot up and did another look around before he continued. "But the strain of jewel you were gifted has never been recorded before in history."

My face scrunched in perplexity at his words. Did he mean the constellastone? That was impossible. Blythe had never gifted her stone to a mortal.

Before I could ask a follow up question, he straightened his knees and abruptly backed away to sit back down in his chair. He must have heard something that I didn't, because as soon as he sat down, the soldier who brought me here had returned, along with the other nine head soldiers and the king.

The soldiers stationed themselves at the front of the dais, bowing at the waist as King Hawthorne walked through the gap they left. He climbed the velvet staircase then set himself down properly on the throne.

I did not give him a chance to settle down before I questioned him. "Why am I here instead of saying goodbye to my family like everyone else?"

"You make quite the first impression." King Hawthorne chuckled. "It is a pleasure to meet you, Maeve Willawood."

I gave him a silent nod of acknowledgment. I probably should have bowed like the soldiers did—or at the very least approached the throne to address the king more formally.

Oh well.

The king's hands clasped together as he leaned forward, elbows on his knees. "Are you aware of the gift you have been presented with?"

"I am not, Your Highness." I rose to my feet and straightened my posture, suddenly intimidated by all of the authority that surrounded me in this room.

He cleared his throat before speaking. "As you know, Blythe is the Goddess of the Mind, and I assume you are aware that she has never gifted her cherished jewel to any mortal?"

I nodded slowly in response.

As it became evident that I wasn't going to approach him, the king rose from his seat. He descended the steps he had only just climbed and advanced on me, stopping inches from where I stood. My spine shivered at the feel of his cold, calloused hand when he reached out and cupped it over my cheek.

He examined me as if I were artwork at auction—like he was trying to decide how much I was worth. The way he rotated my head to see every angle of my jewels made me dizzy. I eventually jolted my neck back. I had enough of being gawked at for one day.

His brows furrowed, but he slid his hand from my face and sighed in obvious irritation.

I glared into his soul, trying to demoralize him as he was to me.

He stared back, unaffected, before speaking in a manner that made it seem like the information made no difference to him at all. "You have been gifted the purest of constellastones from the Goddess Blythe."

I blinked. Once. Twice. Three times, before my eyes widened and stayed that way.

King Hawthorne gave me a moment to process, which was more than appropriate as I was in complete and utter shock. This was obviously an error on Lucan's part. The fact that I was even gifted by a god was a rarity on its own. But the fact that I was gifted by *her*—that was impossible.

I saw my stones. They were diamonds. They had to be. Sure, they had a tint of aqua, but that wasn't uncommon with the gem.

I shook my head, denying his claim. "No. Sorry, Your Highness, but that is not true."

Lucan stepped forward. "It is, Miss Willawood. I have been studying minerals ever since I was a boy. There is no question that the jewels adorning your skin are from the Goddess of the Mind," the advisor said.

I scoffed, rolling my eyes. This was insane. They were delusional. "They are clear. Icy like a diamond," I argued.

Lucan held a finger up. "One moment. Let me just—" He rummaged through his pockets, then pulled out a small mirror, silver and round. He flipped the hinges open then held it up to my face.

"See here. Though they are small, you can make out the colors within the stones. From afar they appear as diamonds, but up close it's clear that they are something much greater."

I took the mirror from his hands, trying to see what he was describing. My hope vanished when the lighting of the throne room made it obvious that my gems were not diamonds. The hint of blue that I had seen was sprinkled throughout the icy stone, along with a dulled shade of violet. There were even some tiny iridescent specks of white captured within the grains of the mineral.

They were exquisite—the most beautiful gems I had ever seen. But their beauty did not make up for the fact that I didn't want them.

I snapped the mirror closed and shoved it into Lucan's hand, then crossed my arms over my chest. "Why?" I asked him, not elaborating because I myself did not truly know what I was asking.

Lucan stuffed the mirror back in his pocket. "Why what?"

I threw my arms in the air. "Why did she choose me? Why do I have *three* stones? Why are they on my face? Just…why?"

Lucan dropped his head, and his voice was soft as he spoke to me. "We don't know. But it is not our job as mortals to question the goddess' choice."

I shook my head again, backing away from the two of them. "This is crazy. It's not possible. This—"

Lucan interrupted my stuttering. "What we *do* know is that as the Goddess of the Mind, Blythe is the most powerful deity. You hold a fragment of her power within your jewels. Even though we don't know what that power is, we can assume that you will be more powerful than any other gifted mortal in this kingdom, or even this world," he said in one long breath.

King Hawthorne rejoined the conversation, just to wreck me even more. "We have no way of knowing what you may be capable of. But regardless, you are now the greatest asset Caelestis holds, and you will be protected at all costs."

Every word the two of them said crushed me more and more. The reality of my situation set in, and I stumbled back as fear swallowed me in one harsh gulp. I began to shake furiously, my whole figure quaking under the pressure that was just placed upon me.

The king did not remove his eyes from me as he rambled on—something about my safety and his son. But my brain screamed, rattling against my skull and causing my ears to ring so loudly that I couldn't make out what he was even saying.

I threw my arms around myself as I glanced around the room. The king's soldiers were watching us—I had forgotten they were there until my eyes met a set of deep blue ones. The soldier didn't look away like he had before, and for some reason unbeknownst to me, the subtle familiarity of his gaze helped me to gather myself.

I took a deep breath, cherishing it in my lungs before fanning it out. A small sense of ease washed over me. Not a lot. But enough for me to snap back to reality.

I dropped my arms and my gaze, refocusing on King Hawthorne, who stood still as he waited for me to contribute to the discussion. My mouth clenched shut when I discovered the expression of smugness set proudly on his face.

He almost looked *excited.* Excited that *my* power would benefit *him.*

That pissed me the fuck off.

My body stiffened as my panic turned to anger and I blurted out a statement that everyone in the room would find downright disgraceful. "You have got to be fucking kidding me!" I yelled, not an ounce of shame in my bones for my language directed at our kingdom's ruler.

Gasps emitted from some of the soldiers.

Lucan's jaw clamped shut.

The king's eyes widened, then narrowed into a scowl at me.

I found some courage and stepped back towards him before

anyone could respond. "Let me get this straight. I was gifted by the one goddess who hasn't even acknowledged mortals in what? Thousands of years?" I paused to breathe. "So *not only* am I damned to a fate like theirs—" I pointed towards the soldiers. "Now I'm your *greatest asset,* too? For the love of the gods." I rolled my eyes.

The irony of my situation was astounding.

And hilarious.

What were the damn odds?

The surprise in the king's face, mixed with the actuality of literally *everything,* drew an unexpected reaction from me. Within seconds I was beside myself, laughing so hard and heavy that my stomach ached. I grasped at my sides, my fingers tangling in my shirt as I fell into a fit of hysterics.

"It's just…just—" I tried to form words.

It wasn't really funny, but I had so many emotions swirling within me that needed to escape. I had promised myself that I wouldn't cry today, so this was my only outlet.

I peeked around the room, observing everyone's reactions to my certainly unexpected reaction. Lucan's bulky glasses didn't hide the way his eyes filled with concern—no doubt for my mental status. The woman soldier's mouth was agape—likely in plain shock that I would speak to King Hawthorne in that manner. The scorching hot soldier had an eyebrow raised and almost looked amused as he fought back a smirk. The rest of the soldiers managed to keep a straight face, indicating their successful training. Lastly, King Hawthorne just looked absolutely bewildered.

I didn't care. Not about any of them—any of it. I hunched over at the waist and my breath warmed the hand that I slapped over my mouth.

"I didn't want this." I laughed into my palm before dropping my arm. I let out a wild gasp of air and pushed off of my knees to stand up, putting myself face to face with King Hawthorne's incredibly displeased expression.

My hands held my cheeks as I looked up at the glorious ceiling above me, shaking my head. "I didn't want this," I repeated in a sigh.

Dropping my head, I lost control once more, but in a whole other sense. "I don't want *any* of this!" I screamed, throwing my arms around in a vague gesture.

My vision narrowed to the floor beneath me as my knees weakened and I crumbled under my weight. The room around me faded as I blocked everyone out and stuffed my head into my hands.

I don't want this.

I finally granted my eyes permission to swell with real tears, and they flowed out of me like rapids after a storm. My body shook with my sobs and I refused to pull my head from my hands. It was too heavy. I would stay here as long as needed. I would rot here in this glorious room if I had to.

I didn't look up when King Hawthorne cleared his throat and excused himself, or when I heard the footsteps of the soldiers filing out after him. I didn't look up when I felt Lucan's hand pat the small of my back, rubbing once in comfort, or when he assured me it would be okay.

Only when my eyes were so puffy that they burned and I was confident that I had been left alone, did I raise my head from my hands. I rolled my stiff neck and looked around, only to find a dark haired soldier sitting in the throne, staring at me.

CHAPTER SIX

I peeled my body from the oak floor and wiped the wetness from my eyes, my fingers grazing my gemstones in the process. I winced at the contact, my skin raw from my tears.

I glared over at the soldier, lounging so casually in the throne that you would have thought he owned it. His mouth was clenched shut, making the sharpness of his jawline appear even more distinguished.

My mouth opened to speak, but immediately closed. There was nothing to say. Instead, I crossed my arms over my chest and turned so that he was out of my view. Now that the dust had settled, I found myself slightly embarrassed over my outburst. Then again, how else was I supposed to react?

My eyes wandered over the floral patterns that lived on the walls and I sighed. What now? The other students were likely already shown to their rooms and given instructions on what to expect for the following days until classes began.

A deep, authoritative voice broke through the chaos in my brain. "I'll show you to your dorm," the soldier said as if he read my mind.

I swiveled around in time to watch him climb down the stairs of the dais. He stopped directly in front of me, and I had to really strain my neck to look into his face. I was tall for a woman, but he had at least a foot on me—the sword he wore strapped against his thigh hardly surpassing his knee.

Dark hair framed his face, a few shaggy strands grazing his forehead. My breath snagged on my ribs at his appearance up close. The word *breathtaking* didn't do him justice.

He stood in front of me for the briefest of seconds before his body turned and strode out of the throne room. He clearly expected me to follow him, and despite my apprehension, I did. There was no other choice. I couldn't change my fate—I just had to live it.

My legs were weak as I trailed after him, needing to take long strides to keep up with his pace. He took me back through the hallways of the castle, and this time I really noticed the magnificent stonework that made up the walls. The bricks were lined up so precisely that I could only assume it took years to perfect such detail. Paintings overlaid the walls, depicting previous members of the royal family along with a few landscape views.

We exited through a set of grand double doors. I followed him through the iron gates and along the cobblestone pathway that I knew would lead us to the dormitories. He didn't say a word to me as we meandered along the path.

The further we descended down the castle grounds, the more the ocean came into view. I could smell the salty air, and in just a few steps, I would be able to see where I sat on the shore early this morning.

It was bizarre how things could change so much in the matter of hours.

When I recognized the rocky area, I came to a halt and peered over the edge of the cliff. Daylight allowed me to actually see the depths of the ocean, unrestrained and flowing freely. The waves crashed against nature's wall, leaving bubbly foam piled on the rocks. I took a deep breath in, inhaling the scent of the sea and letting the fresh air bring me back to a realm of sensibility.

My shoulders relaxed as the rays of the sun melted into my flesh and the wind knotted my hair. At that moment, I had a small glimmer of hope that maybe things would be okay.

You were gifted for a reason. Find it. Use it.

My mother's words would be my objective while stuck at Caelestis Academy. I would find the reason for Blythe picking me and make a purpose of it.

Shade clouded over me. I shivered, snapping out of my daydream. Though unneeded, he cleared his throat to announce himself.

I spun to face the soldier, simultaneously taking a step forward and consequently smacking into the hardness of his chest. He was so large that my body slamming against his didn't even cause him to flinch.

Gods.

"Shit. I'm sorry. I didn't realize you were so close. I—" My cheeks flushed as I stuttered then cut myself off.

He replied with a low grunt, then stepped straight back and pivoted sharply to progress back down the walkway.

"Handsome, but not very charismatic," I mumbled under my breath when I was sure he was far enough away.

He led us the rest of the way down the path, turning at the bottom and guiding me to the front entrance of the academy dormitories.

The building was spectacular, lined with windows five stories high. It looked like a miniature version of the castle except more elongated rather than tall, and lacking towers, of course.

The grassy terrain that surrounded the building was concealed by thousands of wild flowers. They danced in the breeze produced by the beach, which lay just beyond a thick line of dune grass. I caught a glimpse of water peeking through from a sanded pathway that began just a few yards from the entrance of the building.

The soldier held the door open for me, and we stepped inside. The space was already filled with the voices of new students, conversing about their strain of magic and how they couldn't wait for classes to begin so they could learn how to effectively wield. A man on the first floor argued with a blonde haired girl about the size of their gemstones, claiming that his was bigger. A quick glance over my shoulder showed that it was definitely not.

The chatter made my head pound, which did not come as a surprise after the day I had. Shutting the voices out, I focused on the spiral staircase we ascended.

My room was located on the second floor, just steps away from the landing of the winding steps. The soldier stepped in front of me, unlocking the door and then handing me the key while he pushed it open. I shoved it into my pocket and stepped into my new home, which much to my liking, had a view of the water.

The room was beautiful, just like I'd expected after seeing the outside of the building. The walls were painted a faint shade of blue, embellished with an ivory crown molding. The birchwood wardrobe in the corner was accompanied by a matching bed frame, centered on the wall adjacent. My attention snagged on a desk sitting beside a set of windows, which would surely get a lot of use once I got my hands on some writing supplies. Surrounding the windows were a pair of beige curtains, long enough to skim the top of the wooden floor boards. In addition there was a cushioned armchair seated in the corner, along with a plush area rug at the foot of the bed. The appeal of the room somewhat aided in softening the blow of the news I'd received today.

"The king would like to finish his discussion with you tomorrow," the soldier said, interrupting my exploration.

I turned to him and nodded, swallowing the instant flood of anxiety that overcame me at his words. The idea that I would have to face the king again so soon after my outburst was slightly terrifying.

"Someone will collect you in the morning to show you to his study," he stated, then turned and exited the room in one swift motion.

I sighed in relief at the sound of the lock clicking—finally alone.

I pulled my rucksack off my shoulders and tossed it to the side, kicking my boots off as well. My bare feet brushed over the rug as I made for the windows, where I took in the view just beyond the glass.

Everything was quiet for the first time in what felt like forever. I took a few deep breaths, at last allowing myself to process everything that had happened since Jewel-Light.

No logic could explain why the one goddess who was known for never blessing a mortal chose me to be her first. I was bitter that I was robbed of one last goodbye from my family, also furious that my life was now at the mercy of the king. Despite all of that, I couldn't deny that there was a minuscule part of me eager to discover what my magic was. And I *hated* that I felt that way.

Admitting that tiny bit of excitement tore me in half.

My fists clenched involuntarily and beads of sweat slid down my forehead. All of the feelings that I'd been suppressing attacked me at once and my stomach audibly gurgled as a powerful wave of nausea overcame me.

"Oh fuck." I inhaled deeply and clenched my mouth closed. My hand slammed over my lips as I ran for the slim doorway by my wardrobe, which I really hoped was a washroom.

After I'd finished emptying the contents of my stomach last night, I laid down on my new bed and fell asleep within minutes. I had woken up in the late evening and showered, but dozed off again right after, still wrapped in my towel and not waking up again until the next morning, when the sound of a heavy knock filled my room.

Still half asleep, I sat up and stretched, taking note of the brightness that cascaded through my window. It must have already been midday. The fact that I slept for that long didn't surprise me—not after the shock I endured yesterday.

Another knock palpated my door.

"I'm coming," I groaned and removed myself from the warmth of my silk sheets. I pulled on a pair of lounge pants and a baggy cotton shirt then shuffled my feet to the door.

With a yawn, I pulled the handle towards me, expecting to see the same soldier who escorted me here yesterday. To my surprise and slight disappointment, it was the female soldier who was present during my breakdown in the throne room. Her skin was a warm beige and her hair hung to the top of her shoulders in a deep shade of twisted auburn coils. Her teeth shined white as she greeted me with a smile.

I knew why she was here, and I couldn't stop the groan of annoyance that climbed out of my throat over it.

She stepped a few paces into my room. "Hi, there! I'm here to escort you to King Hawthorne," she exclaimed much too enthusiastically.

I didn't bother trying to argue my way out. The king always got what he wanted. Instead I faked a smile, hoping it would mask my irritation. "Okay. Just let me put my boots on."

Still trying to fully wake up, I stumbled across the carpet to where I left my boots, then tied them loosely around my ankles. On my way out the door I stopped to turn my lamp off, but before I could flick the switch, the light dimmed to nothing.

My eyes widened, then rolled to meet the woman in my doorway, who flashed me the topaz on her palm.

"Jesper?" I asked in confirmation of who gifted her, though her ability to manipulate light was a dead giveaway.

She nodded.

I had never really been exposed to magic, except for witnessing a few poor wielding attempts at Jewel-Light. "Woah," was all I managed to say.

The soldier smirked. "My name is Jocelyn, I'm one of the king's head soldiers as I'm sure you've pieced together." She chuckled softly.

I raised the corner of my lips ever so slightly in another attempt to show a smile, but I didn't have it in me to make it convincing.

Jocelyn sighed, and I could sense the sympathy in the air. "I know you don't want to be here, and I know that your whole life just got upturned."

I shifted my head to the side, removing our eye contact.

"I just want to let you know that I understand how you feel. I know everyone seems so happy to be here, but some of us aren't."

My eyebrow raised. "You didn't want this, either?" Her peppy attitude could have convinced me otherwise.

"Not exactly. But I adjusted, and so will you. It gets better," she promised.

The vow eased me a bit, but I wasn't in the mood to have a heart to heart—especially not with the person who was about to deliver me to the man making my life a living hell.

I brushed by her, giving her the cold shoulder as I walked out the door.

JOCELYN TALKED OUR ENTIRE WALK TO THE CASTLE, BARELY EVEN stopping to breathe. The conversation was one-sided. I didn't have a single word to contribute.

We slipped in through one of the side entrances, strolling down a long stretch of hallway and stopping in front of an oak door.

She spun to face me and placed her hands on my shoulders. "This is where I leave you. So nice to meet you! I'm sure I'll be seeing you around." She grinned before turning back the way we came.

I released a chest full of air that had been caught in my lungs ever since she knocked on my door. She was friendly, but exhausting.

I stared at the door before me. Was I supposed to knock? Just go in? I could just turn and run.

"She's quite the chatterbox, isn't she?"

My body jumped into a turn at the unexpected voice.

The soldier from yesterday came down the hall from the opposite way I had. He met me at the door before leaning back against it, raising one knee so that his foot could rest against the wood. He seemed way too informal about the king's property to be one of his head soldiers.

"Yeah, she is," I replied.

"She grows on you."

His eyes latched onto me, and my cheeks flushed as I tried to keep my gaze from roaming down his body. The way his black shirt clung to his abdomen made the task difficult. Not to mention how his leather pants hugged his thighs—

He suddenly dropped his foot from the door, turning to push it open and holding it for me. "After you."

"Thanks," I mumbled, forcing myself to enter the study.

"How am I doing?" the soldier asked in a whisper, following behind me.

I paused in the doorway, tilting my head in confusion. "Huh?"

He smirked, his blue eyes lit up with amusement. "I'm trying to be more charismatic."

My heart dropped into the pit of my stomach.

He heard me say that?

My face went blank, and air shot from his nostrils as he tried to fight his laugh.

"How—" I stammered, trying to gather my response. Before I could, I was interrupted by King Hawthorne who appeared in front of me, taking my hand. His grip was harsh, and he did not let go as he led me to a luxurious armchair positioned in front of his desk.

The soldier followed us into the room. He slammed the door behind him, granting himself an eye roll from the king.

"Sebastian, have you never been taught how to properly close a door?" the king sneered as he took his seat behind the desk.

The soldier—whose name was apparently Sebastian—shrugged his shoulders and half-heartedly tried to withhold his grin. His muscular figure relaxed against the back of the door, the size of him preventing anyone from coming in if they tried.

King Hawthorne sighed and shook his head before addressing me. "Are you in a better position to continue our conversation from yesterday, Miss Willawood?"

I considered apologizing for my rudeness in the throne room, but I wasn't sorry in the slightest. "Yes, Your Highness," was all I said.

"Very well." He scooted his chair closer to the desk and clasped his hands on top of the wood. His eyes scanned over a map that lay splayed on the surface. "As I'm sure you understand from our discussion yesterday, you are a rarity."

"Yes, Your Highness," I repeated.

"To reiterate, in case the information was lost during your fit of *irrationality*, you have been gifted three constellastones by the Goddess of the Mind, Blythe."

I nodded in affirmation. No matter how many times I heard the words, it didn't lessen the blow of them.

"Do you understand the magnitude of your gift, or shall I repeat the information?"

"No need, Your Highness. I understand." My eyes followed his finger to the Kingdom of Draemor on the map.

"The King of Draemor, Cyprian Beaumont, has been making claims of another war ever since we defeated them all those years ago. He promises that he will claim the territory they lost, along with taking over Caelestis." He pointed to the land in discussion. "Recently, King Beaumont has strengthened these threats. We do not know when he plans to strike—it could be days or it could be years." He raised his eyes to me. "As I told you, despite your powers being unknown, you are no doubt the most powerful soul in the kingdom."

My heart began to beat rapidly and an unpleasant feeling filled my empty stomach. I knew where this was headed.

The king's gaze narrowed on me. He let out a deep sigh and leaned back in his chair. "Maeve, you are a gift to our kingdom, and we must not let your name make its way to Draemor. You have something that no Draemornian could ever have, and I fear what they may do if they discover that you have the power of Blythe. I have not made the citizens of Caelestis aware of your gift, but when I do, it will be extremely clear that any traitors to the throne will be executed."

I gulped. He said the word *executed* as if it was something he did more than occasionally.

The king watched my reaction, allowing me a moment to process, but not enough time to allow me to get a word in before he spoke once more. "In regards to your safety, you will be watched over at all times by one of the finest soldiers in our kingdom. Once you complete your two years of academy training and are sworn in as a soldier, we can reevaluate your need for protection."

Now that statement—out of all the bullshit information I had received so far—was the sentence that made my blood boil. I may have been new to this world of magic and battle, but I sure as hell didn't need someone protecting me at all hours of the day.

"Absolutely not!" I shouted, shooting out of my seat.

Here I go again, raising my voice at authoritative figures.

"It's bad enough that you're holding me here against my will, but now I need to be supervised at all times? No. I am not okay with that."

Sebastian, who hadn't made a noise since we entered the room, kicked off of the door behind me and moved to stand by the desk. "Unfortunately, it is *not up for discussion.*" He glanced at the king while making air quotes with his fingers. "I already tried."

Mouth agape and shamelessly stunned, I returned my attention to the king as he spoke again. "Sebastian is correct, it is not up for discussion. We need to take every precaution available to us in the event that Draemor does hear word of your power. I cannot risk you being seized right out of our hands. We must take the proper measures to ensure your safety."

"So you're saying that if he *were* to find out about me, he would do what? Kidnap me?" I scoffed, putting my hands on my hips. That was ridiculous.

King Hawthorne nodded. "That is exactly what I am saying."

This man was insane. And I was livid.

"So what if he does?" I asked, regretting the words as soon as I heard the answer.

Sebastian shuffled uncomfortably and dropped his gaze to his boots.

The king cleared his throat, then lowered his voice. "If that occurs, then what happens to you is completely out of my control. There is no saying what he may do to you. It is possible he may let you live freely in his kingdom, or he may go so far as to try and *steal* your magic." His eyes thinned. "That, my dear, is something you never wish to endure."

I knew what he was talking about. I had heard the story. I just never realized it was true.

Delani had once told me a fable about a set of twins. A sister and a brother. On their twenty-first birthday, the sister found that she was gifted by Emrys, but her brother was not. Out of rage and jealousy, the brother cut his twin's ruby from her flesh and implanted it into his own with the aid of a healer and enchanter. The act of cruelty left her weak and powerless, but her brother was able to wield her magic as his own. It was the one loophole to not being gifted, but it was a horrifically gruesome act. For obvious reasons, it was punishable by death.

The story had many more graphic details, and I squirmed trying not to think too hard about them. "Why would Beaumont want me, anyways?"

"Why wouldn't he? You have something no one else in the world has. If that isn't reason enough, then revenge would be my second guess," the king replied.

"Revenge for what? For the war?" It had been twenty years.

Way to hold a grudge.

"For the war, yes. But I may perhaps be the reason he had to take the throne at the ripe age of twenty-one."

My eyebrow arched.

"He killed Beaumont's parents," Sebastian added nonchalantly when he noticed the confusion on my face.

My other brow followed the first.

"Draemor's former king and queen," Sebastian further clarified, a smug look on his face.

I gave him a sideways glance of irritation.

No shit.

With no other explanation, I swallowed audibly and fell back into my chair.

"This situation is hypothetical, of course. As I said, we will take every precaution to prevent any harm from coming your way. For now I feel as though you are safe living in your dormitory, but if at any point that changes, your room will be moved to the soldiers' housing which is directly attached to the castle," King Hawthorne stated. "And may I remind you, that what happens beyond the borders of Caelestis is out of my control. Which is why I must emphasize that you are forbidden to leave the castle grounds during your time at the academy, unless approved beforehand."

I twiddled my thumbs as I rocked back and forth in my seat. *Angry* wasn't even close to describing the rage I felt. I wanted to fight this, but knew it was pointless. What King Hawthorne wanted, he got.

"So who's my knight in shining armor?" I sneered.

King Hawthorne looked towards Sebastian. "That would be my son. He is the best soldier we have, and he will do everything in his power to keep you well protected and…*intact*."

The realization set in. "Oh, come on."

I had wondered why Sebastian was even here, but it all made sense now. The matching blue eyes and the general lack of regard for the king and his property—Sebastian *was* his son. I had completely forgotten that I asked Delani about that during the ceremony.

Once the shock factor wore off, the denial set in. Sebastian had been nothing but a standoffish ass with the few words he'd even spoken to me. Now I was stuck with him knowing my every move for the next two years? The thought made me fume.

"What about Jocelyn? Can't she be my guard?"

"While Miss Coswell is a talented soldier, she is only one year graduated from the academy. You will be in much better hands with Sebastian."

My nose scrunched and I groaned in annoyance. "Is there anything else you need from me, or may I go?" I had to get out of here. I'd deal with this issue later.

King Hawthorne tapped a finger on his desk as he wracked his wretched brain to see if he missed anything. "Actually, there is one more thing."

"Of course there is," I muttered through gritted teeth.

"The first gala of the year will be tomorrow at dusk in the great hall. I will have a selection of gowns delivered to your room in the morning. Caelestis' greatest weapon must be dressed appropriately," he chimed.

Lovely. I'm expected to be a weapon of war and a debutante.

"Is that all?" I asked again, and when he nodded, I rose from my seat and showed myself to the door, not holding it for Sebastian who I knew trailed behind me. He caught it with his hand regardless, then closed it behind us much gentler than he had on our way in.

I marched to the wall across from the study and laid my hands against it, extending my arms fully and pressing my forehead against the cool rock. I stayed in this position for a minute, focusing on my breathing so that I didn't lose control in front of Sebastian—again.

The amount of stress that I had endured since Jewel-Light should have been enough to break me down. But I kept it together. This was not the place to show weakness. Those moments were to be saved for the confines of my room. Well, besides the throne room, it would appear.

I took a final few deep breaths, then pushed off of the wall and walked straight past Sebastian and down the corridor. I didn't care what the king's orders were.

I don't need a bodyguard.

Sebastian called after me, but I ignored him.

His footsteps echoed behind me, and in an attempt to leave him behind, I picked my pace up to a jog.

I sped down the corridor, taking the same path that I had with Jocelyn. Taking a sharp corner, I picked up speed and raced through the hall. After a minute or so I glanced over my shoulder once and didn't see anyone following me, so I sighed and slowed my legs back to a walk.

I was almost to the main gate when Sebastian was suddenly just *there*—right in front of me and taking the impact of my body as I crashed into him for the second time since we'd met.

My body ricocheted off of his and shock consumed me as I steadied myself and clenched my fists.

"How did you do that?" I snarled.

"There's more than one hallway in the castle," he pointed out with a wicked grin.

I rolled my eyes. *Obviously*.

In an attempt to pass, I stepped to the side of him, but he grabbed my shoulders and stopped me. His hands were large enough to cup the entirety of my joints. His hold on me was firm, preventing me from moving forward.

My brows furrowed as I bent my neck to look at the smugness on his face. My eyes traveled through his, wandering in the shades of blue that swirled in response to the lanterns that illuminated the corridor. He had literal cosmos circulating within his irises, and they were the most captivating eyes I had ever seen.

I snapped out of my admiration for this man and reminded myself of why I had tried to get away from him in the first place. If the king was his father, then the man before me was likely just as corrupt.

Lowering my brows, I snarled, "Let me go."

"Sorry. No can do."

I wiggled my shoulders, trying to get out of his hold. "I don't need you to take care of me," I hissed.

Sebastian tightened his grip. "Good. Because that's not my job. I'm not your house maiden, I just have to keep you alive."

"Let go!" I yelled, not caring if any bystanders heard me.

He didn't budge.

I pursed my lips at him and my eyes started to burn with the sting of salt. "Please," I begged, with no luck.

"I will let you go when you stop fussing. You're causing a scene," Sebastian growled under his breath, his eyes darting around the corridor.

"I don't care."

His grip tightened even more.

The odds were not in my favor, but I dared to ask anyway, hoping the gleam in my eyes and the cracking of my voice would be enough to convince him. "Can I *please* just have this one afternoon alone before my every waking move is monitored by you?"

Sebastian stared at me, pondering my request. His gaze seemed to soften, and after a few moments, his hands went slack, falling from my shoulders. He nodded slowly. "Fine. But you are to go directly to your room and stay there. I'll have lunch delivered to you." He stepped to the side, giving me room to pass, and I didn't hesitate.

I sauntered the rest of the way to the main entrance, and when I looked back, he was gone.

CHAPTER SEVEN

My wakeup call the following morning was from a slender, older woman who made quite the ruckus as she rummaged through my wardrobe. She scurried around my dorm, hanging gown after gown on the rod at the top of my wardrobe. I sat up in my bed and marveled at the way the skirts gathered on the bottom of the chest, pooling into puddles of glitter and silk.

King Hawthorne had said that someone would come to deliver me dresses, but I wasn't expecting their arrival so early into the day. I also had no idea how she got into my room, but I elected to not question it.

Once all of the gowns were hung, she gestured for me to rise with a snap of her measuring tape. My body cracked as I stood and stretched my arms above my head, giving her access. She wrapped the measuring tape tightly around my waist while informing me to browse through the gowns and select one for the gala. She would be back in a few hours to tailor it, and said that she would have the others altered by the end of the week for future events. She let herself out once she was satisfied with her measurements, and I scurried to see what she had left inside of my wardrobe.

Upon opening the doors, I was met by a spectrum of color and a medley of fabric. Corsets of silk constructed a rainbow in my room, shimmering from the sunlight that danced through the window. Chiffon skirts glazed with ribbons and lace filled the dresser, some simple and some covered in intricate designs.

One dress caught my attention almost instantly. I pulled the form-fitting gown off the hanger and laid it flat on my bed. The fabric was an ivory satin scattered with thousands of tiny crystals, their colors ranging from the palest of purples to the deepest shades of blue. The bodice was translucent apart from the bosom area and the boning that stiffened the corset. The gown was completed by a set of thin, beaded straps attached to a sweetheart neckline. I didn't even bother looking at the other gowns. The colors and luster of this one reminded me of the stones that garnished my face. Though I may not have been happy about my gemstones, I had no choice except to embrace them.

I left the gown out for when the seamstress returned, then got dressed for my day. It was then that I realized I had absolutely no idea what I was even supposed to be doing. I had missed the new student debrief while I was meeting with the king. Classes did not begin for another few days—I knew that much. But I failed to ask anyone what was expected of me in the meantime.

I sat on the edge of my bed, contemplating my next course of action. If I left the bounds of my room, there would be a soldier waiting for me and I wasn't sure if I was ready to have my every move watched. But then my stomach gurgled, reminding me of a more dire matter.

I was fucking starving.

I didn't eat the lunch Sebastian had delivered for me yesterday and hardly picked at my dinner, either. I haven't had much of an appetite since Jewel-Light. Not to mention that I had thrown up again last night when I tried to eat—King Hawthorne's orders made me physically sick.

My stomach tumbled again, accompanied by an audible growl. I needed to get some sustenance in me if I wanted to stay standing, so finding something to eat was the first task on my list.

My wardrobe had been stocked with other various clothing items, so I rummaged through the drawers and took out a pair of dark pants. They were a little snug around my hips, but they buttoned. I pulled on a plain cotton shirt and then laced my boots up over my pants. I didn't bother to do anything with my hair. I let the natural waves flow down my back, then left the privacy of my dorm.

I started my descent down the spiral staircase, only to find my newfound guardian propped at the bottom of the stairs, his nose deep in some literature.

"Ugh," I groaned and walked right by him. I pretended that I didn't notice him, and prayed that he wouldn't notice me.

He of course, did, and slammed his book shut as he stood up and walked after me.

I considered trying to get away from him again, but the more I thought about it, the more I realized that he actually could be of use to me right now. I paused my strides and pivoted to face him. "Where can I find something to eat?"

Sebastian scoffed. "Well good morning to you, too."

"Morning," I grumbled.

"I was beginning to think you were going to spend another day locked in your room." He flashed me a half-hearted smirk that should have made my insides melt, but I was too hungry to think about how handsome he was.

"Why would you think that?"

"Because it's almost noon."

My eyebrow raised. *Was it really?* No wonder the seamstress had let herself in.

"Do you always sleep that late? That may be a problem when classes start."

"No," I huffed.

"Should I add wake up calls to your regimen?" He didn't hide his teasing smirk.

"No."

"Are you sure? Attendance is high on the list of importance when it comes to having a successful semester."

"No," I hissed, quickly realizing that he planned on bantering with me for a while. The steady rippling of my stomach couldn't tolerate that, so with a roll of my eyes, I made for the door. The sun slapped me in the face, but I embraced the daylight and started up the cobblestone pathway towards the castle.

"You do realize you have no idea where you are going, right?" Sebastian said, following after me.

He wasn't wrong—I didn't know much of the castle grounds aside from where the festival was held. At that very moment, however, I didn't care. My hunger led my travels.

"You do realize that the information your father keeps blasting me with has me puking up everything in my stomach, right?" I shot back.

I looked behind me just long enough to get some amusement at the way his nose scrunched.

"Lovely," he sneered.

I was teetering at the edge of the castle when he grabbed my hand and yanked me off of the pathway. He guided me through the sun bleached grass, away from the castle's main gate. His calloused palm was rough as it rubbed against mine in tune with the motions of our feet.

If I was being honest, I didn't *hate* the feel of his skin on mine, but I also didn't love it. I knew that once I got my own hands on a sword, that they would feel the same way—thanks to *his* father's orders. I shouldn't have judged him based on his family, but the reminder of who he was still caused me to rip my hand free.

"Where are you taking me?" I asked.

Sebastian didn't answer.

"I may not know the kitchen's exact location, but I know it's not this way," I said.

He stopped in front of the southeast tower. There was a cement door built into it which he pulled open, beckoning me through. My hunger drove my movements, and with the hope that there was food beyond the door, I stepped into the tower after him.

He was silent as he led me through the cramped corridor. We

arrived upon a straight staircase that only led down. He started his descent, and though my brain told me otherwise, I did as well.

We must have climbed down at least ten flights of stairs, and I was out of breath by the time we reached the bottom. Climbing back up would be torturous, but I stepped into a dark tunnel regardless. The only light was that emitted by the lanterns hanging on the stone walls. The air was cool and damp, which felt nice compared to what awaited us back outside.

At the end of the tunnel, I caught a glimpse of a wooden door. I froze at the sight of it, my body refusing to proceed any deeper into the tunnel. Sebastian continued on into the dimly lit underpass, not yet having noticed that I no longer followed him.

I could feel the color draining from my face as a sense of alarm creeped up on me. What if he was taking me to the dungeon until I was needed for battle? Or maybe he was going to cut my gems from my skin, like in the fable.

Those weren't the most rational fears, but I wasn't going any further. Absolutely not.

Sebastian looked over his shoulder. He noticed my hesitation and turned back. "Come on," he urged.

My voice trembled with the increasing angst that had captivated me. "I'm actually not feeling that well, so I think I'm just going to go back to my dorm and rest before the gala," I lied and slowly backed up, not taking my eyes off of him. I had been foolish to put any amount of trust in this man. I didn't know anything about him aside from his bloodline—which wasn't something to put faith in. And if what the king said about my gift was true, I needed to keep my guard up at all times, even with my supposed bodyguard.

Sebastian raised an eyebrow at me. "You just said you were starving." His voice hinted at his confusion.

My muscles were tense and I tried to hide the shaking of my legs as I backed further away from him. "I'm not anymore."

Sebastian took a singular step towards me, and I flinched, the fear I suddenly had for him controlling every movement my body made. He sighed, stepping back when he recognized my apprehension towards him. "Just wait here."

He turned from me and started back down the tunnel. My body relaxed the moment he vanished through the wooden door.

I put one foot back on the staircase. Now was my chance to run if I wanted to. I had no idea what was beyond that door. For all I knew, there could be more soldiers waiting to chain me up in a dark vault. Though I had no reason to suspect that of Sebastian, I decided not to take any chances.

I bolted up the staircase as fast as the weakness in my legs would allow me. I kept a grip on the rail to steady myself as I ran—my hunger combined with the rapid use of energy caused me to feel light-headed, and now would not be a good time to take a tumble down the stairs.

I powered through the dizziness, continuing to climb until I reentered the corridor. I ignored a few bewildered looks as I rushed through the hall, not stopping until I reached the door. I pushed the cement slab open with all of my force and burst through. I was sweating as soon as the raw heat of summer hit me, but relief filled me once my feet touched the grass.

Panting from the exertion I just put on my body, I hunched over, setting my hands on my knees as I took a moment to catch my breath. When I could breathe again, I straightened my torso and found myself face to face with the king's head soldier.

Damn, he's fast.

And he looks pissed.

He held a small satchel which he shoved into my hands. Then he grasped my wrist and dragged me to the side of the tower, out of sight from any bystanders.

"Let go," I spat, flailing my arm.

His eyebrows snapped together. "I'm trying to be patient with you, because I know you are having a difficult time with everything. But what happened back there cannot happen again." His voice was commanding through his gritted teeth.

I glared at him and tried to shake my wrist free of his grip, but he tightened his hand around me, causing a sharp pain to radiate up my arm.

"I don't need you to protect me," I testified, ripping my arm away with such strength that his fingers were forced to unlock.

I tried to put some space between us, but he stepped forward, backing me into the wall of the tower. He put his hands against the wall above my head and leaned forward, putting his face close to mine.

"Do you think I *want* to be your protector?" he snarled. "Do you think I want to spend my time chasing after you and making sure you aren't taken hostage or killed? I'm a soldier, not a damn babysitter," he growled in my face.

My mouth settled into a hard line. The term *babysitter* caused a slight sting in my chest, but I swallowed the feeling.

"Then don't."

Sebastian's jaw ticked. "You think I have a choice about this? Believe me, there are a million other things I'd rather be doing," he contested.

"Oh, poor you," I drawled.

His mouth squeezed shut, and I could tell he was trying not to explode.

"If anyone gets to complain about not having a choice here, it's me," I added.

Sebastian blew out a deep sigh. He didn't break our eye contact as he slid his hands from the wall, setting me free from the cage of his arms.

"My job is to keep you safe. I know you're not happy about it, but too bad—neither am I." He paused to grind his jaw. "I don't need to be by your side all hours of the day, but at the very least, I need to know where you are. Running away without a word of where you're going won't fly with me." Without another word, he turned his back to me and strode away.

He wouldn't go far—I was sure that the moment I moved out from under the tower, he would be there. But with him out of my vision, I relaxed my shoulders a bit, not realizing how tense I was. My spine made contact with the stone behind me, and I slouched down against the wall to sit in the grass.

The shade from the tower offered my skin some shelter as I

untied the satchel Sebastian had handed me and emptied its contents onto my lap. A variety of fruits spilled out of the bag, along with some oat bars and pastries.

My heart sank.

That door had led to a pantry.

Sebastian was actually *trying* to be nice, and I made an ass of myself. Although, he *did* just call himself a babysitter in regard to me, which pissed me off more than it should have.

I didn't quite understand why my disappearing made him so angry, especially considering he clearly didn't want to look after me, anyways. So far he was exactly who I'd expect him to be as the son of King Aldous Hawthorne.

Whatever.

I picked up a glossy, red apple, rolling it in my hands before taking a bite. I savored the taste of it, the ache in my stomach subsiding with each mouthful.

I only stopped eating when the pain from starvation was replaced with a new ache. For a reason I couldn't grasp, my altercation with Sebastian hurt more than I'd ever expected it to.

CHAPTER EIGHT

The gown I had chosen for the gala was hanging back in my wardrobe when I returned from my argument with Sebastian. Just like I had expected, he was waiting to walk me back to my room when I finished eating. Neither of us spoke the whole way back. I had nothing to say to him.

The setting sun snuck into my room through the gap in my curtains. I had just finished showering and sat wrapped in a towel in my armchair, combing through my freshly washed hair. I braided the sides loosely and let the rest hang free. When finished, I dropped my towel to put the appropriate undergarments on, then pulled the dress off of its hanger. I bunched the fabric of the skirt so that I could step into it and pulled the gown over my legs.

The tailor did an incredible job, as the gown slid past my hips and up my torso with ease, fitting precisely as it should for my body type. The satin hugged me in all the right places, emphasizing the indent of my waist and the curve of my hips, while also leaving just the right amount of cleavage at my bust.

I struggled to lace my corset when I heard a female voice coming from the other side of my door. "Is anyone in there?"

I shuffled to the door, expecting it to be Jocelyn standing in the hall, but was instead met by an unfamiliar face.

"Sorry to bother you, but it seems like our whole floor is practically men, and I knew a woman must live here because I saw the seamstress bring in some gowns earlier. Anyways, would you mind buttoning the back of my dress for me? I can't reach the last few," the girl rattled on until she was out of breath. She appeared disheveled, her strawberry hair in disarray on top of her shoulders and her cheeks flushed as if she'd been running.

I was slightly taken aback at the way she rambled like we already knew each other, but she smiled at me and I found myself returning the gesture.

"Of course." I stepped aside, granting her entry into my room.

She sighed in relief, leaving the door cracked open then shuffling to my armchair. Her dress dragged on the floor as she walked, making me question if she had no shoes on yet or if it was just too long for her. She was quite petite, so I assumed the latter.

She sat and twisted her body so that I had access to the line of buttons on her back, then my fingers got right to work, moving meticulously to fasten her gown closed. Her dress was simple—a dark shade of green with no appliqué or shimmer on it.

"Thank the gods for you, I've been trying to button these darned things for the good portion of an hour. Every time I get one done, another one pops open," she complained.

"I've been fighting a similar battle with my corset." I let out a small huff of laughter.

"My name is Pia Hawthorne, short for Piper," she introduced herself as I brushed her hair to the side so that I could reach the buttons at the top.

"Nice to meet you. I'm Maeve, not short for anything." A bit delayed, my eyebrow raised when I recognized her last name. "Wait. Hawthorne?" I asked, stepping to the side of the chair when I finished the last button. "Are you related to the king?" *Oh gods, did Sebastian have a sister?*

Pia rose from the chair and made straight for my washroom. "Yup!" she called back to me. "The king is my uncle."

That made that arrogant ass Sebastian, her cousin. *Poor girl.*

Pia's hair was tidied up when she emerged from the washroom. She positioned herself behind me, lacing my dress without me having to ask. I gasped as she yanked on the ribbons of my corset, cinching the waist way tighter than I would have. I didn't say anything though, and once I got a glimpse of myself in the mirror in my washroom, I didn't question her lacing abilities, either. I'd always loved dressing up, but this took it to a whole new level.

Pia came in to stand by my side. "We look hot," she stated. I chuckled because she was right, and also because that's something Delani would have said.

I chewed my lip to prevent tears from spilling at the thought of my family.

"Wait a second, you're the one everyone's been talking about?" Pia asked, catching a glimpse of my gemstones glistening in the mirror.

"Um, I guess?" King Hawthorne said he hadn't announced my gift to the kingdom yet, but I had disregarded that people may have discovered it for themselves at the Jewel-Light ceremony.

"You are!" Pia put a finger out to feel the jewels on my cheek bone. She was awfully touchy for someone I just met—as everyone in this castle was it seemed—but I didn't shoo her away.

She gaped at my cheek. "I overheard a second year student say that one of the newly gifted had been blessed by Blythe, but I thought it was a joke."

"Really? You're in the royal family. I would have assumed you'd be kept in the loop," I said, her words taking me by surprise.

Pia scoffed. "They don't tell me anything, but I like it better that way, anyways."

"Well yeah…It's me," I confirmed her suspicion. "But if it's all the same to you, would you mind keeping it quiet until the king decides that it *has* to be everyone's business? I'm content knowing that it's still somewhat a secret." I hated being the center of attention, and dreaded the moment that the king decided to announce my gift to the kingdom. "I just would like to pretend that I'm a normal first year for at least a little while longer," I continued.

Pia nodded in acknowledgment and moved her hands back to her hair, adjusting it in the mirror before we both reentered the living space. It was then that I noticed the amethyst burrowed into her hand.

"You're a healer?" I asked in an attempt to change the subject. Before she could respond, a deep, male voice filled the room.

"Pia, what are you doing here?"

I turned to see Sebastian standing with one hip relaxed against the doorframe—he seemed to have a thing for lounging against entryways.

His attire was mostly black, aside from buttons built of diamond that ran up the center of his shirt and also held together the cuffs at his wrists. His slacks were fitted around his thighs, accentuating the muscles of his legs. His outfit was finished by a pair of shining boots, tied mid-calf with silver laces. He looked dashing, and heat flooded my cheeks at the sight of him in his formalwear.

His eyes roamed me for the briefest of seconds, looking away when Pia waltzed over to him. "How do I look?" She smiled before doing a twirl and a curtsy.

He grinned and dipped his chest in a bow. "You look lovely." His expression turned back to all seriousness. "Now, what are you doing here?"

Pia frowned. "Maeve was just helping me with my gown. Why does it—" Her mouth fell open in an epiphany. "Ohhhh," she glanced between Sebastian and me, "Maeve is who Uncle Aldous instructed you to guard?"

Sebastian nodded, still avoiding me as if I wasn't even in the room, which Pia noticed.

She scrunched her nose at him. "Would it kill you to be friendly? You come off as such a jerk."

I couldn't help but snort out a laugh. At least she recognized who she was related to.

Sebastian shot me a look of warning, which I disregarded as Pia turned to me. "Well thanks for your help, Maeve. I'll find you at the gala! Sorry you're stuck with him." She angled a thumb at her cousin and flashed me a smile before leaving.

I watched her go, then turned my back to Sebastian in hopes that he would go, too. He must have gotten the hint, because I heard the click of my door as it latched closed.

I moved for my window, one hand grasping the sill while I used the other to brush a curtain to the side. The colors of dusk crept into the room, painting the walls orange. The moon was a sliver of white in the sky, and a few stray stars twinkled around it in preparation for their time to shine.

I sighed, releasing a breath of anxiety about what Pia had said. I knew that it was only a matter of time before I was the hot gossip of the castle, but the confirmation that I already was didn't sit well with me. I hadn't been overly nervous for the gala, but I was now.

A throat cleared behind me.

My body tensed as I spun around, pressing my back to the window. Sebastian was standing against my door with his hands stuffed into his pockets.

I rolled my eyes at him. "I thought you left."

"No."

"Well I wish you had."

He scowled, but inched forward. "I'm here to escort you to the gala. Are you ready?"

"No."

"Too bad. You have thirty seconds."

Clicking my tongue, I bent down and buckled the pair of heels that the seamstress had left for me, then gave Sebastian a nod of annoyance when finished. He tried to speak to me as I strode by him, but I held my hand up to silence him. I didn't care to hear what he had to say.

Sebastian followed me from afar on our walk to the great hall. When we arrived safely, he strode off to meet with some of the other head soldiers, but still stayed within my sight.

The hall was much larger than I had expected. I spun in a tight circle to take in the entirety of it, every square inch of the space fascinating me.

The wooden walls had vines carved into them, beginning at the baseboard and climbing up to the ceiling. A crystal chandelier dangled over the center of the room, lit with jewel-toned candlesticks. White and gray marble made up the floor that was clustered with students, soldiers, and castle personnel. The room was simple in nature, but the array of taffeta and glittering jewels that swirled around the dance floor made it spectacular.

"Maeve!"

Pia stood in a corner of the room with a group of other first years. She ushered me over and began introducing me to everyone. I really did try to focus on their names, but I could feel Sebastian's eyes on me. My gaze wandered to where he stood with two other soldiers.

They were dressed the same as him, indicating their status as head soldiers. One of them was a few inches shorter than Sebastian—six foot four, if I had a guess. The soldier's fair skin made his light brown hair stand out. The other, who was the shortest of the three, had caramel skin and green eyes so bright that I could see them from where I stood.

They all had qualities that made them nice to look at, but Sebastian was no doubt the most attractive of the group. Too bad he was turning out to be such a jerk, because based on looks alone, he had all the qualities a girl could want.

The three of them were deep in conversation, joking about something based on the expression of the taller man's face.

"Maeve?"

I jolted my head back towards Pia as she said my name.

"Huh? Oh, I'm sorry. Hi, I'm Maeve. Nice to meet you," I said to the man whose hand was outstretched in front of me, holding a drink. I accepted it, flashing him an insincere grin as a thank you, and then pressed my lips to the glass.

I said hello to a few more of the first years, none of which acknowledged the jewels lining my face. I knew that they saw them—the gems were an obvious eye catcher—they just knew better than to gawk.

Our group seemed to grow rapidly as the better portion of an hour passed, and I soon found myself feeling overwhelmed by all of the new faces. The bottom of my dress rippled over the marble as I stepped away from the crowd, needing a few moments of personal space.

I walked by where Sebastian had been stationed with his friends, but he was no longer there. I glanced around, sure that he would be within range of me, but he wasn't—at least not that I could see.

"He's getting into formation with the other head soldiers." Pia's voice startled me.

I flinched and spun around. Was it that obvious that I was looking for him?

"Oh. Yeah. Of course he is." I twirled a strand of my hair nervously, trying to act nonchalant. "Um. Why?"

"My uncle always delivers a speech at the start of his galas. His head soldiers stand behind him. He should be starting any minute."

Releasing my hair, I nodded softly in recognition and turned my head around the room. There were an endless number of eyes pointed at me. People whispered to each other while their gazes held steady on me. I brushed their stares off, fiddling with my fingers as I turned to Pia. "I need more wine," I stated.

"That sounds like an excellent idea." She dragged me to the nearest buffet, also providing a good view of the king when he was to begin his speech.

I drank from my glass. "So have you lived in the castle long?" I asked Pia after I swallowed.

"For about five years," she responded mid-sip. "My mother died from an illness and I never knew my father, so Uncle Aldous took me in."

She mostly seemed unfazed, but her answer made me frown. "I'm sorry. I shouldn't have—"

"No, no, it's fine! I've had years to process it."

It wasn't fine, and she knew that as well as I did. It didn't matter how well you knew the person, or how much time had passed. The aching never ceased.

"I never knew my father, either. He died in the war before I was even a year old," I informed her, hoping to give her something to relate to.

Pia chewed the inside of her cheek, then raised her glass in the air. "Well here's to being fatherless and drunk!" She *clinked* her goblet against mine.

Her comment pulled a laugh free from my chest, and we both took a sip of the sweet wine. I felt very comfortable with her for some reason, so I didn't worry about offending her when I asked, "Why is your cousin such an ass?"

She didn't answer right away. Her eyes widened, and I began to get nervous that I actually *had* offended her. But then her face turned red and she spat out a mouthful of wine in laughter.

"Once you get to know Seb, you'll change your mind about him. He has a really big heart, just a strange frickin' way of showing it," she assured me through her fit of giggles.

"Are you sure about that?"

She chuckled again. "Believe it or not, I am."

We talked for a while longer, thoroughly enjoying each other's company. I described Delani to her and told her how the two of them would get along well. She talked to me about her upbringing and how her and Sebastian had always been really close. I confessed my hesitation about being gifted, and in return she told me how she abandoned her bedchambers in the castle to live at the dormitories with the rest of the first years. The king had tried to convince her otherwise, but she threw a fuss about having the *full academy experience*.

Thanks to her company, the night was going much better than I had expected. That was until King Hawthorne and his soldiers paraded into the center of the hall. "Good evening, students, soldiers, and royal citizens. I hope you are enjoying the first gala of the academy year." His voice bellowed throughout the great hall.

I had no trouble making his words out—I was standing right in front of him and his advisor. Sebastian was stationed beside his father. He fidgeted with a button on his wrist, looking almost uncomfortable.

Having missed the information when the other students received it, I gave the king my full attention as he discussed the expectations for the school year and explained the process of being sworn in as a soldier. He went into detail on his criteria for choosing his head soldiers, and urged all of the new students to strive for reaching that goal.

He briefly introduced the topic of Draemor's war threats, which I already knew from our conversation. Then, just when I thought he was about finished, his eyes darted towards me. He motioned for me to approach with a wave of his finger.

My breath quickened. *Was he really going to do this now?*

My feet froze to the marble floor beneath me, and the strength of my gut was tested as the wine I drank bubbled and sizzled its way up into my throat.

When I still did not move despite his continuous gesture, King Hawthorne leaned over and whispered to the brown-haired soldier I had seen Sebastian with earlier. The soldier nodded and left his formation to come towards me. I looked towards Sebastian as the soldier dragged me forward, but his eyes avoided mine.

King Hawthorne placed his hands on my shoulders, putting me on full display for the crowd standing before us. "I assume most of you have heard the rumors of a new Caelestis Academy student who has been gifted constellastones from the Goddess of the Mind?" he asked the crowd, waiting for the chatter to subside before he continued.

I gazed nervously around the room and watched as hundreds of faces pointed their focus at me.

King Hawthorne took a breath. "I am honored to be the one to confirm your suspicions and introduce you to Maeve Willawood. She contains the most blessed gift of the gods, and as a kingdom, we must do all we can to ensure that knowledge of this gift stays within the boundaries of Caelestis."

He could have worded the following information in a way that made it seem less intimidating, but he said the threat just as bluntly as he had to me yesterday. "If I hear of any traitorous activity regarding this information, then the person responsible will be executed."

That information did not go over well with the crowd, and chaos broke out in spouts of angry heckling.

"So it's true? Why weren't we informed of her gift at Jewel-Light?"

"Freak!"

"Why would Blythe choose her?"

"What makes her so special?"

Those were only some of the comments I heard. There were some words of amazement, but I tuned them out along with the proclamations full of rage and jealousy.

The attention made my body temperature rise as panic started its heated course through my veins. My nails tore the skin of my palms as I locked eyes with Pia, whose face sunk as she noticed my skin fade to the color of snow.

"Are you positive she has constellastones? From here they look like diamonds."

"She's a fraud."

"You mean to tell us that if we so much as speak to an outsider about her, we will be killed? That is the most—"

"*Enough*!" King Hawthorne barked, his voice echoing throughout the hall and making me jump. "I will not tolerate any of this!"

The crowd quieted.

"The rest of the kingdom will be made aware of Maeve's great gift to Caelestis by the end of the week. The Duke will travel through our villages and cities to spread the word. In the meantime, pick your jaws up off of the floor and enjoy the rest of your evening."

I shuffled uncomfortably when the king at last released his grip on me and strode out of the hall, leaving me as the focal point of the room.

His soldiers dispersed into the crowd, and I should have done the same, but my body was paralyzed. The pallor of my cheeks was replaced by a deep shade of crimson and my eyes filled with scalding tears, brought on by the horrified looks directed at me.

I chewed on my quivering lip, trying to release my anxiety through the pain, but it was no use. Suddenly, the room was too bright. The walls were too closed in. My dress was too damn tight. It was all too much. I couldn't take it.

The pressure of a hand grazed my upper arm, and I didn't need to look to see who it belonged to. I didn't care if he would be mad—I shrugged his arm away and forced my legs to help me escape the purgatory I was in.

CHAPTER NINE

I ran as fast as possible in heels. I ran until I was outside of the castle and away from the horrified looks belonging to my classmates.

Going back to the dormitory was my best option, but I couldn't be confined to such tight quarters right now. I needed air. Needed to breathe.

My mind didn't know where to go, but my body did. It took off down the cobblestone path along the cliffside. Sand trapped itself between my shoe and the arch of my foot as I bombarded the beach. I unfastened the buckles of my heels and threw them to the side, then sank to my knees in the sand.

My palm slapped against my chest as the air thickened and my breathing became difficult. I gasped and slid the straps of my dress off my shoulders, trying to remove anything that confined the walls of my chest from expanding properly. In the process, my fingers caught on the pendant from my mother, and the added reminder of how she wasn't here sent me toppling over the edge.

I let out a wail of sheer, emotional anguish.

Tears dripped down my nose. The saltiness crept its way into my mouth, and I could taste it on my teeth as I wept in the sand.

Why couldn't Blythe have chosen someone who actually wanted to be gifted, like Delani? She would have loved the attention and power—and that wasn't a bad thing, that's just who she was.

Me? I wanted nothing less.

I fisted the sand and let it dribble out of my hands as I sobbed.

I felt pathetic.

I *was* pathetic.

If I planned on retaining any dignity, I needed to find a way to prevent ambushes like this from happening. Gods forbid any of the other students saw me like this—they'd sense my weakness immediately. I couldn't allow that. Not when I already had a target on my back.

I took some deep breaths and stared up into the night. The atmosphere was illuminated by a sliver of golden moon that peeked through a fading cloud. My hyperventilation let up with my counting of the stars, but I still choked on air as my tears continued to spill.

In time, the twinkling stars gave me my breath back, and I rose to my feet, wiping the final shroud of wetness from my eyes. Sand fell from the satin of my dress as I secured the straps back into their proper position on my shoulders. My gaze scanned the shore for my shoes, and found them a few yards from where I collapsed. I decided to keep them off. Sand and stilettos didn't mix well.

The few sniffles I had left were hidden by the sound of the waves as I started my walk back to my dorm. Soon enough, the pathway that took me here came into view, along with a very angry Sebastian. His eyes narrowed on me as he stormed across the sand, meeting me where I stood.

"What did we literally talk about *mere hours* ago?" he snarled as he approached, his fists clenched.

He had every right to be angry, and I didn't have the energy to argue. "I'm sorry," I stuttered, not knowing what else to say.

His eyebrows pulled together when he got close enough to make out the swollen features of my face. "Are you okay?" He came to a halt in front of me.

"I'm fine." I brushed him off coldly, turning my head towards the ocean.

"You're crying."

"No. I *was* crying. Now I'm fine."

He sighed. "Listen, I'm sorry that I didn't prepare you for the speech tonight. I was going to tell you about it, but you just really pissed me off earlier and I—"

"Hold on." My gaze darted back to him. "You *knew*? You knew that he was planning to put me on the spot like that and you didn't bother to give me a warning?"

Sebastian stammered, "I kind of figured it was a given after what he said yesterday. I mean, when's a better time to make an announcement than when you already have half the kingdom in front of you?"

My eyebrows arched in anger. The king had never specifically said when he was going to announce my gift, but I figured I would have received some sort of a warning.

"It wasn't *a given*. He was pretty fucking vague about it, actually. And you could have given me a heads up, but apparently you like to hold a grudge," I snapped.

Sebastian rolled his eyes. "Oh, come on," he drawled. "It's not that big of a deal. And it's not my fault you were gifted by the one damn goddess that has never made an appearance. Telling that information to the kingdom would have sucked for you no matter when or where it was told."

I chewed the inside of my cheek. It *was* a big deal for me. "Did you not hear the things people were saying?"

Sebastian stepped towards me. "Who cares what they say? I mean, how did you expect people to react to news like that? They'll all get over it in a few days I'm sure, but did you really think there wouldn't be some sort of backlash when they found out?"

"No. I just didn't expect to hear their comments about it tonight. I don't care what they think of me." I didn't—the attention just stirred something up inside of me. Something my brain wasn't born to handle.

Sebastian scoffed. "Yeah, sure seems like you don't care." His eyebrows gestured to my puffy facial features.

My lips thinned. "Screw you," I growled through gritted teeth. I stepped towards him, raising myself to the tips of my toes so that I could put my face close to his. "If you must be my *babysitter*, then fine. Be it. Do whatever you have to do. But do me a favor—do it so that I have to see you as little as possible."

I lowered myself to my heels and shoved my shoulder into his chest as I strode past him. "Asshole," I mumbled under my breath, though loud enough for him to hear.

He followed me—he had no choice. But I ignored his presence and slammed my door in his face when I made it to my room.

I SPENT THE MAJORITY OF THE NEXT FEW DAYS IN MY DORM WITH PIA for company. She tried to assure me that the talk about my gift had subsided, but I didn't fully believe her. Regardless, classes were set to begin this morning, so I had no choice but to bow to the inevitable.

Sebastian was waiting for me at the bottom of the stairs when I left my room, as he had been every day since I'd arrived here. My throat released a grumble of annoyance at his presence.

I walked right by him to meet Pia outside. She and I had talked briefly about my argument with her cousin, but she didn't have much to say aside from reminding me that he *really was a good guy*. I told her that *I'd believe it when I see it.*

Sebastian trailed behind us on our walk to Caelestis Academy, about half a mile east of our dormitory. The building was massive, built completely of rust-colored brick. There were ivory pillars stationed along the sides of the staircase that Pia and I climbed to reach the entrance.

I turned my head slightly from the top of the stairs when I heard Sebastian call out from behind me. "I'll meet you right here when you're done."

I flipped him my middle finger.

The whole purpose of Caelestis Academy was to prepare its

students to become soldiers, so we would spend most of our class time in either Combat Training or Wielding Education. We also were required to attend Kingdom History and Battle Tactics, but not as frequently.

Pia showed me to the classroom where our wielding classes would be held. We sat at desks next to each other, waiting for our professor to arrive. Students filled in around us, and much to my surprise, a few that I met at the gala said hello to me. Most others didn't acknowledge me, but I received no backlash like I had that night, so maybe Pia was right after all.

A lanky, dark-skinned man entered the classroom shortly after we sat. I guessed that he was middle-aged from the way his head had only a shadow of hair left. He introduced himself as Professor Stoll, giving us the briefest of introductions before he jumped right into the magic of wielding.

"You are all here because a god or goddess has deemed you worthy enough to hold a portion of their magic. As you know, but I am required to reiterate, the gods give a small piece of their power to those they find capable. This is their way of having us mortals aid in the balance of nature. It makes less work for the gods, and a bit of fun for us." He flashed us a grin before continuing. "Your gift has been with you since the moment you were conceived, but only just recently did you discover it, and even more recently, were you able to access it." He clasped his hands behind his back as he started to pace the room. "Now let me ask, how many of you tried to use your magic after the meteor shower last week?"

More hands than I'd expected shot up.

Professor Stoll huffed a laugh. "And how many of you were successful?"

All of the hands dropped.

"There is a reason for your failures. The gemstones embedded in your flesh are why you have the *ability* to use magic, but actually wielding it comes from within your soul."

My eyes glanced around the room to try and see if I was the only one confused. By the looks on the other students' faces, I wasn't.

"Before we begin learning the art of wielding, it is important you understand the physical purpose behind the gift of gemstones." Stoll went on to explain how the jewels symbolized our world at its core and how they were a representation of the essential elements that made up our planet. He went into much more detail, but I tuned him out—I already knew most of this information from the primary school I attended growing up.

When Professor Stoll finished his lecture, he moved the class outside to the grassy lawn behind the academy. He broke everyone into groups based on the god that gifted them, evidently leaving me in a group by myself.

I made eye contact with Pia, who stood with the rest of the students who had been gifted by Eloise. She shrugged her shoulders and offered me an awkward half-smirk, then focused her attention on Stoll as he addressed her group first.

He bounced between all of the groups, instructing them how to harness their magic, and suggesting a few simple maneuvers they could try. I was last, which made sense for obvious reasons. When he finally approached me, he jumped right into business.

"I am assuming you have no ideas regarding what your powers may be?"

I tossed my head side to side.

He sighed in discontent. "I was hoping some indication of your gift may have manifested itself to you in passing, but that was a slim chance. It's difficult to harness magic when you don't know what your magic is." He clapped his hands together. "Here is what we are going to do, Maeve."

PROFESSOR STOLL HAD ME SPEND THE MORNING ROTATING BETWEEN groups, trying to wield the power of each god in the rare chance that mine manifested from attempting the others. Much to his dismay, it did not.

It turned out to be a good thing that we practiced outdoors. A boy from Emrys' group accidentally lit another student's hair on fire.

She suffered minor burns, which the healers were able to practice their magic on. Most of the class was able to harness the basics of their power by using their minds and palms to exteriorize their gift. And no one ended up dead, so that was a plus.

I left feeling discouraged with my failed attempt at discovering my power. I would be lying if I said that I didn't feel left out, but my magic would announce itself within time. I wouldn't see Professor Stoll again until later in the week, so hopefully by then I would have something to show him. And honestly, the longer it took for my magic to manifest, the antsier King Hawthorne would become, which brought me an immense amount of joy.

There was a midday break during which Pia and I enjoyed each other's company under a juniper tree. She was rambling enthusiastically about how amazing it felt to have her magic rush through her when a shadow darkened my vision. Pia raised her eyes to the person standing above me. I rotated my head slightly to see who it was, then rolled my eyes and turned away from him.

"What do you want?" I asked Sebastian while taking another bite of my sandwich, trying to disregard his presence.

Sebastian stepped around me and squatted down so that I was forced to look at him. "Pia, would you excuse us for a moment?" he asked without breaking his gaze from me.

She gathered her belongings a little too quickly. "I'll meet you at Kingdom History," she said to me before scurrying off.

I tried to appear carefree about the presence of the large man crouching before me, but the intimidation in his features was enough to throw my body off center. His eyes were glued to mine, and I held the stare as I grabbed an apple from my rucksack. I raised it to my lips to take a bite, but Sebastian took the fruit from my hands, biting it himself before handing it back to me. Scowling, I took it back, but let it fall from my hand and onto the grass.

The shades of blue in his eyes glistened in response to the midsummer sun as he glanced down at the fruit. His dark hair laid messily upon his head, and the fitted shirt he wore left no room for imagination—I could see every curve of his toned arm muscles.

As he raised his head, my stomach fluttered, my blood rushing to my cheeks. I may have despised him, but he still affected my body in mysterious ways.

"What do you want?" I repeated myself, remembering my anger.

Sebastian released a deep breath as he leaned his back against the trunk of the tree and sat down. "First of all, I told you that I would meet you outside after your class," he said, lifting one dark eyebrow in suspicion.

"We are outside," I said.

He raised his other brow. "Not what I meant."

I shrugged. "You should have been more clear."

Sebastian ground his jaw and fidgeted his back against the tree. "Also I wanted to explain myself. The other night—"

I didn't allow him to finish. I was still pissed about that. "I don't care to hear your explanations, Sebastian."

"I know you don't care, but please just let me—"

"No!" I jumped to my feet. "No. You can't possibly *explain*, because there's no reason good enough for why you couldn't have warned me about the gala. And you can tell me all you want that the way I feel *isn't a big deal*, but you don't know what goes on inside of my brain—it makes everything so much worse than it really is," I ended my sentence in a whisper.

Sebastian rose to his feet as well, keeping his eyes locked on me. I didn't know where my confession came from, but I found myself wishing it had stayed inside.

"I'm sorry for saying that it wasn't a big deal." He rubbed the back of his neck. "And I may not know exactly what you're going through, but trust me when I say that I understand what it's like to be trapped in your own head."

"Oh, please." I shook my head dismissively.

"I'm serious."

"Are you really trying to compare yourself to me? You don't have any idea about what I've been dealing with, and as far as I'm concerned, you never will. So as I said, save your damn explanations, I don't want to hear them." I crossed my arms over my chest.

We stared at each other. And then the asshole smiled.

He fucking *smiled.*

My mouth dropped open and my hands fell to my hips. "What?"

Sebastian looked up and shook his head, biting his lip to prevent a laugh.

I repeated myself in a growl. "What?"

He dropped his gaze, still shaking his head. "I just can't believe I have to put up with this shit for two fucking years."

My fists clenched, and I suddenly felt no shame in admitting to him the hatred that lived inside of me. I was pissed, and he was going to be my outlet.

"You and I both. And while we're being honest, I have a few things I'd like to get off my chest." I paused to suck in a much needed breath. "The way your father forces the gifted to be a weapon of war makes me sick. The way he only sees me as his asset is disgusting," I snarled at him, taking a step forward and shoving him into the tree out of pure outrage.

He could have very easily fought back—his size compared to mine was to his benefit, but he stayed calm and allowed me to blow my temper.

"The way you knew he was going to put me on the spot like that at the gala, but couldn't even warn me about it because you were what, *grumpy*? Pretty immature, if you ask me." I jammed a finger into his chest. "Lastly, the way you just do whatever Daddy tells you is ridiculous. You're his son—you must have a say in how the kingdom is run. You must have a say in all of this!" My arms flew up as I shouted the words in his face.

Sebastian's mouth drooped into a frown and his whole demeanor switched. "That's where you're wrong," he whispered, backing away from me. "I have never had a say about anything in my fucking life." He tucked his hands into his pockets and walked away.

CHAPTER TEN

Myself and the other first years were given some time to adjust to our magic before combat training sessions began. I didn't really need the extra time—I still had no magic to adjust to. But regardless, those weeks had passed and the first training session was today. Pia met me at my room so we could walk together. The early days of fall were approaching, and without the dry heat of summer dehydrating the earth, the grass stayed slick with drops of dew as we trudged through it on our way to the academy.

Sebastian strolled off to join the other head soldiers when we arrived in the combat arena. In all honesty, I had forgotten he had even walked with us. I tried my best to ignore him, and we hadn't exchanged more than a few words since the first day of classes. He escorted me around the castle grounds when needed, but besides that, we basically pretended that the other didn't exist.

Professor Stoll had given us a brief rundown of what to expect for combat sessions, so I knew what to look for when I arrived. The arena was separated into five combat rings, each with a large, painted number in the center. All of the first years would be sectioned into groups. Each group would be instructed by two of the king's head soldiers, making the odds of Sebastian being in charge of my group slim.

Pia stopped at a wooden board by the entrance. "Thank the gods," she exclaimed.

My eyes followed her finger pointing out our names under group three. I sighed a breath of relief, and we made our way to our mat. We sat down along the padded edge and stretched while waiting for our instructors. I tried to ignore the staring eyes of my classmates. Most of the chatter about me had subsided, but not many of the students bothered to talk to me.

Your boot is untied, I mouthed to a girl across the mat.

She stuck her nose up, turning her head and ignoring me.

"Rude," Pia scoffed loud enough for her to hear, then checked the laces of her own shoes.

We were given combat uniforms that were required for training. The uniform was small and tight, designed without any extra material for your opponent to grab on to. The men's outfits were essentially the same except for longer, slightly looser shorts. I shifted uncomfortably and pulled the fabric of my shirt away from my flesh. I hated the way it hugged every part of my body, emphasizing the curves of my stomach that I wasn't particularly fond of.

My eyes rose as I saw Jocelyn waving in my peripheral vision. I waved back, hoping she was one of my instructors, but my eyes sank as they followed her to mat two. The shorter of the two soldiers that I had seen Sebastian with at the gala followed behind her.

His name, according to Pia, was Kohen Sharpe, and I couldn't help but notice the way her lips fought back a smile as he walked by.

I raised an eyebrow at her, but she shouldered me with a warning.

I rose to my feet along with the others in my group as the rest of the soldiers entered the arena. One by one, they walked right past mat three.

"You've got to be kidding me," I muttered under my breath as Sebastian approached my group.

He gave me a side eye like he heard me, and a part of me hoped that he did.

"Good morning, everyone. In case you don't know me, I'm Sebastian Hawthorne. And this," he gestured to the other soldier I had seen him with, "is Sawyer Sinclair."

Sawyer nodded, not offering us even a hint of a smile as his gaze skimmed the crowd. He appeared much more serious today than when I saw him laughing at the gala. The way his eyes narrowed on me sent a rush of distress cascading through my vertebrae.

"Morning. Welcome to Combat Training. Seb and I will be your instructors for the remainder of the year." Sawyer locked his hands behind his back and began pacing around that mat. "This course is designed to kick your ass. If you don't leave today's session bruised and in pain, then you didn't work hard enough." He proceeded to tell us the expectations for class and the next thing I knew, we were in the depths of training.

The drills were designed to work every muscle in our bodies. Within minutes of the first exercise, my forehead was dripping sweat and my body ached deep into my tendons.

One man threw up not even half an hour into the session. Another student tripped during our run and snapped her ankle. One of the healing students tried to fix it, but she ended up needing to be escorted to the infirmary.

Pia elbowed me gently. "I've never broken a bone, and *really* don't want to after seeing that," she whispered.

Today's training mainly focused on endurance, with a bit of strength work added in towards the end of the course. I handled the drills better than most others in my group, but was still completely overexerted by the time I had a chance to glance at the clock. The session was almost over—and a good thing—my body couldn't handle any more today.

Pia, along with the others, were getting ready to pack up. I made for my rucksack to do the same, passing by Sawyer on my way. He whispered to Sebastian, who nodded in response. The two of them then moved past me and positioned themselves in the center of the combat mat. The other students and myself froze.

"Did we say you could pack up?" Sebastian snarked. "We aren't done yet."

Groans over having to exert more energy filled my ears.

"We don't usually start sparring practice until the third or fourth session, but given the circumstances, Seb and I think it would be a good idea to introduce you all to some basics of combat," Sawyer announced, a single eye raking over me.

Circumstances? I hope he means the issue of Draemor and not the issue of me.

Sawyer patrolled around the mat, his hands crossed behind his back. "Any volunteers?"

To my surprise, a dozen hands shot up, eager to be the first to learn some techniques for battle. I kept my arms tightly against my sides.

Sawyer reviewed the candidates, shaking his head. "No. No. None of you." He tapped his finger on his chin, pacing back and forth in front of us. "Willawood!" he bellowed, making a sharp turn of his body and marching to where I stood.

My heart knocked against my ribcage, but I didn't have time to protest. Before I could even truly acknowledge what was happening, Sawyer had my hand in his and was pulling me to the center of the mat.

I caught Sebastian's eyes as they widened. "Woah, Sawyer, wait—"

"Relax, Hawthorne," Sawyer drawled, releasing my hand. He backed up, putting himself a few feet from me. "She's the strongest of all of us. Isn't she?" he said, and I did *not* like the sarcasm in his tone.

"Actually, I don't think I'm the best fit for—"

"I'm going to show you all some basic offensive and defensive moves that you will eventually utilize in real life combat," Sawyer cut me off as he addressed my classmates.

My mouth filled with saliva. *Shouldn't he have been doing this demonstration with Sebastian?*

"Take your stance," he ordered me, his eyebrows sinking into his skull.

I honestly had no idea what to do, but clenching my hands into fists and raising them defensively seemed like a good place to start.

"Willawood here, will show you all her best attempt at defense," Sawyer sneered. As soon as the words slipped from his lips, he was behind me, kicking the sole of his boot into the back of my right knee. My legs swung out from under me, and I landed face down on the mat.

"Hey! What the—" I rolled to my back and tried to sit up, but before I could, Sawyer straddled me, pinning my arms to the mat beneath me.

"Woah, woah, woah! Hey, Sawyer, come on. That's not what we talked about," Sebastian yelled from the edge of the ring.

Sawyer ignored him, tightening his grip on my wrists so hard I swear he could have cracked them.

"Ow." I struggled underneath him.

"Now would be a good time to utilize any weapons you have on you, or your magic." He flashed me a devious smile. "If you have any."

Dick.

His comment struck a match of rage inside of me. I rolled my shoulder over fast, managing to break one arm free from his grip. I used it to grab the back of his neck and fisted his hair, pulling down as hard as I could. I slammed his forehead into the mat beside me, then rolled out from underneath him and jumped to my feet.

Pia was the only one who cheered from the crowd. The others watched us in dead silence.

Sawyer rose, his teeth barred.

I smirked back tauntingly. I'm sure he wasn't expecting me to embarrass him like that.

He growled as he lunged for me, grabbing me by the shoulders and whipping me around so my back was pinned against his chest. He held me there and tightened his grip, squeezing my stomach so hard that if I had just eaten, I would no doubt be throwing it up.

"In this move—" He squeezed me tighter as he spoke to the class. "If you have a dagger on your hip, you may just be able to reach it and stab your opponent between the ribs."

I gasped as his hands locked around me, compressing my body so tight that I could barely draw a decent breath.

"Sawyer, that's enough."

Sawyer ignored Sebastian's plea and instead jostled his arms to try and adjust his grip. He released his hold just enough for me to slide one of my arms between us and uppercut him in the jaw. His teeth rattled against each other, and his arms released me to clutch his chin. I dropped my body down and backed away, raising my arms to block him should he try to strike me again.

Sawyer cracked his neck, scowling at me from across the mat. He stood as still as a corpse, just watching me.

Was that it? Was he done?

He didn't take a step towards me, so I stupidly let my arms down and lowered my guard. I glanced towards Pia for a split second.

Big. Fucking. Mistake.

Sawyer sprinted forward and was on me within seconds, throwing his whole body into mine. My back slammed into the mat, his entire weight falling on top of me. My head ricocheted off the floor, making my ears ring and the room around me spin.

"You need to watch your mouth when you're talking to the king's head soldiers, Willawood," Sawyer snarled, spit and blood dripping from his teeth.

Okay. So this is about me.

Sebastian must have told Sawyer how I'd been mouthing off to him.

I parted my lips to protest, but my jaw clamped shut when Sawyer planted his fist into the side of my face. My vision blurred from the force, my head pounding so hard that I bordered the fine line of consciousness.

"Sawyer, what the fuck!" I heard Sebastian yell, and I vaguely made out his figure as he grabbed Sawyer's shoulders and pulled him off of me.

The release of pressure aided in my vision returning to normal. I sat up slowly, holding my hand to my cheekbone. It stung to the touch, but otherwise seemed intact.

Sawyer spit out a mouthful of blood on the ground in front of me, then wiped his lips and stormed out of the arena.

"At least my punch drew blood, asshole," I called after him.

Kohen's figure appeared above me. His blond-brown hair was matted with sweat against his forehead, and he looked just as angry as Sebastian did. They spoke briefly before Kohen darted out of the arena after Sawyer.

Sebastian watched him go, shaking his head in disappointment. "Class dismissed," he announced to everyone in the arena. "Everyone get the hell out!" he yelled when no one moved.

While the others packed up and filed out of the arena, Sebastian reached a hand out to help me up. "Are you okay?"

I declined, swatting at his palm. I didn't need aid from someone who clearly had a part in this. I tried to stand on my own, but stumbled and fell back to my knees.

Sebastian moved behind me and lifted me up by the underarms.

"I'm fine," I grumbled, shouldering him away from me.

"You're bleeding."

I raised a hand to my throbbing cheek, wet and warm from my blood. Damn. Sawyer's punch actually *did* split my skin—I didn't notice it before. *Awkward.*

"What did I do to deserve that?" I snarled, spinning to face Sebastian as I wiped the blood from my face.

He looked taken aback. "What?"

I scoffed. "Don't play dumb. I saw you two whispering to each other on the mat."

He shook his head. "No, Maeve, I had nothing—"

Pia rushed over to where we stood, my bag thrown over her shoulder. "Are you okay? That was totally kick-ass what you did to him!"

I faked a grin while the soreness in my muscles took over my body. "I'm fine," I repeated myself.

She took my hand. "Let's go back to the dorms. I'll try my healing magic on your wound."

I nodded and stumbled off the mat, paying no attention to the soldier who followed after me.

Pia was able to stop the bleeding on my face, but she hadn't practiced her magic enough yet to fully close the wound. She pushed me to go to the infirmary for sutures, but I assured her that it would heal on its own in a few days. When I finally got her to reluctantly agree, she left and I showered before falling asleep in utter exhaustion.

My head was still throbbing when I woke hours later. I wouldn't have been surprised if I had a concussion from Sawyer bashing my skull into the mat. *Oh well.* There would be plenty of those during my time at the academy.

I rolled to my side and looked out the window. The sun had almost set, meaning my nap lasted longer than planned. I should have gotten up and gone to the castle for dinner, but the idea of having to face Sawyer or Sebastian again today gave me goosebumps.

I let out a long, heavy sigh and pulled the quilt up to my neck. How had everything in my life gone so wrong in a matter of weeks? I was happy before I was gifted. I had spent most of my time at the beach or working with my mother. Now, I was getting my ass handed to me by the king's soldiers.

My fingers lifted to the gash carved into my cheek. "Fuck," I moaned, the wound aching to touch.

A soft knock hit my door, and I jolted upright again, clutching my blanket into my fists. "It's unlocked," I answered mid-yawn, figuring it was Pia returning.

My eyes narrowed on him as Sebastian let himself into my room, closing the door behind him. The corner of his mouth twitched upward in a sad attempt at a smile. He looked out of sorts, and though I hadn't known him for long, he didn't often seem to get frazzled.

"What could you possibly want?" I questioned, obvious annoyance rolling off my tongue. The *audacity* of him to come here—his friend just beat the crap out of me, and I was sure he had something to do with it.

He took a few more steps into the room before he spoke. “Please just let me talk before you say anything,” he insisted.

I didn't have the energy to resist, so I pointed my eyes at the ceiling, doing anything I could do to avoid his gaze.

Sebastian sighed heavily. “First of all, I'm sorry for what happened today on the mat. I had no idea that Sawyer was going to attack you like that. It was uncalled for and an abuse of power.”

I dropped my eyes to him and sat up a little straighter, pushing my back against the headboard. “You didn't know? Really?” I raised my eyebrows in suspicion. “Am I supposed to believe that?”

“I swear to the gods that I didn't know. Sawyer suggested demonstrating some techniques, but he didn't say anything about using you as an example. I never would have allowed that had I known.” The seriousness in his expression was enough to make me believe him.

“Then why didn’t you intervene?”

“That is incredibly frowned upon. The fact that I tore him off of you at the end was dishonorable enough.”

I’ll tell you what's dishonorable.

My lips parted to counter his claim, but he got the first word. “Let me finish,” he demanded and inched closer to me. “I’m sorry for not warning you about my father’s plans to announce your gift during the gala.” He held his gaze to mine, hardly blinking as he went on. “And I'm sorry I was such a dick about it afterwards. You didn't deserve that.”

My blatant shock was obvious. “No. I didn't.”

He held a single finger to his lips and took another step towards my bed. His cerulean eyes were sewn to mine with an invisible thread, and I couldn’t look away.

My breaths quickened. I pulled the quilt up higher to cover my breasts, suddenly all too aware of the thinness of my shirt's material.

“I’m sorry for yelling at you under the tower. I didn't want to, but you have no idea about the implications that my father has set for me. If anything happens to you—" He averted his glorious eyes from me to walk to my window, settling his hands upon the sill.

I watched the way the muscles of his back tightened as he drew a breath, holding it for a moment before setting it free into a deep sigh. His head bowed. "My father will always do everything he can to protect Caelestis. Even if that means putting the kingdom before his family."

Silence overwhelmed us. I wanted to ask exactly what he meant by that, but something told me that now was not the time to pry. He seemed so...*unbalanced. Distraught.* As if he truly was sorry for these things.

When I was sure he was not going to say anything more, I slid out of bed and went to accompany him at the window. He didn't look at me as I joined him in staring out at the twilight.

My breath fogged the glass of the window. "I'm sorry that I assumed the worst of you, and that I've been making your job more difficult, and for all of the terrible things I have said to you." My apology was soft spoken and much shorter than his, but it was heartfelt and I meant it.

Sebastian turned to me, his eyes glistening in the soft light of the moon. A forced smile found his face, though it was short-lived, vanishing when he caught a glimpse of my wound. He reached out to touch it, but stopped himself, putting his hand back on the window sill.

"I'm going to kick his ass," he mumbled under his breath.

I brushed a finger over the injury. "It's not that bad, and let's be honest, it was only a matter of time before someone beat me up," I tried to joke.

He didn't laugh.

The air was heavy between us. Strangled with tension and something else that I couldn't quite name.

Sebastian blew out a deep breath before pushing off of the window sill. He tilted his head in my direction. "Now that that's out of the way, I say we start fresh. We are going to be spending a lot of time together over the next few years, and it will be a hell of a lot more enjoyable if we can get along."

The corner of my lip tugged up. “Sounds like a plan.”

“Good. Okay.” He forced a brief smile as he turned for the door, but I stopped him.

“Wait. Can I ask for a favor? You know, seeing as your friend used me as a mop today?” I chuckled, but he still didn't laugh.

“Sure.”

“Would you be able to get me some writing supplies? I know we aren't supposed to write to family, and I swear that I won't. I just want to…write.”

Sebastian’s forehead creased, but he nodded. “Sure.”

CHAPTER ELEVEN

"Sebastian came to see me the other night," I told Pia.

We sat on a quilt in the sand during our break before wielding class. We'd both been so busy with homework that I hadn't seen her since Sawyer used me as an *example*.

A giant smirk crawled across her face. "Oh really?" she teased with a wink.

I stuck my tongue out and shook my head. "He actually came to apologize." I filled her in on the details of the conversation.

"See, I told you to give him a chance," Pia chimed.

"Yeah, yeah, whatever." My eyes locked on a tiny crab, scurrying along the edge of the water, fighting to keep from being swept away into the depths of the ocean. "What do you think he meant when he said that he's *never had a say about anything in his life*?" I pried, figuring she would know considering she's his cousin.

Pia went rigid.

"What?" I asked. "Sore subject?"

She looked around the beach to make sure no one was within earshot of us. "My uncle has not been the most outstanding father to Seb," she whispered. "I'm sure you know that my aunt Cicily—Seb's mother—was killed during the war against Draemor."

I nodded. Everyone knew about Queen Cicily's tragic end. Her funeral had been kingdom wide. According to my mother, the queen was as pure as they come, which really made me question why she married such a prick.

Pia lowered her voice to less than a whisper. "She was beheaded right in front of Sebastian. He was only about five-years-old at the time, but it was so traumatic that he remembers every detail of it."

My lips parted in shock as my shoulders shuddered. The pain from witnessing an act so gruesome was unimaginable at any age, let alone five. Even worse when it was your own mother.

Pia continued, "In regard to Sawyer, I'm not sure if you know this, but he and Sebastian have been friends ever since they were children. Sawyer's father has been the Duke of Caelestis for years. He is a non-royal, of course, but my uncle and his friendship was strong enough to grant him the title." She paused briefly to make sure I was following. "After Cicily passed, my uncle made Seb a part of things that a child should never be a part of. I'll spare you the details on that though—I already overshared. But Sawyer knows about all of it… he's seen a lot of it."

My eyes rolled at the mention of Sawyer's name. I had only seen him once in passing since our altercation. His eye had been swollen and purple, and though I doubted it, I wondered if Sebastian had something to do with the injury.

I glanced back at the crab who was losing its battle with the waves. "That's sickening," was all I could say. I didn't have the right words.

"Sawyer is one of the few besides myself and Kohen that know details about Sebastian's past. Which is why they are so protective when it comes to him," Pia disclosed.

"That explains Sawyer's attack on me."

Pia nodded. "I would bet my magic on it."

"Can I ask another question?" I waited for her approval before continuing. "King Hawthorne said something about how he killed the King and Queen of Draemor…why?"

"He executed them both the year after my aunt Cicily was killed. Beaumont was the Crown Prince at the time—only twenty-one-years-old and freshly gifted when he murdered my aunt. My uncle decided that the best revenge would be to kill his parents and make him watch." She dropped her gaze to the sand. "Should have killed Beaumont in my opinion. To be honest, I don't know how Uncle Aldous lives with the fact that the person who murdered his wife is still breathing. I sometimes wonder if he even truly loved her."

I wanted to ask more, but Pia's head jumped up, staring down the beach. I turned and followed her gaze to see Sebastian walking towards us.

"Please don't tell anyone that I told you any of this," she begged, her nervousness blatantly obvious as she picked at the sand on her shins.

We stood, and my pulse quickened as he strode towards us, so fluent in the way he walked. His dark hair blew from the ocean breeze, and the vibrant sky joined with the blue in his eyes, amplifying their beauty.

"You two are going to be late for your wielding sessions," Sebastian said as he approached us.

I stared at him intently. He didn't seem like a man who was followed by darkness, but I knew better than anyone that sometimes it was necessary to hide your truth from the world.

Sadness bombarded me. Maybe he and I were more similar than I had thought.

"Why are you looking at me like that?" He raised an eyebrow at me, and I realized that my mouth had dropped into a frown.

My brain somehow managed to create an excuse without hesitating. "I was just thinking about how sad it must be to have nothing else to do besides follow me around all day to inform me of the time," I joked, trying to hide any indication that Pia just spilled some of his deepest secrets to me.

His lips curved up and he gave the sarcasm right back to me. "You know, it *is* quite sad." He took a step towards me, putting his body within inches of mine. His head dipped down so he could speak more directly at me—our height difference made that difficult.

"What's even sadder though, will be *you* when Stoll throws you out of class for being late," he taunted, a mischievous expression taking up residency on his face.

My jaw went slack. Without breaking our eye contact, I reached behind me and grabbed Pia's arm, dragging her across the sand in a hurry.

We made it to Professor Stoll's class without a second to spare. I suppose having Sebastian looking after me did have its perks.

Pia and I were the last two to arrive, so she plopped herself into a desk at the front of the classroom and I made my way to the last empty spot in the back. I slouched into my chair, tossing my rucksack down by my feet.

"Ladies," Professor Stoll addressed us. "Nice of you to decide to join us."

A few students snickered under their breath. I ignored them, crossing my arms over my chest.

Stoll walked around to the front of his desk, pushing himself up to sit on top of it. "I imagine you have all been practicing wielding outside of class, and I would like you to continue doing so."

I shifted in my seat uncomfortably. I had been trying to wield, but when you had no implication of the type of magic you should be wielding, it was extremely difficult. I questioned if the constellastones marking my skin were really a gift at all. So far they had deemed themselves useless.

Pia had tried helping me. She explained how you could feel the magic tingling in your skin. From there, you should be able to use the depths of your mind and soul to harness the magic. She explained it like an expert, but it made no sense to me.

Stoll's voice carried through the room. "Today we will discuss the topic of mental shields. Not always, but there will be times where you may be able to block out magic that someone harnesses against you. If your shields are strong enough, you can stop someone from wielding their own powers against you." He slid off his desk and began to pace up and down the classroom. "It's a very complex use of power. But once you have mastered it, you will be grateful that you have." He stopped when he reached my desk, making eye contact with me for a moment before whirling on his heel and marching back to the front of the room. "Choose a partner, and I will teach you how to apply the power of these shields to your mind."

Everyone jumped out of their desks. Pia rushed to my side, claiming me as hers.

"Are you sure you don't want to work with someone else? I can't even wield yet. It's going to be a pretty one-sided lesson for you if you work with me," I explained in a whisper.

"Just because you can't wield your magic yet doesn't mean that you can't block someone else's," she argued.

"I know, but—"

"We are working together. Shut up."

We followed Professor Stoll out of the classroom and on to the academy grounds. He had decided to keep wielding lessons outdoors until we all get a better handle on our power. Last week, the first death of the year occurred. A student from another class had lost control of their fire magic, burning their partner down to the bone.

I recognized the student as someone in my row during the Jewel-Light ceremony. Anora, her name was. Her body was sent home to her village, Ferolla, where she would be buried.

"Stand across from your partner, about a foot away. Decide which one of you attempt your shield first. The other will harness some of their power against you," Professor Stoll instructed.

"Well I have no magic for you to block, so I guess I'll try to shield yours?" I asked Pia for confirmation, not that it was needed.

"Wielders, please inform your partner on what magic you plan on performing. Shielders, knowing what you'll need to block can help simplify things," Stoll announced as he circled around our groups. "In battle, your opponent obviously will not tell you what magic they plan to use against you. But for the sake of this lesson, the knowledge will help you be successful."

Pia turned her attention to me. "Okay, I'm thinking that I'll try to use my healing powers on the cut on your face. I know I couldn't fully heal it the other night, but maybe now that it's closing up on its own I can finish the job," she suggested.

I agreed. If I could block her magic—great. If I couldn't—at least my face would be healed.

"Now shielders, I want you to close your eyes and focus the depths of your mind on something that makes you feel relaxed. It's important to fully clear your mind when you are blocking out magic."

I squeezed my eyes shut. This would be easy for me. I had been practicing techniques to help relax my body and mind since a young age. My brain drifted into thoughts of the ocean. The feeling of saltwater drenching my skin when in the depths of the sea. The sounds of waves colliding with the shore. The smell of salt and sand coating the air. I fully submerged myself in my imagination, so much so that I almost believed I was really there.

"Wielders, place your hands on top of your partners and prepare to use your chosen magic on them."

I sensed Pia's palms on top of mine, but I was so absorbed in my thoughts that her hands felt foreign against my skin.

"This last step is the most important. Listen up, shielders." Stoll's voice echoed throughout my mind, though it sounded so far away. "As the wielders try to use their magic, I want you to imagine yourself stopping them. Visualize your body physically blocking the magic from reaching you. It sometimes can help if you imagine yourself speaking to the magic, telling it that you are not allowing it to enter your body. When you're both ready, you may attempt this."

Pia palpitated my hands gently. "Are you ready?" she whispered, as to not disturb my inner peace.

I nodded softly, not taking my mind out of its current state of relaxation. I heard her release a breath and felt her adjust her stance as she prepared to try and mend my face.

I centered myself in my mind, visualizing myself mentally speaking to Pia's magic.

Do not heal me.

I imagined the horizon above the shoreline back home—dripping with orange rays of sunlight.

Do not heal me.

Waves rolled over my toes, washing away the sand that covered them.

Do not heal me.

I was so immersed in the experience that I couldn't be sure if I was even doing what I was supposed to. My cheek tickled, but I couldn't sense any alleviation of the gash on my face. Did Pia even try to use her magic yet?

Do not heal me.

I imagined myself blocking out her powers, while keeping my soul tranquil.

Do not heal me.

I thought the phrase to myself again and again.

Do not heal me.

Do not heal me.

"Do not heal me."

A bolt of lightning struck through my veins. The electricity singed my nerve endings and my skin prickled, making the hairs on my arms stand up. My entire body shook as the sensation took over, but I didn't falter from my false reality. I was still on the shore, although it appeared *different* now.

Hands grasped my shoulders, vigorously shaking me. I snapped my eyes open to see dozens of others staring at me, completely mesmerized.

My spatial awareness returned, and Professor Stoll released me. I locked onto Pia, who gawked at me, her eyes fully dilated. Stoll moved to stand next to her and stared at me with a very similar expression.

I raised an eyebrow. "Did I do it?" I touched my fingers to my cheek bone, running them over my constellastones and the injury that still very much hurt.

No one answered me.

"Did you even try to heal me yet?" I directed that question to just Pia.

She clenched her jaw shut and gulped, then shook her head.

I frowned. If I failed at using my mental shield, then why was everyone looking at me like I wore nothing but my undergarments?

Throwing my arms up in confusion, I glanced between the two of them. "So then what's going on?"

Professor Stoll softened the shock on his face. "I believe, Miss Willawood," he lowered his voice so that my classmates wouldn't hear, "that we just solved the mystery of your gift."

CHAPTER TWELVE

Professor Stoll dismissed the rest of our class early. Pia and I followed him back to the classroom, where we sat in silence at two desks in front of the room.

He paced back and forth, tapping a finger on his chin and muttering to himself in confusion. I was scared to interrupt him while he was so deep in thought, but no one had even told me what was going on yet.

"What happened? What does he mean that I may have discovered my gift?" I leaned over and whispered in Pia's ear.

She kept her eyes straight ahead as she spoke to me in a whisper. "I never even got the chance to try and heal you. You kept telling me not to, and no matter how hard I tried, I couldn't bring myself to wield my magic," she said quietly so as to not disturb Stoll, who seemed to be in the midst of an existential crisis.

"What are you talking about?" She couldn't have possibly heard me say that—I never actually said the words out loud.

"You didn't block my magic by putting up a shield, you stopped me from being able to use it at all." Her head ripped towards me, her gaze hollow. "Maeve." She said my name much too seriously for my liking. "You *controlled* me."

I sputtered in complete shock, shaking my head in denial. "No. There's no way. I must have just threw a successful mental shield."

I rotated away from her, turning my attention back to Stoll, who, to be honest, was freaking me out a bit with his consistent pacing and murmuring. All of a sudden, he halted and pointed a finger at Pia. "Go fetch Sebastian Hawthorne," he demanded.

Pia didn't hesitate for a single second. Before I knew it, she was out the door. I watched her go and slouched my shoulders. She seemed really unsettled.

Professor Stoll placed his hands on my desk. "She's absolutely right," he said, referring to what Pia just told me. I was surprised he heard her over his crazed muttering.

I shook my head again. "No, Professor, that's just not possible. Pia must have misunderstood what actually happened. I was trying to put up a shield against her magic, like you said. I was focusing on the ocean. I was telling her magic not to heal me, but it was all in my head. I—" I couldn't finish my sentence.

Did I really say it out loud? I raised my gaze to his as realization dawned on me.

"How?" I asked so quietly that I could barely hear myself speak.

"I've heard rumor that this kind of magic could be possible from Blythe's gift of the constellastone, but it's never been proven. It seemed impossible, so I never truly considered that you may hold this kind of power," he replied with a turn of his back, making for a bookshelf in the corner of the room. His finger ran down the bindings, stopping to pull a deep-blue manuscript from the shelf.

Dust flew into my eyes when he slammed the book down on the surface of my desk. Eyes watering, I blinked away the pain to read the cover out loud, "The Gods and Goddesses of Life."

Without a word, Stoll flipped through the pages as if he knew the book like the back of his hand. He stopped near the end, then read from the page aloud. "*As the strongest of the gods, Blythe is known for honoring the sacred constellastone. The goddess is devoted to captivating the minds of all souls within the realms of nature. Blythe is said to hold the most exquisite power of all the gods, though no one knows precisely what that power is. Every being with a soul is at the mercy of the goddess.*"

He skimmed his eyes to the middle of the page. "*It is presumed through ancient tellings, that if the goddess were to ever find one worthy of her power, the individual would have noticeably different abilities than those gifted by one of the other seven gods.*" He pointed a bony finger to an illustration on the bottom of the page, which showed Blythe standing open-armed under a sky full of constellations.

I moved my face closer to the image. The constellations were shaped as the aspects of nature that the other gods controlled. One constellation was shaped as a wave, representing Thea. Another was a tree, for Sloane.

"*It is also claimed that there may be more to Blythe's power than us mortals even know,*" I read the last line of the page to myself, then raised my eyes to Stoll's face. "How can we be sure about this? Are you *positive* that what I did was more than a shield?"

Stoll nodded and closed the book suddenly, his voice shaking as he spoke. "Today when you thought you were shielding, you instead accidentally discovered the extent of your power. You took control over the psyche of your classmate without even meaning to. Think about it. Blythe's the Goddess of the Mind—the idea isn't so far out there." He stared at me for a moment, trying to see inside of my brain. The examination caused me to twitch in discomfort, and my body tensed until he removed himself from my presence to return the book to its spot on the shelf.

In his absence, I remembered what Pia said happens to her when she harnesses her power. She felt a tingle in her amethyst as her power rushed through her. When I tried to block her out today, I felt something similar in my face—in my constellastones.

"I can manipulate *minds,*" I said the words to myself, needing to speak them aloud to make them seem real.

That will need some time to sink in.

I was already the odd one out with my constellastones. If the other students didn't think I was a mutant before, they certainly would now.

Stoll sat down behind his desk and placed his head into his hands. I took on a similar pose, looking down at my lap and picking the skin on my fingers. Neither of us looked up until the sound of heavy footsteps came marching down the hallway.

I raised my head as Sebastian strode into the room, wearing a look of concern on his face. Our eyes met briefly as he gave me a sideways glance, and he seemed to relax a bit when he saw me alive.

Lowering my head once more, I broke our connection. Unsure as to why, I felt slightly embarrassed. I should have been ecstatic over the discovery of my power, but everyone's reactions didn't make it feel like something to celebrate.

I tuned out their voices as Stoll explained what happened. I did however peek up from the corner of my eye, expecting to see Sebastian's mouth agape with shock, but he didn't look surprised at all. His expression was completely static as he stood there with his arms crossed, his hands clutching the muscles of his biceps. I didn't know how he was able to keep his composure when hearing information as insane as this, but I guessed it had something to do with his years of being a soldier.

I raised my gaze a bit more so that I could really look at him. We had a rough start, but gods…

Everything about that man was impeccable. His broad shoulders. The sharpness of his jawline. The way his dark hair always laid perfectly. Every little detail about him was ethereal.

Maybe it was the way the sleeve of his shirt was rolled up, but I was just now noticing that he had a tattoo on his upper arm. I squinted my eyes to try and see it better. It looked like it could be a dagger, or maybe a sword? Regardless…*hot.*

He was deep in conversation with Stoll, so he didn't notice how my cheeks flushed as I watched him run his hand through his hair. The movement caused his bicep to flex and tighten, which in return caused a chain reaction through my body that began in my stomach and ended in my—

My almost inappropriate thoughts were interrupted by the figure of the man I was daydreaming about hovering over where I sat. Sebastian's body blocked my view of Stoll, but I heard his feet scurry out of the room.

My cheeks paled as I tilted my neck back to look up at him. He was so silent that I feared he knew the things I was just thinking about him.

The intensity of Sebastian's unfaltering gaze created a tension that was begging to be broken, so I spoke. "Turns out my gemstones didn't screw me over after all," I said playfully, although I was sure he could sense the apprehension in my voice.

The corner of his lips raised into a faint smile, and he offered me his hand. I wasn't sure if he even realized that his thumb rubbed across my wrist as he helped me up from my desk, but I did.

"Stoll filled me in," he said, releasing his hold on me all too quickly.

I swallowed the knot in my throat and nodded. "So you're aware that I'm a freak who can control minds?"

"I already knew you were a freak. The mind control, however, is news," he teased, smirking as he stepped aside to let me exit the classroom first.

I fake gasped. "Rude."

He chuckled, moving to walk beside me once we were outside.

"So, what happens now?" I asked him, so many questions clouding my brain.

"Unfortunately, Stoll is informing my father right now about your power emerging. He is going to want to speak with you, which is where I'm taking you right now."

I stopped walking.

He stopped as well, turning to look at me. He didn't say anything, just waited for me to yell at him over having to meet with the king.

I wanted to, but I held my tongue.

"I don't want to see him, either, if it's any consolation."

I chewed the inside of my cheek to hide the smile that his comment sparked. Then I swallowed my pride and forced my legs to continue forward.

The air was warm today, soaked with the smell of fall creeping its way in. I inhaled deeply, also noticing the faint aroma of salt that had drifted its way to us from the sea. There was a refreshing breeze, the same one that was always present when in such close proximity to the shore. The wind blew some hairs free from my braid, and I brushed them aside, tucking the pieces snuggly behind my ears.

We walked side by side, his hands tucked tightly into the pockets of his dark pants. The color of the leather emphasized the tanned glow of his skin as the fading sun beamed into his flesh. He was focused straight ahead and seemed a bit uptight, but I knew from his comment that he was dreading this meeting just as much as I was.

The reality of my powers started to set in as we stepped onto the path that would take us to the castle. "I don't know why the possibility that my magic may be related to the mind never occurred to me," I said, breaking the peace of our walk.

Sebastian glanced over at me.

"I kind of figured that no goddess in their right mind would give a mortal the ability to control people in such a manner. I thought maybe I would be able to read memories, or predict outcomes of events—something less dramatic."

He shrugged. "You couldn't have known."

I clenched my jaw as my hands began to shake, anxiety rushing to my brain. I tried to take control of it, but the weight of my magic added an unbearable amount of pressure on me. The king already thought of me as an asset. What would he think now that he knew what I was actually capable of?

I took a deep breath, slowing my pace so that Sebastian was a few steps ahead of me. I didn't want to lose my composure in front of him. He had already seen me like that once, and I'd be damned if he saw it again.

My legs wobbled and my vision blurred when the panic seeped through my skin. I refused to believe that this was true. There must have been something I was missing. If this was truly my gift, then my power had the potential to be detrimental.

I stopped in my tracks. "I don't want my power," I said softly, hoping that continuing the conversation could aid in calming the tightness that prevented my lungs from expanding properly.

Sebastian stopped as well and turned towards me. "Why not?" he asked, confusion painted on his face with his furrowed brows.

I tried to find the right words to describe my feelings, but so many thoughts were screaming in the back of my head that it was difficult to even speak. "I just don't." I intertwined my fingers behind my back, looking down at the stones beneath my feet.

Sebastian's boots scuffed against the rock as he stepped towards me. "Tell me."

I kicked a pebble off the cliffside to my left and watched it plummet to the sand below. "I compelled Pia's mind, and I didn't even know I was doing it."

"That was the first time you manifested your power. It won't always be like that."

"I could hurt someone." A tear that had threatened to break free, succeeded. I wiped it away quickly with the back of my hand, hoping that he didn't notice, but he did.

"Hey, hey." Sebastian put his hands on my shoulders. His touch was gentle on my skin, the contact bringing me a sensation of comfort.

"You won't hurt anyone unless you want to." He smirked.

A tight laugh released from my chest.

I was beginning to consider that *maybe* Pia was right about Sebastian. Just a few days ago, I would have screamed at him for laying a finger on me—but today, I daydreamed about his arms.

"Okay?" he asked, squeezing my shoulder gently.

I nodded in acceptance of his words, then his arms fell to his sides and we continued up the pathway.

Professor Stoll was just making his exit when Sebastian and I arrived, leaving the two of us alone with King Hawthorne. His hands were folded on the top of his desk while he studied the map under his fists, completely ignoring my presence in the chair across from him.

Sebastian stood, arms crossed in his usual pose against the door. *Should one of us say something*? I mouthed to him, but he bowed his head, shaking it subtly.

As if the king could read our minds, he looked up from the map, planting his gaze on the wound on my face. "I heard you had it out with Mr. Sinclair during combat training the other day?"

My face contorted in confusion. This was certainly not what I thought he'd be wanting to discuss with me. "Uhm…yes, sir, that is correct."

King Hawthorne let out a deep sigh, then pushed off from his desk and took a step towards Sebastian. "I was under the impression that you were supposed to be protecting her."

Sebastian straightened his torso. "Yes, Father, and I am doing as you instructed," he responded coldly.

"If you are doing as you say, then why does Caelestis' greatest treasure have a gaping wound on her face?" he snarled at his son, a vein popping out on his neck.

Gaping was a stretch to say the least. "It's really not that bad," I chimed in, but the glance I got from Sebastian was enough of a warning for me to shut my mouth.

Sebastian did not so much as flinch. "Sinclair's actions were unwarranted, and the situation has been handled."

My jaw tightened. So Sebastian *was* the reason why Sawyer had a black eye.

"Was there a reason that Mr. Sinclair felt the need to brutalize Miss Willawood?"

I gulped. *Yes. I had been an ass to his best friend.*

"I do not believe so. He picked a random first year and it just so happened to be Maeve."

That's a lie.

King Hawthorne glared at his son. "That should have never happened," he spat. "Do I need to bring the duke into this?"

"No," Sebastian hissed back.

"I expect you have learned from this and will do better?"

Sebastian nodded, keeping his head held high and his body stiff during the exchange—very soldier-like. "Yes."

The king returned to his seat. "Very well."

Sebastian laxed his stance a bit, but tension coated the air in the room now. I sat in awe of him. He was a real life example of how years of soldier-hood trained you to be numb. I didn't remember my father, but knew if he ever spoke to me in that manner, that it would sting at least a little.

"Professor Stoll informed me that your power has manifested?" King Hawthorne asked me, changing the subject.

"Yes, sir, I have been told the same," I grumbled, irritated with how he just spoke to his son.

Lines appeared on his forehead. He was clearly not in the mood for my antics. "The ability to alter minds is a gift that people would *kill* to get their hands on." The king put emphasis on the gravity of my gift, and I knew there was some truth in that claim. "It won't be long before news of your power has spread throughout the kingdom. I have already made the citizens of Caelestis aware of what will happen to traitors, but given the circumstances and magnitude of your gift, perhaps I should give them a reminder."

A lump formed in my throat. He meant that he should remind every one of their impending death should they slip up.

"I want bi-weekly reports of how your wielding is progressing," he proclaimed, his eyes bouncing between Sebastian and me. "Professor Stoll will keep me updated, but every two weeks you and I shall have a discussion regarding your progress."

I lifted an eyebrow. "Is that really nec—"

Sebastian flashed me another look, this one telling me not to test my luck.

"Congratulations on your powers, Miss Willawood." King Hawthorne stood and held out a hand for me to shake.

I just stared at it. A handshake was a sign of respect, and this man had not yet earned that from me. Under normal circumstances, I would have never even thought about disrespecting an authoritative figure in this manner. But these were not normal circumstances.

King Hawthorne cherished the ground I walked on. He was undone over a cut on my face, for gods' sakes. I'd be damned if he retaliated against me for not shaking his hand.

So I didn't.

"Enjoy the rest of your day, sir," I said, turning my back on the ruler of Caelestis and escorting myself out of his study.

CHAPTER THIRTEEN

Sebastian walked me back to my room, not saying a word the entire time. He seemed uncomfortable, and I think he felt ashamed that I heard his father speak to him in that manner. Unbeknownst to him, I wasn't surprised to witness their banter after what Pia had told me about their relationship.

It was almost dusk by the time I settled back into my room. Before he left, Sebastian told me he would be back in two hours to escort me to the kitchen for dinner. Finally alone, I changed out of my clothes and into something more comfortable before lying down on my bed. I stared blankly at the ceiling for an hour, trying to process the day.

I went over my wielding session in my head, trying to comprehend how I used my gift without even realizing. If wielding my power and shielding others required me to use a similar mental tactic, how would I distinguish between the two? There must have been a way to channel magic without needing to be in a complete state of relaxation. It would just require more practice for me to figure out.

The clock ticked on the top of my wardrobe, and I peered over at it. I still had some time before Sebastian was back. I could be back in my room before he even noticed I left.

Within seconds, the outside air brushed over my skin, making me wish I had something warmer on. The humid summer nights were almost gone, replaced by the crisp kiss of fall. Goosebumps rose on my arms as I hurried through the thick dune grass that separated the dormitories from the shore.

I kicked my shoes off in the sand to walk barefoot along the edge of the water, keeping my eyes peeled for what I was looking for. About a quarter of a mile from my shoes, my gaze set on two tiny eyes, glowing in the moonlight. I slowed my pace, tiptoeing until I approached the small crab. It scurried back and forth, playing a game with the waves as they rolled up and down the sand. I crouched down a few feet away from it and settled my full attention on the power within me.

I didn't close my eyes like I had with Pia, instead I locked them on the crab and envisioned it turning away from the water. I imagined it scurrying further back on the sand where it was safe, but the command didn't work—the crab just continued its battle with the tide.

With my legs getting sore from crouching, I sat down fully, not caring that wet sand now covered my pants. I closed my eyes and tried to recreate what I had done in class. Relaxing my mind, I said out loud, "Get away from the water."

I squinted my eyes open, only to see that the crab had not moved. Groaning in frustration, I propped my elbow on my knee, resting my chin on my hand. *Maybe my magic only worked on humans?* I considered the possibility, but quickly shot the idea down when I recalled what Stoll read me from his book. Blythe's power worked on anything with a soul.

An aggressive gust of wind blew by, but I ignored the sting of cold air and crawled ever so slightly towards the crab. When it was distracted by an incoming wave, I scooped it into my hands then rose to my feet.

The crab's beady eyes flickered back and forth. It settled into my hands rather quickly, its delicate legs scurrying over my palm.

"Alright, little one, let's try this again," I said to the crustacean as though it could understand me.

Completely still, I focused my full attention on my command. I let the sound of the sea aid in the relaxation of my body and mind. When I felt prepared, I said out loud, "Close your eyes."

My gemstones tickled my cheek as the words escaped me. The feeling was subtle and a tad painful, but a good indication that I had done something right.

In an instant, the roaming eyes of the crab closed tightly. I laughed in excitement, and unintentionally dropped my command, allowing the creature's eyes to reopen. If a crab had the ability to look confused, this one did.

"Damn it," I muttered. I guess I had to really maintain my focus to hold a command. Hopefully that would change with time and practice.

I planted my feet firmly into the ground, steadying myself in the event that a rogue wave tried to knock me down. The hairs on my arms stood up as another blast of chilled wind raced by. I shuffled a little in the sand, pondering my next command for the crab.

Refocusing my mind, I softened my stance. "Freeze."

The crab followed my order, its body instantly becoming rigid. The movement of its legs came to a halt, and its torso collapsed into my palm. I gazed at the tiny life held within my grasp, noting how peaceful the crab looked, though the moment was brief. I lost my focus again and the crab returned to its previous state, crawling back and forth through the trails in my skin.

I stumbled a little, my body suddenly feeling weak. I brushed it off as being hungry and exhausted. Speaking of which, I had to be back to my room soon to meet Sebastian. He'd be pissed if I wasn't there when he showed up.

"Okay, let's try one more thing before I go," I whispered to the crab. I corrected my stance one more time and allowed my brain to unwind.

"Jump."

As soon as the word left my lips, the crab dove from my hand, plummeting towards the sand. I followed it down with my eyes, and gasped at the sound of its tiny carcass shattering when it landed on a rock.

I WAS SHIVERING BY THE TIME I MADE IT UP THE STAIRS AND TO MY room. My arms were weak as they yanked open my door, and I made a mental note to make sure I ate before power wielding next time—also to not sit in wet sand when it was freezing out.

My eyes widened at Sebastian as I stumbled into my room. He was lounging in my armchair, reading a book.

Shit.

His eyes landed on me. Slamming his book shut as he stood up, his long legs began striding towards me.

"Where have you been?"

I expected him to be angry, but his tone was casual as he took in the sight of me. Salt water and sand dripped off my clothes into a puddle on the floor where I stood in front of him.

Sebastian's forehead creased. "Why are you wet?"

I frowned. "I killed a crab."

A dark eyebrow arched. "Oh?"

I bent down to untie my boots, taking them off and tossing them by the door. "Wait a second." I put my hands on my hips as I rose. "How did you get in here?"

Sebastian's lips perked up. "I have a key."

"Of course you do." My eyes rolled as I trudged past him towards the washroom, leaving a trail of water behind me.

His hand caught the door as I tried to close it. "I'm serious. Where were you?"

"Sebastian, I'm soaked and freezing. Can you please just give me five minutes to shower and change before you interrogate me?"

He groaned, but pushed the door closed to give me some privacy.

The heat from the shower stung against my icy skin. I took longer under the water than I'd said, but my body needed the extra time to return to a normal temperature. When finished, I patted my hair dry with a towel and pulled on some loungewear. I didn't plan on accompanying Sebastian to get dinner anymore, I was far too tired.

Once decent, I exited the washroom and threw myself down onto my bed, curling up in the warmth of the quilt that covered it. "Okay, let the investigation commence," I said.

Sebastian approached the foot of my bed, grasping the top of the footboard and leaning over it. "For the third time, where were you?"

"I went to the beach to try and practice my wielding." I sighed, rolling away from him so that he couldn't see my face. "I was planning to be back before you arrived, but I tend to lose track of time when I don't have my *watch* with me."

He snickered at my comment. "Well? How did it go?"

I rolled back to face him again, my face showing my perplexity. "You're not gonna scold me for running away from my *babysitter* again?"

"I thought I was your watch?" he said sarcastically, smiling as he crouched down at the side of my bed, putting us eye to eye. "And what's the point of scolding you when I know you won't listen to me, anyways?"

"Now you're catching on."

"I'm very quickly learning that you don't take well to being told what to do, and that's something I'm going to have to work with."

"Good. Because you'll also learn that I don't take well to not getting my way."

His ocean eyes locked with mine, shades of blue swirling throughout his irises. It didn't matter how many times I saw them, each time I was more amazed at their beauty.

"I told you before that I don't need to be with you every second of every day, but I need to know where you are," he began.

"Ah, here comes the lecture."

"It's not a lecture. I'm just saying that I know you don't think that you need protection, but when word gets out of what your powers are, you will."

The deepness of his voice sent shivers down my back. My focus drifted to his lips, and I hoped he didn't notice the way I admired the fullness of them—and how I imagined what they'd feel like against mine.

Stop it, Maeve. You barely know him.

Refocusing on what he was saying, I nodded in response. It had only been a few days since we apologized to each other, but I already felt as though I was getting to know him. Something about him just made me feel comfortable, and although I didn't need a protector, he did make me feel safe.

"Now don't make me ask again." Sebastian rose to his full height and walked back to the armchair. He slouched into it side-ways, putting his legs over one of the arms. I marveled at him from afar, taking in the way he looked so dashing without even trying.

I sat upright, pulling my quilt up to my neck. "It went okay, I guess." I scratched my head. "I was able to control a crab to do a few simple things. But then it died so—"

"Are you saying that you commanded it to commit suicide?" Sebastian snickered.

"Of course not. I simply told it to jump out of my palm, but it landed on a rock and...*crack*." I imitated the sound of the crab's carcass.

Sebastian bit his lip to prevent a huff of laughter.

"It's not funny," I scowled.

"You didn't do it on purpose," he assured me when he sensed my change of attitude.

"I know, but that's the problem. I wasn't trying to hurt it, but it's dead now, anyways. What's to stop that from happening with someone else?" I raised the question, which didn't receive a response right away.

His pause was not reassuring. "You're going to learn to wield more effectively and accurately. You have only known of your powers for half of a day, cut yourself some slack."

"I guess...but you told me that I wouldn't hurt anyone unless I wanted to," I teased, giving him a fake pout.

"I meant mortals, not sea creatures."

"Good save."

Sebastian's eyes lit up. "Oh, before I forget, here." He rummaged through his rucksack on the floor, then pulled out a roll of parchment along with some quills and ink. He waved them in the air, then put them down on my desk.

"Oh my gods, thank you," I exclaimed, jumping out of my bed.

"Not a problem." He smiled as I approached the desk. "So, you like to write?"

I picked up one of the quills, running the feather through my fingertips. "I wouldn't say that I *like* it as much as I would say that I *need* it."

Sebastian's eyebrow raised in confusion.

"It helps me…deal with…life? I guess."

His other eyebrow followed the first.

"Writing things down helps me cope—helps me process. I get so worked up in my own head sometimes that I don't even know how to describe how I feel. Being able to put the thoughts on paper just…fixes me," I clarified.

"You don't need to be fixed. There's nothing wrong with you."

I scoffed. "You clearly don't know me well enough yet. I'm a mess."

"Doubtful."

"You saw how I reacted in the throne room on my first day here—that's pretty much a prime example of how my entire life has been," I countered.

"Being scared about things to come doesn't mean that you're broken."

"It does when your entire existence is wasted on that feeling," I pinched out, my throat nearly too tight to speak.

Sebastian chewed on his cheek and looked out the window. "My mother liked to write."

"Did she? What did she write?"

"Poetry, amongst other things," he said softly.

"Did she like to read as well?" He always had a book with him, so I wondered if that's where he got his love of reading from.

"So I'm told."

My heart sank. At his core, Sebastian was just a boy who missed his mother.

I moved back to my bed, throwing myself on it. I was exhausted and ready to go to sleep, but he didn't seem like he would be leaving anytime soon. I thought about our meeting with his father today, and I knew that I shouldn't pry, but he said it himself—I was not a good rule follower.

"Can I ask you something?"

Sebastian turned his attention to me. "Anything."

"What's the deal with you and your father?"

He shook his head and pushed out of the armchair, heading for the door. "Nope. We're not doing this," he cautioned.

I jumped up and beat him to the exit, using my body to block him.

"No. That's not fair," I said firmly. "You said I could ask anything. You don't get to question me and not let me do it back. Now spill."

Sebastian shifted uncomfortably, but he didn't try to argue with me any further. He stepped away from the door towards the window, leaving his back pointed at me.

"You know how you have very strong opinions about how those gifted by the gods shouldn't be forced into soldiery?" He looked over his shoulder at me.

I bobbed my head in response and he turned away again.

"I have the same opinions as you."

My jaw slacked. That was not what I expected to hear from the king's head soldier.

"I know that's not what you meant by your question." He looked over at me when I moved to stand beside him. "And seeing how you had the guts to even ask, I'm going to assume that Pia already told you some of it." Sebastian's face looked so dismal that I regretted bringing the topic up. He waited for me to respond, not taking his eyes off of me until I did.

"Yeah. She told me a little bit, but—"

He bit his lip and nodded, looking down at where his hands braced against the window sill.

"If you feel the same, then why do you allow him to do it?" I asked innocently, not thinking anything of the question.

Sebastian scoffed. "I don't *allow* him to do anything. He tells me what to do, and I do it. Because if I don't—"

I could sense the anxiety forming in him simply by observing his body language. I knew the feeling well, and hated myself for starting the conversation that made him feel that way.

His head snapped over his shoulder to look at me, his expression now filled with something like anger. "My father is an ass. Because of him, I've seen things…I've *done* things that would make you absolutely sick." He blew out a deep breath and folded his hands into fists on the window sill.

I brushed my fingers over his arm to try and comfort him, but he jerked his whole body away from me.

"Sorry. I shouldn't have asked that. I wasn't thinking."

His jaw tightened, ticking right before he snapped at me. "Listen, I'm glad you and I can be civil now, but we don't need to have discussions like this. We shouldn't. We aren't friends."

The harshness of his words stung every nerve inside my body. The man he was being right now was a colossal change from the man who humored me just a few minutes ago.

"I'm sorry," I repeated through my quivering lips. "I didn't mean to make you mad. I just wanted to get to know you better."

I don't think he even heard my apology, he was halfway out the door by the time I finished speaking. I shouldn't have cared, considering I barely even knew the man. But for some reason, him being mad at me once more, devastated me.

Tears welled up in my eyes, and I wished I could control my own mind to make them go away.

CHAPTER FOURTEEN

I woke up before the sun. The sky was tinted red from the rays of light that peeked through the clouds covering Caelestis. I could tell the air was frigid just by glancing outside. Fall had entered the atmosphere earlier than usual this year, and I grieved the weeks of beach time that I'd missed out on.

Careful not to wake Pia, who had spent the night after we celebrated the start of the weekend a little too hard, I stretched and slid off my mattress. I moved to my armchair by the window, which had become one of my favorite spots.

My arms ached as I lowered myself into the chair. Overall, I was doing well in combat training, but *gods* the workouts were kicking my ass. After the show Sawyer and I put on last month, he was switched to a new group and replaced in ours by Kohen. Pia seemed to enjoy our new instructor. She wouldn't say it, but it was obvious that she had a thing for him.

Wielding class, on the other hand, had been tough. I'd been successful at blocking out some of the other students' magic, but had trouble wielding my own without feeling completely defeated. It turned out that controlling the mind of another human was much more complex than controlling one of a crab.

Professor Stoll had been giving King Hawthorne updates after every class session, so at least he wouldn't be surprised at our meeting this afternoon when I told him that things weren't going great. At our last meeting, he was fairly dissatisfied with my wielding ability, so I could only imagine how disappointed he'd be this week to learn that not much had changed.

Sebastian had been cold to me ever since I asked him about his father. Every morning he waited for me on the stairs, reading a book. He'd escort me to classes and meals, but other than that, he was giving me the cold shoulder again. The whole situation really sucked seeing as we had no choice but to spend a lot of time together. I had been enjoying his company for the brief period when things were good, and this bothered me more than I let on, though I wasn't quite sure why.

The view of the ocean became clearer by the second as the night dissipated and the horizon came into view. I watched the dune grass as it swayed in the wind and pulled my legs up into the chair, trying to get more comfortable. I shifted my body to find the best position, but stopped when I felt something hard wedged into the cushion. My fingers reached down into the crevice, grabbing a hold of something hard and pulling it free.

My jaw clenched, my finding reopening the wound from Sebastian's cold words to me.

We aren't friends.

I had put it off for a month, but couldn't wait any longer—I needed to vent.

I crawled back into my side of the bed and gently poked Pia in the nose, the moment reminding me of the many like it I'd had with Delani. I wished she were here. She was always better with guy stuff than me.

Pia yawned, slits of her eyes peeling open. “Morning,” she croaked, still half asleep.

“I need to talk to you about something,” I said, the urgency in my voice helping to fully rouse her.

She sat upright, concern pasted on her face. “Is everything okay?”

I waved the book that I found in her face. "He left this here."

"Who?"

"Sebastian," I said as if it were obvious, then passed her the book.

Pia flipped it around in her palms and raised an eyebrow. "Okay? And?"

I released a huff of breath and threw my body down, letting the back of my head hit my pillow. "He left it here a few weeks ago when he told me he wasn't my friend."

She shuffled up onto her knees. "Well, I mean, *were* you friends?"

"We never put a label on it, but I kinda thought we were starting to become friends."

"Why would he say that, anyway?"

I dropped my gaze to the sheets. "I may have asked him why he doesn't get along with his father." I sighed as the words came out, then raised my eyes to see her gawking at me.

"Why in gods' names would you ask him that?" she blurted out.

"I don't know!" I yelled, mostly at myself. "We were getting along. He was being nice to me. We were making jokes." I threw my arms up in frustration. "He's always questioning me about where I am or what I'm doing, so I figured one little question couldn't hurt. But it did, and he stormed out. Now he will hardly talk to me again, just like when we first met, which is a problem because I can't stop thinking about how I upset him and his eyes and his body…and—" I stopped myself abruptly. I most certainly *had not* planned on sharing that information with Pia, but once I started ranting, the words spilled right out of me.

She rubbed her eyes, then stared at me for a good while before her mouth twisted into a smile.

"What?" I groaned, scrunching my face.

"You totally have the hots for my cousin."

I shook my head. "No, I do not. He's absolutely breathtaking—I'll give him that. But that's beside the point." I ignored Pia's giddy smile and sat upright. "The point is that he got pissed and has been cold to me ever since. And what am I supposed to do with this?" I grabbed his book from her, waving the novel above my head.

Her smile faded. "Maeve, I told you that Sebastian doesn't share a lot with anyone. Half of the things I know about him are simply because we are family."

I turned my face away from her, but she stood up and moved in front of me so that I had no choice but to look at her. "I think he struggles with things from his past more than he'll ever let on. He probably reacted the way he did as a defense mechanism to hide that those things actually hurt him," she continued.

She could be right. He told me I could ask him anything, but his mood switched when I brought up his father. If what Pia told me was true, Sebastian had endured a hell of a lot of trauma in his life, and I'm sure there was more than she even knew.

"Well now I feel even worse," I whined, angry at myself for causing him any suffering.

A devious grin formed across Pia's face. She swiped my rucksack from my desk, shoving Sebastian's book into it before handing me the bag and telling me, "Get dressed."

I TENDED TO SLEEP IN ON THE WEEKENDS, SO SEBASTIAN WAITED until mid-morning to meet me at my dormitory. Knowing that, Pia and I were able to leave my room uninterrupted.

"Where are we going?" The crisp fall air had me wrapping my arms around myself for extra warmth as we hiked across the castle grounds. I really needed to start remembering my cloak.

"To get breakfast," Pia said simply, keeping her feet steady on the cobblestone walkway.

"That's it? Just to get breakfast?" My suspicion was obvious.

"Well, after that we're going to give Seb his book back."

I pivoted and started walking back towards the dorms. "Nope. Absolutely not!" I yelled over my shoulder and waved her goodbye.

She chased after me, grabbing onto my arm and dragging me back in the direction of the castle. She was a few inches shorter than me and much smaller, but I had to admit that the girl was strong.

"You see him every day. What's the difference?"

"The difference is that…I—" I struggled to find the words to explain my reasoning.

"Don't be a baby," she teased, flashing me her teeth in a taunting smile.

I rolled my eyes at her, but didn't argue any further. I let her lead me to the castle, where we shoveled down our breakfast and then chatted to kill some time.

"Sebastian usually meets me around ten thirty," I told her as I glanced at the clock hanging on the stonework of the kitchen. It was about ten o'clock now, so he'd be making his way to my room any minute.

Hastily, we picked up after ourselves and gathered our belongings. I started towards the exit, but Pia ushered me through a stone archway on the other side of the kitchen.

"This way. There's another way into the soldiers' housing," she whispered to me.

We traveled down a dimly lit hallway, the lack of lanterns indicating that the corridor did not get used often. She cracked open a steel door at the end of the hall and peered through it. Once she was sure that no one was on the other side, she swung it open with full force and waved me through.

"How do you know about this?" I inquired as we stepped into the corridor.

Her cheeks flushed. "I've lived in the castle for years. And there *may* be someone that I visit here regularly who just so happened to show me a secret way to his room."

"Pia! Who?" I whisper-yelled.

Her eyelashes fluttered. "Kohen Sharpe."

"I *knew it*! For how long?"

"Since the gala."

"What! That long and you didn't tell me?"

Pia blushed. "Sleeping with a head soldier isn't exactly something that would be approved by my uncle. But honestly, I don't care anymore."

The corridor was silent aside from our childish giggles over Pia's fling. A few soldiers glanced at us skeptically, but no one stopped us as we walked down the hall and up a flight of stairs. She took my rucksack from me when we reached the top and fished around in it for Sebastian's book.

"Okay, here's the plan," she murmured under her breath. "I'll give him back the book, and then when I walk off you stay and talk to him."

I raised an eyebrow at her. "*That's* your plan? I would hardly call that a plan."

"It doesn't matter, you just need an excuse to talk to him."

"I wouldn't call that much of an excuse, either."

Pia stared at me, not blinking.

"And what if he refuses to talk to me?" I questioned her.

"He won't."

"You don't know that," I argued.

"Gods, Maeve, shut up and let's go."

We took a corner down the corridor, entering the portion of the floor that held the soldiers' bedchambers.

"Are we even allowed in here?" I asked her, biting my lower lip in doubt.

"Not exactly." She shrugged then stopped abruptly in front of a door on our left. "But everyone brings guests in, so it's an unwritten rule for the soldiers to not squeal." She flashed me a sly grin, and then without any warning, banged her fist on the door.

My body tensed with instant regret about letting her talk me into this. I considered racing away down the hall, but Sebastian would likely see me running, which would arguably be even more embarrassing than what we were doing.

His door was made of a metal so thick that I couldn't hear if he said anything from beyond it. For all I knew, he could already be on his way to my dorm. I kind of hoped that he was. But then the lock on his door clicked and swung open to reveal a very drowsy, and very *shirtless* Sebastian.

I had to clench my teeth together to keep my mouth from falling to the floor at the sight of him.

His physique was even more impressive when it lacked clothing. His abdomen was rigid and well defined, making it obvious that he spent a lot of time training. My eyes fluttered to his arms—purely toned muscle that rippled as he moved his grip to the doorframe above him. I could fully make out the tattoo on his bicep now, which was in fact a dagger. I knew that he had a nice body, but seeing him like this left me speechless. Completely *thoughtless*.

My pulse quickened as our eyes locked. His eyebrows lowered at the sight of me, and my stomach twisted from the intensity of his stare. Then as if I wasn't even there, he turned his attention back to Pia. He was probably angry that I'd left my dorm without him, but he'd just have to get over it.

"What's up?" He dropped his hand from the doorframe to run it over his face and then through his unkempt hair.

"Just here to return your book. Maeve found it this morning lodged into her chair. We went and got breakfast together so I figured we'd drop it off." She reached her hand out with the book in it.

He nodded as he took it, holding it up in a wave of gratitude. "Thanks," he mumbled, then lifted an eyebrow. "How did you get in here?"

Pia smirked, and I choked on a laugh. Her face turned a shade of red, similar to her strawberry blonde hair.

Sebastian shook his head. "I don't even want to know." He turned his body halfway and tossed the book into his room. The muscles of his torso tightened with the movement and I couldn't stop my wandering eyes.

"Alright, well, thanks again," he said, fighting back a smug smirk that told me that he saw how I looked at him.

"Sure thing. See you later," Pia replied, then started further down the hall.

Sebastian paled as he watched her slip into his friend's room. Flustered, he looked back towards me. "I'll be at your dorm around two to bring you to your meeting. I expect that you'll be there?" he asked coldly.

I nodded, my head bowing slightly as I turned and started off down the hall. This was pointless—he didn't want to talk to me, and I wasn't going to make him.

I only got a few yards before he called out for me. "Wait."

"You don't need to walk me back," I argued as I peered over my shoulder, expecting him to be behind me. But he was still standing in the doorway. Just waiting.

"I'm not. Come back."

Though reluctant at first, I overlooked my hesitancy and marched back to meet him. He stepped aside, letting me into his room.

The layout of his bedchambers was similar to mine, but triple the size. The walls were a deep olive green, the color adding a moodiness to the atmosphere. Cherrywood molding outlined the ceiling from which a light fixture hung, leaving a soft yellow glow over the bed below it. His wardrobe and desk looked like mine, except stained a darker brown to match his bed frame. However, the most impressive part of his room was the remarkable bookshelf that covered the entire wall across from his bed.

I knew that Sebastian liked to read, but didn't know he was so passionate about it. I had to stop myself from smirking. The thought of the king's head soldier having such an innocent hobby kind of turned me on.

No, Maeve. No it doesn't. Stop it right now.

Sebastian shut the leaden door behind us then leaned back against it. Our gazes were glued to one another and I had to fight my eyes as they tried to roam his body.

I didn't know what to say. Having thought that he wouldn't want to talk to me, I didn't prepare for what I'd say if he did.

"Was there something you wanted to say?" I asked, my attitude shining through my words. I remembered his disregard for me when I got here, which ticked me off.

He clicked his tongue. "Yes."

Silence.

I crossed my arms over my chest. "What is it then?"

"What's with the sass?" he deadpanned.

"I'm not being sassy."

He snickered, biting his lip as his eyes met the ceiling.

“If you're going to keep me here, can you at least put a shirt on?”

“Why? Don't like the view?”

I sucked in a breath. I loved the view, but it certainly created feelings within me that I wished it wouldn't.

“Could you be any cockier?”

His muscular shoulder shrugged. “Yeah, probably.”

I scoffed and made for the doorway that he still blocked. There was no point in staying here if we were just going to banter back and forth. “Excuse me.”

His eyes softened as they met mine again, and I allowed them to calm the raging storm inside of me. “Hold on.”

Sebastian ruptured the tension by pushing off the door and strutting to his wardrobe, where he pulled a dark shirt over his head, tucking it into the band of his lounge pants. Then he approached me, letting out a deep sigh and adjusting his stance. “I don't want to keep doing or saying things that end with me having to apologize to you,” he confessed.

“Oh, you’re ready to talk now?” I said satirically.

He glared at me, his full lips knitting together.

“I’m sorry,” I huffed, giving in to his honesty, “me either. I should know better than to ask personal questions to someone who only spends time with me because they're forced to.” Sadness coated my voice as the words left my tongue, reminding me how I was nothing more than an assignment to him.

He grimaced and stepped closer to me, not leaving much space between our bodies. The blood in my veins burned in response to the close proximity of his body to mine.

“That's not true. I didn’t mean what I said that night. Sometimes I just get agitated, and I don’t know why. I overreacted. I just…don’t know,” he stuttered through his words.

He may not have been able to put into words how he felt, but I knew what he meant—it was a feeling I knew all too well. “You don’t have to explain.”

“I should explain, though. I—”

“I understand. Really,” I assured him.

He clenched his jaw, but his body seemed to relax a bit, as if the strain between us had been bothering him as well.

My lungs held onto air as I tried to speak. "So…are we good?"

He nodded slowly, chewing the corner of his bottom lip.

Then, time seemed to stop. Sebastian looked at me as if he was trying to memorize every detail of my skin. Icy eyes met mine, sorrow and desire muddled into them. His heated stare made my body tremble, and I had to clench my fists to stop myself from losing my composure. His lips parted ever so slightly, as if he was going to tell me a secret.

He would destroy me if he kept looking at me like that.

I took a step back, putting space between us to avoid doing something I'd regret—like throwing my arms around him and slamming my lips against his.

"Okay, so I guess I'll see you later on?" The words came out too casually, but casual was the only tone of voice that wouldn't give away the array of emotions swirling in my brain.

"Yeah." He stepped back as well, and I gave him a quick glance before turning my back on him.

"You're going straight to your room?"

I nodded, not looking back.

"No stops at the beach?"

A smile tugged at my lips. "Not today. Too cold."

"Are you sure you don't want me to walk you back?"

"Will you get scolded if you don't?"

"Not if you don't get caught." He stepped to my side, opening and holding the door for me.

"I won't. I'm quite sneaky when I need to be." I flashed him a wink over my shoulder. "See you later." As I started out the door, his hand caught my wrist and pulled my gaze back to him.

"I really am sorry," he said softly, his words simple but heartfelt.

My skin quivered from his touch, and all though he noticed, he did not acknowledge the reaction.

"Me, too." I granted him a gentle smile. When his grip went slack, I made my way down the stairs, taking in what the hell just happened.

I'd never had my body react to someone in the way that it just did. I couldn't deny that there was something about Sebastian that made me want to lose all sense of control. I'd known him for two months—most of which had been spent fighting with or ignoring him. But the way I was drawn to him made it feel like I'd known him for years.

I chewed on my lower lip. I didn't want to admit it to myself, but there was no hiding the feelings that arose when he was near me. But he and I would never work. Like Pia said earlier—relationships between soldiers and students were frowned upon. The king would never allow it, and I doubted Sebastian would ever want it, anyway.

This is just a stupid crush because you saw his abs.

But it wasn't. And I knew that.

"Shit, shit, shit," I mumbled under my breath as I stepped outside. There was an undeniable attraction—the reason I had been so upset that we weren't talking.

I was falling for him, even though I didn't want to.

Sebastian stayed true to his word and met me outside of the dormitories mid-afternoon. The air was a bit warmer than it had been that morning, but the bite of cold still nipped at my cheeks. We got lost in conversation as we ventured to the castle as if we'd never spent the past few weeks in silence.

We arrived at the door that separated us from King Hawthorne's study. I took a few deep breaths in an attempt to calm my nerves before entering, but struggled to release the dread that consumed me every time I had to see the king. Sebastian noticed my apprehension and waited for my approval before twisting the golden handle and holding the door open for me.

My sudden halt was unexpected. Sebastian walked right into my back, the weight of his body pushing me forward a few inches. He placed his hands lightly on my waist to steady me. I'm sure he felt the way my body shivered in his grip, but his touch was so gentle that I doubted anyone besides us noticed it.

He released me, and I shuffled to the side so he could enter the room as well.

There were three more attendees at our meeting—Professor Stoll and Lucan being two of them. The other man I had never seen before.

His broad figure stood tall beside King Hawthorne's desk. He lacked hair, but black stubble covered the lower half of his face. He was gifted with an onyx stone that shimmered on his hand as he extended it out to me.

"Maeve Willawood, I presume?" The man shook my hand with a firm grasp.

"Um, yes. That's me."

"I am Duke Sinclair. It's a pleasure to finally meet you."

Sinclair.

"Sawyer's father?"

"That I am," he said with a smile as he directed me to my usual chair. "I assume you have met my son?"

I cleared my throat and sagged onto the chair's plush cushion. "Uhm, yes. We've met." I spared him the details.

My vision scanned the room in confusion, noting Sebastian's blank expression as he stood guard of the door. I assumed he had no knowledge about our extra attendees, either.

"I'm sure you are both wondering why the duke is here with us this afternoon," King Hawthorne addressed Sebastian and me.

I heard Sebastian's sarcasm from over my shoulder. "Very much so." With a quick change of tone, he addressed the duke. "Pleasure to see you, as always."

The duke nodded with a grin. "You too, Sebastian. It's been a while."

"It has. A few months at least, right? Hey, has Sawyer told you about—"

King Hawthorne interrupted their reconciliation with a grumble. "As I was saying," he cleared his throat, looking towards Sebastian and I, "Lucan will be taking notes, and Professor Stoll's part here will come into play later on. For now, I will let the duke take over. I expect you both to give him your undivided attention."

"Thank you, Aldous." Duke Sinclair moved to sit in the unoccupied chair by my side. "As Sebastian mentioned, my absence from the kingdom has come with great reason. I have been stationed in the city Craterra, which if you are not familiar with, borders the southernmost portion of Caelestis." He spoke to me directly. "It is our closest village to the Kingdom of Draemor. Have you heard of it?"

"Of course. I've lived in Caelestis my whole life." *Duh.*

"Very good. Well, due to Craterra's location, we occasionally have stray Draemornian's cross the border. They use the city's lack of wards to their advantage, using it as a passageway to reach us. To spy on us. As you know, they, like us, are forbidden to cross into the other's land, so when they are discovered, we are required by royal law to question. From there, we decided whether to release them, or execute them for trespassing."

I gulped. That was another thing I really hated about how King Hawthorne ruled our kingdom. Innocent lives taken for simply stepping foot over a border—it was so wrong that I didn't even have words for it.

"I'll spare you the details, but you should know that recently, a roaming Draemornian crossed into Craterra, and thus the individual was interrogated." The duke took a deep breath and released it in a sigh. "Long story short, it has been confirmed that there is a traitor in our kingdom."

"What does that mean?" I stuttered, fear gathering inside of me. I had a general idea of the answer, but needed confirmation before allowing myself to freak out.

"Maeve, it has been brought to our attention that word of your gift has been spreading rather rapidly."

My eyes widened, and I gulped as anxiety rose into my chest.

"The Draemornian we questioned had knowledge of a Caelestian being gifted by Blythe," Duke Sinclair confirmed my fear.

My jaw went slack, and I shook my head in denial. I could feel the angst inside of me preparing to send my brain into a spiral. My vision started to blur as it always did when panic clouded my brain.

I turned to Sebastian, hoping he could offer me some reassurance, but he looked just as worried as I was. Actually…angry. He looked *angry*.

"*How*?" he bellowed from behind me. He lunged towards his father's desk, placing his hands on the edge of it.

King Hawthorne sat completely unfazed, remaining calm and ignoring Sebastian. He peered around the side of him to speak to me. "We are unaware of who the traitor is, but we are diligently working to uncover the perpetrator. When the one responsible is discovered, the appropriate actions will be taken."

Sawyer's father piped in, "At this time, we don't believe that King Beaumont is aware of who the gifted individual is, just that there is *someone*."

Sebastian slammed a fist on the desk, blatantly pissed that they were ignoring him. "How did this happen?" he yelled in his father's face, demanding an answer.

"You should be asking yourself that, son. You're the one responsible for her safety," the king spat as he rose from his desk.

"I can't be here watching out for her and in Craterra making sure no one crosses the borders," Sebastian growled back. He stood to his full height, giving himself a few inches on his father.

"That is not what I am asking you to do."

"Well then what exactly are you asking? Do you want me to escort her to classes or to circulate the campus and assault anyone who speaks her name?"

"You seem awfully undone about this, soldier, especially for someone who was recently asking to be reassigned," King Hawthorne sneered.

My jaw tightened, the muscles twitching as I ground my teeth against each other. *Sebastian asked to be reassigned?* His eyes glanced sideways at me, soft and offering me an unspoken apology.

"Gentlemen, please." Lucan looked up from his scribbling to cut in. "Let's all calm down. There is no immediate threat at this very moment."

"While we work on uncovering the traitor, extra measures will be taken to ensure your safety," Duke Sinclair added. Directing his words towards Sebastian, he said, "I must remind you to be aware of her location at all times and within an appropriate distance from her in the event that a threat does become present. Be even more vigilant than you already are."

"Of course, sir," Sebastian agreed. He already did that, anyway.

The king glared at his son, his eyebrows furrowed in irritation. "Stand down. *Now.*" The words came out harsh, as if he were speaking to just another one of his soldiers and not to his offspring.

Sebastian hesitated, but followed his father's order, returning to his place by the door and lounging against it with his arms crossed over his chest. My eyes drifted to the dagger he had openly sheathed against his thigh. I knew it wasn't the best time, but I couldn't help myself from staring. *Hot.*

Duke Sinclair cleared his throat. "Well then, that was all I had. I will let you know if and when I have more information. Have a good day." He nodded goodbye and left the room.

"Have a good day?" I mumbled under my breath. *Yeah right.*

I shuffled in my chair, taking a deep breath—one less body in the cramped room made it easier to breathe. My gaze drifted to Professor Stoll, who had been a silent observer this whole time.

King Hawthorne caught a glimpse of my eyes on the professor. "It has also been brought to my attention that you are having difficulty wielding your powers?"

"Something tells me you already know the answer to that," I replied, noting how Stoll nodded in agreement.

I'd been able to use my powers in small increments during class, but always ended up completely defeated by the end. I hadn't practiced outside of class since the crab incident, having made the decision then and there that I would only use my powers when training or when absolutely necessary.

"Considering the circumstances, Professor Stoll and I believe it would be wise to introduce extra wielding and combat training sessions. Should we need to utilize your power for any reason, it will be to everyone's benefit that you are better trained. These sessions will be one-on-one with Sebastian, and will take place every day until further notice."

My mouth dropped open as I fell forward in my seat. "*Every day*?"

"That is what I said."

"I understand the extra wielding sessions, but why combat?"

"May I remind you of the job Mr. Sinclair did to your face on the first day of training?"

"That's not fair. He would have beat any of us up. It was our first day!"

"Regardless, having Caelestis' greatest asset being well trained in battle can only be to the benefit of the kingdom," King Hawthorne stated, then dismissed us from the room, not leaving the topic open for discussion.

CHAPTER FIFTEEN

My one-on-one lessons were scheduled to begin that evening, just hours after my meeting with the king. Sebastian walked me to my room so I could rest for a while, though Pia met me as soon as I got back. We were sitting on the floor and I was in the process of knotting her hair into two long braids while I filled her in on my conversation with Sebastian from earlier. I considered telling her about my meeting with King Hawthorne, but I was still trying to process the information, so instead I decided to tell her about the thoughts I'd been having about Sebastian.

"Pia," I said her name to grab her attention.

She cocked her head to the side to try and see me, but I pushed her head back forward facing.

"Don't move, you'll mess up your hair," I told her.

She sighed, but obliged. "What were you going to say?"

"It's going to sound foolish." My cheeks began to burn, and I felt like a little girl with a crush.

"Oh, just spit it out," Pia whined. "No judgment here."

My fingers worked effortlessly through her hair. "I think I have feelings for Sebastian," I said under my breath.

"What did you say?" Pia's head shot around, ripping my hands free from her hair.

"*Please* don't make me say it again," I complained through pouted lips.

"No, I really didn't hear you, you were mumbling."

"I think I have feelings for Sebastian," I repeated, only slightly louder.

She stared at me, fighting her smile as she waited for me to elaborate.

"I know it's silly seeing as I hardly even know him, and for most of the time I *have* known him we've been fighting with each other. But after you left this morning and we talked it was *weird*. There's something about him that I just can't shake," I confessed.

She stayed silent for a moment, probably wishing that I hadn't said anything. Sebastian was her cousin, and I'm sure this was an uncomfortable topic for her. But then her face twisted into the biggest grin I'd ever seen on anyone.

"I knew it!" She pointed a finger at me and jumped to her feet, looking ridiculous with one side of her hair still hanging loosely down her back. "I knew it the minute you told me how upset you were that he wasn't talking to you!" Her voice boomed through my room as she clapped her hands in excitement.

"How did you know it when I didn't even know myself?" I had only admitted my feelings to myself this morning.

"You've mentioned how attractive you find him, which I brushed off at first. But then I started to notice the way you look at him. I'd be surprised if he hasn't noticed, too."

Her words made my heart stop. "Shit. Has it been that obvious?" I crossed my arms over myself, hugging my own body and chewing on one of my fingers.

Pia sensed my unease and placed a hand on my shoulder. "Hey, it's okay. I barely knew Kohen when he and I, you know." She winked at me. "Seb is an amazing guy. I know you guys didn't have the best introduction, but that doesn't mean you can't—"

"We can't," I interrupted her.

"Of course you can."

Shaking my head, I uncrossed my arms. Then the feelings that had built up inside of me released in an emotional outburst. "It would never work, not when he's basically my bodyguard. King Hawthorne would never allow that. And besides, there's no chance that he will ever see me in the same way I see him. There's way prettier girls here, and I'm the kind of girl who gets her ass handed to her on the very first day of combat training. I'm the one who's panicking over something new every other day, and I'm the reason he has to deal with his jackass of a father even more than he used to," I announced my insecurities, practically yelling them to her.

My eyes burned, but I refused to cry over this. I looked up at the ceiling and stared at it until the stinginess resolved. When my meltdown passed, I dropped my head to look at Pia despite the redness of my cheeks.

She gawked at me, her arms crossed as she tapped her foot on the ground. "Are you done?" she asked, her voice displaying a tone of fraudulent annoyance.

I stared at her blankly, her nonchalance helping bring me back to reality. "Yeah. Sorry that was pathetic."

Smile lines appeared by her eyes as she tried not to laugh. "Maeve, you are beautiful. Please don't think for a second that you're not. And I promise you that Sebastian isn't the type of man to hold any of those things over someone's head. If he has feelings for you as well, he wouldn't let his father of all people come between that." She wrapped her arms around me in a hug.

I clenched my jaw and nodded in her embrace. I absorbed the comfort, hugging her back tightly.

"Can you please finish my hair? I look like an idiot." She chuckled and released me to sit back down on the floor.

I WAITED ON THE FRONT STEPS OF THE CASTLE AFTER I FINISHED dinner with Pia and some of the other first years. Most of the students in my class had warmed up to me, but I could tell that many of them still used caution around me. Why wouldn't they?

The king had them all terrified that they would be executed if they mis-stepped.

Sebastian's figure sauntered through the castle doors. He wore his steel chest plate, which concerned and intrigued me at the same time.

"Hey," he said, bounding down the steps.

I smiled, returning the greeting. "Hey."

We made our way across the courtyard. It was completely empty aside from the statues of the gods, their figures glimmering in the moonlight and casting shadows on the patio. Light danced off of Blythe's crystalline body, illuminating our skin as we walked by her.

I reached a hand to my cheekbone, making contact with my constellastones. For the first time since I'd been gifted by the goddess, I felt a sense of ease that there was a piece of the world's most powerful individual inside of me.

Sebastian seemed quiet this evening, but I couldn't say I blamed him after the information we received earlier. I didn't feel much like talking, either.

We walked down past the dormitories, continuing until we reached the academy. We entered the brick building and wandered through the hallways, passing empty classrooms as we went. I skated by Professor Stoll's classroom—the only one that still had a dim light emitting from it.

Sebastian stopped walking and pulled a book from his rucksack. "I borrowed this from Stoll. I'm gonna give it back to him since he's still here. I'll meet you in the arena. He likes to chat."

I nodded and advanced through the academy, untying the ribbons of my cloak as I entered the arena. It tumbled from my neck, falling into a pile of cloth at my feet and revealing my training uniform underneath.

Tossing my rucksack down, I dropped to a crouch to tighten the laces on my boots. My heart skipped a beat when I stood up, finding myself face to face with Sawyer.

"Ready for round two, Willawood?" he asked smugly, the corner of his lip curving up.

I glanced towards the entrance of the arena, hoping to see Sebastian close behind me, but he was nowhere in sight.

My airway tightened as I looked back at Sawyer and became all too aware that it was just us here. I'd really solidified some of my fighting skills in the past few weeks, so maybe I'd stand a chance if he tried to kick my ass again.

Standing tall, I puffed my chest out. "Sure. But unlike last time, I have powers now and can turn you into a puppet if I so please, so you may want to rethink that."

He scowled at me for a brief moment, but then his expression warmed. "I'm just kidding." He grinned, moving to the center of the mat where his belongings were.

"Why are you here?" *Please tell me he's not training with us.*

"Just getting an extra workout in," he called over his shoulder. "While I have you alone…"

Oh gods.

"For what it's worth, I'm sorry about what I did to you in combat training. That was pretty fucked up of me, if I'm being honest," he apologized as he gathered his bag.

My mouth fell open. "Am I hearing this right?" I scoffed.

Sawyer walked back towards me. "Seb is my best friend, has been pretty much my whole life." He rubbed his hand over his face, stopping the sweat from dripping into his eyes. "When he told me how you were giving him a hard time, I got defensive."

I gawked at him, speechless. I'd never expected to even have a real exchange of words with Sawyer, let alone an apology.

"Seb is like a brother to me. He's my family, and I get protective over my family."

"Do you think that giving me a reason behind your motives means that I'll suddenly be okay with how you used me as a lesson for the rest of my class?" I asked, crossing my arms over my chest.

Sawyer shrugged. "No, but regardless, there's no excuse for what I did, and I truly am sorry."

"Uh. Thanks, I guess."

He nodded, then with his bag tucked under his arm, marched

towards the exit. Sebastian made his entrance at the same time, stopping to chat with Sawyer for a few minutes. They glanced over at me in the middle of the conversation, then pulled the other into a one-armed hug before parting ways.

I was completely dumbfounded. I didn't completely forgive Sawyer—how could I after what he did? But he was important to Sebastian, so all I could do was try to put the matter behind me. It helped knowing that he got a taste of his own medicine after the fact. He and Sebastian truly must be close if a black eye didn't come between them.

A hand appeared in front of my face, waving back and forth.

The motion made my eyes flutter. "Sorry I—" I raised an eyebrow. "Sawyer just apologized to me."

"Yeah, he told me," Sebastian replied as he walked to the edge of the mat and placed his rucksack down. He released the knot of his cloak and folded it neatly, placing it on the ground next to his bag. "Sawyer means well, but has the oddest ways of showing it."

"I'll say," I muttered.

"You ready?"

"Almost." I took an elastic from my rucksack then gathered my hair in my hands, tying it into a quick braid so that it wouldn't be in the way while we were training. A few strands fell free into my face, but I let them be.

"Okay. Ready." I looked up towards Sebastian who was standing rigid, his eyes roaming my torso. He fumbled across the mat, trying to act nonchalant about the fact that I caught him watching me. My teeth clamped my lip to suppress my grin.

"Do you want to start with battle training or wielding?" he asked, running a hand through his hair, rustling it.

I was tempted to start with power wielding, but it would drain my energy too fast. "Training."

Sebastian nodded and reached down to the sheath hanging against his thigh. He pulled out a dagger, and passed it to me. I gripped it firmly, turning it in various angles to admire it.

The blade was crafted from a polished silver so bright that I could see both of our reflections in it. The hilt was carved from diamond and had sapphires arranged in spirals within the stone. I flipped the dagger around in my hands. "This is beautiful."

"It was my mother's. I inherited it when she died," Sebastian said, hanging his head just enough that I noticed.

I was stunned that he would let me use something so sentimental to him. I didn't feel worthy of even holding something that belonged to Queen Cicily. I tried to hand it back to him, but he shook his head.

"Why are you giving me this, anyways?"

"We are going to practice with weapons during our sessions. You won't do much of that in combat training until next year, but it's just as important to know how to fight with weapons as it is your hands."

I gestured to his chest plate. "That explains the armor."

"Yeah. I don't particularly want to be stabbed tonight."

"You probably should have worn the rest of it then. Your arms and legs are fair game."

"Should I get a healer in here before we start?"

"That would be wise. I don't have the best aim yet," I taunted, waving the dagger in the air.

"I can handle being stabbed in the leg. Just try to avoid any major organs." Sebastian laughed.

"No promises."

I wasn't thrilled with the idea of stabbing the man I was newly infatuated with in the chest, but we got right to work regardless.

"I want you to practice your offensive tactics. Try to hit me in the *armor*," he emphasized the word, "and I'll try to disarm you."

I took my stance on one side of the mat, steadying my legs and bending my arms at waist level. I held the dagger tightly in my palm, angling it towards him. Sebastian did the same on the other side and waited for me to make the first move.

I held a tight breath of air in my lungs and lunged towards him, pointing the blade out. Before I could get anywhere near his armor, his wrist locked around mine. He tightened his grip, and the knife fell from my grasp.

"You didn't even give me a chance." My nose crinkled with my complaint.

Releasing me, Sebastian picked up the dagger and handed it back. "There are no chances in real combat."

"This isn't real combat."

"Do you want it to be?" He smirked and resumed his combatant posture.

"No," I whined, backing up and spreading my feet apart.

Sebastian stared into my eyes intently, waiting for my next attack. I hid my arms behind my back, switching which hand held the blade as I charged at him again.

He noticed my attempt to throw him off and stepped out of my way. His body twisted, his chest pressing against my back as he grabbed me. He held me to him with both arms, then slammed our bodies down on the mat. He was much gentler than Sawyer had been, but the impact still caused me to release the dagger.

"Oldest trick in the book." His words lingered tauntingly into my ear.

"Damn it," I groaned as he lifted his weight off of me and jumped to his feet. I rolled to my back and sat up, scowling at him. "You aren't going to make this easy for me, are you?"

"What's the fun in that?"

"We aren't doing this because it's fun."

His eyes narrowed on me. "Oh trust me, I know. Battles aren't fun. They're messy. Bloody. They reek like death." He smiled smugly then spun to return to his place on the mat. "But training for them doesn't have to be that way."

With his back to me, I jumped to my feet, holding my blade out. I ran at him, slamming my body into his from behind, causing him to jolt forward. I wrapped one arm around his side to hold him still, then lifted my dagger, preparing to stab it in his back. But he was too fast and too strong. He turned his torso so sharply that it tore my arm from his waist and left us standing face-to-face.

I lowered the dagger and stared at him with disappointment on my face. His lips curved up, and I creased my forehead in frustration.

"No wonder you're a head soldier." When it came to combat, Sebastian was really talented.

We spent another hour practicing. Only once did I come remotely close to hitting Sebastian's armor with my dagger, but he deflected the move before I could complete it.

We concluded the session when my movements began to get heavy-handed. The extent of our training left us both dripping sweat and breathing heavily by the end of it.

"I thought I was getting better at combat, but apparently not," I panted.

"You are doing really well. Big improvement from the first day of combat class," Sebastian teased.

"Not funny," I shot back as I let my body collapse onto the mat where I drank from my canteen, taking deep breaths between each sip to try and regulate my breathing.

Sebastian sat down next to me, not nearly as breathless. "Tomorrow we can switch positions and you can try some more defensive techniques."

"Will I get to wear armor?" I asked.

"No need to."

"Why not?"

"Because I don't miss," he deadpanned.

I brushed a few sweat-coated strands of hair away from my eyes and nodded. "Can't wait," I said sarcastically. I was already exhausted. Wielding practice after this was going to completely drain me. The king wanting us to do this every day seemed excessive, but as usual, I didn't get a say.

I took another sip from my flask, and I couldn't stop my eyes from ogling at Sebastian as he stood up. He unclasped the buckles of his armor then lifted the chest plate over his head. The metal made a loud clash as he threw it down on the mat.

"I can't imagine that's very comfortable."

He shrugged. "You get used to it."

Sebastian lifted the edge of his shirt, using it to wipe the sweat on his forehead. The ridges of his abdomen flexed and heat rose inside of me as I admired his physique.

Fuck.

I choked on my water. To muffle my cough, I turned my head and wiped my mouth, trying to rid myself of dirty thoughts.

"You good?"

I bobbed my head, my eyes watering. "Yeah. I just… I…too much water."

His shadow darkened the light around me. "Ready to try your luck at wielding?" he asked, not waiting for my answer before stalking out of the arena with his cloak draped around his shoulders.

With red cheeks, I pushed myself up from the mat, running after him and throwing my own cloak on. "Where are we going?"

"You'll see." He led me outside, past the academy, and along a path that I'd never been on before.

The only light left in the sky was from stars that twinkled over us. A gust of frigid air made me shiver, and I wrapped my cloak tightly around myself to preserve heat.

The further we got from the academy, the more the starlight fizzled away under the network of branches above us. It was eventually so dark that I couldn't see much beyond my hands. I fumbled my steps, almost falling.

"I can't see anything."

My heart jumped when Sebastian reached his hand behind him. He slowed his pace to match mine, taking my hand and guiding me through the darkness.

"Can I ask you something?" I inquired in an attempt to distract my mind from hyper fixating on his skin against my palm.

"Sure."

"Why did you ask to be reassigned?"

A deep sigh filled the silence of the wilderness. "Because sometimes I'm just as stubborn as you."

"I'm not stubborn."

"Oh, yes, you are." Sebastian's hand squeezed mine a few times. "And sometimes I just do things out of frustration."

"Maybe you should try writing, too. It helps to prevent making rash decisions."

"Yeah, maybe I should." He released a huff of laughter, and I shivered in his grasp as we took a turn.

"Sorry. I know it's cold, but we're almost there."

"Where is *there*?" My teeth chattered as I spoke.

"I find it easier to wield when I'm in a location that relaxes me." A faint glow of moonlight illuminated his face just enough for me to make out his features. "For me, the castle archives do the trick. For you, however, I think this is much more fitting."

Sebastian dropped my hand to push apart a thick field of dune grass, ushering me through. I instantly forgot about the cold air when I stepped into the hidden oasis.

Before me was a beach of golden sand—the most beautiful piece of earth I had ever stepped foot upon. The ocean raged beyond the shore, the glow of the cosmos bouncing off of the water. Shells glazed the sand, adding a prism of color to the already stunning ambiance. The entire coastline was hidden by an array of grass and shrubs, concealing it away from the rest of the world.

"Sebastian…" I started, but had no words to describe this. I wandered towards the edge of the water, gazing into it and being reminded of the night I discovered my stones.

"Amazing, isn't it?" Sebastian appeared beside me. The starlight made his features even more alluring, and I found the air gone from my lungs.

I drew in a deep breath, exhaling slowly to gain control of myself. I had to stop. If I kept thinking about him like this then I'd truly fall for him. And I couldn't allow that. The next few years would be miserable if I ruined things by letting my feelings get in the way.

I put my attention back on the waves, watching them bounce off of the boulders to the right of the coastline. "Amazing doesn't do it justice. How did you know I'd like it here?"

"I pay attention. You spend most of your free time on the beach."

"Oh," I breathed, my voice shaking. "How did you find this place?"

"I ran away from my father when I was eight. Found myself here. Took them an entire day to find me."

Though I wanted to ask him why, I learned my lesson from last time. He only shared as much as he was comfortable with, though I wanted to know more of that Sebastian. The version of him that had feelings too large to release. I wanted him to confide in me. To know him at his core. I wanted to know the things he believed would make me sick. What book he was reading, and how he reacted when he found out he was gifted by Caius. I wanted to know every minuscule detail about him. But instead of asking, I changed the subject.

"Maybe we should start wielding. It's getting late, and I'm cold," I whispered, sudden sadness sticking to my words like honey.

Sebastian agreed. "Let's start with some shielding first. I'll throw some of my magic at you. Do everything you can to stop it from reaching you." He kept his eyes wide as he spoke, making sure I comprehended his instructions.

I bobbed my head yes, liking that suggestion. Once we started wielding, I wouldn't last long. In fear of seeming weak, I had been quiet about how draining my powers were.

"Ready?" he asked, pivoting in the sand to look at me.

I closed my eyes and focused on calming my mind, body, and soul. "Ready."

A chill much icier than the fall air caressed my skin. Pricks of ice bit my flesh before my body's heat melted them away. I recognized the droplets as Sebastian's magic, and imagined myself telling the storm to dissolve. I used every ounce of my focus to concentrate on stopping the snowflakes he summoned.

All at once, the goosebumps on my skin faded away. I opened my eyes to meet Sebastian's gaze, tilting my neck up to watch the snowfall over the beach, landing everywhere except for where I stood.

"Good job." He smiled proudly, and as he lowered his hands, the snow vanished.

I grinned from ear to ear, relieved that I was able to shield properly on the first try. "I'll be honest, I wasn't sure how I would differentiate between shielding and wielding, but between class and now this, I think I'm starting to get it."

"Don't be so quick to assume. I was making it easy on you."

"Oh, so *now* you decide to take it easy on me? Where was that mercy back on the mat?"

"If I make things too hard on you, you may request a new guard."

"I might just do that, anyway."

Sebastian snickered, letting a smile slip free.

He didn't give me any time to celebrate my achievement before he harnessed more magic for me to block.

I successfully shielded a few more times, some of which I was able to keep my eyes open for. Happy with the progress, we took a few minutes to rest before starting to wield.

My mouth opened to let out a yawn, the exertion from this evening had begun to consume me.

Sebastian grinned apologetically. "We'll make this quick. I know it's late, and you must be really tired from having your ass handed to you on the mat."

"Well maybe if someone wasn't such a try-hard, I would have stood a chance," I retorted, laughing at the same time.

Sebastian's lips quirked up once more as he held his hands out to me. "Come here."

"I don't need to be touching someone to use my magic against them." I was hesitant to take his hands again in fear that I'd do something I'd regret.

"I know. But you're still new to this and contact makes it easier. Come on." He gestured me over with a wave.

I gulped but stepped towards him. My hands were so small compared to his, fitting inside of his palms with room to spare. Before I could lose myself in his face, I squeezed my eyes shut and aimed my focus on relaxing my body. "What should I try to make you do?"

Sebastian spoke to me softly as to not distract me from my inner peace. "Whatever you want."

"Whatever I want? That seems a bit bold to tell someone who can do exactly that."

"I saw how you reacted to the crab incident, so I know you won't do anything too harsh," he replied.

Air blew from my nostrils in a subtle laugh. "That crab didn't body slam me to the mat while training, though."

"Valid point."

I shuffled my feet to cement myself in the sand, then loosened my limbs, letting my arms go slack and using the support from his hands to keep them from dropping to my sides.

I completely relaxed myself, calming the thoughts in my head that never seemed to rest. My jewels sent jolts of energy throughout my face, signaling that my magic was active, ready to emerge and take control of the man in front of me. I imagined my command, repeating the words inside my head, and when I was ready, opened my eyes and said, "Drop your cloak."

Sebastian released my hands and raised them to untie the knot that held his cloak around his neck. He meticulously moved his fingers to release the strings, then it fell to the sand in a puddle at our feet.

"Woah," was all he managed to say, his blue eyes opened wide, showcasing his amazement.

He hadn't seen my magic yet, so this was an entirely new experience for him. I couldn't relate, but I imagined it must be bizarre to have no control over your actions.

A gust of wind passed us, and he shivered as he picked up his cloak, shaking the sand off of it before wrapping it tightly around himself. "Alright, let's do a few more then we can go."

"The cold air catching up to you?" I teased. The adrenaline from using my magic was enough to warm my body.

Sebastian smiled. "Yeah, actually it is." He stuck his hands back for me to grab. "Ready when you are."

I laid my palms on his, feeling the warmth of his skin on mine. My heart urged me to pull him closer, but my brain granted the thought to release as quickly as it came.

I removed all of the air from my lungs, and repeated the steps I'd been practicing ever since my magic manifested.

"Show me your tattoo."

Sebastian released one of my hands, using it to bunch his cloak up, revealing his shirt to me. He slid his arm out of the sleeve and flaunted me the dagger tattoo that covered his bicep. The lines of ink soaked into his skin were intricate and detailed, perfectly representing his mother's dagger.

Reaching a hand out to touch him, I ran my fingers along the edge of the inky blade that marked his body. The contact caused electricity to blaze through me. I'd touched him before, but this felt different. Almost intimate.

He shivered, and I wondered if he felt the same thing that I did when our skin made contact. But maybe me caressing his arm made him uncomfortable, or maybe it was just the cold air.

I tore my fingers away from him. "This time can you try blocking my magic as I use it?" I asked in a desperate attempt to break the one-sided sexual tension.

He cleared his throat, adjusting his shirt and putting his arm back in his sleeve. "Sure."

I prepared myself to wield once more, and when ready, spoke my command.

"Tell me a secret."

Nothing happened.

I tried again. "Tell me one of your secrets."

Sebastian didn't speak, proving his shield successful. I dropped my command.

"Good thing I was able to block that one."

"Why? Got a bunch of dirty secrets up in there?" I tapped his forehead.

"Wouldn't you like to know."

I would.

By the end of our session, my body felt so broken that I had trouble walking. I tried not to let Sebastian notice me stumble as we made our way to the dormitories. He walked me all the way up to my room and unlocked my door with his key, holding it open for me. I lost my balance a little as I entered, but caught the door frame, using it to keep myself upright.

"You okay?" His eyebrow raised.

"Yeah. I'm just exhausted, it's been a long night." I disregarded his concern and glanced at the clock. "We really have to do this every single night?" I moaned.

He smiled apologetically, his eyes studying mine for the briefest of moments. "You should get some rest."

We said our goodbyes, and as soon as the door sealed behind him, I collapsed onto my bed and didn't rise until late morning the following day.

CHAPTER SIXTEEN

Weeks had come and gone since Sebastian started training me privately. Fall was in full force now, and the colors of nature darkened with each passing day, preparing for the gloominess of winter to arrive in a few short weeks.

We had been steady with our wielding practice, and though exhausting, it was going well. I had solidified my skills on the basics of my power, but was yet to try more challenging commands. Sebastian kept pushing me to, but wielding took so much out of me that I didn't know if I could handle it.

Thankfully we said our goodbyes outside last night after our session, as I threw up the moment I got back to my room. The overexertion was beginning to affect my whole body, and no one knew about it besides myself. The whole thing perplexed me. None of the other students seemed to get nearly as depleted when they used their magic.

I had gotten fairly good at using my mental shields as well. Most times I could keep my eyes open, not needing to concentrate nearly as hard as I did when I first began shielding. I learned the hard way however, that losing my focus could be detrimental. One evening Sebastian was summoning icicles for me to block, but I had gotten distracted and one pierced between my shoulder blades. He felt horrible, but the ice shard only drew a little blood, which Pia was able to heal with hardly any effort when I got back to my room.

Sebastian had agreed to start doing our combat training in the morning and wielding at night. This schedule definitely helped me retain my energy, but with classes in the mix, I still felt my body get weaker with each passing day. I had shown some improvement though, having successfully blocked Sebastian from stabbing me with a training sword twice in a row. He was dumbfounded when the weapon fell from his clutch, and the look on his face was one I wouldn't soon forget.

My week of classes had come to an end and I was looking forward to having some down time the next few days. Although I'd still have my nightly sessions with Sebastian, the days would be free to spend as I pleased—aside from a certain soldier accompanying me everywhere.

He was waiting for me this morning in his usual spot on the staircase. My heart fluttered when I saw him reading a book—like always.

I found it incredibly charming that one of Caelestis' most talented soldiers had such a knack for reading. He could take an enemy down with a singular swing of his sword, but spent his downtime doing one of the most virtuous hobbies.

I smirked and made my descent down the stairs. "Whatcha reading?"

Sebastian slammed the book shut and tilted his head up. His eyes followed me down the spiral of the stairs. I sat down on the step next to him and though he tried to fight me, I tore the book from his hands.

My lips trembled to fight back a smile. "I didn't peg you for a romance reader."

He shrugged as he took the book back, tucking it into his rucksack. "What can I say, I'm a hopeless romantic."

"Yeah right," I laughed with a roll of my eyes.

Sebastian smirked sheepishly and rose from his spot on the steps. "Breakfast?" he asked.

"What about combat training?"

"I'm giving you the day off."

"Why?"

"I have something to do this morning," he said, and I trailed behind him as we commenced our daily hike across the castle grounds.

Exhaling deeply, my heated breath turned to mist from the chill of the air. I had my winter cloak on, which provided me a thick layer of protection, but it didn't block the frigid wind from blowing my hair in every direction. I regretted not braiding it today as some strands got stuck in my eyelashes.

Sebastian noticed me quivering and sped up so that he could walk in front, blocking the wind from hitting me. It turned out he was hot *and* chivalrous.

"So do you read anything besides obscene literature or is that what really gets you going?" I broke the silence of our travels.

Sebastian stopped in place, pivoting to look at me. He bit his lip, smiling at me bashfully. "It's not *obscene*. It's a work of art that you are clearly too young and immature to appreciate."

"I'm not that young."

"You're only twenty-one."

"You're only four years older."

"Yes, and it shows in my ability to read mature literature."

I raised an eyebrow. "You're really showing your age, soldier."

Sebastian's eyes rolled up and with a shake of his head, he turned and started walking again. I trudged along behind him, appreciating how his large frame kept the wind from knocking me on my ass. I also appreciated the view of him from behind.

"What do you have planned for today?" I tried to make conversation to avoid dwelling on my skin that would soon be blue and frozen.

"I have a consultation with the other head soldiers and my father." Sebastian looked over at me. "Then the rest of my day depends on yours, I suppose."

"Oh." Guilt overwhelmed me. As annoying as it could be to have someone knowing my every move, it was arguably worse to be in his position. I liked Sebastian and didn't mind his presence, but I wasn't sure he felt the same about me.

"What is your meeting about?"

We took a corner on the cobblestone path, putting the wind behind us and allowing my hair to settle. Sebastian slowed his walk so that he was by my side.

"That's nothing for you to worry about."

My eyebrows lowered. "I wasn't worried. But should I be?"

He let out a chuckle. "I just said that you don't need to be."

"Well, it seems like there's always something for me to worry about nowadays."

Everything went silent aside from the crashing of waves below the cliffside. I had been trying not to think about what the duke had said about the traitor, but a pit formed in my stomach when I realized that I hadn't heard anything about the situation in weeks.

"Do you know what it's like to constantly have a target on your back?" I asked out of nowhere.

Sebastian sighed. "I do."

That was a stupid question. Of course he did. He was his father's target.

"And I wish I could take that feeling away from you," he said under his breath.

Me too.

"Have you heard any more about the traitor? Have they discovered who it is?" I asked the question that was really on my mind.

Sebastian audibly gulped, causing suspicion within me.

"Is that what your meeting is about?"

He glanced over at me. "Remember thirty seconds ago when I told you not to worry?"

"Oh gods." Panic overtook my body.

He halted his movements and took hold of my shoulders, lowering his head so that his eyes were in line with mine. "My job is to protect you, and I swear to you that I am going to do that. You don't need to worry." His eyes widened. "Do you understand?"

I bobbed my head in response.

"Good. Now, I'm not supposed to be telling you this, but I know if I don't that you'll spend the rest of your day agonizing over it."

He was right.

"Duke Sinclair sent word that they uncovered the name of the traitor. They are in the process of trying to locate the individual now."

I relaxed a bit, but not enough for him to release his hands from me. "Okay, so this is good news?"

His face told me that there was more before he even opened his mouth to speak. His lips sealed into a tight line, like he was trying to stop himself from telling me the rest of it.

"Tell me," I demanded.

"There's been no mention of your name by any Draemornians that we've encountered, which is good. That means it's likely that word of your gift hasn't spread any further and that King Beaumont still doesn't know who you are," he reassured me.

I let out a sigh of relief. That was also good news, but Sebastian's face still looked all too serious.

"What is it?"

He stared at me blankly and I stared back, not releasing him from my gaze until he blew out a breath and responded. "Beaumont has sent a letter to my father with a proposal."

"Okay?"

"He wants Caelestis to turn you over to Draemor, and in return promises to remove their threat of declaring another war."

"*What*?" I blurted out. My knees threatened to collapse beneath me as my entire body weakened with fear. I couldn't go to Draemor. I'd heard horror stories that I certainly didn't want to experience on my own.

Sebastian lifted a finger to his lips, his eyes scurrying back and forth. "Shh."

"I'm being used as a *bargaining tactic*?" Though I already had no control over my life, something told me that it would be so much worse if King Beaumont had me under his reign. I promised myself that I wouldn't lose my composure in front of Sebastian again, but I couldn't help but panic.

"Shit."

I heard Sebastian curse. Clearly realizing that I was about to lose it, he grabbed my hand and practically dragged me along the rest of the pathway and to the side of one of the towers. I sank down against the stone, holding my knees to my chest and tucking my head between them.

If King Hawthorne handed me over, I'd never see Delani or my mother again. They would have no idea what happened to me. He would probably just tell them I was dead—that I had an accident in wielding class.

My eyes began to burn. I tried everything in me to keep my cheeks dry, but the tears spilled over them.

The problem was that King Hawthorne *should* give me up. It was the smartest thing to do for the kingdom. Sacrificing me would grant all other Caelestians safety.

"Maeve? Talk to me."

I tried with everything inside of me to hold myself together, but my body shuddered when the power of my fear became too strong.

"Fuck," I swore, frustrated with myself for being unable to control this feeling. I had been doing well, using writing to help me cope throughout this whole transition. I'd been able to stop the torment of panic before it consumed me. I'd been able to work through moments like this and come out stronger on the other end. I had been pretty damn resilient—until now.

I didn't lift my head to look at Sebastian as he slumped to the ground next to me. He put one of his arms over my shoulders, pulling me close to him. "I told you that you don't need to worry, and I meant it."

The gesture was comforting, and pretty unexpected from a man who seemingly never showed this type of emotion. The strength of his biceps holding me sent chills throughout my core, and although I would have much rather focused on the feel of his body against mine, I couldn't right now.

Just a few months ago—hell, even a few weeks ago—I would

have slapped his hands away if he laid a finger on me. We'd been so on and off that I was almost surprised at myself for accepting the contact now. I wondered what he truly thought of me—the girl who had given him so much trouble since she crashed into his life. The girl who was cowering against his father's castle.

"What are you thinking?" he spoke softly.

I heard his words, but was still as motionless as the statue of Blythe in the courtyard.

"Look at me."

I didn't want to. Didn't want the man I'd developed feelings for to see me like this.

Mortified, I shook my head between my knees. "Leave," I whispered, doubting he ever lost control of himself in this way. He must have thought that I was a pitiful excuse of *Caelestis' greatest asset*. And he would be right in thinking that—I was pathetic.

"Please look at me," he pleaded.

I didn't.

"Please leave," I begged.

He didn't.

I shuddered when a drop of rain fell on my head. Or maybe it was snow. It was still fall, but with the temperatures lately it wouldn't have surprised me. Whatever it was tumbled from the sky, dampening my hair and cloak. I tried to ignore it, but my body began to shiver uncontrollably. Shouldn't the tower have prevented the weather from hitting me?

I looked up from the comfort of darkness to see the snow Sebastian created as it fell over us. With my emergence from my knees, the snow vanished.

I turned my eyes to him, despite the puffiness of them. "That was mean," I said in a hush.

He grinned apologetically, then rotated his torso so that he faced me more directly. His arm slid off of my shoulders, drifting beneath my cloak and landing on my forearm. "Breathe," he said, taking a deep breath of his own in an example.

I sucked in a shuddered inhale.

"What are you thinking?" He stared at me, trying to decipher my thoughts from the look on my face.

I ran a hand over my face, removing the dampness from my cheeks and wiping my swollen skin. "The king would be wise to follow through with Draemor's proposal."

"My father is not a wise man," Sebastian tried to joke, but I wasn't in the mood.

I met his eyes with my own, finally accepting the ease he offered me. I absorbed the qualities of his face, soaking in every detail of his skin, my own body calming in response. Maybe it was the adrenaline, but I so badly wanted to be rash and put my lips on his. By the way he was looking at me, I wondered if he wanted the same thing.

He squeezed my arm gently. "I'm not going to let anything happen to you. You have my word."

I nodded, and he took his hand off of me, leaving an unsuspected emptiness where it had laid.

Why was *he* the catalyst that caused a full body reaction inside of me? I didn't think I'd ever understand it, so I brushed the feeling off, reminding myself why we would never work.

Something told me that I'd be reminding myself of that until the day I died.

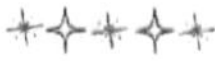

Once I collected myself, Sebastian and I grabbed a quick bite to eat from the kitchen before parting ways. I would be accompanying Pia to the archives, and he would meet us there when he finished his meeting.

Picking at my muffin, Pia and I wandered through the corridors of the castle. I didn't have much to say after the news I'd received this morning, and she noticed. "You okay?" she asked.

"Mhm," I muttered through a mouthful of my pastry. I wasn't too hungry, either, but knew that I'd regret not eating tonight at wielding practice.

"You're awfully quiet this morning."

"I'm just really tired from all of the extra training." I hated lying to her, but I promised Sebastian that I wouldn't tell anyone what he told me until the king made it known to the rest of the kingdom.

"Yeah. Okay," she scoffed, but dropped the subject.

We arrived amongst a set of towering golden doors. Pia pulled one towards her, and I entered the archives for surprisingly the first time since I arrived at the castle. My mouth fell slack as I took in the thousands of books before me.

The room was cylindrical, manuscripts lining essentially every inch of the walls. Any space that didn't have a bookshelf was filled with glass panes that overlooked Caelestis. In the center, past the oversized wooden desk, was a staircase that led up to four more floors, each one just as open as the first. There was absolutely no privacy in the room.

"This place must give Sebastian wet dreams," I quipped. I'd never met someone who admired books as much as he did.

"Ew." Pia grimaced, then laughed. "But yeah, you're probably right."

We climbed all the way to the fourth floor. I threw my bag down in an armchair then explored the archives for a while, roaming aimlessly through the floors and studying the curved walls of books that seemed to have no end.

Back on the fourth floor, I came across a small section with manuscripts about the gods and goddesses. A row of narrow-binded books caught my eye. There were eight of them in total, each a different color. Sliding the green book off the shelf, I read the title, *The History of the Goddess of Nature.* I flipped through a few pages, then pushed the book about Sloane back into its slot.

I ran my finger along the other bindings, stopping at a pale blue book and plucking it from the shelf before returning to Pia.

Aimlessly flipping through the pages about Blythe, I tried to distract myself from thinking about Sebastian's meeting. Just like writing, reading helped to clear my mind of the worries that took up too much space.

Blythe was known as the strongest of the gods and goddesses. She was granted this title from her ability to compel the brain matter of all things living.

Blythe's power is the most advanced of all the gods, and thus her gift of a constellastone is unheard of in a mortal.

They'd have to update that.

I glanced up and at Pia, who was hunched over and smiling while she scribbled on a piece of parchment. She giggled to herself, then looked up at the sound of my book slamming shut.

"What in the gods' names are you writing over there?" I asked, my tone accusatory.

"I'm writing to Kohen."

"What's so funny about writing to Kohen?"

Pia passed me the parchment, her cheeks flushing as she did. My eyes widened at the incredibly provocative words she had written.

"Pia!" I whisper-yelled.

She giggled and held a finger to her mouth. "Shh."

Dumbfounded, I passed her erotic love note back to her. "I didn't realize you and Kohen were that serious."

"We aren't. Well, not really." She raised an eyebrow. "I actually don't really know what we are. But I do know he's good in bed."

I smirked and shook my head. I wished for the nerve that Pia had, then maybe I could make something of my feelings for Sebastian.

I returned to my book, only to be interrupted seconds later by a very distraught Sebastian who just so happened to look over Pia's shoulder at her letter.

"Oh my gods, Pia, what the actual f—"

"SHH!" Pia raised her finger to her mouth once more, her face turning the brightest shade of red that I'd ever seen.

"You and Kohen? Since when? He didn't tell me," Sebastian stuttered, his eyes practically bulging out of his head.

Pia shoved the letter into her bag, crumbling it so much that Kohen wouldn't be able to read it, anyways. "Oh, please. Like you didn't see me go into his room a few weeks ago."

"I thought that had something to do with classes!"

"Relax, Seb." Pia rolled her eyes. "It's nothing serious, at least I don't think it is." She shrugged the situation off and her face returned to its normal hue.

Sebastian, however, looked awfully pale. "If that's what you write to someone you aren't serious with, then the gods help me if I ever see what you write to someone that you are."

The disgusted look on his face was enough to make me burst out in laughter.

He murmured something while turning his attention to me. His face settled into an expression that told me he needed to talk to me. My pulse raced as I rose from my chair.

"I'll be right back," I told Pia, and she flashed me a confused look as Sebastian and I walked off.

He led me out of the archives all together, down the hallway and into an empty corridor. He glanced around to make absolutely sure no one else was there before speaking to me. "I know that you won't meet with my father again for a while, so I wanted to fill you in so that you don't spend your week worrying."

My heart fluttered at his act of kindness, but I forced it to return to its normal sinus rhythm.

You and him will never work.

"My father has no intention of going through with King Beaumont's proposal. You're much too important to him."

My shoulders relaxed as relief washed over me. "Oh thank gods."

"I told you not to worry." He smiled and my insides melted like the wax of a burning candle. "Also the duke has a lead on where the traitor is hiding, and he solidified the plan for when he's in custody."

He didn't need to explain the plan to me—I knew what happened to traitors when they were caught.

"Do you know who it is?" I doubted that I would know the name, but was curious who ratted me out to Draemor.

"Yeah um…something Fletcher. Edward, I think."

"Shut the fuck up," I swore, my eyes popping out of my skull.

Sebastian took a step back, eyebrows drawn together. "Excuse me?"

"I grew up with him. He's from my village. That prick! Why would he do that?"

"You'd be surprised what people will do for wealth. For power. I don't know his motives. It doesn't matter, really. He will be taken care of."

Killed. He would be killed.

Sebastian changed the subject. "There was also more discussion about moving your housing for safety purposes, but I convinced him to hold off on that for now."

"Thank you." I sighed in contempt, having grown to like my room and not wanting to leave it.

"One more thing." He took a step closer to me, leaving only inches between us.

My breath lodged in my chest. He had to know exactly what he was doing to me.

"I really need you to be careful. I know you hate having to tell me where and when you are going somewhere, but I need you to take this extra seriously now. *Please.*" His face was the most serious I'd ever seen. He was worried.

"I will," I assured him, and meant it.

CHAPTER SEVENTEEN

"No more bullshit!" Sebastian yelled across the arena as he took his position on the mat. "Tonight, you're trying to use your power to its full ability."

"Ugh," I groaned. I saw that coming. He'd been trying to convince me to perform more difficult commands on him for a while now.

The past two weeks had been rough, to say the least. Though wielding had gotten easier with practice, I still struggled with the aftermath. I had been putting off using more complicated compulsions in fear that I'd show Sebastian how fragile I was, but tonight he would get his way.

"It's going to be fine," he assured me.

"What if I can't do it?"

"Only one way to find out."

"What if I accidentally compel you to jump off a cliff and then we have the crab incident all over again?"

"We're inside. And you're really hung up on that crab, aren't you?"

"Well yeah, I don't particularly enjoy taking innocent lives."

"That's good. I'd be a bit concerned if you did."

I crinkled my nose. “Well what if—”

He held a hand up to silence me. “Enough.” Realizing that he wasn't getting anywhere with this conversation, Sebastian came towards me. “First of all, you didn't *kill* the crab. You told it to jump and it did. It's not your fault that it had bad aim.” He took a step closer. “Second of all, I have very effective mental shields. They're always up, except for when I'm training with you. If I don't want someone's magic affecting me, it won't.”

“Why do you keep them up all the time?” I knew he had to let his guard down while we trained, but he even kept his shields up with Sawyer and Kohen?

He ignored my question, moving his body to stand behind me. My blood rushed to my core, sending my mind into a frenzy. I gasped as he brushed my braid over my shoulder.

Then, time froze for a moment. All I could feel was the rise and fall of his chest against my body, and all I could think about was how badly I wished he’d spin me around and pull my lips to his. I trembled so obviously at the thought that there was no way he didn't notice how my body shook from his touch.

“Third of all,” his words slipped into my ear, his breath tickling the back of my neck, “you're going to want this back.” With a flick of his wrist, he unclasped the star pendant from my neck then rushed back to his place on the mat.

Asshole.

He waved the silver chain in the air. “Whenever you're ready,” he taunted with a wink, knowing damn well what he just did to me. “And don't just tell me to give it back. Make it more complicated. No more simple commands.”

I rolled my eyes. What did *not simple* mean to him? Asking him to give the necklace back was too basic. Telling him to drop it on the ground was quick and easy.

I contemplated my options and when ready, allowed my powers to flow through my soul. My cheek prickled as magic pooled into my bloodstream. “Put my necklace back on,” I commanded.

I held my ground as Sebastian did what I instructed, the feeling of his fingers creating the same reaction as before.

I've got to get control of myself.

He finished and I released him from the grip of my powers.

"That was perfect," he exclaimed with a smile.

"Thanks," I mumbled, trying to pinpoint any part of me that felt weak from using my powers. So far I felt fine.

"Ready to try something else?"

"No, but sure. Any ideas?"

"Whatever you want."

My shoulders slouched. "I hate when you say that. The free range stresses me out."

"It's fine, I trust you."

I sighed, but focused on my powers again. I didn't need to, but closed my eyes while I thought about Blythe and how she chose *me* to give a fragment of her soul to. Though I may have felt weak, the stones on my face were enough proof that I wasn't. I had a goddess within me.

My command played on repeat in my mind before I spoke it into existence. "Run a lap around the arena."

My eyelids flipped open to watch Sebastian take off running. This command was difficult because I had to maintain my focus on it the entire time, and the arena was large.

His leg muscles rippled as he ran. His biceps tightened and released with the movements of his arms, and I bit my lip as I watched him. How did he make something so simple look so appealing?

He was almost finished with the lap, but my magic slipped as I became more focused on how his arms would feel holding me down against his mattress.

"Shit," I muttered, flustered.

"It's okay." His breathing was labored as he leisured towards me. "I could feel when the pull of your magic broke. But that was a good start. Try it again."

I kept my eyes closed this time and was able to hold my control over him for the entire lap.

"Nice. Let's take a break for a minute. I need some water," Sebastian said as he made for his bag.

I bent down to tighten my shoelaces, and when I stood up, my head started to spin. I braced my hands against my thighs, pushing myself upright as my vision blurred and my whole figure wobbled. I blinked through the dizziness and tried to find my center of gravity, praying Sebastian didn't notice.

"You good?" he called out to me.

Gods damnit.

How was he so observant?

"I'm fine!" I yelled back over my shoulder, the words slightly slurred.

Get it together, Maeve.

I tucked my hands into my pockets so he wouldn't notice them shake, then returned to my spot on the mat, keeping my mouth shut about what just happened.

"That went pretty well, so I'm thinking we should try something a little harder," he said.

Great.

"Sounds good," I lied. "What are you thinking?"

"How about trying to compel me to use my magic? I know you stopped Pia from using hers, but I would think controlling someone to use theirs would be more challenging."

I didn't blink. He had to be joking. That was way too much for me after what just happened.

He stared back, waiting for my answer.

"Seriously?"

"Why not?"

"That sounds pretty complicated."

"Scared of a challenge?"

"No. I just—"

"Sounds like you are." He smirked tauntingly.

"I'm not. But I already did what you asked. I tried some harder commands and was successful. Let's just accept the victory tonight."

A cocky grin appeared across his face. "It's okay to be scared, Maeve. No need to lie."

He knew exactly what he was doing.

"I'm not scared," I growled, staring him down.

One of his shoulders shrugged. "If you weren't scared, then you would do it."

"Are you really trying to peer pressure me into this?"

"Is it working?" His eyes widened on me, matching my antagonistic glare.

"No. You—I—" My face scrunched and I stomped my foot down. "Fine, you jerk. Let's give it a try," I agreed, knowing damn well it would be a mistake.

The pounding in my head didn't cease as I got back into position. I focused on the tingling in my face, using the familiar feeling to ignore the blood rushing to the surface of my skin as I harnessed my magic. "Use your magic to craft a dagger."

Sebastian's hands got right to work, using his powers to form a blade of crystalline ice. He waved his hands like he was conducting an orchestra, crafting tiny icicles and carving details into the weapon he created.

My eyesight began to falter, tunneling into darkness for a moment before tearing me back into the arena's bright light.

I held on to my power, only letting it go limp when Sebastian's hand was outstretched in front of me, dripping as the weapon of ice melted from his body heat.

My vision blurred again when I reached out to take it, making me miss his hand by inches. My head pulsated, and though I could hardly see anything anymore, I made out the look of fear on his face.

"Maeve?"

I couldn't form the words to respond. I tried to grab the dagger again, but my body went slack and crumbled to the mat.

✦✧✦✧✦

My eyes fluttered open. I rubbed the sleep away and glanced around my room. *How did I get here?*

The glow of the crescent moon poured over my skin as I rolled to my side in my bed. My gaze caught on Sebastian. He looked exhausted, lounging in my armchair reading a book.

I sat up and hung my legs off the side of my bed to try and stand, but his shadow appeared above me.

He looked worried. And kind of pissed.

He grabbed my legs, pulling them back onto the bed before taking his seat on the edge of the mattress. "How do you feel?"

"Um. I—" I cleared my throat. "Fine, I guess. What happened?"

"Does your head feel okay?" He peered around to the back of my skull.

"It's fine, why?" My hair crunched beneath my fingers when I felt where he was looking. There were flakes of dried blood on my hands when I pulled them back into view.

"Oh fuck." My eyes widened as I recalled what happened.

He scooted a little closer to me. "What do you remember?"

"We were training. I compelled you to make a dagger." I looked up at him for confirmation.

"Yeah. And then?"

I chewed the inside of my lip. I knew what happened, but didn't want to say it.

"You passed out, Maeve. You wouldn't wake up. I had to carry you back to your room. You've been unconscious for hours."

"Oh."

"Why didn't you tell me?" he asked angrily.

"Tell you what?"

"Why didn't you tell me that harnessing your power hurt you?" His eyebrows were furrowed as he questioned me.

"I'm sorry, Seb." My cheeks flushed as I caught myself using his nickname. "I didn't want you to think I was weak, and in all honesty, I didn't know the extent of it." I felt a little guilty for not warning him about how draining my power was, but never expected for it to knock me out.

Sebastian shot up from my bed. "Well shit, Maeve!" He started parading around my room, running his hands down the front of his perfectly chiseled face. "Does anyone else know?"

"No."

He nodded slowly. "Good." He sighed in relief as he roamed my room.

I gathered all of my strength and stood up as well. "Is it really that big of a deal? I'm sure with more practice I will—"

"Yes, Maeve, it *is* a big deal! You could get hurt! You could get killed!" He stormed over to me. "You can't keep stuff like this from me! Not when I'm the one pushing you to your limits on a daily basis!"

"I'm sorry," I said again, the anger in his voice triggering something in me. "That's never happened before. Usually I just get sick or get a bad headache."

"Gods…I've been working you so hard and I had no idea it was hurting you." He hung his head, and not even the oceans in his eyes could hide the sorrow that took over his expression. "How didn't I see this?" he asked himself. "I mean, I should have known something was up by the way you were fighting back there."

"I didn't want you to know." I shrugged. "Why are you so upset over this?" He had never shown me any indication that he truly cared for me until now.

He pivoted so he could face me head on. His hands collapsed around my upper arms, his fingers so long that they wrapped all the way around. "Fuck, Maeve! If my father finds out, I'm worried that he'll change his mind and go through with the deal with Draemor."

My blood froze in my veins. Seeing Sebastian lose control caused instant panic to overwhelm me.

"I never thought of that…" My voice quivered. If King Hawthorne found out that I wasn't as powerful as he had thought, he'd have no reason to keep me here. My eyes started to gloss over.

Sebastian's expression softened when he realized that I was getting upset. "Shit, no. I'm sorry. It's going to be fine, please don't worry." He pulled me into his chest, holding me there and resting his chin on top of my head.

I held my breath, trying to work through the weight of my emotions. I allowed the embrace to comfort me and wished it would never end.

Sebastian rubbed a palm over the back of my head, his fingers gliding slowly over my hair. "I'm not saying that would be the case, but we can't take any chances. It's going to be fine, I promise you. I'll think of something."

I nodded into his chest. Being this close to him caused my heart to slow and my mind to calm. I breathed him in—his unique scent of pinewood and fresh snow.

He pulled away from me suddenly, and I found myself missing the warmth of his body against mine. We gazed at each other, and the way his eyes drifted to my lips made me realize that there was something between us—something more than just a soldier and his responsibility.

He sensed it, too. I know he did.

"You should get some sleep. I'll check on you in the morning. Don't worry about training tomorrow. We'll take another day off."

"Okay." I still felt frail and depleted, and sleep was the only solution to that problem.

I laid back in my bed, snuggling into the warmth of my sheets. Sebastian flicked my lamp off before the door locked behind him.

Pinewood lingered on my clothes as I drifted off to sleep.

CHAPTER EIGHTEEN

The brightness of the sky told me that I'd slept through breakfast. Lunch, too. I dragged myself out of bed and into the shower, ready to wash off the failure from my wielding session. The water ran red as I washed away the blood mangled in my hair. The injury hurt, but wasn't deep enough for me to need a healer.

My scalp burned, but I spent longer in the shower than I'd like to admit, trying to work through the array of emotions stuck in my head. What was the point of having a power like mine if I couldn't even use it properly? Is that why Blythe never gave her constellastone to anyone—because they couldn't use it, anyway?

The pondering of my existential crisis continued outside of the shower, following me to my desk where I sat and picked up a quill. My fingers twirled a strand of my hair as I wrote down my thoughts on the parchment Sebastian had given me.

I wrote about my successful wielding last night, and then about how I fainted right after. I wrote about the way Sebastian was looking at me like he wanted to kiss me, and how I wished he would have.

When I finished spilling my feelings, I tucked the paper away in my desk along with the others, then crawled back into my bed. I didn't have the energy, physically or mentally, to do anything else today. I pulled the blanket over my head, but as soon as I got comfortable, a soft knock hit my door.

"Who is it?"

Their response was muffled by the blanket covering my ears. I reluctantly pulled myself out of my bed and shuffled my feet to open the door, revealing Sebastian.

His eyes had shadows under them and his dark hair laid messy atop his head. I was pretty sure that he had stayed awake the whole time I was unconscious, and by the looks of him now, he didn't sleep much when he got back to his room.

"Can I come in?"

I nodded and spun around, returning to my bed. "I'm surprised you even knocked when you have a key," I grunted, pulling the blankets back over my head.

The door slammed and his footsteps echoed in my room. I was mortified about pretty much everything that occurred last evening and wanted to pretend it never happened. Maybe if I was quiet enough, he'd get the hint and just leave.

My false hope was crushed as he tore the blanket off of me. "We need to talk. Get up," he demanded, seeming annoyed.

"I'm tired," I whined.

"I don't care. Get up."

I stuck my tongue out at him. Childish, I know, but I was not in the mood to be bossed around today. I crossed my arms over my chest and stared blankly at the ceiling.

"Maeve, I'm serious. This is important. Get up."

I rolled my eyes down towards him. "Whatever it is, you can tell me while I lay in my bed."

He huffed a laugh of frustration, and shook his head. "Fine, stay there. I'll wait." He threw himself down in my armchair, rubbing his forehead with his fingers.

Rolling to my side to look at him, I stated the obvious, "You seem stressed."

"Good observation," he grunted.

My nose scrunched at his tone. “What's up your ass?”

“You,” he shot back, and I started to feel bad for how I was acting. None of this was his fault—I shouldn't have taken it out on him, but he seemed to be lacking patience this morning, which irritated me.

I sat up. “I don't know why you're so annoyed with me right now.”

Sebastian glared up at me through his hands, then slid them down and away from his face. “I'm not annoyed, Maeve. I'm scared, and you're acting like it's a joke.”

“Why are *you* scared? You're not the one who could be shipped off to Draemor any day now.”

He stood up and stormed towards me, bracing his hands on the edge of my mattress and leaning into my face. “Did it ever occur to you that maybe I don't want anything bad to happen to you?”

I gulped. “I—”

“Because I don't.” His jaw twitched as he stared into my soul.

Did he really just say that? This seemingly unbothered man actually cared about me? “I'm scared, too. Actually, *scared* doesn't do justice to what I’m feeling,” I said with a pout.

His arms flexed as he pushed off the bed and took a step back, shoving his hands into the pockets of his black, leather pants. “I know you are, but you can't shut down. You need to help me help you.” His frustration seemed to ease with the release of his words.

“How?”

“My father wants us to train your wielding daily, but after what happened last night, that's clearly not going to work.”

I nodded in acknowledgement. “Not if you want me practicing more challenging commands.”

“It’s not that I want you to, but it's that you need to. You need to learn to use the full extent of your power, but it can’t be done as often as I’d like.” He began pacing the room. “We’ll keep our combat sessions in the mornings, but we will only train your magic every few days. That way you'll have time between sessions to recuperate. We'll be able to practice more effectively and prevent another episode like last night. You'll get the experience you need without the negative side effects…hopefully."

"How will we get away with that?" I asked. "King Hawthorne has eyes all over the castle. Don't you think that he'll learn rather quickly that something is going on?" I'd noticed that we sometimes had peering eyes on us during our training sessions.

He paused to think, swaying a little where he stood. "We won't say anything, but if he asks, we'll tell him that we're training in various locations to get you used to having distractions while you wield."

"What will we actually be doing and where?" I questioned him.

He shrugged his shoulders. "I don't know. The archives are pretty empty at night, we can go there or to one of our rooms. It doesn't really matter where, it's just important that we are together in case someone sees us. If they do, we can pretend to be practicing."

"So we just lie?" This was actually not a bad idea. It was a simple plan, but sometimes simpler was better.

"We lie," he confirmed. "I'll tell my father that you haven't been feeling well. We can't push it too long or he will get suspicious, but it will buy you a few days to get your strength up before we start training again. Sounds good?"

"Yeah. Thank you."

He turned towards the window, and I could see the tension falling off of him with the confirmation of our plan.

I finally removed myself from my bed to stand beside him. My fingers grazed over his hand that grasped the window sill, trying to reciprocate the comfort that he always gave me. Right now, he seemed to need it more.

"Why do you care so much about what happens to me?" I asked, my voice so faint I wouldn't have been surprised if he couldn't make out the words.

He intertwined his fingers with mine, rubbing his thumb across my knuckles. "You know damn well why."

My heart pounded against my ribs.

Is he implying what I think he is? What I hope he is?

I wanted to ask, but we were interrupted by another person banging on my door.

His hand slipped from mine, and we jumped apart just in time for Pia to waltz through my doorway.

She raised her eyebrows, sucking her lips in to fight back a smile as she glanced between the two of us. "What's up?" she chimed, not acknowledging how close we were to each other.

Sebastian shuffled to the side, putting even more distance between us. "I was just about to leave," he stammered. "I was going to walk with Maeve to the castle, but she said she's not going for lunch this afternoon."

Pia nodded slowly. "Ahh. Of course." Her tone said that she didn't believe him.

Sebastian cleared his throat and turned to me. "I'll see you later," he said with a nod, then strutted out the door, hands stuffed in his pockets.

Pia beamed at me when he was gone.

"Nothing happened."

"Bullshit. The tension in the air here is *thick*."

"Nothing happened," I repeated.

"Mhm."

"I'm serious."

"It smells like sex."

My nose scrunched as my head shook.

She frowned and stomped her foot, believing me at last. "Damn it. I'm really rooting for you two."

SEBASTIAN MET ME AT MY ROOM TO WALK ME TO HIS FATHER'S STUDY for my biweekly meeting. Neither of us had much to say this afternoon, but the look he gave me when we arrived said enough. He went to grab the door handle, but King Hawthorne opened it from his end.

"Good afternoon, Miss Willawood."

"Hello, Your Majesty."

The king turned his attention to Sebastian. "I will be speaking to Maeve alone today, soldier."

Anger flared inside of me. I ground my jaw, hating when he referred to Sebastian as anything other than his son. It just seemed so wrong to me.

The look Sebastian gave his father suggested that he wanted to argue, but knew better than to even try. "I guess I'll just wait out here then," he said, then sank against the wall and to the ground, where he reached into his bag for his current read.

The king held the door open for me and I entered his study, sitting in my usual seat. He sat down behind his desk, crossing his hands in front of him. "I heard you have not been feeling well the past few days?"

I cleared my throat. "No, sir, I have not."

"I trust you are feeling better now considering you made it to our meeting?"

"I am."

"Good. I believe it is long overdue that you and I have a discussion just the two of us." He granted me an insincere grin. "There are a few matters I have been meaning to discuss with you. First and foremost, I wanted to let you know that we have uncovered the name of the one who spoke of your gift to the Draemornians. Duke Sinclair has been working day and night to locate the traitor, and believes he is close to doing so. Once captured, he will be executed."

I clenched my fists. I already knew this. *Fucking Fletcher.*

"In addition to this good news—"

I scoffed. Good news? Since when was killing someone considered good news? Don't get me wrong, Edward Fletcher deserved some sort of punishment, but death seemed a bit harsh.

I coughed to try and cover my ass.

King Hawthorne glowered at me, but disregarded my rudeness. "There is a more serious matter to discuss. The King of Draemor has presented me with an option to cease his threats of war against Caelestis." He paused to watch my reaction, which was a fake look of alarm as I already knew that as well.

"Cyprian Beaumont did not address you by name, meaning he

still does not know who you are specifically. However, he did request that Caelestis hand over their constellastone-gifted individual, in return for a peace treaty."

I yawned, showcasing my boredom with the conversation.

"I would be a fool to release the most powerful individual Caelestis has ever seen into the hands of our enemy. So naturally, I declined this bargain."

He stared at me, awaiting a thank you to leave my lips. He was an idiot if he thought he would ever hear those words from me.

"Is that all?" I asked him, disregarding everything he'd told me. Why couldn't Sebastian be here for this meeting? He already knew all of this, too.

He scowled at me. "No, Miss Willawood, there is one more thing I wish to discuss with you."

I adjusted my posture in my seat, suddenly uncomfortable from his words.

"May I remind you that in less than two years, you will be a soldier of Caelestis, and I expect you to act as one. That title does not come lightly."

I had to avoid rolling my eyes. He was acting as if I wanted to become a soldier—as if it were a privilege.

"If war does commence, you *will* utilize your gift in whatever means necessary to protect my kingdom. If that means you must use your power to kill every single Draemornian who threatens Caelestis, then that is what you will do. If that means you need to train around the clock to be superior in combat, that is what you will do."

That comment almost made me laugh. He had no idea what Sebastian and I had planned in regard to my training.

"If that means destroying the ones you love for the sake of my kingdom, then that is what you will do," the king spat the words in my face, then leaned closer. "Lastly, do not *ever* expect mercy from me again. I do not care if you are so sick that you cannot stand. I do not care if you have two broken arms and struggle to hold a sword. I do not care if you are laboring your child. The ten-year mandated service does not apply to you. For as long as I am alive, if I call upon you for service, *you will show up*." His voice bellowed throughout the room, ricocheting off of the walls.

Just when I thought I could not hate this man any more, he proved me wrong.

"How dare you," I growled, shooting up from my seat. "How dare you take the only ounce of freedom I have left. And for what? Because I have a different gift than your other soldiers?" I shook my head, refusing to accept that fate. "I'll be damned if you truly believe that I will comply."

The king chuckled. "Oh, you will comply. You have no other options, my dear. Not if you would like to see your loved ones again."

My eyebrows rose. "What do you mean by that?"

"You know exactly what I mean."

"Don't you fucking touch them," I hissed.

"Watch your mouth, young lady." He bared his teeth, standing as well.

I didn't say another word. I turned my back to him and exited the room, slamming the door behind me. I contemplated flipping him my middle finger, but decided silence was better in this scenario.

Sebastian jumped to his feet when he saw me. "What did he say?"

I strutted by him, too pissed to even put into words what just happened. Not to mention that I felt a bit nauseous.

Picking my walk up to a run, I moved my legs as fast as possible, trying to make it outside before I got sick.

Sebastian chased after me, calling my name.

I barely made it out of the castle. As soon as my feet touched the grass, I held my hair back and hunched over, bringing up everything in my stomach.

"Oh shit." I heard Sebastian curse as he approached behind me.

I waved him away with my free hand. He, of course, ignored the gesture and was soon by my side. He took my hair for me so I could use my hands to steady myself on my thighs as I heaved again and again.

When there was nothing left to release, I wiped my mouth with the back of my hand. The grass, frozen from the air, crunched underneath my weight as I sat. I crossed my legs and hung my head, feeling slightly dizzy.

Sebastian sat next to me and wrapped part of his cloak over me. He didn't say anything. Just tucked me into his side, allowing me to steal the warmth from his body. With all of the adrenaline coursing through my blood, I hadn't even realized that I was shivering from the cold.

I puffed out my cheeks and released a deep breath. "I hate him," I snarled coldly.

Sebastian looked over at me. "You and me both."

My shivering had yet to cease, so he pulled me closer to his body, closing the cloak around us.

"I think I left my rucksack and cloak in his study," I said.

"I'll get it later."

"Thanks." I sniffled as my nose dripped from the cold air. My silence was surely killing him, but Sebastian didn't pry. He let me wallow in my own self-pity for as long as I desired. Time faded away as I replayed the king's cruel words in my head over and over.

"If we stay out here much longer, you'll be frozen to the ground. We should move inside," Sebastian suggested when he realized I wasn't ready to divulge any details. He helped me up, my knees wavering as he led me back into the castle.

We stopped briefly at his father's study to grab my things, then Sebastian directed me through countless twists and turns of hallways and corridors. At first, I thought he was taking me to the archives, but that was in the opposite direction of where we were headed.

I recognized the door we approached as the entrance to the soldiers' housing. My stomach rolled in queasiness again. *Was he taking me to his room?*

He didn't unlock his door, though. Instead, he walked right by it, stopping in front of a different door which he hit hard with his fist.

Giggling came from beyond the wall, then someone yelled at us to go away.

Sebastian banged on the metal even harder. "Kohen, open up."

Kohen was in the midst of buttoning his pants when he opened the door. He ran a hand through his disheveled hair and granted us an awkward smirk when he saw that Sebastian wasn't alone.

"What's up, Seb?"

"Busy?" Sebastian asked, his voice laced with sarcasm.

"Yeah actually, a little."

"I need to steal Pia."

"Can we at least finish first?" Kohen taunted with a grin, knowing his comment would get a rise from his friend.

Sebastian huffed a breath of disapproval. "Pia?" he called into the room.

"Hey, Seb," her mortified voice responded.

Sebastian turned to me. "I'll deal with Kohen, go talk to Pia. Blow off some steam."

"No. I just want to go back to my room."

He pulled me to the side. "I don't know what happened in there, but I can tell that you need someone to talk to right now. If you won't talk to me, at least talk to her."

"I can't tell her anything, anyways. You told me not to."

"I trust her. Go ahead."

He looked worried for me. I would tell him tonight at wielding practice what his father said to me. Right now I just…couldn't.

"Are you sure?"

"Positive."

"Okay," I said softly, and Sebastian's lips turned up faintly at my agreement.

"I'll come back in a few hours to get you for our session." He ran a hand up my arm for a second before dropping it back to his side.

We turned back to Kohen, still standing shirtless in the doorway. Sebastian grabbed his wrist and dragged him out. "Come on, let's go find Sawyer."

"What the hell, man. We were in the middle of—"

"I don't want to know what you were in the middle of."

I slipped into Kohen's room, which looked very similar to Sebastian's, except it lacked a bookshelf and his walls were navy blue.

Pia stepped out of the washroom, brushing her obvious post-sex hair. Concern coated her face when she saw me. "What's going on?" she asked, climbing onto Kohen's bed and patting the spot next to her.

As soon as I sat down, I spilled every single thing that I had been keeping from her. I had no control over the words as they flew out of me. She let me vent, listening intently to every detail I shared.

"To top it all off, I just vomited all over the castle lawn and now I'm fucking famished," I finished, out of breath.

Pia stared at me blankly. "Woah…That's a lot to unload."

I flopped backwards on the bed, not caring about what she and Kohen just did on it.

"Yup," I said flatly.

Pia laid back, too. We turned our heads to look at each other.

"Want some liquor?" she asked.

"Absolutely."

CHAPTER NINETEEN

Sebastian and Kohen arrived back a few hours later with Sawyer in tow.

"Gods," Kohen whispered when he saw us.

Pia stood up on wobbly legs and stumbled over to him. She held an open bottle in her hand, drops spilling out of it as she moved. "Yay, you're back!" she chimed, planting a kiss on his lips.

Sawyer grinned from ear to ear, but Sebastian looked unamused. "This is not what I meant by blowing off some steam," he said.

I stood up, too, my legs not nearly as wobbly as Pia's, but I definitely had more to drink than I should have. "Ready to wield?" I asked Sebastian, running a finger down the side of his arm.

Drinking made me *way* too confident.

He shuddered at my touch, but he took my wrist in his hand and removed it from his body. "Absolutely not." He almost chuckled, but kept his face serious. "You need to sober up before I let your magic anywhere near me."

"Boo," I drawled, and he fought back a smile.

My heart raced as I stared at his lips, biting my own as temptation overtook me.

Sawyer swiped the bottle from Pia and took a swig. She was too busy rubbing her hands all over Kohen to notice. "This could be really fun if we're all down," he joked, picking up on the obvious sexual tension in the room.

Sebastian elbowed him in the side hard enough for him to spit out his drink.

"Lighten up, Seb, it's just a joke." Sawyer moved deeper into the room and laid down on Kohen's bed, drinking from the bottle thirstily. "You couldn't handle me anyway," he muttered.

"Can't you guys skip training tonight?" Pia inquired. She knew that I could really benefit from one more night off.

The alcohol granted me some courage, and I took Sebastian's hands in mine. "Please," I begged, fluttering my eyelashes at him.

Kohen waved a bottle of liquor in front of Sebastian's face. "Come on, Seb. I have your favorite."

Sebastian looked at me, almost convinced. I pouted my lips, and that was all it took. He grabbed the bottle from Kohen and took a drink. Sawyer cheered and Pia came to stand by my side, pulling me into a hug.

"Let's forget about everything you told me for tonight. Make it tomorrow's problem," she advised me in a whisper.

I agreed with her, but there was one problem from today that couldn't wait to be solved. If I was going to be hanging out here for a while, I needed to change my clothes. Mine had seen more than enough for one day.

I turned to Sebastian, slurring my words a little as I spoke. "I'm just going to run back to my dorm quickly and grab something else to wear."

Sebastian dropped the bottle from his lips and shook his head. "Nice try."

I should have known better by now to even try going anywhere alone. "Come on, I'm disgusting right now and you know it," I complained.

He chuckled, then took my hand in his again. "You could never be disgusting, but come with me." He started to lead me into the hall, calling back to the others, "We'll be right back."

"Have fun, you two," Sawyer teased with a wink, implying exactly what I wished we were going to do.

The feel of Sebastian's skin against mine sent heat surging through me as he guided me down the hall. He could have let go, but didn't, which sent my mind scattering with inappropriate thoughts. I quickly shut them out, blaming the liquor.

When he at last dropped my hand, it was to unlock his door. Following him inside, he made straight for his wardrobe and rummaged through it, then passed me a pair of lounge pants and a cotton shirt.

"Put these on. They'll be big on you, but for tonight they'll have to do." He showed me to the washroom.

I stumbled over my own feet as I pulled the pants on my legs, rolling the waistband so that the bottoms didn't drag on the floor. The scent of him lingered on his shirt as I slid it over my head and breathed it in.

Sebastian was lounging at his desk, his legs spread apart, waiting for me when I finished.

"How do I look?" I smiled and spun in a circle.

He adjusted himself in his seat and my stomach filled with knots from the way he looked me up and down, fighting to suppress a smirk.

"You're shorter than I realized."

"I'm quite tall for a girl, I'll have you know."

One side of his mouth jerked up. "Oh really?"

"Yep. Five foot six."

He rose to his full height and approached me, towering over me and proving just how small I really was compared to him.

"Point taken," I said, looking up at him.

His eyes dipped to my face, and his voice turned gruff and serious as he spoke. "Listen, I'm up for having a fun night. But before we go back there, are you okay?"

I wanted to, but didn't lie to him. "No. I'm not okay."

He inched forward, closing the gap between us. "You don't have to tell me what he said if you don't want to, but if it comes down to your safety, I really wish you would."

I chewed the skin inside my cheek. Pia said to forget about everything for the night, but I didn't think I'd be able to do that until I told Sebastian what his father said to me.

"I'm surprised you didn't go ask him yourself."

"That would have been an invasion of your privacy."

"My privacy?" I half scoffed, half chuckled. "Any ounce of privacy I had was destroyed the second you became my guard."

Sebastian's head tilted to the side, a lock of his deep brown hair falling over his brow. "You know what I mean."

Pursing my lips, I gave in. "He told me about the traitor and King Beaumont's bargain deal," I began, but paused to contemplate if I really wanted to tell him the rest of it. I could have just saved it for my journal.

Sebastian didn't ask for more information, he just gave me his undivided attention and waited for me to choose to give it.

I unclenched my jaw and found the courage to continue. "He also told me that for as long as he lives, I'm expected to work for him. That I'm expected to show up when he calls upon me—basically that I'm under his control indefinitely." I released a breath, the words hanging heavy on my tongue as I said them. "He threatened my family. Told me that someday if I'm pregnant and I'm labor, that if he calls upon me, I'm still expected to be there."

I filled him in on the rest of the details from the conversation, quoting the king word for word. When I finished, Sebastian looked just as sick as I had been this afternoon.

He cracked his knuckles and anguish overwhelmed his face. His rough hand tousled his hair and then turned his back to me, the room silent except for the tapping of his foot. I watched him stand so effortlessly balanced and wondered what he was thinking.

"I hate him," he muttered under his breath, copying my exact words from earlier today. When he turned back to look at me, I swear his eyes looked glossed over. "I fucking *hate* him!" he hissed, his nostrils flaring as he yelled so loudly that I was sure the others could hear him from down the hall.

A vein popped in his neck. "Where does he think he gets the

damn right?" he shouted, then began pacing back and forth through his room.

"It's okay, Seb." I stepped forward and placed a hand on the small of his back, stopping him in his tracks.

He spun on his toes and grabbed my shoulders, leveling his face with him. "It's not fucking okay, and you know it. His words made you *sick* for fuck's sake. He threatened you and your family. Nothing about that shit is okay."

He drew a heavy breath, then dropped his arms and stormed out the door and down the hallway.

I definitely should have waited to tell him about this.

"Where are you going?" I yelled after him.

He didn't look back. "I'm going to talk to him."

I sobered up extremely fast. For once since we'd met, I wasn't the one losing their composure.

I chased after him, cutting him off before he reached the staircase and putting my arms out to stop him from going any further. "No."

He tried to push past me, but I copied his movements to block him.

"Maeve, stop," he said through gritted teeth.

I stood my ground. "No. If you talk to him, you'll just make the whole situation worse for so many reasons."

A muscle in his jaw ticked. "Move."

"No."

"Move or I will make you move."

I put my hands on my hips, but stood static at the top of the stairs.

"Last chance," he growled, grinding his jaw.

When I didn't budge, the man picked me up by the underarms and tossed me over his shoulder.

"Put me down!" I yelled, kicking my legs to get out of his hold.

Sebastian carried me back down the hall, putting me down outside of Kohen's room.

"Go have a fun night. I'll bring you back to your room when I get back." He narrowed his eyes on me before turning to make his way back down the hall.

I caught him by the sleeve of his shirt. "Sebastian, please! I shouldn't have even told you."

He crossed his arms over his chest, ripping his shirt from my hand. I tried not to gawk at the way his biceps flexed, but he made it damn near impossible.

He didn't seem to notice my wandering eyes. "He can't do this." He sighed, calming a bit.

"Unfortunately, he can. And if you go speak with him right now, he's going to wonder why you aren't currently helping me wield, and also how you even know about what he said to me."

My words seemed to get through to him. His shoulders laxed a little and he dropped his arms to his sides.

"Regardless of what he said, I'm stuck here for the next two years, anyway. So I have until at least then to figure it out." I gave him a fake smile of hope.

He tilted his head up and gazed into my eyes, absorbing my words. "He won't harm your family. I'll make sure of that."

I offered him a soft grin of appreciation. "Thank you."

"And I won't let you be stuck here for your whole life. I promise you."

"Everything okay?"

I turned my head to see Sawyer standing in the doorway.

"Yeah, everything's fine," I replied.

Sawyer stepped into the hall. "You sure? We heard yelling and—"

"We're good man, thanks." Sebastian waved him away. Sawyer stared for a moment, but ultimately did what was asked.

"I'm not in the mood to go back there." Sebastian gestured towards the room.

I didn't blame him. I wouldn't have told him all of this if I had known it would cause such an unrest within him.

"That's fine. Will you just walk me back to my room then?"

"Of course." He shoved his hands into his pockets and initiated our mute walk to the dormitories.

My fingers were sore by the time I finished writing down everything that had happened the past few days. I massaged my knuckles while I sat on the edge of my bed, waiting for my escort to arrive. I'd spent most of the day tucked away in my room, writing and reading. Doing anything I could to take my mind off of the past week.

I'd been trying not to think too hard about the situation I'd found myself in thanks to Aldous Hawthorne. I kept reminding myself that despite his new orders, I was already mandated as a soldier for a decade after graduation, anyway. Unless he died before then. One could only hope.

I looked up at the sound of my door unlocking and watched Sebastian step into my room unannounced.

"You're lucky I'm decent," I teased, but he didn't laugh. He didn't even try to smile.

He'd been in a bad mood all day. He hardly said a word to me during combat training this morning.

"Ready?" he asked, not waiting for my answer before he walked back out of my room.

"This is gonna be a fun night," I muttered under my breath, trudging along after him all the way to Caelestis Academy. Winter was approaching fast, and the chill of the air was unbearable to spend more than a few minutes in. I walked fast, trying to keep up with his pace.

"Training went well this morning," I said to break the silence. "I expected to need more time to reestablish my skills after having last week off, but I feel like the movements are slowly becoming second nature to me."

"That's good," Sebastian grunted.

"Yeah. So if wielding goes well tonight, should I plan for the archives again tomorrow?"

It'd only been a week since we commenced our new training schedule, but we'd continue for as long as needed, switching locations on our off days to keep the suspicions from others at bay. The hope was that I'd be able to wield more powerful and more effective magic if I wasn't harnessing every single day. I was confident that the plan would work—at least for a while.

"Mhm."

"I'm a little nervous to wield," I said as we stepped into the warmth of the academy.

"It will be fine."

"We've only tried it once since I passed out, though." At least if anything happened tonight, he would be there.

"Yeah, and it went fine."

I untied my cloak as we entered the arena, letting it fall to the floor along with my bag.

Sebastian unsheathed his dagger and bent down to tuck it into his bag ever so carefully. Something was wrong, and I wanted nothing more than to comfort him. But it was hard to comfort someone when you didn't know what was bothering them. Unless *I* was what was bothering him.

"Whenever you're ready," Sebastian said, avoiding eye contact as he took his position across from me on the mat.

The lack of communication started getting to me. "Did I do something?"

"No."

"Why do you seem so angry then?"

"I'm not angry."

"Did something happen with Sawyer or Kohen?" I pried, even though I knew I shouldn't.

Sebastian rolled his eyes towards the ceiling. "No. Are you going to interrogate me all night or can we just get this session over with?"

"I might," I retorted, crossing my arms over my chest. I knew Sebastian well enough by now to understand that his attitude was a defense mechanism. Something was bothering him, and I was going to get it out of him.

"Is it your father?"

"Oh for the love of the gods, Maeve—" He threw his arms in the air, mumbling to himself.

"Well I've been agonizing over it all week, and seeing as it bothered you so much when I told you, maybe you have been, too."

"For fuck's sake," he muttered.

My fists clenched by my sides. *That's it.* If he was going to be cold to me, then I'd do the same. I didn't give him any warning. I relaxed my mind and blasted him with the full force of my power.

"Tell me what's bothering you so much," I commanded.

He didn't flinch and his mouth didn't open to comply.

What the hell?

I raised a hand to my cheek bone. My gems tingled with the exertion of my power, so why didn't my command work on him?

My heart sank with realization.

His eyes narrowed on me and through a clenched jaw, spit out a growled, "Seriously?"

I shrugged my shoulders in innocence. "You have hardly said a word to me all day!"

"I just have nothing to say, Maeve."

"Enough of this." I stomped towards him. "That's bullshit and you know it. Why are your shields up?" I jammed a finger into his chest and demanded an answer.

He stilled, the only movement coming from him was the blinking of his beautiful, blue eyes. He was completely shutting down.

Starting to worry, I softened my voice. "Please, Sebastian, tell me what's wrong."

"Drop it."

Frustration consumed me and I turned my back on him, returning to my spot on the mat. "I knew I shouldn't have told you about my meeting."

"That's not what this is about."

"Then what *is* this about? Because I'm getting a lot of mixed signals from you. I thought we were on good terms. I thought we had even become friends, but now I'm not sure because you will hardly speak to me and I know damn well that I did nothing in the past twenty-four hours to deserve that."

Looking up at the ceiling, he puffed his cheeks full of air. "Fuck, you are relentless." His head dropped and he stepped towards me, giving in to my nagging. "Duke Sinclair has located the traitor. I'm expected to leave in the morning to go to Craterra and oversee the execution."

My mouth squeezed into a tight line.

"As I'm sure you can understand, this is not something that I'm particularly looking forward to."

I swallowed the knot that had formed in my throat, feeling horrible now for calling him out.

"How long will you be gone?"

"I don't know."

"What will I do about my wielding while you're gone?"

"I don't know."

"Who's going to train me? How will I hide my weakness when I use my magic with them?"

"I. Don't. Know," he said, and with the enunciation of each word, his eyes filled with more fear.

His fear passed through to me. "Shit." The rest of my words escaped me.

"Yeah. *Shit* is right," he scoffed.

This was bad. No wonder he'd been acting like an ass all day. If there was anything I'd learned about Sebastian, it was that he had trouble expressing his emotions.

I took a deep breath. "This could ruin our whole plan."

"I'm trying to make sure that doesn't happen."

"It's going to be fine. I'm sure you won't be gone too long," I said, trying to reassure him and myself while a whole other thought took up residence in my mind.

Sebastian noticed my pondering. "What are you thinking?"

"What's going to happen to him? To Edward Fletcher?"

"You know what happens to traitors," he replied.

"I know, but like, what *specifically* will happen?" Would they behead him? Hang him? Torture him to death? I didn't like the man for obvious reasons, but we grew up together. And although I was pissed that he sold me out, I still hoped they didn't make him suffer.

"You don't really want to know that, Maeve, trust me."

"I do—"

Sebastian shook his head, and his voice was a stern threat not to argue. "No. You don't. And I'm not going to tell you." He moved closer. "Listen, I'm sorry. I shouldn't have taken my stress out on you. This isn't your fault."

My mouth lowered into a grimace. "It is kind of my fault, though. If it weren't for my gift from Blythe, there wouldn't even be a traitor to begin with."

He took another step towards me. "It is also not your fault that you were gifted."

"Doesn't change the fact that I was." I blew out a breath and looked into his eyes. "Well anyways, I'm sorry, too. I just assumed that you were still upset about—"

Sebastian held a hand up to stop me, then reduced the space between our bodies. "You have nothing to apologize for."

He gazed into my face, and the hardness of his expression softened into one of affection. Tension hung over us, soaked with a passion that neither of us could deny.

"Maeve," he whispered my name, and the deepness of his voice made me shudder with overwhelming desire.

I bit my lip, trying not to act on my need for him. My eyes closed, needing a second of peace to stop myself from doing something rash.

"Yes?" I asked breathily.

"We *are* friends." He broke our heated tension by denying my claim from earlier, and I blinked to look at him just as he returned to his side of the mat.

Friends.

I couldn't help but wonder if he wasn't being completely honest. Because you didn't look into the eyes of a *friend* in the way that he just looked into mine.

CHAPTER TWENTY

Sebastian must have left early the next morning, because Sawyer showed up in his place for combat training. We never had time to figure out a plan before he left, so I would use my magic as little as possible until he got back. I'd keep to the basics while wielding, which should work because Sawyer didn't know any better.

Combat training left me completely defeated. Sebastian didn't take it easy on me by any means, but Sawyer showed me absolutely no mercy. He threw me on the ground too many times to count. I thought my offensive skills were improving, but maybe I was just learning to predict Sebastian's next move.

I collapsed to the mat, dropping my head between my knees while I tried to catch my breath. "Gods," I said through labored breathing. "You're a little too good at this."

Sawyer huffed a laugh. "I've been training since I could walk, Willawood. I better be good at it." He tossed me my rucksack and I removed my flask from it, finishing it off within seconds.

Sawyer had grown on me, which was good considering he was one of Sebastian's best friends. I sulked at the thought of him. He was so distraught yesterday, and I just hoped that he was okay.

"He'll be fine," Sawyer said, noticing the melancholy that had consumed me. He offered me his hand and I let him pull me to my feet.

I didn't bother trying to play dumb. "How long does it take to get to Craterra from here?" I asked him, trying to estimate when Sebastian might be back.

"Two or three days by horseback."

I nodded, looking down at my feet.

"He should be back in a week or so." Sawyer did the math for me. "In the meantime, you're stuck with me."

"Oh joy."

"Hey, you should consider yourself lucky to be training with me. I'm one of the best soldiers in Caelestis."

I chuckled. "Best at what? Punching new students in the face?"

Sawyer pointed his dagger at me. "You had that coming. You were being a brat."

"My whole life just got upturned. You would be a brat, too, if that happened to you," I argued with a laugh.

"Yeah, yeah, sure." He handed me my cloak and I threw it over my shoulders, wrapping it tightly around myself to prepare for the cold front that awaited us outside.

"Let's go get some breakfast, Willawood, you'll need to replenish your energy before I kick your ass again tonight." Sawyer draped an arm over my shoulder and we started for the castle. "So, tell me a little more about yourself."

"Pfft. What could you possibly want to know that Sebastian hasn't already told you?"

His arm fell to the academy's door handle, swinging it towards him and holding it open for me. "He hasn't told me much to be honest. The basics, sure. And how much of a pain in the ass you were when you guys first met."

My eyebrows sank.

"My words. Not his."

"Okay. Well, um, I love the ocean and—"

Sawyer paused on the stone walkway, shaking his head. "No. None of that bull crap. I want the good stuff. Tell me the worst thing you've ever done, or your family's dark secret, or about when you lost your virginity."

A laugh shot out of me. "I am most certainly not telling you about my past relationships."

Sawyer's arms crossed under his cloak and his neck tilted. "Aw. Virgin? Cute."

Scowling, I pushed past him, resuming my journey to the castle. "Not that it's any of your business, but I am not a virgin. And as for dark family secrets, we have none. Worst thing I've ever done? Yet to be determined, so don't piss me off."

Sawyer's laugh trailed after his boots as he scuffed the walkway to catch up with me. "Wanna know the worst thing I've ever done?"

"Is it the time you beat a new student up on the first day of training?"

"You hold a grudge, huh? But no. Not even close." He chuckled as if my suggestion was so far out there. Still a hundred yards from the castle, he kept the conversation going. "How are you liking it here so far?"

"I hate it," I said bluntly. "I want nothing to do with any of this. I don't want to be living here. I don't want my powers. And no offense, but I don't want to be training with you."

"Ouch." Sawyer clutched a hand to his heart. "Tell me how you really feel."

"It's nothing against you. I don't want to be training with anyone. I don't want to be training at all, or wielding, or going to galas, or living in an unfamiliar room, or—"

"I get it." Looking over, he held a hand up to silence me. "If it helps, most people feel that way when they first get here. But I swear, once you graduate, it's really not all that bad. Aside from the battles and stuff."

"Ah yes. Living the dream, huh?"

"Sure. Food's decent. The girls are hot. Free room and board."

"Decent food with a side of shitty rules and execution," I snorted.

Sawyer shrugged. "You can't have it all."

"I'M EXHAUSTED," I YAWNED WHEN PIA AND I ARRIVED AT THE dormitories.

"*I know.* And you're welcome, by the way. If I didn't wake you up, then you would have missed Stoll's lesson about combining mental shields with wielding."

We pushed through Pia's door. "Sebastian started teaching me that weeks ago. It wasn't entirely new to me, anyways." I shuffled across the room that looked essentially the same as mine, and slouched into her armchair, releasing another deep yawn.

Pia took a quick shower, and I studied my kingdom history text while I waited for her. She returned wearing loungewear shortly after, indicating that she didn't plan on going anywhere else this evening. She flopped down onto her bed and turned her head so that she could see me. I stared back at her, and we both released a sigh of exhaustion.

"Tell me some good news," I said, closing my book. I needed something to take my mind off of literally everything in my life right now. "Something that doesn't involve your sex life," I clarified before she could respond.

Pia laughed. "But—"

"The last thing I need is a reminder that I don't have one, so please spare me the details."

"Ugh fine, let me think." The silence that followed was deafening. "Guess things are pretty lousy right now, aren't they?"

I scoffed. "No kidding."

Pia rolled to her stomach. "If you don't want to talk about my sex life, can we talk about yours?" she asked innocently.

I burst out laughing. "I literally just told you that sex is nonexistent in my life right now."

She laughed as well. "Well, it doesn't have to be. Maybe a little action will lift your spirits."

"I'm sure it would. But with who?" I rolled my eyes.

"I'm sure Sawyer would take one for the team."

"Ouch. Would sex with me really be considered charity work?" I smirked and clutched my chest to dramatize my exclamation.

"I'm kidding about that part, but I'm sure he would, though."

My head shook with my laughter, but my smile faded shortly after. I had no interest in sleeping with anyone except for one certain individual, and I knew that was never going to happen.

"You could just be straightforward with Seb. Tell him that you have feelings for him," Pia suggested.

Sometimes I swore that she could read my mind.

"Nope. No way."

"Come on," she groaned. "Why not?"

I answered without hesitation. "There's too many reasons why he shouldn't know the way I feel about him. Hell, I don't even know exactly how I feel. Besides, it would complicate things too much."

"Too many reasons? Care to elaborate?"

"Well for starters, if King Hawthorne found out, he'd replace Sebastian as my guard. With my luck it would be with freaking Sawyer, and I don't think I could handle him full time. He asks too many questions. And if I tell Sebastian how I feel and he doesn't feel the same, it would make for an incredibly awkward year and a half."

Pia's eyebrows rose. "Is that it?"

"No. He's like, four years older than me. I'm sure he would want someone who's closer to his age."

"Four years is nothing, and I'm sure Seb would agree. Try again."

"He doesn't break down over every minor inconvenience like I do, and he's seen me puke. That's gotta be a turn off for him."

Pia gave me a sideways glance. "When did he see you puke?"

"Never mind that." I puffed out my cheeks, then released my breath. "I guess that's all I got."

Pia pulled herself up and slid off her bed, moving to stand in front of me. She crossed her arms over her chest. "Those are the absolute most ridiculous excuses for not telling someone you love them that I've ever heard!" she shouted in my face.

I jumped to my feet. "Who said anything about *love*?"

Pia gave me a knowing look, and I shook my head in denial. I was about ready to argue with her when I caught sight of the clock on her desk.

"Shit, I gotta go," I said frantically. Sawyer was likely already waiting to collect me for wielding practice. I gathered my cloak and bag, and raced down the hall to my room.

I was right.

"You're late." Sawyer tapped his imaginary watch.

"Sorry. Lost track of time."

"I'll cut you some slack this time, but don't let it happen again."

"Oh, whatever. Let's go." I made my way down the spiral staircase and led the way to the combat arena.

We both got situated then stood across from each other on the mat. He bent down to tie his boot, and I tried to mentally prepare myself for the outcome of this session. I had no idea what to expect.

Sawyer, along with mostly everyone else in the kingdom, didn't know much about the powers I had from my constellastones. I should be able to get away with just using some basic commands on him, which in theory would prevent me from overexerting myself. It worked on Sebastian—until it didn't. I'd have to find a balance though. If I kept it too simple, I risked Sawyer asking questions.

"Alright, Willawood, let's do this!" Sawyer hollered with a clap of his hands.

Anxiety tried to creep up inside of me, but I shoved it down. If I lost my composure now, it'd be a dead giveaway that something was up.

I secured my footing, cementing myself firmly to the ground in preparation for harnessing my powers. "You have to drop your shields," I reminded him.

Sawyer raised an eyebrow. "I would if they were up."

"Oh. Sebastian usually—" I cut myself off. Keeping your mental shields up around the clock was not typical. Sebastian had a personal reason for why he felt the need to do so.

Probably because of his damn father.

"Never mind," I said. "Give me a second to think of a command."

Stick to the basics.

Although I no longer needed to, I clamped my eyes closed and brought my mind into a state of deep relaxation, focusing on the things that granted my soul tranquility. Usually this step required me to imagine the ocean, but today my mind jumped straight to Sebastian. I didn't fight my subconscious, letting the thought of him consume me. I relived the feeling of his hands in mine. The way it felt to be wrapped in his arms while he embraced me. How his clothes smelt like snow and pinewood when I wore them. I soaked in the reminders of him and felt all the tension in my blood vanish.

When content, I spoke my order into the air. "Throw your dagger at the practice target."

Succumbing to my trance, Sawyer unsheathed his weapon. He spun his torso and threw the blade straight at the chest of the mannequin to his right. He stared at the dummy, then at me with his mouth agape. He'd never been on this end of my power, so even the simplest compulsions were bound to amaze him. "That's a badass gift, Willawood."

I shrugged off his compliment and got back into formation, just wanting to get this lesson over with.

Sawyer retrieved his dagger, and I tried a few more simple commands on him. I made him run a lap around the arena like I had Sebastian do before. I also compelled him to use his magic to make a rainstorm fall over himself, finding quite a bit of joy in knowing that he'd have to spend the rest of our session soaked.

We'd been going at it for over an hour, and although I was exhausted, my body wasn't getting weak yet. Hopefully that meant my plan to use simple magic would keep me conscious for the rest of the week.

"Let's try one more before we call it a night," Sawyer told me, water dripping from his forehead.

"Haven't we done enough?" I groaned.

"What's wrong, Willawood? Tired already?" Sawyer taunted.

"Yeah," I scoffed. "Actually, I am."

"Seb must be taking it easy on you if you think this is hard."

"I guess so."

"One more then we can be done. I swear."

I reluctantly agreed, and racked my brain for another command to use on him.

Sawyer didn't give me any time to think before his sapphire magic blasted me with a forceful stream of water. The pressure knocked me off of my feet, and I fell to the mat with a force so strong that I felt my tailbone bruise at the contact.

I tried to scold him, but couldn't speak. I could barely breathe from the flood of water in my face. I fumbled around on the mat, trying to get away from the lake, but the water followed me. I knew that his intention behind this was to have me harness my powers to stop him, but I didn't comply. I couldn't risk it.

Crawling around on the mat, I tried to position my back towards Sawyer so that I could get some air in my lungs. He moved with me, keeping his magic aimed at my face. It became evident that he wasn't going to stop unless I made him, and if I didn't want to drown, there were no other options but to use my power to retaliate.

Searching for a sense of peace within the chaos, I grasped hold tightly to the minuscule amount I could find and commanded Sawyer to, "STOP."

The wave came to a sudden halt, dripping to the mat before disappearing completely, leaving me drenched from head to toe.

I spit out a mouthful of water and clutched my chest, gasping for air. I tried to rise to my feet, but decided from a brief moment of dizziness that I would stay down.

"Sawyer, what the hell?" I gasped, scowling up at him.

He smirked, and looked awfully devious as he did. "Nice job. I didn't expect you to be able to gain control of your magic that easily."

An ache in my temple started to form, and I took the pain as confirmation that stopping someone's magic did *not* count as a simple use of my power. I'd have to keep that in mind for the rest of the week.

I furrowed my brows at Sawyer as he approached me. He grabbed me by the shoulders and lifted me to my feet. We were both sopping wet—the walk back to my dorm was going to be dreadful.

"You could have killed me," I snarled, taking my hair in my hands and twisting it, wringing the water out over his shoes.

He stepped back. "Oh please, do you really think I would let the girl my best friend fancies die?"

My jaw went slack. "What did you say?" I asked, my cheeks flushing at his accidental spill.

Sawyer's eyes widened and he smacked his hand against his mouth. "I didn't say that," he sputtered, his face filling with panic over his unintentional admission.

I strained to hide the smile that fought its way onto my face. Did Sebastian tell him that he had feelings for me, or was Sawyer just making assumptions? Either way, I obviously wasn't meant to know that information.

"It's okay." I waved my hand in a gesture that disregarded what he said. I tried to act nonchalant, though everything inside of me was screaming and giddy.

Sawyer combed his hands through his hair. He looked way more stressed about this than he should have been.

"Sawyer, it's really fine. You were just messing around. Right?" I knew that he wasn't, but if he agreed with me, maybe it would help kill the fire inside of me.

He gulped and nodded.

"Alright so let's just forget it," I told him—and myself. Because for all the reasons I told Pia earlier, I *really* needed to forget this.

CHAPTER TWENTY-ONE

By the end of the week training with Sawyer, I was utterly defeated. My muscles felt like they were being twisted any time I made a sudden movement. Sebastian and I trained hard, but Sawyer trained on a whole other level—one that left me beaten and exhausted.

Sawyer and I bonded better than I ever thought we could after our initial introduction, making our week together not as painful as I anticipated. Although our wielding sessions had been almost unbearable, there was only one incident where my vision tunneled. I thought for sure I was going down, but somehow managed to hold it together. *Thank gods.*

The days had blended into one. Train, eat, class, wield, sleep, repeat—my schedule was exhausting. Luckily, my meeting with King Hawthorne had been canceled this week as he had accompanied Sebastian and Duke Sinclair to Craterra.

My feet dangled over the edge of my bed, my thighs burning with the movement. I peered at the clock—Sawyer was late. That was odd. He hadn't been a second late all week.

I did not question his absence. Instead, I changed out of my winter training uniform and released my hair from its braid, shaking the waves free. I laced my boots over my ankles, then went down the hall to Pia's room to see if she wanted to get breakfast. I knocked, but she didn't answer, meaning she probably had spent the night with Kohen.

It seemed as though I had the morning to myself, so I embraced the lack of a bodyguard and made my way to the castle.

It felt strange to have no one walking with me as I strolled the corridors of the dormitories and down the winding set of stairs. Sebastian would be pissed if he knew I was escorting myself to the castle without a guard. The thought made me chuckle.

Sawyer and I never further discussed what he let slip about Sebastian, which was for the best. I'd been trying not to think about it, not wanting to get my hopes up. If my calculations were correct, Sebastian should be arriving back to Caelestis tonight. I was optimistic that I'd hear from him when he returned, but didn't get my hopes up over that, either.

A gust of frosted air smacked me in the face when I stepped outside. I shivered fiercely, frost crunching under my feet as I crossed the lawn. There was no denying that winter was among us.

I hiked through the barriers of icy air that left my cheeks raw by the time I reached the kitchen. The drastic change in temperature caused my skin to sting, so I grabbed a cup of tea and settled on a warm breakfast pastry, then secured myself an empty table that just happened to be near the secret soldiers' housing entrance.

"What are you doing here?"

I looked up from my breakfast to see Sawyer standing over me, baffled.

"I could ask you the same thing," I replied through my mouthful of food.

Sawyer sat himself across from me, one eyebrow raised. "What are you talking about?"

"I waited for you for over an hour. When you didn't show, I took advantage of it and came here to get breakfast."

"Sebastian didn't show up?"

"He's back?" My heart calmed in knowing that he made it home safely.

Sawyer's face transformed from confused to concerned. "Shit," he muttered, setting his elbows on the table top. He rubbed his hands over his face and released a groan.

"What's wrong?"

Sawyer glanced around to make sure no one could hear us. "Sebastian doesn't always handle this stuff well."

"What stuff?"

He leaned in closer and whispered, "Performing an execution."

I almost spit my food out. "*What*?" I said much louder than I intended.

Sawyer shushed me. "Quiet, Willawood, you're drawing attention to us."

Peering eyes surrounded us. *Screw them.*

"He told me he had to *oversee* the execution, not that he would be the one *performing* it," I whisper-yelled back.

Sawyer didn't say anything more. He just sat twiddling his thumbs.

"Well, do you care to elaborate a bit, Sawyer, or do you plan on leaving me hanging here?"

"It's not my information to give."

"I don't give a shit. Spill it. Now," I demanded.

He leaned back against his seat, crossing his arms over his chest. "Seb's father has been making him do this kind of thing ever since he was a kid."

"What kind of thing?" I leaned across the table to make sure I was understanding him correctly. "Killing people?"

Sawyer nodded.

My hand found my mouth, blocking out my gasp.

"King Hawthorne forced his child to murder people?" I understood that killing was unfortunately one of the responsibilities that came with the title of being a soldier, but as a kid?

"He's pretty numb to it now, but sometimes even now when Seb has to kill in the line of duty, the trauma of doing it as a kid rehashes. He just…shuts down. Sometimes it takes days for him to come out of it. Battle is one thing, that's life or death. But the executions are always brutal to watch, never mind performing one."

Anger boiled up inside of me, and I clenched my fists under the table. "Who makes their child kill people? That's fucking horrific to say the very least." King Hawthorne just kept giving me more and more reasons to despise him.

"He's done worse," Sawyer replied nonchalantly.

My appetite vanished. "What do you mean?"

Sawyer shook his head. "Now *that* is really not my information to share."

A grimace found my face, but I respected the boundary. "So what do we do?"

"About Seb?" Sawyer shrugged. "Nothing we can do. Kohen and I have tried to snap him out of it in the past, but it's nearly impossible to get through to him when he's like this. Just have to wait it out."

I didn't like that answer. No wonder Sebastian could be so temperamental. I would be, too, if I was consistently traumatized while growing up. Between watching his mother be killed, and then being forced to do it to others—the whole thing made me feel nauseous.

I've done things that would make you sick, he had said, and I guess he was right. But none of those things were his fault. He didn't choose his father.

I scrapped the rest of my meal and rose from the table, my one-track mind marching me through the archway that would take me where I needed to go.

Sawyer jumped up in front of me. "Where do you think you are going?"

"I'm not just going to let him wallow in misery for days," I said, pushing past him.

Sawyer moved in front of the entryway, blocking me from going through it. "Bad idea, Willawood," he cautioned.

I ignored his warning and squeezed by him, entering into the dimmed hallway and only stopping when I stood in front of Sebastian's door. Sucking in a deep breath, I prepared myself for whatever reaction I might receive when he opened the door.

The corridor was so silent this morning that I was actually able to make out Sebastian's disgruntled response when I knocked.

"Go away, Kohen," he grunted.

I'm going to go out on a limb and assume that Kohen has already tried to talk to him.

I knocked again, even harder.

No response.

Unsure if it would even work, I contemplated using my magic on him through the door to make him open it, but he without a doubt had his shields up right now. I didn't want to aggravate him more, but I risked doing so by knocking one more time.

"For fuck's sake, Kohen. I told you to leave me alone." The door swung open, and Sebastian's jaw snapped shut when he saw me.

I had almost forgotten how breathtaking he was. Even now, his face twisted into an expression of distress.

His hand tightly grasped the door frame. His dark hair was a mess of curls and his eyes that normally gleamed were full of dismay. He wore gray lounge pants—that was it.

I didn't want to admit it to myself, but I'd missed him the whole time he was gone.

"Sorry. I—"

"Can I come in?" I interrupted his apology.

He bobbed his head and the muscles of his back flexed as he turned and walked back into his room. I followed him in and closed the door behind us. The curtains were drawn, the only light emitted being from a single-bulb lamp on his desk. His bed was disheveled, a few open books lying on the sheets.

"I didn't know you were back," I stated.

Sebastian pulled his desk chair out, sitting down and avoiding eye contact with me by burying his face in his hands. "I got back late last night," he said, his voice muffled by his palms.

"I saw Sawyer at breakfast."

Sebastian groaned. "Great. I'm sure he had a lot to say."

"He did."

His hands found his hair, ruffling its waves. "What do you want, Maeve?"

I took a few steps towards him. "Are you okay?" I pried, worry coating my tongue.

He didn't look at me. Nor did he make a sound.

Gently, my palm cupped his shoulder. "Listen. I know that you have things you don't talk about with anyone, but—"

His head whipped around, making me jump as my arm fell back to my side. "You don't know anything about me," he snarled with a tic of his jaw.

I didn't let his tone faze me. I stayed calm as we locked eyes.

"I know you better than you think," I retaliated. "And I know this feeling all too well. I might not understand exactly how you're feeling, but after what Sawyer said…I'm worried about you and—"

"Please," he scoffed, turning his head back to his desk. "If this is why you came here, then please. Just. Get. Out." He punctuated each word to show how much he meant them.

A fire fueled by frustration lit inside of me. I wasn't taking this from him right now.

"No," I said sternly. "You're not doing this to me again. You don't get to just shut down, and I won't let you shut me out."

My arms crossed as I stood still, observing him. His head was back in his hands and I swore that I saw his body shudder.

"Seb, please just talk to me." My voice softened with each syllable that I spoke. It was bizarre to me how natural the urge to comfort him came.

"Why are you even here?"

"I told you why."

"And I told you to leave."

"Yeah. And *I* told *you*, no."

"Gods, are you always this damn stubborn?" He finally looked up at me with glossed over eyes. No tears were falling, but I suspected that they would be soon.

I tapped my chin in false contemplation. "Yeah, I can be."

He scoffed. "I'm not talking about this with you."

"And why not?"

Neglecting me an answer, he reiterated his question from before. "What do you want from me, Maeve?"

How did I answer that? There was so much I wanted from him. I wanted him to open up to me—to tell me the things about him that he thought I didn't want to know. I wanted him to tell me about his trauma—I could handle it. I wanted to know what book he was currently reading, and which was the worst that he'd ever read. I wanted him to desire me in the same way I desired him. For him to crave my touch on his skin in the way I craved his. I wanted him to kiss me passionately and to never stop. I wanted every single thing that he had to offer.

"Do you want me to split myself open like a journal and spill you all the deep, dark secrets that are written in smudged ink? Do you want me to cry on your shoulder and be all, *woe is me*? Do you want to sit there and watch me throw a damn pity party over my life?"

"If that's what you need, then sure." It *was* what he needed, but I wasn't sure he realized that.

Sebastian's eyes widened, as if he was surprised that I would actually want him to confide in me. "Well I'm not going to do that," he snarled, dismissing my gaze and looking back at his desk.

I was beginning to think Sawyer was right. There was no getting through to him while he felt like this. Maybe it wasn't really my place, anyway. Plus, he was kind of being an ass. Not that it surprised me.

My teeth scraped against my lip. "I'll go," I said with a shrug of defeat. I really thought I could help him.

The doorknob was already in my clutch when he spoke.

"I'm sorry. Don't go."

My heel revolved to see him standing next to the desk. Only a few feet separated our bodies, but I felt so distant from him. Amidst the turmoil in the room, I'd almost forgotten about his lack of clothing. I lost control of my eyes as they wandered to his chest, and I had to bite the inside of my cheek to prevent my mouth from going slack. Who gave him the damn right to look so good?

Gaining control of my vision, I focused my attention back to his face. He looked so broken, and I would do anything to fix it.

"I don't know what Sawyer told you, but I'm sure it's more than I was hoping you'd ever find out."

I moved towards him, stopping only inches from where he stood. "You're a good person, Seb. I don't think there's anything you have done, or could do, that would make me think less of you." If you had asked me that a few months ago, my answer would have been very different, but today, I meant what I'd said.

"I am not a good person." Sebastian bent his neck back, turning his head towards the ceiling. I could tell he was trying not to break down.

"Talk to me. You can tell me anything you need. I can handle it. I'm not going to run my mouth about it, either. Whatever you say, I'll keep between us." I pleaded my last attempt at getting him to open up.

With a quiver of his jaw, he at last stopped fighting his emotions and let himself lose control. "Fuck!" he shouted, weaving his hands through his hair and spinning so I couldn't see the tears flowing from his eyes, though he was too late.

He stormed to the window and placed his hands on the sill, bowing his neck down. The angle he created with his spine made the muscles of his back go rigid. I watched his figure quake and I'd never felt more useless.

"I'm a soldier, for the love of the gods!" he yelled. "Killing is part of the damn job. It shouldn't get to me like this. Not anymore. Not after everything I've done." He looked over his shoulder, and I recognized the look on his face as one of panic.

He turned to face me, leaning back against the window as I approached him. His hands were static on the sill, making his biceps unintentionally flex. I placed a hand on top of his, attempting to offer him some comfort.

"You can't blame yourself for the things you did to protect yourself. At the time, they were the only way you knew how to keep yourself safe," I told him.

He lowered his neck and blinked away the stray tears from his eyes. His lip quivered slightly as he stared at me, no longer caring that I could see his sadness.

I know it killed him inside for me to be there while he was so vulnerable, and seeing him like this hurt me more than I'd ever imagined it could. I had to fight my own eyes from producing tears.

"Those things were not your fault." My voice choked, but I held myself together for him.

The calmness returned to his skin. He wiped his eyes and said while shaking his head, "You don't know the half of it."

"I don't need to. Not unless you want me to." My hand slid up his arm, my finger lingering near his elbow, studying a line of raised skin running across it. I flicked my eyes towards the rough edged scar that bisected through his elbow.

"I got that when my mother died." He twisted his arm to give me a better look. "I tried to stop Beaumont from killing her."

Five-year-old Sebastian trying to save his mother's life, and in return being sliced open like that—I choked down the horrific thought.

Five. Years. Old.

"Still want to know everything?" he asked in response to the pallor that had appeared on my face.

I moved my gaze back to his face and granted him a soft smile. "Yes." His past didn't scare me.

My fingertips felt the tension in his body ease with my answer. He captivated my gaze, so deeply, so immersed in me, that it prevented me from looking anywhere besides at him. The closeness of his body sent my senses into overdrive and created feelings inside of me that were very much inappropriate at this moment in time.

His eyes glimmered with the same desire that mine did, and my blood warmed as his gaze moved to my mouth. He grazed a finger along my waist, silently dragging me closer to him. I parted my lips ever so slightly, longing to feel his crashing against them.

It was at that moment when I realized what Sawyer told me was true.

I had feelings for Sebastian, and he had them for me, as well. Whether his feelings for me were pure lust or if they entailed something more, I didn't know. Though right now, it didn't matter. The closeness of his body to my breath. The way his gaze lingered on my blushing lips. I didn't care what he wanted me for—as long as he wanted me.

There was a joint understanding of the tension that encapsulated the room.

"Maeve," Sebastian whispered my name, seducing me with the roughness of his voice.

"Yes?" My response was almost too breathy to be heard.

"I'm not good enough for you."

"That's not true."

"I'll hurt you."

"No, you won't."

"What if I do?"

"I don't care."

He leaned forwards, dipping his head to make it level with mine. He took my hands in his, pulling them up to rest on his shoulders. My fingertips roamed the back of his neck, and I didn't have time to think before his lips brushed gently against mine, teasing a kiss.

The faint touch sent a rush of sensation straight to my core, but before either of us could deepen the contact into a true kiss, I pulled away from him. I wanted him more than anything in the world, but not like this. Not when his emotions were in such disarray that it was unknown if he was even thinking clearly. Now was not the right time.

I shook my head subtly, and he released a breath as he straightened his posture. "I know," he murmured, as though he could read my thoughts.

My lips smiled gently and his did the same, although his face was still laced with traces of sadness.

"I should go," I squeaked out, shuffling a step back from him. I had a feeling he'd be okay with me breaking the rules and walking back to the dormitory on my own.

"Are you going to be okay?" I asked.

"Yeah." He cleared his throat, and didn't argue my leaving as he removed his hand from my waist.

"I assume that I'll be seeing you tonight for our wielding session?" I asked, putting air quotes around the tail end of my sentence. He knew as well as I did that I needed a night off after the week I'd had with Sawyer.

He nodded in reply, then I backed out of his room. I didn't break my attention from him until he turned from me to return to his desk.

I closed the door and pressed my back against it, shutting my eyes and releasing a puff of passion filled breath from deep within my chest.

When I blinked my vision open, I was met by Pia's cheesy grin and Kohen's suspicious brows.

"Not what you're thinking," I shot her assumption down.

She scowled. "Damn it."

CHAPTER
TWENTY-TWO

It took a few days for Sebastian's mood to improve after his experience in Craterra. We still hadn't discussed our *almost kiss*. I wanted to, but it likely only happened because emotions were high. At least that was the bullshit excuse I kept telling myself.

Sebastian met me at my room at a little after seven, and we made our way to the castle for our *wielding session*. We decided on the archives tonight which pleased me. I wanted to study the book on Blythe again. With everything going on, I had forgotten about trying to discover why I was given my constellastones in the first place. Although considering the fact that I could barely wield without knocking myself out, I was leaning towards the idea that Blythe just made a really big mistake.

We stepped into the cylindrical room, the shelves lined of manuscripts ranging from fables to bibles. The bookkeepers dimmed the lights in the evening, adding an alluring ambiance to the space. I inhaled the smell of dusty parchment and snickered to myself as I remembered the joke I made when I was here with Pia.

Sebastian gave me a sideways glance. "What's so funny?"

I waved him off. "Nothing."

"It's clearly not nothing."

"I can't repeat it in front of you." I sucked my lips in to prevent my laughter from breaking free.

"Why not?" he asked as we ventured further into the library.

"It's just a dumb joke."

"I like jokes," he replied, starting his ascent up the stairs.

"Do you like jokes that are at your own expense?"

Sebastian chuckled softly, and we climbed to the top floor. The entire room was empty besides us, making for the perfect aid in avoiding being caught.

"You seem to be in a better mood," I pointed out.

"Turns out pity parties do actually help." He huffed a laugh.

Sebastian chose a set of chairs stationed in front of a large window, the glass creating one of the only gaps in the bookshelf. He sat down in one of the seats, but I wandered towards the view, flattening my palm against the cool glass as my eyes journeyed outside.

I could see everything for at least a mile away. The waves of the ocean crashed along the shore, starlight glimmering on top of the water. The dormitory was so clear that I could tell which rooms were occupied by the windows that emitted light. In the forest on my other side, trees danced in the wind, a parade of greenery that flowed all the way to the academy.

The heat of my breath created a film of fog on the glass as I sighed. Delani would have adored this view. I wondered what she'd been doing while I was gone. My mother probably tried to rope her into taking my position at the village's archives, but she would never accept.

Sebastian, suddenly, was awfully close, and my body was well aware of it. I sensed his presence before even turning around.

"Beautiful, isn't it?" his voice whispered near my ear.

I nodded, looking back towards the sea, red from the remnants of the setting sun. "It is. Deceiving, though. The kingdom looks so breathtaking from this height that it almost tricks you into believing its innocence, that there's not a ton of bullshit going on behind closed doors."

"From my experience, beauty is almost never accompanied by innocence."

His breath warmed the back of my neck, and my skin pricked up from his words cascading down my spine. He had no idea the effect he had on me by simply speaking.

"Where did you learn that? One of your dirty books?" I teased, toying with the hem of my shirt.

"How did you know?"

I shot my head around and he flashed me a tantalizing wink. "I can joke, too." He chuckled.

"Very funny." I rolled my eyes. "But really—where did you learn something *so wise?*"

His torso moved in a half-shrug. "Beauty is never just how it appears at first glance. Everything that is beautiful has a secret. Something that balances it. The sky has its storms. The sea has its waves. *You* have an attitude." His lips tipped into a smile before he turned suddenly and returned to his chair.

My heart battered against my ribs.

Did he just call me beautiful? He also said I have an attitude, but I guess that proves his point.

Flustered and needing a distraction to prevent myself from doing something stupid, I took off through the archives, making straight for the section I required. Scanning the shelves, I found the book with ease, right where I'd left it. Having likely been the last person to hold it, a film of dust had accumulated on the cover. I blew it off, then flipped through the pages while I meandered back to where I'd left Sebastian. I threw myself into the chair beside him and unlaced my boots, wiggling them off my feet and letting them drop to the floor beside my chair.

"Comfortable?" he asked from my left.

"We're gonna be here a while, so might as well be." I pulled my legs up so that my whole body was in the chair and settled the book on my lap.

Sebastian cleared his throat as he removed his own book from his rucksack, the cover of it showing an illustration of a crown. All of a sudden, something dawned on me.

"Oh my gods," I said, completely and utterly dumbfounded.

He raised an eyebrow and adjusted himself to face me more head on. "What?"

I gawked blankly at him, not saying anything more and heartbeats passed.

"What?" he asked again.

"You're a prince," I stated.

"Yeah? And?"

"I just realized it."

Sebastian's lips curved up into a smile, the first true one that I'd seen from him in days. "You're kidding me, right?"

"Well, I didn't *just* realize it. Your father is the king, so obviously you're the prince. But it's not something I really ever think about—no one ever refers to you in that way."

"That's because I've asked them not to."

"Why? Sebastian Hawthorne, Crown Prince of Caelestis, has a nice ring to it."

"I don't use the title because I have no intention of following in my father's footsteps," he said seriously.

"Well I'd sure hope not. He's a royal fucking jackass."

My comment broke Sebastian. He released the most heartfelt laugh I had ever heard from him. "I would pay anything to hear you say that to his face."

"I'll do it for free," I scoffed, turning more in my chair. "Why not, though? Isn't it every man's dream to have all of *this*?" I gestured vaguely with my arms.

He shrugged. "For most maybe, but I want a simple life. I don't need any of this. I don't want to rule a kingdom that has ruled me my entire life."

Understandable. His father hadn't set the best example.

"Plus, politics really aren't my forte."

That, I agreed with. "Mine, either. I don't quite understand it all, if I'm being honest. I've never stepped foot outside of Caelestis, and why? Because it would be considered treason? Seems stupid to me. I hardly think traveling across the continent should be considered trying to overthrow our government."

"You're safer in our borders, anyway."

"Who's to say it's not safer elsewhere? Like Mealioria?

"I've been to Mealioria. Trust me, you have it better here. There's no beaches in Mealioria."

"How have you been there?"

"Long story."

I crossed my arms over my chest. "Oh, whatever. All I'm saying is, if I were queen, things would be different around here."

"How so?"

"Well, for starters, I wouldn't hold the gifted on the castle grounds with a tall, mysterious guard watching their every move."

"You forgot charming," Sebastian pointed out with a grin. "What's your next order of business, Queen Willawood?"

I tapped a finger to my chin. "I would secure the eastern territory and safeguard it from harm. Keep the land free of mortals and allow it to just exist as nature wishes."

"Wouldn't that be nice."

"It would. I also would scratch this whole *kingdom* bullshit and just rule the entire Prilarean empire alongside my sister. Maybe a man, too, should I find one worth keeping around."

Sebastian snorted a chuckle. "I know I said politics aren't my forte, but they certainly aren't yours."

"Why not?" I raised my brow. "It sounds like a solid plan to me."

"How would you execute it? How would you get all of the kingdoms to follow you? What would you say or do to prove to their citizens that they should trust you with their lives? And what would you do about an army if not enough citizens volunteered willingly?"

I sucked my lip under my teeth. "I haven't gotten that far yet. Tell me, though, why is the crown prince also one of the king's head soldiers? Your father wouldn't bend the rules for his son?"

"That was somewhat of a compromise for my refusal to take on most of my royal duties, but also I chose to be a soldier."

"Why?"

Sebastian looked me dead in the eyes. "Revenge, I suppose. Justice."

For his mother, no doubt.

Tapping a finger to my chin, another question struck me. "Do you have a crown?"

"I do."

Hot.

"Can I see it?"

"Next time you inevitably find yourself in the soldiers' housing without permission, sure."

"Can I try it on?"

"You are full of questions tonight." Sebastian laughed.

"Questions and hypotheticals *are* my forte. Get used to it. So can I?"

He smiled. "Sure."

Can I wear it alongside nothing else while you throw me down on your bed and—

Oh gods, Maeve, stop.

"I must say, I quite like that the first thing that comes to mind when you see me *isn't* that I'm the prince."

"You may wish otherwise if you knew what really came to my mind," I shot back.

"Is it that I'm the most handsome and talented soldier you have ever laid eyes upon?" he asked with a teasing smirk.

Yes.

"No," I lied. "It's that you're the strange man who reads erotic novels outside of my bedchambers every morning."

Another laugh burst free from Sebastian as I jumped out of my chair, tossed my book to the side and dropped down on one knee in front of him. "I am at your service, Your Highness," I said with a bow of my head.

He let out a breath of silence before he cleared his throat. "Get up," he demanded, shaking his head with a tantalizing gleam in his eyes.

I hesitated, raising my head and scanning my eyes slowly up his body. I could tell by the glimmer in his expression that he liked the sight of me kneeling before him. "Whatever the Crown Prince wishes." I flashed him a sarcastic wink before returning to my own chair.

Sebastian shuffled in his seat, adjusting his pants a bit before burying his face back into his book. The pages of mine bounced off my fingertips as I searched to find my place once again. We read in silence for a while, keeping a lookout for any peering eyes in case we had to quickly act like we were wielding.

I soon was bored with reading an in-depth history about the goddess, so I performed an act that would have caused any avid book lover—specifically Sebastian—to roll in their grave.

I skipped to the end.

My head tilted as I read something that piqued my interest and sent anxiety to my bones all at once.

The prophecy as foreseen by the Goddess of the Mind.

I peeked over at Sebastian, who was so engrossed in his book that he'd probably forgotten I was even here. Then, looking back to the manuscript in front of me, I brought the pages closer to my face.

The word of Blythe has been passed down through centuries. It is claimed that the one who fulfills her prophecy, will be the most blessed mortal to roam the lands. The goddess will grant a single mortal her precious gemstones if the chosen fulfills every aspect of the prophecy.

A wave of unease roamed through my veins, but I kept reading, squinting my eyes to make out the writing better in the dimly lit room.

In a kingdom of salt and stone, the chosen will be birthed midway through the year, at precisely the same moment that the first rainbow meteor falls from the cosmos and disintegrates into the seas. Blythe's chosen will be presented with the gift of constellastones, embellished into their skin in a manner that was previously unheard of. At a time unknown, this soul will be presented with an unparalleled dominance in return for a sacrifice. The chosen mortal will be treasured by the gods and goddesses, and will have the ability to reclaim tranquility and restore the balance of the world.

I lifted my eyes from the book and frowned. What the actual hell did that mean? I fulfilled at least two parts of the prophecy—my birthday and my gemstones—the rest of it however, I was unsure about.

My anxiety definitely did not subside by reading the rest of the prophecy, but instead went through the roof. I stood up abruptly and marched to Sebastian, waving the book in his face. "Read this."

He glanced up from his novel in confusion. I swiped his book from his hands and threw mine into his lap, then crossed my arms over my chest and watched as he absorbed the text. His eyebrows rose as he read, and I brought a hand to my mouth to chew on my nail.

Sebastian's forehead wrinkled when he looked up from the manuscript. I waited for him to say something, but he didn't speak.

I began parading around the archives with my hands on my hips. "*The chosen will have the ability to reclaim tranquility and restore the balance of the world*? That seems like an awfully big task for one person, don't you think?"

Sebastian's eyes flared at me in bewilderment. "Well yes, but—"

"*Embellished into their skin in a manner unheard of.*" My head bobbed as I quoted the text. "That one's obvious."

"Maeve."

"I need to find out what time I was born." My body shuddered in response to the angst rolling through me.

Sebastian stopped my roaming by placing his hands on my shoulders. "Maeve," he repeated my name.

"Actually, no I don't. She wouldn't have given me the constellastones unless I fulfilled all of the parts of the prophecy," I mumbled to my feet.

"*Maeve.*" Sebastian squeezed my shoulders harder, shaking me a little and bringing me back to life with the little lakes that swirled in his eyes.

"What?" I yelled back.

"You're freaking out. Take a seat and calm down," he demanded, his voice firm—and kind of sexy.

I did as he said, swiveling my body and returning to my chair. I propped my head up on my bent arms, in a complete daze trying to decipher the cryptic ending of the prophecy. "A sacrifice? I'm not sacrificing shit. I've already given up enough. What does that even mean?" I looked up at Sebastian, questioning him as though he had an answer.

He shrugged. "I dunno. But it might not even be true. I've never heard anything about Blythe having a prophecy before. Have you?"

"No. But that doesn't mean it's not true. I mean, I fulfill all the criteria. We live in a kingdom of salt and stone. Salt as in the sea, and stone as in the gemstones I'm assuming."

"Yeah, or the cliffside maybe?"

"Either way. Doesn't matter. And I was born during the Jewel-Light Meteor Shower. Sure, I don't know the exact time, but my jewels didn't appear until the shower began. It all lines up."

"This is also just one text," Sebastian pointed out. "It could be false."

"It's not false. Every word of it makes sense."

He knelt in front of my chair as anxiety took control of every part of my body and mind. "Oh gods," I whispered when a horrific thought struck me.

"What?"

"Oh *fuck*!" I bellowed and shot back out of my chair.

Sebastian threw his hand out over my mouth. He held a finger to his lips, quieting me and guiding me back down into my chair with his free palm.

"Maeve, I know you're freaking out, but please try and calm down. If someone finds us here when we are supposed to be wielding, we could blow our cover." There was not an ounce of leeway in his tone. "Okay?"

He pulled his hand back when I nodded in agreement that I wouldn't draw any more attention to us.

"I'm going to die," I whispered my epiphany.

"What?" He sounded rattled at my sudden pessimism.

"The prophecy pledges sacrifice. Which means I'm going to die." The reasoning was not exactly logical, but the only explanation that made sense to me right now.

I gestured for the book, and he passed it to me. I tore out the page that had the prophecy on it, then reached over the side of my chair to shove it into my rucksack. Sebastian would likely have something to say about me degrading such a precious piece of history, but right now I couldn't care less.

The panic inside of me reached an all-time high, and I visibly shook as the air in my lungs thickened, making it hard to breathe.

"Look at me."

Tears hot as embers rained from my ducts. "I'm going to die," I said so hushed that I wasn't even sure I said the words aloud.

Sebastian tilted my chin up with his thumb and forefinger, rubbing his other hand over my knuckles. "You are not going to die. That prophecy could mean so many things," he assured me.

"You don't know that," I argued.

"No. I don't. But my job is to protect you, and *I* will die before I let anything happen to you," he promised me, sliding his thumb up to wipe the tears from my cheeks.

I closed my eyes and blew out a quivered breath, nodding in acknowledgment that I'd heard his words. He was right. The prophecy could mean so many things. I wasn't doing myself any favors by jumping to the worst possible conclusion.

I took a few deep breaths, and once calmed, opened my eyes. "Maybe the sacrifice is referring to the—"

Sebastian cut me off, sarcasm lacing his words. "If you bring up that damn crab again."

"How did you know?"

"Lucky guess."

The brief moment of humor faded, and I returned to the dread that had followed me ever since summer. Sebastian's gaze met mine, and I allowed the beauty of his features to comfort me, feeling so undeniably safe with him.

"Why is it that you always see me at my worst moments?" I asked him, though my lips trembled.

"Oh, you mean like when you destroyed a perfectly good piece of literature a few moments ago?"

"I knew you wouldn't let that slide." A grin broke free from my lips. "You know what I mean though."

Sebastian exhaled deeply through his nostrils. "You saw me at one of my worst moments the other day, so I think we're even."

Sniffling, I fiddled with my thumbs. "I can't keep living like this," I confided in him. "I'm exhausted spending every single day of my life worrying about what's to come."

Sebastian smiled sadly while he brushed a stray piece of my hair behind my ear. "I know."

"When I got here—to the academy—I contemplated if death would really be worse than the fate I was given. For a moment, the thought of being buried gave me some peace…My life may be over, but it wouldn't be controlled by the hands of someone else."

Sebastian stared at me, unmoving.

"The guilt I feel for thinking that—" I bowed my head. "I don't want to die."

"You won't."

"But what my life has turned into…" I tilted my head to the ceiling and shook it in denial. "Living like this is not living at all." The feelings that consumed me when I first found out that I was gifted came rushing back.

Sebastian rolled back off of his knees to sit on the ground, giving me some space. "I know," he repeated.

"Someday I'll live again," I promised myself, dropping my head to see him.

"Me too."

"Someday *we'll* live again."

CHAPTER TWENTY-THREE

"How do you *almost* kiss someone? You either do or you don't," Pia argued with me as I followed her to a table in the kitchen and sat down with my lunch.

We hadn't seen each other much this past week, so I was just getting to fill her in on everything. I decided to keep the prophecy between Sebastian and I for now, at least until I got a better understanding of it.

"I dunno, that's just what it was. An *almost* kiss."

"Well did your lips touch?"

"Urm, yeah I guess kind of."

"Then it was a kiss," she said, tossing her hands up.

"No…it really wasn't," I fought back.

"You are ridiculous, you know that?"

"Why?" I exclaimed, flashing her a look of confusion. "*He* almost kissed *me*, not the other way around."

"Whatever." She finished chewing. "How long do you plan to dance around the fact that you like each other?"

"I'm not dancing around anything. That's not something you just blurt out to someone."

"Well, why not? Look at Kohen and I. We started off as friends with benefits and now we are soulmates." Her eyes brightened at the claim.

"Does he know this?" I asked sarcastically, followed by a laugh.

She flipped me her middle finger.

"Well last I heard you two *weren't that serious*," I imitated her previous claim.

"Things have changed."

I leaned back in my seat and took another bite of my food. The way things had been going lately, it seemed like Sebastian might have feelings for me, too. What was the worst that could happen if I told him? Besides him turning me down, or his father finding out and appointing me a new guard.

Pia waved her fork in front of my face. "What's going on in that head right now?"

"Nothing," I lied and took a mouthful of my lunch.

Pia rolled her eyes again.

"Someone's feisty today," I snorted.

She looked back at her own food, picking around it with her fork. "Whatever, Maeve, but I swear to the gods, if you don't tell Sebastian, then I will."

"Tell me what?"

I almost choked. My eyes widened on Pia as she looked up behind me.

You suck, I mouthed to her, before turning around and flashing Sebastian an innocent smile.

"Good afternoon, *Crown Prince Hawthorne*," I greeted him facetiously.

He looked unamused. "Any chance you'll soon let that go?"

"No. Probably not. I rather like your formal title."

The black pants of his uniform tightened around his leg muscles as he sat down next to me, his diamond dagger glistening in the binding around his thigh. "Did you have something to tell me?"

I caught a glimpse of Pia's smirk, which vanished quickly when I kicked her from under the table.

"Nope." Pia was not getting her way today.

"Huh…that's interesting. Because I swear I heard—"

"You heard nothing."

Pia groaned, tossing her head back and shaking it. I was sure I'd hear later about how annoyed she was at my determination to keep my feelings harbored within me.

Sebastian looked at her. "What's your problem? Kohen finally come to his senses?"

She stuck her tongue out at him, not responding to the satirical comment. The two of them acted just as siblings. Picking and prodding at each other every chance they got.

Turning back towards me, Sebastian asked, "Are you almost ready?"

I swallowed a sip of water and groaned, "Unfortunately."

"What? Don't fancy meeting with the king of Caelestis this afternoon?"

"Never have and never will," I replied, pushing up from my seat. I waved goodbye to Pia, who looked fairly displeased, then meandered after Sebastian through the cool corridors of the castle, an uncomfortable silence joining us on our travels.

Eventually Sebastian cleared his throat, disrupting the tranquility of our walk. "Should I be worried about what you're not telling me?"

My pulse quickened. "No. Drop it."

He, of course, did not drop it.

"What were you two talking about?" he pushed.

"Nothing. Really."

"Then why are your cheeks turning red?"

Damn it. I could feel the heat of my blushing skin, but hoped he wouldn't notice. "I'm hot."

"Really? The snow on the ground outside would beg to differ. Maybe you should take your cloak off."

"No, thank you."

Sebastian stuffed his hands into his pockets and bobbed his head as he tried not to smile. Or was he trying not to laugh?

I came to a halt, crossing my arms over my chest and tapping my foot. "What's so funny?"

He stopped walking, too, and turned his torso to face me, grinning. "You told her."

"Huh?"

"You told Pia about the other day in my room."

My face went blank. Keeping anything from this man was damn near impossible. Not to mention that I was taken aback that he even brought it up.

I stuttered to find something to say. "How do you—"

"I know Pia almost too well. She's easy to read and she loves butting into my personal life. It was an easy assumption to make, and your reaction proved me correct." He turned on his heel and continued back down the corridor.

I demanded my feet to unfreeze and hurried after him, not stopping until we stood feet before the king's study.

"Wait." I grabbed his arm to stop him from going any further. "I didn't tell her anything else. Nothing about what happened before we..." My voice trailed off. I didn't even know what to call what happened between us.

My arm fell when he turned to face me. His eyes gleamed animalistically as he slowly stepped towards me, backing me into the wall.

"Before we *what*?" he asked, the deepness of his tone sending my body into survival mode. He looked at me the same way he had in his room, with an expression full of lust and longing.

I wriggled in my skin, shaking to release the pressure his attention was building inside of me. His face was demanding and a smirk developed on his lips while he watched me struggle to form a sentence.

"Before we almost kissed," I blurted the words out. I didn't mean to, but knew he was waiting for me to say them.

He came closer, keeping me trapped against the wall. Even if I wanted to get away from him, I couldn't. "Is that what we did?" his voice taunted, a hint of seduction laced between the syllables, slipping off of his tongue like a smooth, antagonizing kiss.

He placed a hand against the stonework above my head and I glanced down to free myself from the heat of his gaze. I worried that if I looked back at him, that I would turn our *almost kiss* into a real one.

"I thought so…Wasn't it?" The words stumbled from my mouth. The same tension that filled the air during that moment together seemed to have followed us here, and I couldn't fucking breathe.

"Well that won't do, now will it?" Sebastian put a finger under my chin, guiding my head back up to look at him. My lips fell apart as my attention was drawn to his mouth.

"What do you mean?"

"I don't like to leave things unfinished," he breathed into the side of my neck, his lips sweeping across my skin.

"Here?" I questioned. "Your father—"

"I don't give a fuck about him."

We were seconds away from finishing what we started in his room, when the door to the study flew open. We jumped apart, and despite his claim, Sebastian sighed in relief when he saw Sawyer's wide eyed expression instead of his father's.

Sawyer closed the door behind him, kicking off of it as he strutted for us, a devious smile drawn out on his face. "Whatcha guys doing?"

Sebastian shot him a look of warning, ignoring his question. "Why were you in there?" He gestured towards the study.

"Our fathers called a conference to the throne room in ten minutes. I'm on my way to collect Kohen and the other head soldiers." Sawyer turned his attention towards my beet red face. "You've been instructed to attend as well."

"Did they say why?" Sebastian asked.

"Something about Beaumont, but that's all I know."

My body tensed at the mention of the king of Draemor's name.

"Oh, and heads up, they are still in there. So you may want to take your public displays of affection elsewhere." Sawyer winked, then turned his back to us and continued down the hall.

"Are you doing okay?" Sebastian questioned me while he unlocked the door to my new room—my *safer* room—in the soldiers' quarters. My rucksack that one of the handmaidens had packed for me hung from his shoulder.

I nodded as he pushed the door open. My room was on the same floor as his, just a few doors down. The king wanted me to be as close to Sebastian as possible in case he needed to "*rush to my rescue*" in the middle of the night.

I scoffed at the thought. When did everyone decide that I couldn't protect myself? They never even gave me a chance to prove that I could.

Sebastian entered the room first, and I stopped in the doorway to take it in. I had grown to like my old room and dreaded leaving, but the size of this new space made up for it.

The layout was the same, but the walls were painted a dull white. A singular ceiling fixture illuminated the entire room, and the scent of wood from the caramel furniture warmed my senses as I stepped onto the bronze carpeted floor.

"Your clothes will be delivered by the end of the day," Sebastian informed me, swinging my bag off of his back and passing it to me.

I swiped it from him and moved towards my new bed, dumping the contents out onto the duvet. There wasn't much in the bag as most of my belongings were confiscated when I arrived.

I stacked my emotion-covered parchment sheets, which looked as though they had been read by the one who packed them, and shoved them into the desk, leaving one blank sheet out to write on when I was alone. Then, I tried to ignore Sebastian in hopes that he'd leave me alone. I heard the door close, but knew he hadn't left.

"Maeve, you're kinda freaking me out."

He didn't need to worry. I was fine. It wasn't like the news that King Beaumont had learned of my name came as much of a surprise. It was bound to happen eventually. Everyone else who had been in the throne room seemed more overwhelmed at the information than I had. Lucan's eyes had turned bloodshot and his skin paled when he took in the news. The whispering soldiers should have terrified me, but I hadn't even flinched. I understood the severity of the situation, but was too used to being a war pawn by now.

"You haven't said a word since the throne room."

There was nothing to say. There was another traitor in the kingdom—someone who likely knew me just as well as Edward Fletcher did. Someone else who took it upon themselves to inform the king of Draemor of my name. My powers. Everything they knew about me. What could I possibly say that would change the fact that my world just collapsed under my feet again? Just as I was getting used to the way things were.

I ignored Sebastian's concern and headed back for the bed, fiddling with the rest of my belongings. He sighed, and I recognized his heavy footsteps as they shuffled across the room, stopping at the opposite side of my bed so that he could see my face.

"Can we please talk about this?"

I blinked at him, emotionless.

"You're in shock," he stated.

Is that why I felt so empty? Shock?

I looked down and continued rummaging through my belongings, pausing when my fingers touched the crumpled book page that had the prophecy written on it.

Sebastian noticed my finding. "You've had a lot thrown at you lately, between what my father said to you, then the prophecy, and now this…"

I made back for the desk, shoving the paper into it, then returning to my bed to continue organizing.

Sebastian blew out a breath of frustration at my silence then sat on the edge of my bed. "Okay. I'll talk then. Here's what happens now. There will be soldiers stationed around the perimeters of the castle grounds at all times in the event that Draemor attacks. We can make the assumption that Caelestis has other traitorous civilians living among us, so we will also be working to remove them. Can you look at me please so I know you're following?"

My head upturned. I could see him, but it was like he wasn't really there.

His ocean eyes narrowed on me. "I know you're not a rule

follower, but I need you to be careful, now more than ever. We don't know how Beaumont will react to us denying his offer again, and we need to take every precaution to keep you safe."

His words were just echoes in the dark cavern of my mind.

"I know that you won't say it, but you're scared that my father will turn you over to Draemor. Please believe me when I tell you that he won't comply. He doesn't trust that a peace treaty would truly be dealt. And regardless, I'm not letting them take you anywhere."

I couldn't help but wonder if my fate would be better in Draemor. Beaumont extending his offer again made it evident that he was eager to have me under his reign. Would I be granted freedom if I was no longer in Caelestis? Or would the bounds of my control be worse on the other side? These thoughts should have rattled my mind, but no fear consumed me.

No anxiety coursed through my brain.

No anger heated my blood.

I couldn't feel anything, and no wonder.

There was nothing left to feel.

I'd experienced it all already. I'd fought with fear and panic from the moment I arrived at the castle. I battled despair and discontent every time I thought of my family. I've pulled on the constraints of my life, bound against my will ever since I met King Hawthorne. None of these feelings were new to me.

"Sit down. Tell me what you're thinking." Sebastian gestured for the armchair, his brows furrowed with the fear apparent on his face.

I wished he would realize that I was fine—that I was always going to be fine. There was no other choice.

It was apparent that he wasn't going to budge. I assumed he had his mental shields up, but there was only one way to be sure, so I took a gamble and focused all of my attention on calming myself. The act turned out to be pretty easy when emotions didn't cloud your brain, consuming you.

"Leave," I demanded with the help of my magic, and because his shields were in fact down, he did.

I didn't fall asleep until almost dawn. My mind whirled but was uncomfortably empty at the same time. I could hardly think straight. Couldn't do anything other than gaze outside. I only truly slept for an hour or two before I was awoken by Sebastian who let himself back into my room.

A moan escaped me, remembering that we had combat training this morning. I sat up in my new bed, which I couldn't lie—happened to be more comfortable than the one in my old dorm.

"Morning." He smiled half-heartedly.

"Morning," I said my first word in half of a day.

I expected him to be angry that I had used my powers on him last night, but I had needed the space. Despite the lack of sleep, I felt a bit better this morning and owed him an apology.

"I'm sorry about last night," I murmured, looking down at my sheets, embarrassed about how I acted towards him. "It wasn't you, I just—"

"You don't need to apologize."

"Yes, I do. I used my magic on you when we weren't training. It was an abuse of power."

"I've used my magic on you before."

"That was different," I replied.

"Maeve, it's really okay. Please don't even think about that right now."

I blew out a breath and sat up a little straighter. "Why weren't your shields up? I thought you always kept them up when we weren't practicing?"

He shrugged, stepping towards my bed. "It's different with you."

Everything is different with you, too.

What would have happened yesterday if Sawyer hadn't showed up? I had such conflicting ideas about what to do with my feelings for Sebastian. If I acted on them, I risked so much. If I didn't though—that felt like an even bigger risk. Besides, now clearly wasn't the time to be focusing on men, anyways. I had more important things to worry about. Like *my life*.

"Why?" I asked my delayed question.

He moved to sit at the edge of my bed, his vision still clouded with worry for me. He watched me intently, like he was waiting for me to break. Like he was anticipating the contents of my brain to spill out over the bed into a pool of emotions.

"I'm fine," I assured him, even adding a fake smile to make it more convincing.

"You're so full of it," he said, shaking his head.

"I swear."

"Don't lie to me."

"I'm not."

Sebastian blew out a long, drawn out breath. "How can you just be fine after everything that's been thrown at you lately?"

I don't know. But you help.

I shrugged my shoulders. "It was only a matter of time before this happened. I would be a fool to believe that King Beaumont would never learn who I was."

Sebastian laid a hand on top of mine, the warmth of his calloused skin soaking into the softness of mine. "You know you can be honest with me, right? If you aren't okay?"

"I am being honest. I really just don't want to talk about it anymore."

"We haven't talked about it at all. This is the first we've spoken about it since it actually happened."

I blinked at him, the rest of my body still.

"Alright." He released my hand to stand up, towering over where I sat. "I can't make you talk, but if you need to, I'm here. In the meantime, get your ass up and dressed. We have a training session to get to."

CHAPTER TWENTY-FOUR

The harsh curse of winter struck every time I stepped foot outside of the warmth of indoors. Snow was thickly layered over the sandy beaches, preventing me from enjoying the company of the waves until spring returned.

Caelestis Academy offered all students a winter break, the week off ending with a gala to commemorate a successful first semester. Sebastian convinced the king into allowing me a break from our combat sessions as well, though we weren't able to get away with less wielding sessions. Not that it really mattered—we only practiced every few days, anyway.

Our plan had been working out to my benefit, and I was incredibly thankful to Sebastian for devising it. I was getting a better handle on harnessing my magic, and only having to wield every few days increased my stamina—in return preventing me from getting ill. We did almost get caught once by a bookkeeper who arrived late in the archives, but I threw a simple command at Sebastian to throw them off.

Aside from wielding sessions, I spent most of my break in the comfort of my room, going over and over the words written in Blythe's prophecy. I'd been racking my brain, trying to make sense of the ending, but had no success. Sebastian had done some research as well, but we were both at a loss.

After our second *almost kiss* in the hall last week, I was even more confused about what was going on between him and I.

Maybe Pia was right. For all I knew, I could be shipped off to Draemor or caught in the midst of a war any day now. It would really suck if I died before getting a chance to tell Sebastian how I felt.

Admitting my feelings to him used to seem unimaginable, but it was beginning to seem more crazy to live in denial of them. If I wanted to take back control of my life—whatever parts possible—I could start by telling him how I felt. When the time was right, of course.

Releasing a deep breath, I stretched my arms up and stood from my desk chair. I'd been sitting here for an hour, writing about all the bullshit that had been going on and my predictions about the prophecy, though none of them felt right.

I peered out the window in front of me, missing the view that my old room had. This one didn't show the ocean at all, just some trees left bare from the cold. I still hadn't fully processed all of the changes that had taken place lately. Instead, I avoided the thoughts when they swelled in my brain. Sometimes it was easier to just pretend everything was fine.

"Hey."

A voice startled me, forcing my body to jump around and released a scream.

Pia stood in the middle of my room, her arms full of dresses. "Gods, Pia, what the hell?" I exclaimed, clutching a hand to my chest.

She threw the dresses down on my bed. "I knocked. You were too invested in your daydream about Seb to hear me."

I rolled my eyes. "That's not what I was doing."

She waved me off. "Yeah, sure. Wipe the drool from your mouth and come look at these dresses."

My duvet had been replaced by an array of taffeta and silk. All colors of the rainbow, drenched in lace and glitter that shimmered in the light of the chandelier.

"Which one should I wear tonight?" she asked, and before I could even respond, she picked up a lilac ball gown by its hanger. "You're right, this one will go well with my eyes."

Glancing at the clock and realizing what time it was, I turned to my wardrobe. I hadn't looked through my gowns since the first gala. Swiping through the hangers, my fingertips paused on a deep blue gown, so dark that it would appear black in the evening light.

Pia unbuttoned the dress for me while I stripped to my undergarments. I must have gained some muscle tone since I started the academy, because the gown was pretty snug around my curves. I wriggled my hips into the fabric, then Pia helped me with the buttons again.

The dress was jaw-dropping with beaded straps that laid off the shoulder, revealing the sharp lines of my collar bones. The neckline dropped into a deep plunge that was more revealing than I was used to, but grew on me swiftly. The gown hugged my waistline, then dropped into a dripping flow of fabric, cut with a slit on each side that ran up to the middle of my thigh. The dress shimmered with glistening swirls of black and silver sequins.

"Nice ass," Pia interrupted my admiration of the gown.

I snickered and turned my body to get a look at my behind. The back of the dress was completely open, the fabric not covering anything above the dimples on my back.

I felt beautiful, and for reasons I couldn't deny, I couldn't wait until Sebastian saw me.

Fighting back a smile, I combed through my hair, leaving it wavy aside from two small braids on the sides, connected in the back with a silver hair clip I borrowed from Pia. I covered my lips with a sparkling, pink gloss and finished off my look with a pair of silver heels.

"I'm not sure that I'm ready for this." I shuddered a breath, trying to ignore the memory of the last time I wore a pretty dress.

Pia gave me a look of consolation. "I know the last gala didn't exactly go well, but try to have an open mind."

"Easy for you to say."

I let her apply a thin layer of hair glitter to my scalp and cheeks before we left. Though I was skeptical at first, the added sparkle really completed my look.

Since I now resided within the four walls of the castle, Sebastian gave me permission to escort myself through the castle as long as he knew where I was going. Leaving the building was another story. There was extra security around all corners of the castle now, anyways. I had more than just his eyes watching over me now. I tried to disregard the way the guards glared at me while I walked by, but we all knew that I was the reason for their new orders.

Pia and I descended down the staircase just as Lucan was climbing up. He gave me a nod of greeting, but nothing more as we passed by each other.

"Why is he in the soldiers' housing?" I whispered to Pia when we reached the ground floor.

"I dunno. Maybe he's seeing someone," she snorted.

"That would be quite the age difference." I laughed. The oldest soldiers that lived on the castle grounds were twelve years older than myself, and Lucan had at least twenty more years on them, if I had a guess.

My mouth fell limp upon my entrance to the great hall. The room was unrecognizable with its exquisite decor that outdid the last gala by miles. Drapes of sparkling cloth hung from the ceiling, accompanied by garland weaved of greenery and white roses. Twinkling lights dripped from the side walls, resembling icicles so clearly that it was as if Caius himself put them there. The gemstones of the gods were depicted throughout the room by clusters of colorful streamers and tinsel. Light reflected onto the dance floor, twirling off of the satin gowns and suits of the galas attendees.

"This is incredible," I exclaimed in awe, spinning in a tight circle to absorb the room in its entirety.

"Always is." Pia grabbed my hand, dragging me to the nearest buffet station and selecting a goblet of rose-colored wine for each of us. We sipped on our drinks, waltzing through crowds of people who swayed to the whimsical tunes that saturated the room.

My thighs peeked through the slits in my gown with every step I took. In my travels, I glanced around, searching for a certain soldier. My breath caught at the sight of him, standing with his poised posture, his dark hair shining against the contrast of the tinsel and lights. Sebastian was deep in conversation with Sawyer and Jocelyn, laughing and looking as though he was truly enjoying himself.

Good. He deserved some fun—most of his free time was consumed by looking after me.

Kohen joined the group, his hands full of liquor which he passed out amongst his friends. Sebastian flashed his teeth in a thank you before sipping his drink. He looked dashing in his charcoal uniform. The jacket of his ensemble was unbuttoned, revealing the ivory dress shirt he wore underneath. His boots were black, their silver laces matching the buttons that cuffed the sleeves tightly around his wrists.

As if he could sense my wandering gaze, Sebastian peered up from his glass and his cerulean eyes caught mine. I jerked my head away, praying that he didn't notice me staring. When I finally got the courage to glance over once more, his back was towards me.

I finished my drink in one swift gulp. "I have a feeling I'm going to be needing a lot of this tonight," I said to Pia, just as she caught sight of Kohen. She grabbed my arm, pulling me across the dance floor to join him and the others.

My heart collided forcefully with the walls of my chest as my adrenaline-thickened blood pumped. "Wait. I'm gonna go get some more wine first," I stammered.

"Oh come on," she groaned, pausing her motion but not releasing my wrist.

"I am not nearly drunk enough to talk to Sebastian right now."

"You talk to him every day. The only difference now is that your boobs are out." Ignoring my plea, Pia tightened her grip and led me straight to the group of head soldiers.

She released me to throw her arms over Kohen. She kissed his cheek, who blushed from the contact. I smiled faintly to myself as I watched them. They seemed really happy together.

"Maeve! You look gorgeous!" Jocelyn addressed me, admiring my dress selection.

My head tilted down with my grin. "So do you," I complimented her burgundy gown. My gaze avoided Sebastian, though I was unsure why I suddenly felt so nervous near him.

"You clean up nice, Willawood," Sawyer said, pulling me into a one-armed hug. I suppose we could be considered friends now, which was a bit ironic all things considered.

I gave Sawyer a modest thank you, then despite my best efforts, found myself looking into Sebastian's face. I released a soft breath full of angst as I prepared to address him.

"You look charming tonight." My voice reflected my insecurity.

The hall was filled with so much noise that I was unsure if he even heard me, but Sebastian took another sip of his drink and stepped towards me, leaving some distance between us and the others.

"Thank you." His gaze roamed over my body, unashamedly taking in every inch of me. He pulled his glass away from his mouth then moved to stand by my side.

I inhaled deeply and my body relaxed from the familiar aroma of frost and pine, now mixed with the sweet sting of whiskey. We both looked straight ahead, observing our group of friends mingle with one another.

Sebastian's arm brushed against my waist as he leaned his lips to my ear. "With all of the books I've read, you'd think I would have discovered the words to express how beautiful you look this evening. But I don't think such words exist." As he stood straight up, he slid his hand up the side of my waist, trailing his fingertips to the middle of my back where he let them linger. His touch sent an exquisite sensation flowing through my body, coating every inch of my skin before settling amid my thighs.

"Maybe you should be in the archives then, instead of here sipping on whiskey." My breathing shook on my exhale as I made light of his compliment.

He snickered into his glass then tilted it back to take a drink, saying after he swallowed, "In all honesty, I would choose the archives over one of these parties any day."

"Me too. I'm not one for crowds."

He explored my bare skin, his thumb tracing down the curve of my spine, stopping when it reached fabric. "What's keeping us here then?"

A gasp escaped my throat as he hooked his finger under the fabric of my dress, just enough to make me shiver.

"I would say your duty as a head soldier and crown prince," I answered breathlessly, wriggling a bit to distract myself from the wetness forming between my legs.

His finger explored deeper down my dress, skimming the dimples of my back. His whiskey-coated breath tickled my neck when he whispered, "My duty is to look after you. Wherever you lead, I will follow."

I couldn't speak.

Then, without any notice, Sebastian slid his hand away from my skin. Sawyer gestured for him, and he stepped away without another word, leaving me frozen to the marble floor, trying to rid myself of the lust that had devoured me.

What the hell just happened?

I tried to shake it off, but was pretty sure that Sebastian just hinted at the two of us *getting out of there*. My cheeks puffed full of air that I blew out heavily as I watched him return to our group of friends. None of them noticed what just occurred between us. Thank the gods.

I was right in thinking that a lot of wine would be needed to make it through this night. I got Pia's attention to let her know where I was going, then wandered away to find the nearest buffet that could fulfill my need.

The evening seemed to drag. What happened with Sebastian left me even more perplexed, and in all honesty, just wishing the night would end. I should have just left, but that wouldn't go over well with the king, who had just finished giving his speech to the crowd. His words were full of a bunch of bullshit that I doubted anyone cared about, especially seeing as everyone immediately scattered amongst the dance floor at his departure.

I leaned back against a wall, sipping on my fourth drink while silently observing the dancers. My blood was warm, but I was not nearly intoxicated enough to get Sebastian out of my mind.

"Where's Kohen?" I asked Pia as she appeared by my side, not moving my eyes from the crowd of dancers.

"He *was* taking shots with Sawyer. *Now* they are dancing with each other." She pointed to the two of them on the dance floor, blatantly drunk and holding each other as they swayed to the music.

I struggled to keep my drink in my mouth, laughing at the sight of them. "They are going to regret that in the morning."

"Yep." Pia swiped my drink and took a sip. "I've been replaced."

We watched them until the song ended and they vanished, likely off to find more booze. When they were out of our field of vision, Pia turned to me with her forehead creased. "Why are you standing here all alone?"

I shrugged. I didn't want to tell her about what happened with Sebastian earlier, but at the same time, keeping it inside was killing me.

She handed me my drink back. "Out with it," she demanded.

I didn't try to fight her. "Sebastian's been giving me very mixed signals."

"How so?"

"He had his hands all over me earlier." I stopped myself from divulging anymore when we were interrupted by a very drunk Kohen.

"There you are," he slurred, pulling Pia into a sloppy hug.

Sawyer arrived behind him, just as intoxicated but not nearly as clumsy. "Someone can't hold their liquor." He chortled, angling his thumb at Kohen whose arms were wrapped tightly around Pia's neck while he danced to the music.

With my brows raised, I eyeballed the two of them. Maybe if I took a few shots I'd be as carefree as them and get Sebastian off my mind.

"Whatcha drinking, Maeve?" Kohen peeled himself from Pia and reached out for my goblet.

"No way." She swatted his hand away. "You've had way more than enough."

"Don't be a buzzkill, Hawthorne." Sawyer took my glass instead and downed it in one gulp.

"You'll thank me in the morning when you remember how you two embraced each other on the dance floor," she retorted, annoyance coating her tongue.

"You guys are a mess. How much did you drink?" I snickered.

"I dunno. Six…seven…maybe nine," Kohen garbled.

"Nine *what*?" Pia asked him.

"Nine," he simply replied.

"For fuck's sake," she mumbled, holding Kohen tightly so that he wouldn't fall.

"Who wants one?" Jocelyn chimed as she appeared from midair, holding a tray of more shots.

Pia snatched Kohen's wrist out of the air. "Why don't we go get some water," she said through gritted teeth, then proceeded to drag him away from the rest of us.

Sawyer swiped a glass from the tray and extended the offering to me. "You want one?"

Screw it. I took the glass from his hand and shot down the liquor, allowing it to coat my throat like honey.

I suppressed a gag. "That shit is strong."

Sawyer chuckled at the disgusted look on my face, then drank his. "That *shit* is Seb's favorite."

"He has bad taste," I groaned.

Within seconds of swallowing, the warmth of the alcohol in my stomach caused the thoughts in my brain to ease. I should have had one of these earlier in the night. It certainly would have made the evening more enjoyable.

"Here, take another." Jocelyn handed Sawyer a shot.

I couldn't help but notice the way he looked at her. His eyes were full of the same longing that mine had when I looked at Sebastian. I wondered if there was something between the two of them.

"I'm all set, thanks," I declined her offer when she tried to pass me another glass.

Sawyer took his, then Jocelyn wandered off, leaving just him and I. The way he watched her go made it undeniable that he felt something for her.

"She's really beautiful, isn't she?" I asked once she was out of earshot.

He didn't take his eyes off of her crimson gown as it vanished into the crowd. "Yeah, she really is."

My heart softened at the idea of Sawyer liking someone. He had such a rough exterior—it was sweet to see him with his guard down.

"Have you told her?"

"Told her what?"

"That you like her."

Sawyer glared at me, chewing the inside of his cheek. "Have you told Seb?"

My lips fell into a tight line.

"Actually, have you seen Seb?" Sawyer changed the subject before I could answer.

I shook my head. Come to think of it, I hadn't seen him since his father's speech.

"Here." Sebastian's voice broke through the crowd. His figure appeared through the parade of streamers and greenery. The lights glimmered off his skin, bringing my attention instantly to his eyes that so often seemed to captivate me. His hair laid in delicate waves over his forehead, curling around the backs of his ears. *Gods.*

He removed a hand from his pocket, and reached out for me. "Care to dance?"

I tried my hardest, but couldn't suppress the smile that tugged at my lips. "Sure," I said softly, taking his outstretched hand and allowing him to guide me to the dance floor.

Glancing back at Sawyer, I mouthed, *ask Jocelyn to dance.*

He rolled his eyes, but the suggestion turned his cheeks pink before he sauntered off after her.

Sebastian took us to a crammed corner of the dance floor, out of the blatant view of his father. He kept his hold on my hand and swung his body to stand in front of me, placing his other hand on my waist.

"Where have you been all night?" I asked as we started to move with the hum of the music.

"Where have you been?" he countered.

I looked down, watching our feet move as we danced. "Drinking."

"I thought it was you that I saw throw a shot back like it was water."

"Just something to help calm my nerves." I smiled at the ground.

"What's there to be nervous about?"

You. I am terrified that I'll never have you in the way I need you.

I shrugged, raising my gaze back to him. "What isn't there?"

He released his hand from my waist to spin me into a twirl. Our bodies moved together in such grace that you would have thought we'd been dancing together all our lives. When the twirl concluded, he grabbed my waist again, pulling me closer to him—so close that our bodies were flushed against each other. I tilted my neck up to see his face, and I didn't think I'd have the willpower to ever look away.

"I told you that you don't need to worry. That I would protect you," he said.

That wasn't it at all, but I nodded. "I know."

He was absolutely perfect. Every single thing about him. Breathtaking to look at, yes, but who he was at his core was the most attractive thing about him. And no, I didn't know everything about him, but I didn't need to. None of our past mattered to me. I needed this man more than I needed air.

I was entirely consumed in him.

"How have you been feeling about everything?" he asked me out of the blue.

"Are you going to ask me that every time I see you?"

"Until you tell me the truth, yes."

"Well you caught me at a good time, because I'm tipsy and feeling honest." I adjusted my hand in his, fiddling with his thumb.

"I'm so pessimistic about everything that I'm having a difficult time enjoying myself tonight. Well, I was at least."

"My dancing skills really cheered you up that much?" Sebastian chuckled, the gravel in his voice creating shivers all over my skin.

"More so Kohen and Sawyer's dancing skills, but yours helped."

We spun in circles, gliding along the marble floor, not speaking again until the song concluded.

"In case I didn't make it clear earlier, you look exquisite. Ravishing. Stunning. Breathtaking."

I flushed at his words, both externally and internally. "So was it the archives that you ran off to? Looking through texts to find the words you seemed to have lost earlier?"

He twirled me again, and when he pulled me back in, we were somehow even closer than we were before.

His lips curved into a grin. "How did you know?"

He dropped my hand so that he could hold my waist from both sides, and I raised my arms to his shoulders, clasping my hands behind his neck. I studied his face, trying to read him. Did he want this just as much as I did? Or was I just a piece of his puzzle—waiting to be completed so that he could shatter it and shove the pieces back into its box.

I frowned unknowingly at the thought.

"What's wrong?" His forehead creased.

I should have told him how much he affected me without even realizing it—how I wanted to be more than just his training partner. More than his friend. But I didn't. It wasn't the right time.

I faked a smile. "Nothing at all."

He leaned down, placing his head in the crook of my neck. His body was so close to mine that I could feel the pounding of his heart against my own chest.

"I know you well enough to know that you're not telling the truth," he breathed. "Why do you insist on lying to me?"

I bit my lip in a shudder as his words kissed my collarbone. He moved his hands down to my hips, pulling my thighs into him so that they were grinding against his groin as we danced.

Fuck.

"You don't want to know the truth. Sometimes it's better being left in the dark," I replied, my puckered lips skimming his jaw.

"I am the dark," Sebastian muttered, his tone empty and hollow. "You are the light. And when it comes to you, I don't want to be in the shadows."

I rolled my shoulders back and he removed his head from my neck to stand upright. When we were face to face once more, I analyzed his expression.

His eyes were full of want, but mine were full of need. And I couldn't tell if he wanted to be with me, or just *wanted* me. That information alone made it evident that we weren't on the same page—we couldn't have been. And the thought shattered me.

Despair settled in my bones. I needed to get out of here. Needed some air. This was getting to be too much.

I pulled away from him abruptly, pushing off of his chest with my palms. "Excuse me," I choked on my words and backed away.

Uncertainty clouded Sebastian's features as I spun on my heel and left him alone on the dance floor.

CHAPTER
TWENTY-FIVE

"Maeve!" Sebastian called after me.

I hurried out of the great hall, holding up the sides of my gown to avoid tripping. Ignoring his voice, I moved as fast as possible in heels, needing to get away from him. I couldn't handle another moment of wanting him without actually having him. Not tonight at least.

When confident I had left him behind, I stopped in a corridor far away from the shining lights and loud music. I swallowed a few deep breaths, blowing them out shakily as I slouched against the stone wall. I clasped my hand over my star pendant and looked up towards the heavens, shaking my head to the gods. I couldn't keep doing this. Even if it broke me, I needed to know what he felt.

"Maeve?"

My gaze dropped towards Sebastian, his eyebrows drawn together as he approached me.

"What's going on?" He crouched in front of me, reaching a veiny hand out to stroke my arm.

My instincts told me to pull away, but I couldn't bring myself to follow through. Fiddling with my necklace, I avoided his eyes. "I just…I just need you to—" My voice quaked, struggling to find the words to explain.

"Did I say something?"

I shook my head. I could keep telling myself that it wasn't the right time, but would the time truly ever be right?

"Then what—"

Rising on my feet, I threw my arms in the air and spun my back to him. My hands pressed against the wall and I dropped my neck to my chest, my body shuddering to expel the pent up emotions that had accumulated within me.

"Talk to me."

Fuck it.

"I don't know what you want," I said at last, punctuating each word and turning back to him. "You almost kissed me, not once but twice. Then a week later it's like nothing even happened. Then tonight you're making suggestive comments and touching me. But as soon as Sawyer waves his hand, you leave my side like you didn't just have *your hand* in my dress."

His jaw ticked, but he didn't speak.

"I know what I want, Seb. But I have no idea what the hell *you* want." I pointed a finger at his chest, then stopped myself from saying more.

My breathing was heavy with the release of desire that had been brewing inside of me. A sense of calm flooded me for a brief moment before replacing itself with nausea from the anticipation of what he was going to say.

Sebastian closed the gap between us, staring at me deeply. Eagerly. "You really have no ideas about what I want?"

"No. I don't. Every time I think that I do, something happens that makes me think otherwise."

His head dropped, lowering his eyes so they were level with mine. "I want you," he stated, leaving no room in his tone for me to misunderstand.

I was sure that my heart stopped beating.

"I want you so bad that I can't think about anything else when you're near. You walk into the room, and I have to force my eyes to focus on anything but you." He brushed the hair off of my shoulders, then skimmed his lips over my neck. "I can't breathe when you look at me the way that you are right now."

I couldn't breathe either. My body trembled as his touch slid over my flesh.

Pulling back ever so slightly, his eyes dipped to my mouth, and before I could say anything else, a needy sound escaped my throat as Sebastian's lips captured mine in a long awaited kiss.

He pushed us back against the wall, his hands moving to cup my jaw. Our tongues were already entangled when he tilted my head back to deepen the contact. He kissed me like he was a part of me —like we were two halves of a soul, absorbing each other to make one.

His hands dropped from my face, grazing my skin as he moved one to my waist and used the other to cup the back of my thigh. He lifted my leg with his calloused palm, hooking it around him. My gown shifted to the side, the slit in the fabric revealing more of my skin to him than I'd intended.

I couldn't even tell if I was breathing anymore. He kissed me so hard that air was no longer a priority. I was certain that even if my lungs dried up, I would be able to thrive as long as he kept kissing me.

"I've wanted you since you first challenged me all those months ago," Sebastian uttered into our kiss. His hand ran up my exposed leg, slipping under my dress and moving up my thigh. I gasped as his fingers teased the lace of my panties, his knuckles skimming beneath them, subsequently creating a pool of wetness from my core.

"I never should have let it get to this point. I swore to myself that I wouldn't let myself feel this way about you," his lust-enhanced voice spoke between the movements of our tongues.

"But why?"

"Some may call it an abuse of power, or me taking advantage of you."

"It's not being taken advantage of if I want it, too."

He gave me a look that made me liquify, then he growled into me, the guttural tone making my body crave more. I moved my arms to his shoulders, grasping the material of his jacket and pulling the sleeves down. I tossed the coat to the floor and ran my hands up the hardness of his chest.

"Seb," I moaned his name into his mouth as his tongue laced with mine in an exquisite dance of lust. Our hips ground against each other, the hardness that lay beneath his slacks rubbing against me.

This is what I'd always imagined it to be—him and I. He was everything my soul needed, making me feel whole for the first time since the summer. Though I didn't want the moment to end, before it went any further, I needed to tell him the true extent of my longing.

"Seb?" I repeated his name in the hint of a question.

"Maeve?" His voice ached with lust, but he forced our mouths to break apart. His hand still gripped my thigh and he directed his kisses to my neck while I spoke.

"I didn't finish what I wanted to say."

"I'm listening." His tongue traced my neck through his words.

"I want all of you. Every piece of you," I practically moaned as his mouth explored my skin.

He separated his lips from my skin so that he could lock eyes with me.

"I feel things for you that I've never felt in my life. Things that I didn't know were possible to feel."

He dropped my leg to the ground, not breaking his gaze.

"I want to be with you. I want to know everything about you. I want you to me show the parts of you that you think will scare me—the parts of you that scare *you.* I want it all." Reaching my hand out to stroke his face, I leaned in close, whispering to him, "I need you."

His jaw clenched, and his whole demeanor shifted to one that I couldn't even describe. He grabbed my wrist, removing my hand from his face so he could back away from me. "I can't give you that," he said flatly.

My stomach twisted in agony. "What?" I stuttered. I was

certainly not expecting that to be his reaction after the way we were just kissing.

"I may be what you *think* you want, but trust me when I say that I'm not what you need." His fists clenched by his side as he shook his head.

"You don't get to tell me what I want," I argued.

"No. I don't," he started, taking a step back. "But you can't tell me what I want, either."

My entire being crumbled at his words. He didn't want this, too? Despair flickered off of me like sweat. "You just said you wanted me—"

He cut me off. "It doesn't matter what I said. I can't do this. I can't have you. I won't," he snarled, his words so harsh and so cold that the temperature of the hallway dropped.

"So what? You just wanted to screw me? Is that it?" I spat in his face, suddenly consumed by anger.

"No," he scoffed. "I'm not that much of a prick."

"Are you sure? Because seconds ago you said that you couldn't breathe when you were around me, and now you're denying it." My face tightened to hold back a flood of tears.

Sebastian didn't say anything else. He bent down and picked his jacket up, shrugging it over his shoulders as he turned his back to me and strutted away down the corridor.

"You can't just act like an ass and push everyone in your life away every time you get scared!" I yelled after him, but he didn't look back.

Once he was gone, I broke down, collapsing to the floor in a pile of fabric, where I pulled my knees to my chest and sobbed.

I had a brief taste of what I could only imagine life beyond the veil was like, just for it to disintegrate moments later. My body trembled uncontrollably as I mourned the one person who I'd come to need more than anyone.

He felt the same way about me—I knew he did. It was impossible to kiss someone that passionately if you didn't feel deeply for them. I knew him better than he'd like to admit, and he was scared.

He felt like he didn't deserve this and was letting those thoughts get in the way of him being happy.

Someone cleared their throat from my side. My head jumped up to see Sawyer standing at the end of the hall.

"Oh gods, please tell me you didn't see any of that," I groaned, tears still spilling from me. My throat burned at the thought of him seeing what Sebastian and I just did. However the feeling faded quickly as my sorrow was too fierce to stay away.

"No. But I heard you yelling from down the hall, so I put two and two together." Sawyer crouched down by my side. He put an arm around me and pulled me into him, allowing my tears, which fell so vigorously that they could have been mistaken for a river flowing rampant during a storm, to soak into his shirt.

"Did you hear everything?" I managed to get out through my sniffling.

Sawyer sighed deeply. "Yeah, Willawood, I did."

"I don't know what I did wrong," I cried into his shoulder.

"You didn't do anything wrong. That's just…Seb. He refuses to see the good in himself." Sawyer reached into his jacket pocket and grabbed his handkerchief, offering it to me.

I used it to wipe my eyes, though the tears didn't cease. "Why won't he let anyone in? Why can't he let himself be happy?"

"Wish I knew."

"It's not fair," I muttered. "To either of us."

Sawyer squeezed me a little tighter. "No, it's not."

"He's an asshole."

He chuckled softly. "Sometimes, yeah."

I cried until I was so exhausted that my eyes wouldn't stay open. Sawyer didn't leave my side, and I was almost asleep against the cool rock of the corridor by the time he convinced me to go back to my room.

He pulled me to my feet and walked with me back to the soldiers' housing, leaving me once I was in the safety of my room.

I stripped out of my gown and threw myself onto my bed, where I stuffed my head into a pillow and released my anguish into more tears. I sobbed until the fabric was soaked and I had fallen asleep to the sound of my own heartache.

THOUGH I DOUBTED HE WOULD HAVE HAD THE GUTS TO SHOW UP anyways, I decided to blow off my wielding session with Sebastian the next day. I couldn't be near him. In fact, before Sawyer left last night I asked him if he would take over my one-on-one sessions. I knew that this meant I'd no longer have off days for wielding, but I'd prefer being weak and defeated over having to face Sebastian.

I spent the day tucked away in the privacy of my room, planning to study Blythe's prophecy while fighting the melancholy that had me in a chokehold. Stationed at my desk, I read over the crumpled parchment holding the words that granted me so much uncertainty.

The mortal will have the ability to reclaim tranquility and restore the balance of the world.

How could I restore the balance of the world when I could barely compel someone to flick a lamp on without walking the line of blacking out?

At a time unknown, this soul will be presented with an unparalleled dominance in return for a sacrifice.

I read the words over and over, attempting to decipher what it could possibly indicate. Eventually too frustrated to continue, I stuffed the page back into the drawer of my desk. I'd have to check the archives again to see if there was another manuscript that could help me.

I jotted a quick journal entry then slid my chair back and rose to my feet. I took a shower, attempting to wash away the feel of Sebastian's hands as they explored my skin, though his touch was a feeling I didn't think I could ever forget.

Cheeks puffed out with a sigh, I glanced at myself in the mirror. My eyes were red and itchy, the skin around them inflamed from crying.

My gems glimmered as I turned my head. I'd come to ignore the jewels that embellished my swollen cheek. They'd become a piece of me, even though I cursed the goddess who granted me them. If she hadn't, I would not be here right now, full of so much sorrow that I couldn't breathe.

A soft knock hit the door of my bedchambers. I shuffled out of the washroom to open it, praying it wasn't the one person I couldn't stand to see right now.

Pia's eyes widened when she saw me. She crept into my room, shutting the door quietly behind her. "Who do I have to kill?" Her eyebrows furrowed in anger.

"Take a guess." I turned from her and settled myself in the armchair by my window.

"Oh. Well, I can't kill *him*, but I can fuck him up. What did he do?"

My legs dangled over one side of the chair, my head resting on the other. "I don't want to talk about it." I really didn't want to rehash everything right now. My heart couldn't handle it.

"Too bad," she countered, sitting on my bed and staring at me until I broke.

"I told him how I feel." I sighed. "Then we kissed…Well, it was pretty touchy to just be considered a kiss, but I'll spare you the details."

She clapped her hands giddily. "I want the details."

"No," I said flatly as Pia fought a smile that would soon vanish.

"He said he wanted me the same way I wanted him." I paused to scoff. "But then I told him how I *really* feel and he freaked out, saying that he can't have me. That he won't have me. He basically disregarded everything he said."

I closed my eyes to keep the tears locked in. "He told me this would happen. He said that he would hurt me, but I didn't listen. I didn't listen because it didn't matter. I wanted whatever he could give me, even if it was hardly anything at all." I sniffled, wiping my nose with the back of my hand. "Well it turns out that it *does* actually matter."

The barrier of my eyelids was not strong enough to keep my tears from breaking free, and a few slipped past by mistake. I blinked them away, opening my eyes to meet Pia's fixated stare. "I don't know what I expected. I knew this could happen, so I shouldn't be so hurt."

"I'll talk to him," Pia chimed in, her tone so blank that I couldn't tell what she was thinking.

"Don't bother," I rejected her offer.

"I'm not trying to defend my cousin being an ass, but hear me out." She moved to sit in the chair at my desk, closer to me. "Seb is *never* going to feel worthy of love. He truly believes that he doesn't deserve it."

Sawyer had hinted at the same thing.

She continued, "I know. It seems ridiculous to us because we don't understand it. And be thankful that you don't."

A tiny bit of my anger was replaced by sadness. "Everyone deserves to be loved."

She ground her jaw. "I know."

"Well, I'm not going to spend my life waiting around for him to love me back." I tried to convince myself of the lie, knowing damn well I would wait for him until the oceans dried up.

Pia's eyes bulged and my hand hit my mouth when I realized what I said. Is that why this hurt so much—because I was in love with him?

"I didn't mean to say that," I denied the words as if they didn't just come pouring out of me in pure admission. "You can't be in love with someone you've only known for months, that's absurd."

The corners of Pia's lips curved up gently. "Sure you can. Some souls are simply designed to love one another. Like the stars are destined to love the heavens."

Though I wanted to believe her, I was still too angry at Sebastian to accept that what she said could be true.

"How was the rest of your night?" I changed the subject.

Pia went off about how drunk Kohen was when she got him back to his room. I lost focus shortly into the conversation. My mind just kept wandering back to Sebastian.

I wouldn't pine for him. I wanted him to let me love him, but he would have to decide that for himself. Until then, I'd focus on my studies and decoding the prophecy while I pretended that I'd never met Sebastian Hawthorne.

CHAPTER
TWENTY-SIX

Exhausted did not come anywhere near explaining how I felt.

Two months of training without a day off had left me completely beaten down. I knew Sawyer went hard when he trained, but having sessions with him for weeks on end might result in the death of me.

The risky pattern was worth it if it meant that I could continue avoiding Sebastian. I hadn't spoken to him since the gala. He'd tried to talk to me a few times, the most recent being after my last meeting with King Hawthorne, but each time I pretended not to hear him and gave him the cold shoulder.

Without him as my escort, I hadn't seen Sebastian much except for my meetings and occasionally at meals. He seemed to be keeping to himself. *Good.*

I'd been trying to ignore my feelings for him, hoping that they'd vanish as quickly as our kiss did. However they stuck around, refusing to relinquish me from the weight they put on my soul.

"One more go around, Willawood?" Sawyer circled me on the mat.

We'd been multitasking by training my combat skills and wielding together, practicing what it would be like to combine the two in the field. I hoped I'd never have to, but considering King Hawthorne damned me to a life of soldier-hood, it was only a matter of time before practice turned to reality. I preferred training this way though—I didn't have to wake up as early.

I took my stance across from Sawyer, holding a practice dagger in my hand and waiting for him to make the first move. I blinked, and when my eyes opened, he was directly in front of me.

My heart raced as I lifted my arm to block his punch aimed at my side. The deflect was successful, and I twisted my body to position myself behind him.

My attempts in compelling him to release his dagger had failed all night. Though it seemed simple, the command was easier said than done when someone was trying to beat the crap out of you. With the added pressure of our battle, I'd been unable to focus on the command long enough for him to fulfill it.

I kicked my foot into the back of his leg, causing him to stumble and fall down on a knee. He caught himself before fully hitting the ground, cursing as he tried to regain his footing. While he was down, I concentrated on finding a district of peace in my mind, then tried my command on him again.

"Damn it," I murmured, failing yet again. Sawyer's mental shields were not nearly as strong as Sebastian's, and I was usually able to break through them if I tried hard enough.

"Not doing so hot tonight, Willawood," Sawyer taunted from his end of the mat.

I was already pretty much spent and eager to get this session over with, but Sawyer said he wouldn't set me free until my command was successful.

"Shut up," I replied, and as he repositioned himself, I came up with my battle tactic.

With my fist clenched around my dagger, I pointed it towards his chest and charged at him. He expected me to aim for his sternum as I had been, but I veered to the side to throw him off. Before he could twist his torso towards me, I was behind him once again, my arm hooked around his neck in a choke hold.

"Drop your dagger." My jewels pricked my skin as my magic

coursed through my veins. I held on tightly to the compulsion, but my magic began to waver as Sawyer's shield fought it off.

I bit back a wince as he jutted his elbow back under my ribs. He wriggled his body to release himself from my hold, but I dropped my own dagger and wrapped my other arm around his waist, tightening my hold on him. He was much larger than me, but I had him in a position that would make it hard for anyone to get out of.

"Drop your dagger." My face stung with the words as they left my lips with force. I could feel my magic breaking through his shields, right before there was a release of pressure in my mind.

Sawyer's hand unclenched, and the dagger fell to the ground with a clang.

I smiled down at the glinting blade, then released my grip on him. My legs wobbled as I backed off the mat. This session took more out of me than I expected it would.

Sawyer wiped the sweat from his face with his shirt. "Hell yeah. Nice job."

I gave him the thumbs up as I hunched over, clasping my knees and gasping to catch a hold of my breathing. Darkness blocked my vision when I stood upright, my blood pressure plummeting. I paused to let it subside, but it only passed to be replaced by a headache so intense that I thought I might vomit.

I swiftly packed up my rucksack, needing to get back to my room as soon as possible.

The sky was black as death when we left the arena. I thanked the stars for not shining tonight and allowing me to hide the pallor of my skin. The temperature had begun to warm in preparation for early spring, making for a more pleasant walk than a few weeks back.

I followed Sawyer back to the castle and into the soldiers' corridor. His room was on the floor below me, so we parted ways when we entered the building. I gripped the railing tightly while climbing the stairs in the event my vision failed me again. What a pitiful death that would be—tumbling down two flights.

My shaking hands struggled to unlock my door, but when the lock clicked free, I tossed a hand over my mouth and raced for the washroom. I threw up—as I had almost every night for the past month and a half. Harnessing my magic daily had caught up with me very shortly after I began training with Sawyer.

When the heaving ceased, I washed the sweat from my skin with a cool shower. I learned the hard way to avoid hot water after wielding. Last week after one of our sessions, I collapsed in the shower, only to wake up an hour later with a large bruise on my ass and no recollection of what had happened.

I dried off in a plush towel, not ignoring how the fabric now wrapped around me almost twice. I'd been getting sick so often that I'd been losing weight. Eating had become difficult as well. The more I ate, the more I threw up later on, making it hard to stomach much food.

I moved the towel to my hair, wrapping it around the brittle strands that had yet to fall out. My waves had thinned significantly, but tying it into a braid prevented anyone from noticing.

In the mirror, I observed the reflection of my bare body that felt so foreign. My curves had slimmed down so much that I could feel the bones of my hips starting to protrude. My stomach that had never been completely flat, now sucked in towards my lungs. My finger traced the outlines of my ribs as I puckered my lips, my once rounded cheeks now pale and slightly sunken in.

Sickly was the only word to describe my new figure. Though I used to be self-conscious about my curves, I missed not being able to feel every bone in my body. I could only imagine how I'd look in a few weeks if I kept up like this.

I should have stopped being so stubborn and gone to Sebastian for help. I could ask him to start our wielding schedule up again, but my pride wouldn't let me. He didn't need me, so I didn't need him, either. At least that's what I told myself. But it was bullshit and I knew it.

I pulled a cotton top over my head—the baggy fabric long enough to be worn with just underwear—then went to climb into bed. My vision wavered as I stepped for the mattress and my balance escaped me. My knees hit the ground, and not having the strength to stay on them, I fell sideways, landing on my hip bone.

Sitting up, I groaned in pain and watched a bruise form on my knee. "Fuck," I cursed, fed up with feeling so weak.

While down, I caught a glimpse of something underneath my bed, shimmering from the moonlight that passed through my window panes. I reached my arm out, grabbing hold of the hair clip Pia had let me borrow for the gala.

I turned the accessory around in my palm. Pia received the clip when she was a young girl. She said that she wasn't upset, but I knew it bothered her when we thought it was lost at the party.

The clock ticked on top of my wardrobe. It was almost ten-thirty, but Pia was right down the hall in Kohen's room, and I didn't want to wait to give the clip back to her.

Using the edge of my mattress, I pulled up and steadied myself on my feet. The throbbing in my head was yet to subside, but I powered through it, as always.

I cracked open my door and peered into the hall to make sure there were no soldiers around to catch a glimpse of my underwear. The corridor was dark and silent, so I tiptoed down the hall and knocked on Kohen's door, knowing that Pia would be the one to open it. The knob turned and she slipped out the room, closing the door gently behind her so as to not wake Kohen.

"Everything okay?" she asked, her brows drawn together.

I tossed her the hair clip, and a smile tugged on her cheeks. "You found it?" she cheered, unable to hide her joy.

"Under my bed."

"Why didn't we think to look there." She chuckled. Her eyes roamed over my body briefly before returning to my face. She looked as though she had something to say, but couldn't bring herself to say it.

I raised an eyebrow at her. "What?"

"You look different lately," she stuttered.

"That noticeable?"

She gulped and nodded slowly. "Are you—"

"I'm fine," I cut her off.

"Maeve…Maybe you should talk to Sebastian. Go back to your old training schedule."

"No," I said flatly.

"I'm worried—"

"Pia, please. I'm fine. I promise. Okay?"

She crossed her arms over her chest. "You are barely eating and—"

"Okay, goodnight." My dainty fingers waved her goodbye as I removed myself to go back to my room. I heard Kohen's door shut just before I found myself frozen in the middle of the hallway.

Sebastian's legs came to their own halt when he noticed me walking towards him. He was heading to his room, and unfortunately I had to pass him to get to mine.

"I picked quite the night to roam the halls in nothing but a shirt and underwear," I muttered before sealing my lips. Grabbing the edges of my shirt, I pulled it down further as I resumed walking. I was covered enough, but one wrong move and I risked flashing him more skin than I'd prefer to.

Head down, I moved to squeeze by him, but he reached out and grabbed my wrist, stopping me from going any further. The contact sent a jolt of electricity through my body. It didn't matter how much time had passed or how much anger had been stored within me. My attraction to him was magnetic. It was more than just physical. He was embedded in my soul.

"You're bleeding," he said. His expression was bland. Emotionless.

"Huh?"

He gestured with his eyes and I followed their direction to my knee, leaking drops of crimson blood.

"Shit." The skin must have split when I fell.

He released his grip on my wrist. I held my shirt down with one hand and used the palm of my other to apply pressure to the wound.

"Thanks," I muttered, looking behind me to avoid eye contact and noticing the trail of blood I'd left.

"Sure," he said under his breath. "Do you want a bandage or—"

"I'm fine."

In silence, I held the broken skin until a clot formed, then stood up straight, pausing briefly to let the pounding in my head cease before trying to walk away. My legs trembled when they started to move, but the concern in Sebastian's voice stopped me from proceeding.

"Are you okay?" His wide eyes looked me up and down. "You look…*not* okay."

Weeks ago, I would have told him the truth. But tonight I lied. "Yup," I quipped and brushed past him with nonchalance.

"You're making yourself sick," he called out after me.

"Why do you care?" I didn't think he heard me, but his response told me otherwise.

"Because I care about you."

Raising a brow, I turned my body halfway to look at him. "Really? You have a strange way of showing it."

He frowned, and though I wanted to release the fortress of anger and frustration that had built inside of me ever since the gala, I didn't. It wasn't worth it. It was not like anything would change.

He bit the inside of his cheek then whispered, "Goodnight," before stuffing his hands in his pockets and leaving me in the darkness of the corridor.

Back in my room, I dug my nails into my palm until it bled, grief making my veins swell. I hated this. I hated being so angry with him. Actually, I didn't know if it was even anger I felt towards him anymore. Maybe I was just sad. Disappointed. I didn't know what I felt aside from the fact that I missed him, which was the worst part of all.

CHAPTER TWENTY-SEVEN

"Willawood, get up and put your combat uniform on. Now!" Sawyer's voice screamed through my door, jolting me awake and inducing anxiety all at once.

I flew upright and to the side, falling out of my bed with only the sheet wrapped around me as a cushion. Moaning in pain, I glanced up at the clock. "Fuck, Sawyer, it's five in the morning. What happened to training at night?"

"This isn't for training. Get up and meet me in the hall."

Normally I would argue, but the severity of his tone told me not to.

Wiping the crust from my eyes, I fumbled around in the darkness for my uniform, pulling it on along with my boots. I searched for my cloak, but still half asleep, had no luck in retrieving it.

When I had fulfilled his request, I met Sawyer in the hall, slamming my door behind me. "What could you possibly want from me at five in the morning?" I sneered, a blatant scowl residing across my face.

"I don't want anything. The trials are today."

"Trials?" I asked mid-yawn.

"Soldier trials for the first years."

"First I'm hearing of this."

"Yeah, that's the point. *Surprise.*" He waved his fingers in the air.

"Pretty shitty surprise," I grumbled, shaking my body loose and then following Sawyer's heavy strides.

He led me outside, back to my old dormitory building, where all of the other first years were gathered. We met up with Pia and Kohen, who both looked as exhausted as I felt.

"What exactly happens during these *trials*?" I asked, though I couldn't help but notice the wide-eyed look Kohen and Sawyer gave each other.

"Yeah. And why weren't we told about it?" Pia questioned.

"No one knows when the trials will occur except for King Hawthorne. And we are forbidden to speak of them. The first years aren't allowed to have any time to prepare," Kohen answered.

"What will we be doing?" I asked, reiterating my previous question through my chattering teeth. *Fuck, it was cold for spring.*

"Battling each other," Sawyer replied simply.

"That's it?"

"Well, yeah. Except for the weakest participants will be killed," he added.

My eyelids peeled from my skull and my blood heated enough to stop my shivering. "You're joking." I was so weak right now that I could hardly eat, let alone fight for my life.

"Wish I was."

"How many get killed?" *A.K.A., how many would I have to beat to stay alive?*

"Five."

Five. Just five. Okay. Even at my worst, I was confident that I was stronger than the weakest five—I hoped.

"That's so incredibly fucked up," Pia spat, her skin turning green with nausea.

"We should have at least had a warning," I added with a scowl directed at the head soldiers.

"We can stand here and debate this or you both can shut up and let Kohen and I give you the rundown," Sawyer said as he crossed his arms over his chest.

"I thought you were *forbidden to speak about it*," I mocked, crossing my own arms.

"Do you want to die? Because no offense, Maeve, but you certainly aren't the strongest in your year right now."

"What's that supposed to mean?"

"It means I've been kicking your ass in our training sessions for weeks. Am I wrong?"

My arms fell to my sides in submission.

Kohen interrupted Sawyer and mine's bickering. "You'll each be given a random opponent. You can use your magic and weapons to fight. You win your first trial, you're safe. If you lose, you'll fight another loser. Win that battle, then you're safe. So on and so forth until only five are left."

"Why kill the losers? Why not just let them go home?" Pia asked, her worry adamant in her voice. She didn't need to worry. She was one of the best wielders in our class. She wouldn't be killed, I had no doubt about that. Myself, on the other hand…

"King Hawthorne believes they are too weak to be effective soldiers, but still too much of a threat with their jewels to be kept alive."

"Remove their jewels then," Pia pleaded.

"That's forbidden. You know that," Kohen reminded.

"Oh, but killing innocent people isn't?" I jeered, my eyes rolling so far back that I swear I could see my skull.

"I'll have to have a word with uncle Aldous about this," Pia complained, her face scrunched into a deep scowl.

"Do they do this in our second year, too? Or can you not tell us that either?" I commented, my tone fairly rude.

Sawyer cut in, "Gods, will the two of you just shut up for two damn minutes? We are trying to keep you both from dying!"

With our attention pointed at him, Sawyer continued. "Don't use your magic unless you have to. Preserve your energy. You'll get a choice between a sword and a dagger. I know you don't have much experience with it, but pick the sword."

"Don't be afraid to get some blood on your hands. Do what you have to do to stay alive."

Everyone's head shot around at the sound of Sebastian's voice, except for mine.

Pia won her first trial.

I lost mine.

I lost my second trial, too.

And my third. I was too weak. Too sick.

I hadn't used my magic at all. I wanted to preserve my energy for when I really needed it like Sawyer said. I also didn't want anyone to see how weak I was, but that had already backfired.

There were twenty of us left. If I lost this next battle, I would be in the bottom ten. Only one more loss away from my death.

"You're scaring me, Willawood," Sawyer cautioned.

"Join the club."

"What's going on with you? Stop being stubborn and use your damn magic. It's almost like you *want* to die," he replied.

"You said not to."

"No. I said don't use it unless you have to. And, uh, news flash, you have to."

"He's right. If there's ever been a time to use it, it's now."

With gritted teeth, I slowly spun on my heel to face Sebastian. "No shit."

"Oh sorry. Did I scare you? I meant to approach with caution, I know you can be grumpy in the morning," Sebastian's sarcasm slivered off his tongue with his words.

"What do you want?"

Sebastian scoffed. "Can I have a word alone?"

Not seeing a choice, I stepped away with him.

After making sure no one could overhear us, Sebastian's tone lowered to one of concern. "What's going on? You could have won your first trial if you used your magic. Mind compulsion versus an earth wielder—they would have stood no chance."

"Yeah, maybe I could have won. Or I could have passed out and blew my cover. I'm better off fighting with just my hands," I retorted.

"Just do a simple command, make your opponent freeze in their tracks or some shit. I dunno. Anything!"

I blinked at him. Did he not see the way my muscles had atrophied? Or how I could hardly stand with him now without wobbling on my feet.

"I can't," I said under my breath, not needing to elaborate any further.

"This is exactly why I should be training you. You wouldn't be so weak that you—"

"Maeve Willawood and Deane Jursen, please make your way to mat four," the announcer's voice cut through Sebastian's.

"Gotta go." I practically ran from him, then crouched alongside mat four, taking a few calming breaths in preparation to face my next opponent.

A hand grazed my shoulder, and I looked up, surprised at the company.

"You seem to be having a tough time today," Lucan whispered to me.

"You could say that again."

"What's going on? You haven't even touched your magic."

"I wanted to prove that I could beat my opponents without it," I lied to the king's advisor. "However, I am yet to be successful with that." I rolled back to a sit, drooping my head between my knees. "This is certainly not how I thought I'd die," I whispered back.

Lucan followed my form, clasping his hand over my own. "You will not die." His fingers fumbled around, and he tucked something into my palm before pulling his hand back.

I looked up at him, confusion plastered on my cheeks. "What—"

He held a finger to his lips. "Our little secret," he said, then stood up and left without another word.

I glanced around to make sure no one was looking before I unclenched my fist. I held a small capsule, turquoise and shining in my palm. Ridgeroot—I would know the color of the crushed herb anywhere. Where did he get such a delicacy? And why would he give it to me?

It didn't matter. Ridgeroot had power enhancing abilities, which the gods knew I could use. If I took the capsule, it was cheating. If I didn't, I very well could die.

Quite the moral dilemma.

THE FAMILIES OF THE LOSING SOLDIERS WERE INVITED TO COME TO their executions later that evening.

The wails released from their loved ones as the losers were hung were sounds I would never erase from my memory. I could hear them all the way from my bedchambers, despite closing my window tightly when I arrived back.

I was bloody and bruised from my last trial. I had almost lost again—my attempt to break through my opponent's shield failed. There was too much chaos for me to effectively wield, but I did try. Luckily, I was able to jam the tip of my sword in his thigh, just deep enough to make him bleed, but lame enough to keep him from bleeding out. When he stumbled and fell to his back in agony, I was declared the winner.

He lost his last trial.

I bet it was his mother's sobs I heard from my window.

I cried in the shower, though my tears were not as heavy as those of the losers when they discovered that they would soon die. They tried to run, tried to fight the guards as they pulled them towards the dungeons, but they had no say in their fate.

Dressed but still in shock, it took me a moment to react to the soft knock on my door. I shuffled to the entryway, pulling the handle open to reveal Sawyer.

"Hey."

"Hey," I answered.

"You okay?"

I choked back the truth and nodded.

"Need some company?"
I nodded once more.

CHAPTER TWENTY-EIGHT

The clock hanging on the stone wall ticked loudly, the sound cursing my ear drums. Only minutes left until noon. I leaned against the corridor across from King Hawthorne's study, waiting eagerly for the meeting to begin, simply so I could get it over with.

Footsteps thudded along the floor of the corridor. I didn't look towards the sound, knowing it was Sebastian by the way his boots echoed on the marble.

Even though I hadn't been training with him, he still came to my meetings. The king didn't know that Sawyer had been training and guarding me for the past two and a half months. At least I don't think he did. He probably wouldn't have minded much anyway, as long as I was still doing what he wished.

I stared straight ahead, focusing on the door of the study so I didn't have to make eye contact with Sebastian as he approached. Of course he decided to come stand right beside me, leaning back against the wall and tilting his head to the side towards me.

"Good afternoon."

When I didn't return his greeting, he said, "I'm glad you didn't die."

"Huh?"

"During your trials."

I nodded once, then took a step away from the wall to put some distance between us.

"How long do you plan on avoiding me?" Sebastian asked, grabbing my arm and pulling me back to the wall.

"I'm not avoiding you."

He scoffed. "You're spending time with Sawyer by choice just so you don't have to train with me."

I rolled my eyes, not breaking my gaze from the door. "I like spending time with Sawyer. We're friends. And I just talked to you the other day."

He moved in front of me so that I had no choice but to look at him. I glared into his face, scowling, making sure he knew how unamused I was.

"That was two weeks ago and I hardly consider that a conversation," he argued.

"What could you possibly want to have a conversation about, Crown Prince Hawthorne?"

He ground his jaw at the use of his formal title. "You know what."

I looked over his head at the clock. I'd never been so eager to see the king in my life. I tapped my foot. It was noon. He should open his door any—

"Good afternoon." King Hawthorne's voice bounced off the walls of the corridor as the door to his study flew open.

I sidestepped and marched by Sebastian as if he was not even there, then took my usual seat and crossed my legs. The other two filed in after me, the king shutting the door and moving behind his desk.

He got right to the point, not wasting any time before completely fucking up my day. "Duke Sinclair has located three more traitorous Caelestians, whom he has dealt with. However it seems that Draemor is still receiving information about our kingdom and you, Maeve. We are unsure how he's obtaining this information."

I sat still and silent as he went on.

"We suspect that there could be someone within the walls of the castle who is delivering this information to Cyprian. The things he's aware of are not things that are public knowledge to most Caelestians."

I twiddled my thumbs as Sebastian moved to take a seat next to me. I fought my eyes from wandering to him as King Hawthorne slid a piece of parchment across his desk to me—a letter from King Beaumont.

To the Ruler of Caelestis,

I present you with one last opportunity to turn over Maeve Willawood to the Kingdom of Draemor. As I have previously offered, in return, I will cease all hazards that threaten your civilians. If you decline, prepare your soldiers for relentless bloodshed. My army will not fall back until the eastern territory belongs to Draemor, and until Maeve Willawood is under my reign.

All the best,

Cyprian Beaumont

I pushed the letter back to him, disregarding Sebastian's hand that tried to grab it to read as well. Unfortunately the king ruined my pettiness by passing him the letter himself.

Sebastian scanned the paper, showcasing how fast of a reader he was. "This is just the same shit he's been threatening us with for months."

"I am aware," the king responded calmly.

A muscle in Sebastian's jaw ticked. "I thought you were supposed to be taking care of this."

"I have it under control."

"Clearly you don't. Beaumont is just getting more insistent that he'll have Maeve no matter what—war or no war."

"He will not take her. Unless there's a good enough reason for me to give her up willingly, that is." King Hawthorne raised an eyebrow. "Is there?"

Sebastian crossed his arms, his muscles flexing under his shirt. "There's not," he growled.

"Then I suppose we best prepare for war."

"Seriously? That's the best you got?"

"What do you suggest, soldier?"

"Hm, I dunno maybe—"

I sighed loudly at their bickering, interrupting them.

"Something wrong, Miss Willawood?" King Hawthorne diverted his eyes to me.

I covered my mouth and yawned. "Nope, just waiting for you both to finish so I can go get lunch." I smirked under my hand, knowing my comment would piss them both off.

He glowered at me, removing his attention from Sebastian and changing the subject. "How are your wielding sessions going, Maeve?"

I shuffled in my seat. The king had never called me by my first name before. "They are going well, Your Majesty."

"Are you sure? Because you look even weaker than when I saw you two weeks ago." He squinted his eyes at me. "I can imagine it's difficult to harness effective magic when you look like you haven't even eaten lunch in days."

Ouch.

"Not to mention how you embarrassed me at the trial. That was absolutely *pitiful*," he spat.

I swallowed audibly and could feel Sebastian's eyes on me. "I am sure, sir. That was just an off day. I have become very successful with harnessing my magic."

King Hawthorne looked down at his desk. "Good to hear, however…" The corner of his lip quirked up in a devious smile.

My heart pounded in my chest, anticipating what he was about to demand from me.

He pushed off from his desk, towering over where I sat. "While I have you here, I would love for you to show me an example of your power. Seeing as you seemed to have an *off day* at the trial."

Yeah. Saw that one coming.

I shoved down the feeling of panic that began to overcome me. It would be fine. I'd just use a super basic command. He wouldn't know any different. He just wanted to make sure I could actually use my powers.

"Of course, Your Highness."

The king gestured to Sebastian, who looked awfully pale all of a sudden. "Assist her please," he demanded.

Sebastian and I rose to our feet, facing each other. There was something unspoken between us. I knew he was worried about me using my magic, but wouldn't say it in fear of what would happen if his father discovered how strenuous it was for me. We could have faked it, but the risk was not worth it. So we stared at each other, both on the same page about what we needed to do.

"Whenever you're ready," the king said.

I adjusted my posture, racking my brain for a command that I knew wouldn't take too much out of me, but found it difficult to think of one. Training as much and as hard as I had been has made almost every compulsion draining.

Sebastian noted my apprehension. "Make me unsheathe my dagger," he suggested.

I nodded. That was a good idea. Simple.

The king interfered before I could begin. "I was thinking something more like," he tapped a finger on his chin, "commanding my son to utilize his magic to…hm…coat the floor of this room in a layer of ice."

Shit.

Shit. Shit. Shit.

Queasiness flooded my stomach, but I had no choice but to do as he said. Sebastian's skin turned even paler, and though I know he wanted to, he didn't argue with his father.

Please don't pass out. Please don't puke. Please just keep it together until you're out of this room.

I took Sebastian's hands in mine, knowing the contact would

make this at least a little bit easier. I shivered at the connection, but focused on what I needed to do.

The waves of the ocean pooled in my mind, the feel of them flowing over my skin as I dived beneath the surface. Delani laughed by my side as we swam. My mother stroked my hair, whispering my nickname to me as I dozed off. My star. My star.

I created visions in my brain of the things that usually calmed my thoughts enough to release my powers, but none of them worked.

The king cleared his throat.

My breathing shook. I was about to blow this.

Sebastian squeezed my hand lightly, either encouraging me to start, or in acknowledgement of my doubt.

You got this, he mouthed to me.

I breathed in deeply, and thought of the one thing that never failed to calm me—even when I was in the midst of a mega argument with that person.

Closing my eyes, I relived the first time I saw Sebastian at the Jewel-Light Ceremony, and how he quite literally stole my breath. I recreated the feel of his arms around me when he first embraced me. I thought of the soft plushness of his lips against mine when we kissed.

I may have still been hurt and angry, but I missed him.

The softness of Sebastian's voice cracked through the barrier of my mind. "Ready?"

Nodding hesitantly, I blew out a breath and released the compulsion onto him. "Cover this floor in ice."

The temperature of the room dropped as soon as the command left the confines of my mind. Sebastian released me, using his diamond to harness the magic I'd requested from him.

My eyes flinched open at the sound of ice crackling beneath my feet. Shards of frosted glass pooled from his fingertips as Sebastian formed a crystalline sheath over the marble tiles.

I held my concentration on the command, and he was about halfway done when I started to feel lightheaded. Sweat dripped from my forehead as an influx of nausea came and went. I clenched my fists, trying to disregard the sickness that threatened to break my control. I fought through the pain, rolling over my memories of Sebastian again and again until I felt my magic halt with the commencement of his powers.

I opened my eyes slowly, my lashes wiping away the darkness that clouded my vision. A translucent blanket of ice stood firm under my feet, shining so clearly that I could see my reflection. I smiled at my success.

Sebastian studied me intently, waiting for me to show any signs of collapsing. The all too familiar twinge in my skull appeared, and I knew that if I didn't get out of here soon, I risked showing the king how much the command took out of me.

"Amazing," King Hawthorne said in awe as he inspected the frozen floor of his study. He came towards me, close enough that I could smell the fear mongering on his breath. "If you continue training as you are, soon you will be the most powerful mortal in the world. The things you will be able to do to others, will make you unstoppable."

With a sudden shift in disposition, he stepped back and clasped his hands together. "That's all for today. You both may be excused."

Relief washed over me, and I had never moved as quickly as I did then. I burst through the doors and into the corridor which luckily, was empty. Sebastian followed me out of the study, making a point to close the door tightly behind him.

My vision blurred again with my sudden movement. I stumbled to the nearest wall and pushed my temple against it, using the stone to try and block out the agony that was cracking my skull.

Firm pressure from Sebastian's palm rubbed my back. I wanted to push him away, but had no extra energy to waste. My stomach was in shambles, and I needed to find a washroom before I created a mess in this hallway.

Just when I thought I was getting some control back, my head sent a shooting pain down my nerves and my eyesight tunneled. I began to waver in and out of consciousness.

Sebastian's voice said my name, but I was not lucid enough to respond. My body shook with fragility. I was close to blacking out when I recognized the feel of his arms as they wrapped around me, unsticking me from the wall and pulling me upright.

He supported most of my weight as he rushed us through the hallway. We stopped in an abandoned corridor away from the study, though I was too senseless to make out exactly where we were.

My head bobbed as Sebastian helped lower me to the ground. I struggled to stay awake, my surroundings fading from my view. Was he talking to me? I couldn't make out the words. Why was he speaking so softly?

Everything was so dark. Black like the night, aside from two twinkling, cerulean stars that shone right into my eyes, trying to rope me back in.

There they went, flickering away with the rest of the world.

I came jolting back when something bone-chilling grazed my clammy skin. My eyes snapped open and I lifted my heavy head to meet Sebastian's gaze latched on to me.

His hand was pressed against my forehead, the other resting on my shoulder, preventing me from toppling over. I shivered as he pulled his hand from my temple and flashed me his palm, coated in a thick layer of ice.

I glanced around, allowing myself a moment to recall what happened. I was too weak, but tried to stand up anyway, only for Sebastian to hold me down.

"Don't get up." His voice was stern and demanding.

I cleared my throat. "Let me go. I'm fine."

"Absolutely not," he growled. "You are *not* fine, Maeve. Stop telling me that you are. Nothing about any of this is fine."

I looked away from him, but he grabbed hold of my face and forced me to listen.

"You are going to kill yourself if you keep this up. You're *sick*, and it shows. You think I haven't noticed that you can't eat? And I know why, so don't even try to give me some bullshit excuse."

My heart skipped a beat at the idea of him paying attention to me in such detail that he knew if I was showing up to meals or not. But I rolled my eyes at him. Who was he to act like he cared now? "I know how I look. You and everyone else have no trouble telling me that I look like crap," I snarled.

He released me and his expression softened into a more sympathetic one. "I don't mean it like that." He laid his hand on my arm, but I shrugged it off.

His mouth drew into a tight line. "You need to let me train you again. That's an order."

"You of all people don't get to order me around."

"At least let me tell Sawyer what's going on so he can take it easy on you. You two can stick to the plan we had."

"I'm surprised you haven't told him already," I croaked out.

"Oh trust me. I want to and am very close to doing so if you don't let me help."

I could tell that he was struggling to have patience with me, but I didn't give him the satisfaction of agreeing. I stared at him blankly, telling him no without verbally responding.

Sebastian rose to his full height and ran his hands through his hair. "Fuck, Maeve!" he shouted out of pure frustration. "I hate seeing you like this. Please just let me help you," he begged.

Not caring if I pissed him off, I gave him the two-word answer that he was no doubt sick of hearing. "I'm fine."

He threw his arms up, and I just sat and watched him in awe. How could someone who went from wanting me, to wanting nothing to do with me in a matter of minutes, now stand here and claim that he cared. It didn't make sense. *He* didn't make sense.

I pushed myself off of the ground, fighting my knees as they quivered and quaked. Once stable, I stepped towards him. He straightened his posture, and I looked right into his face.

"I don't understand you," I said with a shake of my head.

"I don't understand *you*! You're being so damn stubborn, it's unbelievable. I don't know why you just won't let me help you!"

"Have you considered that maybe I'm not being stubborn, that maybe I really just don't want to be around you?"

I can't be around you.

"I don't care if you want me around or not. You need help and—"

"You have made it perfectly clear, Sebastian, that you don't care what I want," I flared, and he knew exactly what I was referring to.

His lips parted slightly as if he was going to speak, but I dismissed myself from the situation before he got the chance.

The walk back to my room made for quite the journey as I stumbled over my own feet and battled the blurriness of my eyes. Fortunately, I made it back just in time for me to black out on my bed.

CHAPTER TWENTY-NINE

"We're taking the night off, Willawood! Get your ass to Kohen's room. We're getting drunk tonight!" Sawyer's voice called through my door.

"I literally just finished putting my training uniform on," I yelled back through the wall. I couldn't complain though—everyone and their mother knew that I could use a break from wielding.

"Do you need help getting it off?"

My head shook with my laughter. "I think I'll manage."

I discarded my uniform, switching it out for a pair of black lounge pants and casual shirt, both of which hung off of me. I wondered if the tailor would take my clothes in. I'd have to remember to ask next time I saw her.

Pia and Jocelyn were already sipping on a glass of wine when I arrived at Kohen's room. Sawyer lounged on the bed, throwing his dagger in the air and catching it between his fingers. "See you got your uniform off all right," he sneered with a smirk.

"Screw off."

Jocelyn jumped up when she saw me. "Hey, Maevey baby! How are you?" she slurred and squeezed me into a hug.

My eyes widened. Was she drunk already?

Maevey baby? I mouthed to Pia over Jocelyn's shoulder.

I don't know, Pia mouthed back with a shrug.

Jocelyn seemed to be part of our group now. I wasn't fond of her at first—I found her to be almost *too* nice. But her personality added something peppy to our friend group, and I was pretty sure that Sawyer still had a thing for her as well, despite his joke about my uniform.

Kohen came out of the washroom to join us, drying his honey brown hair with a towel. "No Seb?" he asked, and Sawyer shook his head.

Sebastian's absence didn't surprise me. I would have been more surprised if he *did* show up.

"He's been so antisocial lately, it's driving me crazy," Kohen complained.

My mouth lowered unwillingly. I shouldn't care, but I couldn't help but wonder if Sebastian was okay.

"Maybe he'll come by later," Pia chimed in, glancing at me with half a grin.

"Doubt it," Sawyer muttered, then turned to me with a forgiving smirk. "What can I get you to drink, Maevey baby?"

I flipped him my middle finger.

"Something strong? Coming right up."

Sawyer didn't mess around when it came to training, and he didn't mess around when it came to making drinks, either. The room was spinning under my feet within an hour of my arrival.

"I swear I'm telling the truth!" Pia yelled.

"I call bullshit," Sawyer retorted.

We'd been playing a drinking game, and Pia was trying to convince everyone that she had a vision as a child that she would be gifted by Eloise.

"No one believes you, Pia. Just drink," Kohen decided her fate.

"I swear! She came to me in my dream. Like floating through the air in a violet gown."

"Yeah. And Thea showed up at my first birthday party to light the candles," Sawyer mocked.

"I believe you," Jocelyn sputtered, waving her drink in the air.

Pia looked at me for my approval.

"Sorry," I shrugged, "I'm gonna have to agree with the guys on this one."

"Oh whatever," Pia grumbled but gave in, the others cheering as she finished her goblet.

"I'll ask Sawyer one next," Kohen said.

"Oh great." Sawyer rolled his eyes. "Go for it."

Kohen tapped a finger to his chin. "Last time you had sex?"

"Would you believe me if I told you last night?"

"Hell no. I was with you last night, and we sure as hell didn't fuck," Kohen snorted, then passed him the bottle. "Drink up, liar."

Sawyer pointed his bottle at me. "Your turn, Maevey—"

"Shut up."

His lips quirked up.

"Yeah, Maeve, it's way past your turn!" Pia squealed.

They were all so drunk that I'd been able to convince them for the past half hour that it was someone else's turn whenever mine came up, but they finally caught on.

"Ugh fine. Who's asking the question?"

Jocelyn raised her hand then stood up and walked over to me. Stumbled over to me, rather. The girl should have been in bed—she had no idea what was going on. She wouldn't remember a thing in the morning.

Jocelyn plopped herself down on the floor in front of me. I could smell the wine on her like she was wearing it as perfume. Someone had better cut her off.

"Okay, Maevey baby." She contemplated her question, then smiled and asked after taking a sip of her drink, "Have you ever been in love?"

Everything inside of me shut down. Yes—I'd been in love. I *was* in love. Unfortunately the guy I was in love with didn't love me back.

"Why would you ask that?" Pia whispered to her, although it was loud enough for me to hear.

All of the eyes in the room were on me, waiting for my answer, but I would not give it. Alcohol and feelings didn't mix well.

There was no point in trying to convince them of a lie. I reached my hand out to Sawyer. "Pass me the bottle."

"Oh, come on," Kohen complained. "That was a stupid question. We all know she's in love with—"

Pia slapped her hand over his mouth.

I gestured for the bottle again, drinking more than I should have when it was finally in my hand.

It was well past midnight by the time we all cleared out of Kohen's room and made for our own. The rest of the evening was a mess. Our game—which rules seemed to change with each round—ended with Jocelyn's hands all over Sawyer's suddenly bare chest. We called it a night when Jocelyn got sick. Luckily she made it to the washroom, but Kohen was still undone over it.

Sawyer walked with me back to my room, shirt slung over his shoulder. He tugged it on when we stopped outside of my door. "Do you need any assistance getting into pajamas?"

I snorted in laughter. "You are the definition of a typical guy."

Sawyer chuckled. "Night, Maevey—"

I punched him in the arm. "Don't say it."

He smiled. "Goodnight."

"Night."

I let myself into my room and flopped down on my bed, gazing up at the spinning ceiling. I closed my eyes, but just as it did every evening, my mind wandered to Sebastian.

He never showed up to join us and I wondered why. Him and I were at odds, but it was still not like him to miss out on an evening with his friends.

I rolled to my side. Where did everything go so wrong? Things were good before all hell broke loose at the gala. The way he kissed me...You didn't kiss someone like that if you didn't want them—if you didn't *need* them.

I knew he felt something for me—his blatant concern lately made that obvious. He was denying himself in a sick and twisted form of self-sabotage that I wished he would give up so he could admit he liked me, too.

Oh well, I guess. I was too drunk to care.

That's a lie. I do really care. Way too much.

I sat up right, my feet dangling over the edge of my bed. This was ridiculous. At this point, being angry at Sebastian was a waste of energy. It'd been over two months of silence, when it could have been two months of us being together or at least being friends.

Maybe the alcohol was altering my thinking, or maybe I'd just finally had enough. Either way, I was going to talk to him.

I crept out of my room and down the hall, stopping in front of his door. I raised my fist to knock, then dropped it. I lifted my hand again, only for it to fall back at my side. It was late and he was probably sleeping. This could wait.

Pivoting on my heel, I began to walk away. But then, my courage grabbed me by the throat, and against my better judgment, I took a deep breath and banged on his door.

I realized my mistake as soon as I retracted my fist.

Fuck.

I should have ran back to my room. Locked myself in it and never allowed myself freedom again. This was stupid. I was stupid and drunk.

I was ready to make a run for it when the door pulled open with such force that it startled me.

Sebastian's hair was disheveled and his abs…*Focus on his face, Maeve, not the fact that he's not wearing a shirt.*

"Everything okay?" he questioned, his voice rough from sleep and his eyebrows raised.

I should have lied, said yes, and turned around. But I already made it this far. "No, *Crown Prince Hawthorne.* Everything's not okay."

His eyes scanned me up and down. "Are you hurt?"

"No." I pushed by him, inviting myself into his room.

He closed the door and leaned against it, folding his arms over his chest. "Then what are you doing here?"

I copied his movement, crossing my arms over my own chest. "I'm here because I'm mad."

"Shocking," he quipped.

My brows furrowed at him.

He sighed, pushing off of the door and moving towards me. "Why are you mad?"

"I'm mad at *you*." I pointed a finger at him.

"Yeah, I've gathered that from how you've been avoiding me for two months."

"It's been longer than that."

"Oh, I'm well aware. Seventy-nine days, to be exact."

"Woah…That's a lot of days," I slurred, tottering a little where I stood.

"Are you drunk?"

"A little, but that's beside the point."

Sebastian pulled the chair out from his desk. "Sit down," he instructed, then brought me a glass of water as I pulled my legs up into my chest.

He sat down on the edge of his bed, leaning back on his arms, watching me with a slight smile on his face.

"What?" I asked.

"Hm?"

"Why are you staring at me?"

He spit out a laugh. "I'm waiting for you to tell me why you're here."

"Oh."

After a few moments of silence, I said, "Things are already pretty shitty between us, so I suppose I can't make it any worse, right?"

Sebastian's smile faded. "Maeve, listen—"

"No. Let me talk."

He closed his mouth and nodded, giving me his undivided attention.

"What you did to me really sucked," I stated, sucking in a breath of air before continuing. "The reason why I think you did it sucks even more."

Sebastian leaned back further on his hands and drew in a breath, his abdomen flexing and rippling. "And what reason might that be?"

"Well, I can only assume, seeing as you keep your feelings under lock and key, but *I think* that *you think* you're unworthy of love. That because of your past you don't deserve love. And I don't know who you used to be, but I know who you are now, and I know that you are a good person who deserves good things."

"This probably isn't the best time to talk about this," Sebastian murmured, shuffling on the edge of the mattress.

Rising from the chair, I took a few wobbly steps towards him with a silencing finger held against my lips.

"Despite how you may feel, to deny yourself of being happy..." I shook my head. "It's not fair to yourself. It's not fair to me or to anyone else you're with, if there is someone."

The alcohol in my stomach bubbled up my throat at the idea of him being with someone else. Maybe I'd misread the whole situation. Maybe he really just didn't want to be with me. Maybe he just wanted a hookup that night. Regardless, I swallowed the spit in my mouth. "I don't care how much you try to deny it, I know the truth. I know the night of the gala that you wanted me just as much as I wanted you—as much as I *still* want you."

His mandible ticked as I moved close enough to smell his skin. "So stop being an ass and pushing the people you care about away. Allow yourself to be happy. You deserve it, even if you think you don't."

Sebastian looked up into my eyes, which gleamed with a few stray tears. I hadn't even realized I'd been crying. As I said before, alcohol and feelings didn't mix.

He reached a hand up and brushed a lock of hair behind my ear. "First of all, there's no one else," he whispered, and I exhaled in relief. "Second, I'm sorry. For all of it. For pushing you away time and time again. For the crap I pulled at the gala. For not apologizing to you sooner."

I bit my cheek. "That part is my fault. You kept trying to talk to me and I wouldn't let you. If I hadn't been so stubborn…" My head shook. "I've lost so much time by being angry with you."

"None of this is your fault. I just get so caught up in my own head that I—"

"I know." He didn't need to elaborate. I knew how complicated his mind was. How complex his thinking could be.

"What you said to me at the gala, it freaked me the fuck out, for lack of better words. I realized that I felt the same about you and just hadn't admitted it to myself yet. It's been eating away at me since that night, but I didn't want to push too hard for you to talk to me. I figured I'd blown my chances with you. And you and Sawyer have gotten pretty close, so I figured maybe something was going on there. Hence why I've been kinda a dick lately."

My nose scrunched. "Me and Sawyer? No chance." Him and I were just friends. Nothing more than that.

Sebastian huffed a deep breath, then dragged his eyes back to mine. "I want to be with you more than I want anything else in the world, and that is the truth."

I sniffled at his admission and suddenly felt very sober.

"Don't cry."

"I'm not crying."

"Right." He grinned as he wiped the tears from my cheeks.

When he removed his hand, I placed my back towards him and took a few steps away. My heart stuttered in my chest, my palms sweating. I should have let him talk to me when he tried. Instead, I spent months being stubborn and foolish.

"Come back here." His demand was soft spoken.

I hesitated, knowing what would happen if I did. But despite the what ifs, I turned back around and as our eyes locked, the months of agony and uncertainty dissipated. It was just him and I.

"Why?" I asked under my breath.

"To make up for lost time."

Was I ready for this? After everything?

Yes.

I lunged for him and he grabbed the back of my knees, pulling me down onto his lap. My arms wrapped over his bare shoulders, clasping behind his neck. He pulled my hair into his fist and pushed it behind my neck, then his lips crashed into mine.

Our mouths moved in an exquisite dance of lust, enhanced by the unspoken love that I knew we both felt but were yet to admit to each other. My neck tilted back and he leaned forward to deepen the kiss. His tongue explored my mouth in a tangled frenzy, hastily discovering every part of it.

"I worry I won't be able to give you enough—what you deserve." His voice was light and airy when it broke through our kiss.

"I'll take whatever you have to give, and that will be more than enough."

He stared intently for a few seconds, like he was trying to decide if he believed me. He should, as I meant every word of what I'd said tonight.

"Gods, you are beautiful," he growled before needily resuming our kiss. I flushed at the compliment. Knowing that he saw me as such even though I'd become so frail made me want him even more.

His hands roamed delicately down my back, pulling me closer to his chest. He kissed me like I was the reason he was alive. My nipples peaked under my shirt as his hands moved further down my body, stopping to cup my ass. My body was serenaded in new sensations as he held me down on his lap.

Gods.

My fingers slid from his neck and down his chest, lingering on the hard ridges of his muscles. I adjusted myself on his lap—he was hard beneath me as my hips gyrated on him. He released a breathy moan into my mouth, which sent shivers of euphoria straight to my core.

This.

This feeling was what I'd been missing my whole entire life.

Him.

He nipped at my bottom lip then pulled away without notice, breaking the pure exhilaration that I drowned in.

My eyebrows drew together. "Why'd you stop?" I asked, my lips swollen from our kiss.

"Because you're drunk, and if we go any further, I don't know that I'll be able to stop."

"I'm not that drunk." I frowned.

He chuckled. "You're drunk enough."

As badly as I wanted him, he was right. We should wait. We had time.

He locked his arms around me and laid back on his bed, pulling me down with him. I rolled to my side and laid there absorbing his features, memorizing every detail.

I released a deep breath, letting in the exhaustion I'd been fighting off. I put my hand over my mouth as I yawned, hoping he didn't see how tired I was. I was not ready for this to end—not when I'd waited so long for it.

"Now what?" I asked through another yawn.

He pulled me deeper into his chest, and I rested my head in the crook of his arm, soaking in his scent as he weaved his fingers through my hair.

"Now we sleep."

I WOKE UP WITH A THROBBING HEADACHE FROM MY NIGHT OF drinking. Though the elation I felt from finally being in the arms of the man I'd yearned after for months, helped lessen the ache. I blinked the sleep from my eyes and peered over at him.

Sebastian looked so tranquil lying there, and I wondered if sleep was the only time he truly felt at peace. If I could take the pain of his past and place it in my own soul, I would. I'd remove all the horrible memories from his brain and harbor them within mine.

His eyes fluttered open, brightening when they saw me. "Good morning," he said groggily, his voice coarse.

I couldn't help but grin. "Good morning."

He rolled to his side to face me, reaching a finger out to stroke my chin. "Did you sleep okay?"

I nodded. "You?"

"Best I have in a while."

My cheeks flushed. He stared at me for a while, absorbing me like I had just done to him, before placing a light kiss on my lips.

"Does this mean you're going to let me train you again?" he asked when he pulled back to yawn and rub his eyes.

"I don't know how much training we'd get done." I giggled.

"That may be a good thing. You need a break."

"Fine." I sighed. When it came to him, it didn't take much for me to surrender.

"Good. Your first instruction is to take a week off." He rolled on top of me, planting a kiss on my nose. "We'll keep it on the down low, no one has to know if you don't want them to."

"Are you talking about training or about you and I?" I teased.

His face turned serious. "Both, I guess. If you don't want anyone knowing about this, then that's your choice and I'll respect it."

I pushed my hand on his chest and he backed up a bit so that I could sit up on his lap. His arms wrapped around me, supporting me from behind. "It's not that." I shook my head. "I'm pretty sure Sawyer and Kohen have an idea about what's going on with us, anyway. And Pia knew I liked you before I even did."

"She's too good." Sebastian shook his head in amazement.

"I'm just worried about what will happen if your father finds out."

"Screw him."

I flaunted the worry in my eyes. "What if he just sees us as a distraction to each other? He could choose to give me to Draemor if he thinks I'm not going to be useful to him anymore."

His voice was stern. "Remember when I told you that I wouldn't let anything happen to you?"

I bit my lip. How could I forget?

"I meant that to the very depths of my soul. I know you don't need me to, but I will always protect you against anyone, or anything. Including my father."

My heart very literally melted at his words. I leaned up and kissed him softly. I loved him. Eventually I'd tell him that, but not yet. I'd already poured enough of myself out and didn't want to overwhelm him.

My lips reluctantly pulled from his and found themselves instantly missing the feel of his mouth, but I had something I needed to take care of.

"Where are you going?" He raised a brow as I climbed out of bed.

Knowing that I had the day free of wielding and therefore, puking, I stated, "To the kitchen. I'm fucking starving."

CHAPTER
THIRTY

Chaos surrounded me.

In the courtyard of the castle, I stood alone aside from the statues that circled me. Unsettling screams of cruel agony circulated the air. The inescapable smell of burning flesh filled my nostrils as I spun around, absorbing the massacre before me.

"Sebastian?" I called out, though he was nowhere to be seen.

I crossed the cobblestone over piles of deceased bodies. Cartilage crunched under my feet as I stepped on the charred skin of someone's loved one, the corpse still burning when I walked by it.

Hot blood sunk into my eyes, turning my vision red. I looked up towards the heavens. The sky was ablaze, though not with flame, but with death.

Caelestis was under attack. That was the only explanation for this. Draemor finally struck when King Hawthorne refused to hand me over.

I gazed at my feet, watching as the death beneath me was swallowed by fog.

This was my fault.

Recentering myself in the courtyard, I ignored the cracking

bones under my boots. The world was being consumed by a thick veil of haze, and I couldn't see anything within a few inches of me.

"My star." My nickname called to me in a whisper.

My mother—the only one who called me that. I gazed sightless through the haze for her, but she was not there.

Pain swelled in my chest. I couldn't stop it. Couldn't stop the death. The agony. My face twinged with the feeling of false magic—I had no power in a battle this large.

I was useless.

"Maeve," the same shrouded voice hummed my name. A feminine hand reached out of the clouded space, shining and white, beckoning for me to take it.

I did. Without hesitation.

Spindly fingers of stone weaved themselves between mine. *"You can stop this,"* the voice said, and though I couldn't physically see a face, I could picture her.

Her image flashed through my mind. Illuminated silver hair flowed down past her back with strands of aqua that matched her glittering eyes. Her lips and cheeks were pale, and her skin sparkled despite the darkness around us. She was ornate with her aura of peace.

"I am too weak."

"You are far from weak." Her mineral fingers wiped the blood from my face, her light skin contrasted by the deep crimson.

"You have the stars on your side." Her voice echoed within the walls of my mind.

I shook my head in denial. "The kingdom's on fire, and I'm the one who caused it."

"Maybe so, but you will also be the one to stop it. Do not fight the sacrifice, as it is well worth the reward."

Her voice faded away as her hand pulled back into the veil of nothingness. She absorbed back into the mist, leaving me alone in the turmoil of war to be swallowed by a bloodcurdling scream.

My own scream.

I shot straight up in my bed, panting and choking on my own lungs. My forehead was soaked with sweat, stray pieces of hair plastered to it. I clutched the star pendant to my chest, rubbing it beneath my fingers as I settled my breathing. My insides burned like they were on fire.

It was just a dream. A nightmare, rather. Though it seemed more real than that. Like a horrific, twisted hallucination.

My gut told me that the woman I saw was the one responsible for my constellastones, but I had not envisioned her face long enough to know for sure.

The horror of the dream clung to my brain like sap. I gagged at the smell of rotting flesh that I swore lingered in my nose.

Although only a dream, it raised more questions about the prophecy, specifically the sacrifice. I'd been meaning to search the archives for more information, but have been too exhausted from all of my wielding. I also worried that I'd find something that I was better off not knowing. Outside my window, the obsidian sky was completely starless, the only light was that of the silver moon. Sleep seemed impossible after what I just experienced, so I decided now was as good of a time as ever to make my way to the archives.

I crept through the soldiers' corridors, down the staircase, and into the foyer of the castle. The halls were dimly lit, making it difficult to recognize where I was. I'd never really walked the castle this time of night, but was surprised to see there was no one else out for an evening venture. There were guards stationed throughout, but they did a good job at staying hidden. I reached the archives without seeing a soul.

Like the corridors, the library was vaguely lit this time of night. I looked up along the cylindrical walls of books, noticing that one floor was brighter than the rest—the one floor I needed to be on. Of course someone was up there.

I considered going back to my room, but ultimately decided against it. I wasn't doing anything wrong by being out this late. As long as whoever was up there didn't get nosey about my book choices, there was nothing to worry about.

I made straight for the portion of the endless bookshelf that had the manuscripts on the gods. My finger ran down the spine of my chosen book, sliding it off of the shelf. I studied the cover as I had many times before. There must have been an answer to explicitly explain why Blythe chose me. Out of everyone in our world, why did I have the characteristics she wanted fulfilled to grant her gift? I must be missing something.

"What are you doing here so late?"

I jumped, dropping the book from my hands at the sound of Sebastian's voice behind me.

I turned to face him, adrenaline coursing through me. "On the gods, you just scared the life out of me."

He bent down to pick up my book then passed it back to me. "Sorry."

When I got a good look at him, my head cocked to the side and my body tensed. He wore a pair of brown, square-framed glasses that somehow made him look even hotter. "You wear glasses?"

"Shit, uh yeah." He reached up to take them off, but I caught his wrist, guiding his hand back down.

"I didn't know you had glasses." I smirked, releasing my grip and accepting my book from his outstretched hand.

"Just for reading. Even then, I usually only wear them if I'm going to be studying for a while."

"Is that why *you're* here so late? Studying?"

The corner of his lip tugged up. "Not particularly. Just reading." He turned, walking back to where he had been sitting, and I followed him.

His reading material laid open on the chair. The book was small, and the pages looked handwritten.

"More obscene literature?" I teased, thinking back to the romance novel I caught him reading when we first met.

His cheeks flushed as if I embarrassed him, but he smiled. "Once again, it's not obscene," he argued.

I peered over, trying to get a better look, but he grabbed the book and hurriedly shoved it away into his rucksack, taking a new book out to replace it.

"Now why are you here?" he asked while lowering himself into his chair. "Without a guard, I should add."

"I couldn't sleep." I shrugged, choosing not to tell him about my dream. Or my vision? Hallucination? Whatever it was, I refrained in the fear of sounding crazy.

He glared at me through the tops of his glasses. "Why not?"

I took a deep breath in, releasing it and then sealing my lips tightly shut. I didn't want to relive that nightmare again.

"Got it. I won't keep asking."

I gave him a half grin and sat in the chair next to him, turning my attention to the reason I was really here. The pages of my book skimmed my fingertips as I looked for something to solve the mystery that'd been consuming so much space in my brain.

Sebastian and I sat in silence while we read, simply enjoying each other's presence. About an hour in, I became too frustrated to continue and slammed my book shut with a groan of annoyance.

Sebastian looked up from his novel. "What's wrong?"

"This book is useless. I've read it time and time again, and there's no indication on what the sacrifice is," I complained.

"Maybe it's not meant to be solved until it comes true."

"Maybe…"

He stared at me, knowing that I was not done.

"How is it that no one seems to know about the prophecy?"

"This archive in particular holds centuries worth of manuscripts, many of which just get lost in time. Forgotten about. There's also never really been a reason to study Blythe until you."

"I'm going to go see if there's anything else in that section that might be useful before I leave," I said as I climbed from my chair.

I searched the shelves high and low, but came across nothing that could be of any use to me. Maybe Sebastian was right—the prophecy wasn't meant to be solved.

The thought sent me spiraling in fear over my potential impending death, but I clung to the words from the woman in my dream. *Do not fight the sacrifice, as it is well worth the reward.*

I turned back towards our chairs to tell him that I was leaving, but did not see Sebastian. I scanned the space until I spotted him on the other side of the room, putting his novel back on the shelf.

"You finished that already?" I questioned as I approached him.

"I'm a fast reader."

His finger beckoned me closer to him, and when I obliged, he wrapped his arms around my waist, pulling me into his chest. He smiled down at me, then dipped his head to kiss me. I welcomed the contact, my lips parting just enough for his tongue to slip between them.

It was a brief kiss, though it felt more intimate than our others. He pulled away too soon, leaving my lips aching for more.

"I really screwed myself out of kissing you while I was being stubborn for all those weeks," I snarked while tucked away in his arms, my head resting against his chest.

"It's okay. Gave me more time to practice."

My eyes widened. "You better be joking."

He laughed, "Of course I am," then pressed his lips to the top of my head.

I glanced up from the warmth of his chest to the bookshelf behind him. "What erotica do you plan to read next?"

"How many times must I tell you that I don't read erotica?" He chuckled, fighting back a smirk.

"Are you sure? You tucked that book away awfully fast earlier."

Sebastian leaned towards my ear, dropping his voice to a whisper. "I don't need to read erotica when I can make my own."

I chewed on my lip, understanding what he was suggesting, but not acknowledging it.

Leaning back, I bent my neck up to get a better view of the bookshelf behind him. My finger tapped against my chin, stopping to point at a novel that grabbed my attention. "How about that one? Sounds dirty." I winked at him.

His head shook with laughter, then he moved his arms down my back and under my behind, scooping me up in one swift motion. I raised my arms to his shoulders and locked my legs around him, giggling as I clung to him like a vine for support. He spun us around, placing my back against the bookshelf and holding me there. Our heads were at the same height, so when his lips captured mine in a needy kiss, neither of us were straining our necks.

My eyes fluttered closed as my tongue slipped between his lips. He kissed me back greedily, as if he could never have enough of me.

Books fell from the shelves around us, but neither of us gave the interruption any attention.

His lips were smooth as they caressed mine in jumbled, enticing movements. Sebastian moved one arm from underneath me, tearing his glasses from his face and throwing them to the side, the lack of barrier allowing us to deepen our kiss.

He returned his hand to my ass, holding my back against the bookshelf for support. I fisted the front of his shirt, trying to pull him closer despite there being no gap to close.

We devoured each other hungrily. Desperately. I couldn't possibly get enough of him.

He smiled into our kiss as I grasped the back of his neck and intertwined our tongues even more. A gasp quietly escaped me as he squeezed my ass and slid me up higher on his torso. The friction sent a jolt of heat between my thighs, and I already felt myself getting wet for him.

"Seb," I moaned his name into his mouth. I needed more. More of this. More of *him*.

He sensed my need and carefully lowered me to the ground, not breaking our kiss. With my feet planted to the floor, he moved his lips from mine and trailed them down my neck. My whole body tingled from the feel of his mouth nipping at my skin.

Sebastian pulled his mouth away from my flesh to look at me, gazing into my eyes, full of desire for him.

"Please," I begged, not needing to say what for.

He smirked in satisfaction at how quickly I was coming undone for him. Then, as if I wasn't already craving him enough, he dropped to his knees before me.

Gods. Seeing this man—this powerful force of a man—kneeling before me sent me into absolute shambles.

I chewed my lip, anticipating what he was going to do to me—how he was about to make me feel.

He looked into my face, smiling deviously with the knowledge that he had full control as he gripped the sides of my lounge pants, pulling them down past my knees. I trembled as his hands cupped the inside of my thighs, applying gentle pressure to spread them apart.

His fingers traced up my legs, moving for my panties and hooking under the lace. He slid them down to join my pants at my feet, leaving me on display to him.

He took in the sight of me, bare and vulnerable. "Beautiful," he whispered into my flesh as he planted kisses on the inside of my thighs, working his way up.

Fuck.

I was a silent observer as his head dipped forward, closing in on me. I shook as his breath warmed my core, teasing me.

He looked up at me with his glorious eyes. "Are you sure you want this?"

I nodded eagerly, unable to speak.

At my approval, I was met with my own gasp, brought on by the sensation of his tongue trailing over the most sensitive parts of me. He started off slowly, savoring me with his mouth.

My head dropped back, reveling in the euphoria he presented to me.

"You taste even better than I imagined you would," he said breathily as he continued to ruin me with his tongue and teeth.

"You've thought about this?" I breathed amidst my moans.

"You haven't?"

Of course I have.

I tangled my hands through his hair as he moved his tongue in faster, tighter circles over my clit. He was going to utterly destroy me.

Sebastian pulled his mouth away to trail a single finger up the inside of my thigh, moving it to my center and rubbing the sensitive bud of my core. He played with me in taunting, tantalizing motions before slipping his finger inside of me. I let out a breathy moan as it entered me, sliding in easily. "You're so wet for me, Maeve."

His mouth began licking me again, damning me to complete silence as I lost the ability to form words. He worked his fingers and tongue together, moving them meticulously to bring me to the edge.

"Please." I couldn't take it anymore. I grabbed a hold of his hair and lifted his head to look at me. "I need you," I pleaded. "Now."

Sebastian chuckled, his finger still moving inside of me. He shook his head. "No. Not here."

My mouth opened to argue, but cried out instead as he inserted another finger. My neck fell back and I returned to that undeniable sense of euphoria as his fingers worked within me.

"I want you completely bare and sprawled on my bed when I take you for the first time," he spoke into my skin, his voice primal and demanding.

Without any warning, his mouth was back on me. He flexed his fingers inside of me while he focused his tongue on my clit. He was so close to bringing me into oblivion.

"Fuck, Seb," I cried out, dangerously close to climaxing.

He moved his other hand up to cover my mouth, quieting me—we were in the archives, after all.

"That's it, baby. Give in to me"

It wasn't long before I was whimpering into his hand as I came around his fingers, falling apart for him.

"Good girl."

I grabbed his wrist and moved his hand from my mouth, sucking in air to try and catch my breath.

He pulled his fingers from inside of me, bringing them to his lips and licking me off of him. He slid my panties back up, then my pants as he rose from his knees.

His swollen lips laid on top of mine, and I tasted myself on him as he kissed me passionately.

Sebastian pulled back, grinning at the sight of me. I couldn't move—or speak, for that matter. He'd left me in complete wreckage.

"Think you'll be able to sleep now?"

CHAPTER THIRTY-ONE

When I had collected myself, Sebastian and I packed up our belongings. The early hours of the morning had crept in, and to no surprise, I felt like I could sleep again.

Sebastian took my hand and guided me down the staircase. We made it to the second floor when he suddenly froze. He held his finger to his mouth, shushing me as he pulled us off of the staircase. I followed his pose and ducked alongside the balcony, keeping quiet to try and make out the hushed conversation below us.

"And what should I report back to King Beaumont in regard to the girl, sir?" a male voice asked his counterpart.

"Please inform Cyprian that last I've been told, Aldous has received his final offer. I believe he plans to decline, but we won't be certain until he does."

My breathing quieted even more. They were talking about me.

"While we wait for his response, tell Cyprian to prepare the Draemornian troops to move in on Craterra. Should Aldous be a fool and reject the offer, we don't want to waste any time," the same voice informed the first.

"As you wish." The man paused, reducing his tone even lower. "And what of the prophecy?"

My heart stopped.

They know of the prophecy? I mouthed to Sebastian, who just held his finger up to his lips again.

"The prophecy is not common knowledge to most. As long as we get to the girl before the sacrifice is complete, there should be no complications."

The voices trailed off, and we watched from the balcony as the cloaked figures came into view briefly before exiting the archives.

Nausea struck me viciously. I turned to Sebastian, my eyes wide and full of fear. He stroked my hair in silent affirmation that everything would be okay, and once we were sure they were gone, we stood from our crouch.

"Those must be the insiders giving information to Draemor," Sebastian huffed, rubbing his forehead.

"Do you have any idea who they were?"

"No. Everything echoes in here, I couldn't recognize the voices."

"How do they know about the sacrifice?" I asked him while I tried to ignore the sinking feeling in my stomach.

"I mean, it's possible they read the book of Blythe before you ripped the page out, but it's doubtful. I have no idea." He took my hand again and I followed him down the rest of the staircase.

We reached the doors of the archives and he cracked one side open, peering out to make sure no one was in the corridor before we made our exit.

He didn't let go of my hand. He used it to practically drag me through the hall, bringing me back towards my room.

"What do we do?" I asked him, my nerves starting to take control.

"*We* don't do anything," he said, turning a sharp corner and picking up his pace. "I'm bringing you back to your room, then going to inform my father of what I heard."

I. Not *we*. He didn't plan to tell his father that I was with him.

We hurried through the darkness. "I want to help." This was partly my fault, after all.

He didn't look back at me. "You can help by keeping yourself safe. Don't go anywhere alone, stick to our plan." The protectiveness in his tone threatened me to not argue with him, though I wanted to.

Sebastian threw open the door to the soldiers' corridors and we burst through. He slowed his pace a little when we were in the safety of the corridor, but I could tell his nerves were still in control.

We reached the staircase that led to our floor. Sebastian began climbing, but I stopped in front of the steps as I was met with an unwelcome thought.

"What if King Hawthorne decides to just hand me over when you tell him?" It wasn't an unreasonable question. "If giving me to Draemor prevents Craterra from being attacked, it would be in the best interest of our kingdom."

Sebastian climbed back down, stopping in front of me. "That will not happen." He gripped my face with his hands. "I will not *let* that happen. I promise you." The assertiveness of his voice almost reassured me.

"How can you be so sure?"

"Because I know my father. I know his tactics. And we have the upper hand here. Beaumont doesn't know that we know his plan. We can make it to Craterra before his army gets there," he explained.

I gulped and nodded, but another worry appeared. If he told his father about the prophecy, that could change things drastically. If King Hawthorne knew that I may die, he still might choose to follow through with Beaumont's request.

Sebastian sensed my concern before I voiced it, and eased my nerves without me even having to ask. "I'm not going to tell him about anything more than the attack on Craterra. The prophecy stays between us."

I nodded again and stepped onto the staircase after him. He unlocked my door for me, ushering me inside of my room. "Stay here. Keep the door locked. Don't open it for anyone unless it's me or Sawyer. Understand?"

"There must be something I can do besides sitting here. Please let me help," I begged, though I already knew the answer.

He pulled me into an embrace, shaking his head. "No. I'm sorry."

I sighed and wrapped my arms around him, allowing the scent of him to absorb into my clothes. He kissed the top of my head.

"I'll see you in the morning then?" I looked up from his chest.

Sebastian smiled sadly. "Goodnight, Maeve." He put his lips on mine in a much too brief kiss before shutting the door behind him.

Displeased with his quick exit, I couldn't help but feel like this was not a goodnight, but instead was a goodbye.

The first thing I did when morning arrived was disregard the promise I made to Sebastian.

I would only go down the hall to his room. I just needed to know how it went with his father.

As soon as I stepped into the hall, I was met by Sawyer, lounging against the wall across from me.

"What are you doing?" I gave him a sideways glance.

"He's not there." He gestured his head at Sebastian's room.

My mouth dried up as Sawyer stepped towards me. He observed me, so much being said between us without needing a single word.

"How long?" I asked.

He raised a brow.

I don't think he realized that this news didn't shock me. "How long will he be gone?" I clarified.

Sawyer looked down at his feet, exhaling a breath of remorse. "I don't know."

I bit my lip and nodded in denial, fighting a battle with the dampness in my eyes.

Sawyer reached into his pocket, grabbing his handkerchief and holding it out towards me. I waved his hand away. I wasn't going to cry. I wouldn't let myself.

"About one-hundred troops, including half of Caelestis' head soldiers, were sent to Craterra early this morning," he informed me, stuffing the handkerchief back in his pocket.

"You're still here, so who else went?"

"Jocelyn went, Kohen stayed." He named a few others, but I didn't care to listen.

I sighed in relief, looking back at the wall. Good. Pia would be a mess if Kohen had to go. I sensed the sadness in Sawyer's voice when he said Jocelyn's name. I wanted to tell him that she'd be okay, but I didn't like to promise things that only the gods had a say in.

My cheeks filled with air, holding it for a while before I blew it out with an unplanned laugh. What were the damn odds? Sebastian and I finally were together, and then he got sent on a combat assignment with no indication of when he'd be back. Better yet, the reason he even went was because of me.

I wondered how much Sawyer really knew. "Did you see him? Before he left?"

"Yeah. He came knocking on my door after he dropped you off. Filled me in quickly before doing the same to Kohen and then went off to see his father." Sawyer turned his torso towards me, looking me in the eyes all too seriously as his voice dropped to a whisper. "He told us about your powers, how harnessing them too much makes you sick. And about the plan you two had in place so that we can continue it."

My body froze, but my eyes widened. Why would he do that? For over two months he let me train with Sawyer without so much of a word of my weakness to him. Granted, Sebastian was still around to keep an eye on me, but why did he decide to tell him now? My gut churned. Unless he thought he would be gone for an unforeseeable amount of time…or that he wouldn't be coming back. *Oh gods.*

Sawyer recognized my shock and waved his hands dismissively. "It's okay, we're not going to tell anyone. Seb just wanted me to know so that I didn't train you so hard that you get sick…er." His eyes were apologetic as they roamed the frailness of my figure, caused by his training.

He raised his attention back to my face. "Anyways, King

Hawthorne called us all to the throne room at three in the morning. Told us how Seb overheard a conversation from some of the traitors, and that he needed half of us to volunteer to go to Craterra."

My heart fell out of my chest and rolled across the floor. It bled through the cement, the heavy weight of it burying into the dirt underneath.

Sebastian *volunteered*?

Why would he do that? I knew it was my insecurities talking, but I couldn't help but think he just wanted to get away from me, especially after what we did in the archives. Was it too much for him? Maybe this was his sick way of trying to push me away again—because he realized he couldn't handle it.

Sawyer's eyes widened as he realized what I was thinking. "Gods, Maeve, no." He put a hand on my shoulder in comfort. "He did this to protect you. I promise."

"How can you protect someone if you aren't here?" My question did not warrant an answer. I dropped my head to my feet, watching my toes as they wiggled in my socks.

I sniffled, and this time, I accepted the handkerchief when Sawyer tried to pass it to me.

"Why didn't you volunteer?" I asked through shuddered breathing.

"Seb asked me not to. Asked me to stay and watch after you. He wanted to make sure that no one else was responsible for training you so that you don't get sick again."

"He could have stayed and did that himself," I complained, the words coming out ruder than I meant them to. "I'm sorry, I—"

"It's fine. You have a right to be angry, hurt, sad…whatever you're feeling."

There were a few moments of silence before Sawyer asked, "Why didn't you say anything?"

Knowing immediately what he referred to, I shrugged as my response. My reasoning didn't seem good enough anymore.

"How bad was it? Full transparency, right now."

"Sawyer, that doesn't matter now. Everything is okay—"

"Tell me," he demanded in a tone I had never heard from him. And that was saying something, considering our introduction.

I sighed in defeat. As much as I didn't want to divulge this information, he deserved the truth. "I passed out more than I'd like to admit. Got sick almost every night after we trained. I couldn't eat because it was just more for me to throw up later on. The pain I got in my head when I wielded too hard was unbearable, yet somehow I pushed through it night after night."

His eyebrows furrowed in dismay, his freckled cheeks sinking into his skull. "I had no idea."

"I'm good at hiding things I don't want people to know. I could have just as easily told you what was going on, but I didn't. And the only person to blame for that is myself."

"If I had known how bad it was…Fuck. I would have stepped in. I—"

"Can we not talk about this anymore, please?" I fiddled with the handkerchief between my fingers. "Did he tell you…about us?" Sebastian and I were so new that I hadn't even told Pia about us yet. I'd been soaking it all in, enjoying having this secret between him and I.

"He didn't need to."

"That obvious, huh?" I forced a chuckle.

Sawyer draped his arm over my shoulder, pulling me into a one-armed hug against the wall. "For some reason, your sarcastic ass really does something to him."

I gave him the side eye.

He continued, "You can get through to him—break open the barriers that Kohen and I have never been able to. It doesn't take a genius to know that there's something special between the two of you."

"Then why did he leave?" My voice quaked.

Sawyer pulled me in a little tighter and I laid my head on his shoulder. "Because you make sacrifices to protect the people you love."

Love.

"Didn't you want to go so that you could be with Jocelyn? Why didn't you argue with Sebastian when he asked you to stay?"

Sawyer sucked his lips in, releasing a sigh before he said under his breath, "Love."

CHAPTER
THIRTY-TWO

"Have you heard anything?" I asked the same question I'd been asking every day for the past month.

Sawyer shook his head, as usual, and I scowled at his lack of knowledge, as usual.

I groaned, grabbing my rucksack from my bed before storming out of my room. I hadn't heard anything from Sebastian since he left. Not even a letter. Pia assured me that writing a letter was not the number one priority when stationed at an outpost fighting a battle, but whatever.

King Hawthorne had postponed our meetings until further notice. He had been too preoccupied dealing with the Draemor and Craterra issue to have time to bicker with me. I was not complaining. The less I had to see that man, the better.

A week after Sebastian left, King Hawthorne announced to the kingdom that Draemornian troops were seen moving in on Craterra, which confirmed his rejection of Beaumont's final offer. It had been a month, and no official declaration of war had been made yet. I could only assume that meant good news out of Craterra, and that maybe our army was able to keep the Draemornian soldiers at bay.

The hope was to stop Craterra from becoming a pile of ruins, and destroy enough of the Draemornian troops in the process that King Beaumont rescinded his threats against Caelestis. *Thanks* to King Hawthorne's orders placed on anyone gifted, Caelestis' army was much stronger and larger than it was two decades ago, so we had a good chance at being successful.

I walked alongside Sawyer while he escorted me to the academy for my classes. He'd been keeping incredibly close tabs on me due to Sebastian's orders. I didn't mind, though. What I heard in the archives that night frightened me, and for the first time, I felt that the extra protection was truly needed.

The air had warmed with spring, making a cloak unnecessary on most days. The sun shone with the promise of the ocean being ready to divulge in soon. Although I had trouble being excited with everything that's been going on.

"Not to be dramatic," I started.

Sawyer huffed a laugh. "Oh right, because Maevey Baby is *never* dramatic."

I punched him in the arm. Hard.

"I think I'm going through the stages of grief."

"By the way you just hit Sawyer, I'm going to guess you're in the anger stage right now?" Pia caught up with us, hugging me from behind as we walked.

Sawyer rubbed his arm. "You don't have to guess about that," he mumbled.

Pia moved to my side, taking my hand in hers and swinging our arms as we trailed through the freshly grown grass. She beamed from ear to ear as she pointed her face towards the sun.

"What are you so happy about?" I raised an eyebrow of suspicion.

"Oh nothing," she hummed, her smile widening even more.

"Tell me. I need some happy news so I can move onto the bargaining stage."

She gave in too easily. "Okay fine. Since you asked, Kohen and I just had the absolute most mind blowing—"

Sawyer flashed an expression of disgust and cut her off, "I don't want to hear this." He quickened his pace, his leather pants reflecting the sun as he moved to walk in front of us.

I chuckled. Sometimes I forgot that Sawyer had known Pia almost as long as he'd known Sebastian. She was like a sister to him.

Pia rolled her eyes. "Anyways, best sex ever."

"I should have known that's what you would say. You tell me this every day, I swear."

When I had told her about Sebastian and I finally getting together, she was ecstatic, to say the least. I could only imagine what she would have said if I told her the details of what we did in the archives.

I bit my lip to suppress my smile as I remembered that night. The way he kissed me. The spontaneity. The feel of his mouth and tongue as it licked all over my body.

Pia noticed the color of my cheeks change. "You have a secret."

I slowed my walk a little to make sure Sawyer couldn't hear us. I started to tell her about the archives, but my nostalgia was soon replaced by the reminder that he was not here, and I stopped myself.

A few days.

We only had a few days of truly being together before he was whisked away from me.

Pia noticed my sudden change of mood and squeezed my hand in hers. "He's going to be okay. He's a strong fighter," she assured me.

"Yeah, I'm sure he's fine," I said. But I was not.

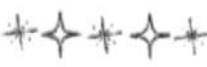

I'D BEEN HERE BEFORE.

I glanced around at the familiar sight of human carcasses, completely bled out and shattered into bits of bones, lying in their final resting place on the cobblestone patio of the courtyard.

The hairs on my arms stood up as the temperature dropped in response to the heavy fog rolling in, covering the cadavers just as it had before. I reeled in a deep breath, steadying myself to continue my journey to nowhere.

The air was plastered with the stench of mortal rot. It bit at my nose, a constant reminder that I was not truly alone.

Wind lashed around me, tangling my hair into knots. Some of it stuck to my forehead, caked with the blood of myself and others. I walked around the edge of the patio, familiarizing myself with the eight figures of stone that surrounded me. They had me cornered, and I saw no exit through the haze.

Flames burned through the mist covering my feet, responsible for turning some poor soul to ashes. I stood centered in the wreckage of death, waiting for a voice to call to me, just as she had before.

"Come to me," the euphonious voice sang, as if she knew I was expecting her—perhaps maybe she did.

The hum drew me in, and I halted in front of Blythe, wiping my face as my own blood dripped into my eye. "I'm here," I announced to the goddess made of stone.

Her hand broke out of the mist, the same as before. This time, however, the stone severed from her fingers, crackling off in chunks as she reached out for me. I accepted her outstretched hand, my gemstones sparking when our skin collided.

"Why am I back here?"

Her voice was hushed as she spoke to me. *"I have a message for you."* She tightened her grip, pulling me closer. I couldn't see anything but her hand and a silver-blue eye watching me through the mist.

"What is it?"

"The prophecy will soon become a reality, and you must be prepared for when it does."

I gulped. She meant that I should be preparing for my death.

"That is not what I'm referring to."

Did she just read my mind?

"I am the Goddess of the Mind and Stars," she stated. *"Are you so surprised that I know your thoughts?"*

A shuddered, "Woah," escaped my chest.

Wait. Did she say mind *and* stars?

"*There is no time to explain that now, but listen to me closely, Maeve.*" The eyeball twisted and churned through the mist, watching me while its owner spoke.

"There's a book—you've seen it before, in a classroom, from what I can see."

I racked my brain, trying to decipher what she referred to. "Yes. Professor Stoll showed me a manuscript when I first discovered my powers." I recalled the large textbook he had shown me back in the fall. "*The Gods and Goddesses of Life*," I said the title back to her.

"He did not show you enough of it."

Before I could ask what she meant by that, I was transported out of my dream state and sitting straight up in my bed, screaming.

I patted the sheets by my sides, trying to familiarize myself with my surroundings. I drew in a few shaky breaths, blowing them out even more shuddered.

My door burst open, startling me even further.

Sawyer ran in, his eyes bulging. "What's wrong?" he panted.

I clutched my blanket, holding it against my stomach. "Nothing. I—"

"I heard you screaming when I left Kohen's room. Is someone in here?" Sawyer drew his dagger and started parading around my room, checking behind my curtains and in my washroom.

"What? No. I just had a bad dream."

"Oh." He dropped his blade, sheathing it against his thigh.

"Sorry, I didn't mean to scare you."

"You probably scared the whole floor. You got some strong vocal cords." Sawyer moved towards my bed, slumping to the bottom of my mattress. "What was your dream about?"

"I don't remember."

He raised an eyebrow. "You're dripping sweat and still breathing heavily. You remember."

I pulled my blanket up higher to hide my chest. "It was just a dream."

"Uh huh," Sawyer mumbled in a tone that said he didn't believe me. He laid the back of his hand against my forehead. "You're burning up," he said when he pulled it away, placing it instead around my wrist.

I gulped and forced a small grin. "Just a bit under the weather, I guess."

His fingers unfurled as Sawyer rose to crack my window open, allowing some fresh air into the room. "Alright, well if you need me, you know where to find me."

I nodded. "Thanks."

He was halfway out the door when I stopped him. "Actually, would you mind just staying until I fall asleep?" To be completely blunt, the revisitation of my nightmare had my anxiety at one level below panic.

"Of course." Sawyer settled himself into my armchair, and when I woke up in the morning, he was gone.

After my wielding session that evening, I stopped by Professor Stoll's office, planning to break in. Unfortunately, I had to take Sawyer with me as he refused to let me walk back to my room by myself.

Stoll usually left the door to his classroom open, but tonight, of all nights, it was closed and locked.

"What are we doing here?" Sawyer asked as I fidgeted with the lock.

I held a finger up to my mouth, shushing him as I twisted and turned the knob. A heavy groan escaped my lips when I realized it was not going to work.

"Move over." Sawyer waved me away.

He used his magic to create a powerful stream of water from his fingers. The liquid leaked into the knob, and the pressure of it cracked the lock. Sawyer turned the handle and pulled the door open.

I guess having him here turned out to be pretty useful.

I made straight for Stoll's bookcase, rummaging through it.

Sawyer walked up behind me, observing as I scanned my eyes over the bindings, in search of the familiar text.

"Yes!" I whispered excitedly when I found it. I removed the manuscript from the shelf and started flipping through the pages, not lifting my eyes as I moved to sit at one of the desks.

Sawyer mirrored my movements, taking a seat next to me. "Willawood, what are we doing—"

I shushed him again, and this time, he listened.

I found the page Stoll had shown me, with the image of Blythe and the constellations. I read it over a few times, not finding anything beneficial. I flipped through the next few pages, still not finding anything.

I huffed a breath, reconsidering that maybe my dream was really just a dream, but I flipped a few more pages, and my eyes widened as I read.

Although there is no written proof, word of mouth has told a fable of Blythe, passed down through centuries of storytelling. Centuries ago, as the creation of the world became more meticulous, the brothers and sisters of the goddess believed her to be too powerful. She could erase their doings with the use of her mind and she would often do so if the balance of nature and humanity was being threatened by her siblings.

The seven of them before long, had enough. They could not see the bigger picture of what their sister was doing for the world, and took action to stop her. Blythe predicted her fate and set a prophecy in place to ensure the use of her magic was never truly lost when her soul was hidden.

Of course, this is just a fable, but one may consider the possibility that all stories start from some truth.

Unbelievable.

I leaned back in my chair, absolutely dumbfounded. How had I been in the same room as this information for months, but never discovered it? This proved that my *dreams* weren't really dreams at all. They were visions. A gift from Blythe to prepare me for what was to come. She had mentioned that the prophecy would be fulfilled soon. The visions may have been her twisted attempt at preparing me to meet my demise. If that were the case, I'd haunt the shit out of her when I was gone.

Sebastian would scold me if he were here, but I ripped the page from the book anyway. I'd add it to the collection of notes and various manuscript pages that I'd seemingly created.

I skimmed the pages to see if there was anything else useful. When I determined there was not, I tucked the book safely back into the shelf, just one page shorter.

"I'm done," I stated, turning my back to Sawyer and exiting the classroom.

He followed after me. "Woah, woah, woah. Stop."

I kept moving.

"What the hell was that about?" he called after me.

"Don't worry about it." I left the academy, stepping onto the grass outside.

"I am absolutely going to worry about it!"

"Trust me, you'd rather not know," I said to Sawyer, then muttered to myself, "I sure wish I didn't."

Sawyer caught up to me and grabbed my arm, stopping me in my tracks, pulling my attention towards him. "I'm all for a bit of sneaking around, breaking and entering, you know—all kinds of illicit activities. *However*, I do like to know *why* I'm doing them."

"Any chance you'll let this go?"

"Fuck no."

"Fine," I growled. "But are you actually capable of keeping a secret?" I recalled when he let it slip that Sebastian had feelings for me.

Sawyer hesitated, and that was a good enough answer for me.

"Yeah, that's what I thought." I pulled my arm from his grip and resumed walking.

"No wait." He stopped me again. "I can."

I glared at him in suspicion.

"I promise."

"Fine. But if you tell even your imaginary friend, then I will compel you to cut your own tongue out," I cautioned him, not entirely serious but not fully joking, either.

Sawyer grimaced. "Point taken, you psycho."

I breathed out deeply, praying to the gods that he didn't make me regret telling him this. "I found a prophecy a while back in a book in the archives. It describes me perfectly and is claimed to be the word of Blythe."

Sawyer stared at me, letting me continue.

"It says that there will be a sacrifice, but I haven't been able to figure out what or why. Then I remembered this book that Stoll had shown me at the start of the year, and I figured there might be something useful in it." I shrugged. "Turns out there was." It wasn't the entire truth, but I was not going to tell him about my visions—I hadn't even told Sebastian about those yet.

I passed him the page from Stoll's book, then gave him a moment. Sawyer looked flustered as he read, his forehead furrowing and rising repeatedly. He handed the parchment back to me, shaking his head in confusion. "I feel like you're leaving a lot out," he said.

I stuffed the paper back into my pocket. "Basically I'm just trying to figure out if I should be arranging my own funeral."

Sawyer gawked at me. "How are you so casual about this?"

"I've had a while to process it, and worrying about the situation won't change anything." As the words escaped me, I realized how much I'd changed since the summer. All the shit situations I'd been put in since I got my jewels must have desensitized me.

Fear coated Sawyer's expression as we continued walking. "You're right. I would rather not know."

CHAPTER THIRTY-THREE

"No. I haven't heard anything," Sawyer answered my unspoken question before I had the chance to ask.

I flipped him my middle finger.

"Woah. Don't be mad at the messenger," he exclaimed, following behind me after I brushed past him.

We left the castle for the combat arena to start our wielding session. I didn't talk our whole walk, and he accepted my silence as a threat not to mess with me right now.

I had too much on my mind this evening. King Hawthorne announced last night that Duke Sinclair discovered two more traitors in the kingdom. They were seen conversing with Draemornians in Elscara—a village close to Craterra. They would be put to death by fire in the dungeons later this week. I wondered if they were the men Sebastian and I overheard in the archives months ago. I hoped so.

I used to feel empathy for those who were executed for simply spilling a secret that was not theirs to share. But not anymore. Maybe I'd become numb to it all. Or maybe it was the fact that if it weren't for these traitorous, greedy mortals divulging information on me to Draemor, then Sebastian would be here and I wouldn't be worrying for my life.

So let them burn.

Sawyer and I had been sticking to the wielding schedule that Sebastian had put in place. The king has resumed our meetings, but kept them short and sweet. He has also been too preoccupied to have any suspicions, so our plan has been working well.

I put my stress into training, and it showed. I was no longer sick after every wielding session. I gained some weight back and was starting to look more like myself, though I'd never felt less like myself. I'd spent two months absolutely terrified about so many things. Sebastian and the prophecy, to name a few. *Was he okay? Was he even alive? What if the prophecy played out before he returned?* He'd be welcomed back by my shallow grave in the castle's crypt.

I haven't had another vision from Blythe since I discovered the fable. I guess she got her message across—whatever it was. At first, I thought the new information helped clear up some of my confusion, but it turned out that I just had even more questions now.

Sawyer held the door of the academy open for me, and I stepped in, heading straight for the arena. I had a lot of pent up emotion to let loose this evening, some of which I was not even sure how to describe. To put it lightly, I was a mess.

I tossed my bag down on the mat and tied my hair into a tight knot. "Ready?" I asked Sawyer.

He glared in my direction. "You good?"

I ignored his question altogether. "Drop your shields," I demanded. Sawyer now put his mental barriers up the moment we entered the arena with the purpose of adding an extra challenge to our sessions. I clenched my jaw together. Even if I tried, I couldn't hide the array of emotions that I wore on my face.

I'd gotten really good at wielding my powers without giving it much thought. I didn't need to focus as hard and the whole process was becoming second nature to me. Turned out that Sebastian was right. Less but stronger wielding sessions have really helped progress my harnessing abilities.

Sawyer stared blankly at me. "Willawood, what's wrong?"

"Nothing's wrong."

Everything is wrong.

He took a step towards me. "Are you sure? Because you seem kind of uptight."

I scoffed with a roll of my eyes. "Just drop your damn shields, Sawyer!"

He stilled, but did not let my yelling faze him. "No. Not until you tell me what's bothering you."

Screw this. If he wouldn't drop his shields, then I'd just break through them.

I closed my eyes and focused on my command, which was going to be telling him to screw off, but before I could speak the words, my back hit the mat.

Sawyer tackled me to the ground and when I opened my eyes, he was way too up close and personal with me.

"What the fuck, Sawyer?" I yelled at him again, palming his shoulders to push him off of me.

"What the fuck to you, Willawood!" he shouted back, rising to his feet. "You were about to break through my shields!"

"You weren't dropping them!" I complained as I sat up.

"We *literally* just got here," he huffed. "Why the rush?" He reached a hand out to me and pulled me to my feet. "You're never this eager to practice. Something's up. What's your problem?"

"I already told you. Nothing," I snarled.

He threw his hands up in the air. "Oh for fuck's sake, Maeve. We're friends, you can talk to me."

Emotions climbed a ladder up my throat, trying to force themselves out. I tried to swallow them back down, but there were too many. "Can we please just practice," I begged softly, hoping he'd drop this whole thing if I asked nicely.

He crossed his arms over his chest.

I pouted my lips and crossed my arms as well. "Do I really have to say it?"

I shouldn't have had to. He should know from my daily interrogation that I was worried about Sebastian. Actually, *worried* wasn't even the right word. I was catastrophically *terrified*. Every waking moment was spent agonizing over him and the prophecy, and it was overwhelmingly exhausting.

I spun on my heel, putting my back towards my friend. "Two months. I haven't heard from Sebastian in two months." Not a letter. No indication that he was even still alive. Nothing. I wiped a salty tear away before Sawyer could see it. Damn my eyes for being so weak.

Sawyer's hand patted my shoulder. "You know, I'm scared, too," he said.

His words granted me some compassion, and I felt a slight bit of shame for treating him so poorly tonight. Sometimes I forgot that he was missing someone, too. Two someones, rather.

I turned back towards him, letting his hand fall from my shoulder. There was a gleam of wetness in his eyes, and I wondered if his emotions had been just as untamed as mine.

My sympathy was short-lived. I didn't need a heart-to-heart right now. I needed a distraction.

I only needed to ask once more before he gave in. "Now please, just drop your shields."

"I KNOW HE'S NOT HERE, BUT WE SHOULD CELEBRATE ANYWAY." PIA raised a bottle of whiskey in the air, then dropped it to her lips. Today was Sebastian's birthday.

"Turning twenty-six in the middle of battle," Sawyer shook his head as he took a slug from the bottle. "What a pitiful fucking excuse of a birthday party."

Kohen chuckled as he was handed the whiskey. "Sure is." He took a sip. "I'll make sure to let him know when he's back that we celebrated for him by sharing his favorite drink."

He passed the bottle out to me, but I dismissed him. "No thanks," I said quietly. I wasn't in the mood.

"Come on, Maevey baby, you love this stuff," Sawyer encouraged.

I glared at him, my eyes narrow slits. Gods, I *hated* that damn nickname. "No."

"You don't have classes tomorrow, just have a drink with us." Pia batted her eyes at me.

I knew they were all just trying to get my mind off of things, but it was pretty fucking irritating. They were all acting like everything was fine. Pretending that things were normal and that life wasn't just one big fucking mess.

"Actually I think I'm just going to go back to my room, I'm pretty tired." I rose to my feet.

"What? No!" Pia cried out. "You just woke up from a nap, you can't be tired."

"Yeah, Maeve? What's your problem?" Kohen said only half-jokingly.

"*My problem*?" I huffed, glancing between the three of them. "It's pretty fucked up, isn't it?" I shrugged my shoulders. "To celebrate the birthday of someone who very well could be dead."

I regretted the words as soon as they left my lips, disgusted at myself for even speaking such a thought into the world. They were all worried about Sebastian, too. And Jocelyn, for that matter. If drinking their worries away helped them, then who was I to take that away from them.

"I…I'm sorry…I don't know why I said that," I stuttered, trying to form an apology. Why *did* I say that?

My uncalled for comment acting as a reminder that Sebastian's status remained unknown left Pia looking like she was about to cry. "Don't say that. He's fine…I know he is," she sniffled.

Kohen set a scowl on me before wrapping Pia in a hug. "What the hell, Maeve?" he growled, wiping the tear that trailed down her cheek.

I didn't even dare look at Sawyer as I backed up towards the door, twisting the knob and busting through it. The metal slammed behind me, blocking the horrified faces of my friends from my view. They may have been upset right now, but I knew they would forgive me. They all understood what I was going through—not that it was an excuse.

Sawyer would kick my ass when he realized I didn't go back to my room, but I didn't care. I hurried out of the castle, and once my boots touched grass, I took off running.

Down the pathway along the cliffside I sprinted, listening to the waves as they crashed amongst the rocks. My old dormitory peered into my peripheral vision as I moved towards the sound of the water, following the whisper of the sea.

I broke through the patches of dune grass that tried to conceal the beach from those like me. I peeled my boots from my feet when my eyes caught sight of the water, my toes burying themselves into the earth.

The tension secured in my chest calmed with each step I took towards the sea. The air was humid tonight, hinting at the impending summer season. With that in mind, I stripped to my undergarments and didn't stop running until my body was submerged in the water.

The waves rolled over me. I dipped my head back, saturating my hair while gazing up at the stars. I envied them. They didn't feel pain, heartache, or sorrow. The stars didn't feel regret. The stars had never known anything other than peace.

I floated until the sea salt had dehydrated me and my skin shriveled up, leaving me just as drained physically as I was mentally. Only then, when I was completely empty, did I return to my room.

Aside from classes and meals, I refused to leave my room, and no one could make me. Pia tried. Sawyer tried. Kohen even tried. I was not moving until he came home. Alive or dead.

Ridiculous, I know, but my anxiety had me in a chokehold.

King Hawthorne gave word last week that Draemor had ceased their attack on Craterra. Caelestis' army was too strong for them. Had we not known about their plan to attack ahead of time, things could have ended differently.

I *was* relieved, but then a few days passed and Sebastian had not come back. Now it had been an entire week since the announcement, and he still wasn't back. I'd seen some of the other soldiers who'd made it home, and I knew Craterra was only a few days' ride by horseback, so my mind went to the worst.

My brain told me that he was dead, but my heart told me that I would feel it in my soul if he were. I didn't know which organ to believe, so until I saw him in the flesh, or saw his corpse, I would lie in bed.

I rolled to my side, taking the plush quilt with me. I stared blankly out the window, watching the clouds roam by ever so slowly. The sun was vibrant and trees blew wildly in the midseason breeze. It looked like a beautiful day out.

I couldn't stand the sight of it.

I climbed out of bed to pull my curtains shut, blackening my room then crawling right back into my sheets to rot. Sleep has been impossible lately, so I didn't even try. I just laid in bed, withering away over the man I loved.

It truly was pathetic, but that was me—the woman who let love completely consume her, even if it spit her back out in pieces.

The day wasted away before my very eyes, and I ignored the rumbling in my stomach that reminded me I needed to eat. Instead, I counted the divots of plaster on the ceiling.

One.

Two.

Three.

Fifty-four.

Any light that had made its way through the crack in my curtains vanished, meaning the evening hours had rolled in.

Three-hundred and thirty-one.

I closed my eyes tightly, hoping if I kept them shut long enough, I'd drift into a dream.

Sleep had almost taken me when my body flinched upright in response to a knock on my door. I knew by the sound of the fist that my visitor was not Pia.

CHAPTER THIRTY-FOUR

I shot upright in my bed, my eyes glued to Sebastian as he slipped into my room. Jaw clenched and white knuckled as he approached, my heart pounded, trying to escape from the dungeon of my ribcage.

He looked the same as when he'd left, aside from his hair desperately needing to be cut. The metal armor plate still covered his chest, which led me to believe that he came straight here when he got back. His battle leathers creased around his thighs as he inched towards me. "Hey," he announced himself, his voice hoarse and dark.

I climbed free of my sheets and stood at the end of my bed, leaning back against the footboard. Everything that had been building up inside of me for months tried to break free. My body tensed, but this was a battle I shouldn't fight.

Anger. Grief. Depression. Fear. Love. All built up so high that I couldn't control myself. The emotions begged to scatter out of me, so I stopped fighting myself and set them free.

All of my strength came through my biceps as I took a long stride towards Sebastian and shoved him in the chest. He stumbled back a few steps, losing his footing.

"How could you!" I screamed, salty tears pouring from my eyes like rivers.

Sebastian held his arms up in surrender and tried to approach me again. "Maeve, let me explain—"

"NO!" I wailed, pointing a finger at him. "You just *left*, without so much as a word! Better yet, you *volunteered*!" My fingers grasped at my scalp, tangling in my hair. He reached a hand out for my shoulder, but I turned to avoid it.

Every cell in my body was conflicted, unable to process this. I was relieved that he was back, alive and in one piece. So unbelievably relieved. But I was also so fucking angry that he left in the first place.

"Three months," I whispered, raising my eyes and three fingers to him. "*Three fucking months*, of not knowing if you were alive or dead." I shouted the words, then sucked in a few shuddered breaths to console myself. My body fell onto my mattress, sagging down so that I could place my head in my hands.

He came back.

He was safe.

That was all that mattered right now.

I heard a clang of armor as it hit the floor, then the mattress shifted underneath me. Muscular arms wrapped around my waist, pulling me into the chest of the man I had missed for months.

He held me tightly, stroking my hair as I sobbed into his chest. "Shh, baby. Everything is okay."

He is alive.

I wept in relief for what felt like an hour, though it was only minutes.

"I'm sorry," Sebastian whispered, and I knew he meant it. "I had to go. I'm one of the best soldiers Caelestis has, and I needed to ensure things were done right. I needed to keep you safe."

I breathed him in. Despite all the death he just endured, his skin still smelt fresh and crisp, like frost.

"You didn't *have* to leave. You chose to," I contested.

He breathed deeply, pulling me in closer to him. "I didn't make that decision lightly. I didn't want to leave you, but I knew you would be safe here with Sawyer."

I lifted my head up, letting him see the gleam in my eyes. "You didn't even write."

"I couldn't. It's so much worse than you even realize, Maeve." Sebastian shook his head. "The Draemornian soldiers retreated for now, but this is not the end of it."

"What took you so long to get back?" I sniffled.

He pressed his lips together, hesitant to answer me. "I had some things to take care of before I left."

"*Things*?"

His brows furrowed, and his face filled with sorrow as he hung his head. *Bodies*. He meant bodies. He had to bury the corpses of his fellow soldiers.

"Oh."

He looked back up at me, faking a small smile to show that he was okay. I saw right through it. He fidgeted with his thumbs and looked at me as if he had more to tell me, but didn't want to.

I wasn't sure that I wanted to know, but asked anyway. "What is it?"

"Beaumont still wants revenge against Caelestis, but he wants you more. He desires your powers, and it seems as though he will go to the extreme to get what he wants. We don't know how to stop him without full blown war." Sebastian looked stressed as he continued. "The things I heard over there…about you…" He shuddered, as if he couldn't stomach saying the words. "The entire Draemornian army has a one track mind to get to you, and the things they are saying they'll do to you if they get their hands on you…I can't even—" His skin paled and he looked as though he might be sick.

His arms loosened so that I could sit up, using the back of my hand to soak up my tears.

He didn't want to elaborate on what he heard, and I was fine only being able to imagine what would be done to me. The news of more war didn't surprise me—I'd never expected King Beaumont to simply give up, and my visions showed me a glimpse of what was to come.

I may have been hurt that he left, but Sebastian was right. I'd been safe here at the castle while he went through something unimaginable.

My finger grazed across his jaw, edging along the sharp bone. "I'm glad you're safe. But are *you* okay?"

"I'm fine." He nodded, though a muscle in his jaw twitched under my finger tip.

"Are you really fine?" I asked him the same question he'd asked me too many times to count.

"Yes." He pulled me back into his arms and dragged us down onto the bed.

I wanted to pry, but knew better than to try and get information out of him that he didn't wish to share. I'd ask him again at a later time.

"I've missed you more than you could ever imagine." He leaned forward to kiss me softly. Our first kiss in months, and *gods,* was it worth the wait. His mouth was soft and subtle against my own, and he tasted just as I remembered.

"Are you sure? For a while I thought that you leaving was your last attempt to get away from me," I teased, letting my lips linger against his.

Sebastian's grin interrupted our kiss. "Never."

In one swift motion, he pulled me on top of him and rolled onto his back. Straddling him, I hunched forward to press my mouth to his, this time more passionately as I released the longing that I'd been holding inside since he left.

Our tongues worked together in sync, as if no time had passed at all.

His hands roamed along my body, stopping at my waist and holding me down even closer to him. My lips moved to his neck, and he shivered in response to my touch. My stomach swirled with arousal, knowing that he reacted to me in the same manner that I did to him.

My teeth skimmed across his throat, then back to his mouth,

reclaiming our kiss. As his hands moved down my back to cup my ass, mine slid down his chest, stopping at the hem of his shirt. My fingers looped underneath the fabric and I broke our lips apart to pull the barrier off of him, revealing his toned abdomen. I bit my lip at the sight of him.

"If you keep looking at me like that, there's going to be a lot more than just kissing going on in this room," he warned, his gaze a tempting threat.

"Good."

Our eyes captured each other, staring for a lust-filled moment as we recognized each other's needs. I could tell he wanted this as much as I did, but was waiting for me to give him the go ahead.

I pulled myself up on his lap, grinding my hips and causing him to quietly groan in response to the friction. Not breaking our eye contact, I pulled my shirt over my head, leaving my breasts full and bare, showcasing my desire for him. Though my self-consciousness told me to hide, there was no need to conceal myself with him.

Sebastian sat up hastily, careful not to throw me off of him. I could sense his arousal growing stronger as his eyes drifted over my naked torso. He hardened against my ass, and the feel of his desire caused my own to saturate my panties.

He clenched his jaw, breaking his gaze from my breasts and moving his eyes to my face. "Maeve, are you sure—"

I interrupted his words by leaning forward, settling my hips down into him as I did. My nipples grazed against his chest as I brushed my lips tauntingly against his neck.

"I've been waiting three months for you. Yes, I'm sure," I whispered into his skin.

"I just don't want you to regret it if we—"

"I won't."

"I still think you deserve better."

Was he serious right now? I appreciated the chivalry, but I wanted this—probably more than he did.

I sat upright on his lap, staring at him starry eyed. "Seb, just fuck me already," I demanded.

His eyes widened with desire, and he wasted no time pulling me down over him and capturing one of my nipples with his lips. It stiffened as his tongue flicked over it. My hands weaved into his hair as he licked me, the dampness of his tongue sending shivers over my whole body.

I didn't know how he did it, but the next thing I knew, he was on top of me, his mouth claiming mine again as he worked my pants down my legs. I was so eager to have him that I kicked them off myself, not wanting to waste any time.

"Someone's impatient," he groaned teasingly into my mouth.

"I've been patient enough. I need to feel you. *Now,*" I pleaded, not caring how desperate I sounded.

He smirked as he forced his mouth away from mine, watching my reaction as his fingers dipped into my panties and began to massage my clit. My mouth fell open in pleasure as he stroked me.

"So wet already," he said breathily, moving his hand down further. Two of his fingers pushed inside of me, and I gasped at the unexpected feeling as he slowly pulled them in and out.

"Is that what you were doing in bed when I arrived? Touching yourself while you thought about me?" Sebastian's words lingered in the air as he taunted me. I couldn't respond.

I flailed beneath him, but the palm of his hand splayed on my stomach, holding me to the mattress. My neck strained to watch as he ruined me with his fingers, and he smirked when he noticed.

"Do you like watching me play with you?"

I moaned a breathy *yes* as he flicked his fingers back and forth. Then much to my displeasure, he removed his hand from my panties, but only so he could take them off of me, leaving me fully naked beneath him.

His tongue grazed my navel, trailing down lower with each kiss he embedded into my skin. My breath caught with anticipation of where he was headed, but he pulled himself back, denying me the pleasure he was moments away from delivering.

I frowned at the abrupt removal of his mouth from my skin, and Sebastian smirked deviously in response.

His hands dropped to his pants and I pushed myself up on my elbows as he worked to unbutton them. I chewed the inside of my cheek when he released his length, marveling at the size of him as it sprung free from the leather, hard and swollen with lust.

I forced my eyes to move to his face as he bent over me, claiming my mouth in another kiss, this one sloppy and full of need.

He reached his hand back down to my clit, rubbing with it in circular motions. He explored me sensually, toying with every part of my core. A moan escaped me as his touch alone threatened to push me off the edge before we'd even really begun.

"You're going to make me come if you keep doing that," I said breathlessly as he tormented me with his fingers.

"No." His hand gleamed with my wetness as he took it away. "I'm going to make you come by fucking you."

My breath stopped. Fuck. *The mouth on this man—*

Our eyes kidnapped each other while he waited for my approval, which I granted him by clasping my hand around his girth and guiding it to my entrance. He accepted the invitation and crashed his lips back into mine as he pushed into me slowly. I moaned into his mouth at the feel of him filling me.

"Gods," I groaned in satisfaction. Everything about this moment felt so undeniably right. Just him and I. Alone in this room. Finally fulfilling the desires we'd both held on to for so long.

He settled himself inside of me, giving me a moment to adjust to the feel of him stretching me. "You good?" he asked with restraint.

My eyes closed against my will from the feel of him stilled within me. As soon as I nodded my answer, he started pumping his cock inside of me. He started off slow, allowing me to acclimate to the size of him.

I moaned, craving more. He grasped my aching for him, and increased the power of his strokes.

He fucked me needily, pulling himself in and out in a perfect rhythm. I glanced down to where our bodies were joined. The sight of him inside of me was everything. I tossed my head back, reveling in the indescribable ecstasy.

His hands slid over my torso, cupping around my breasts. "Fuck, Maeve," he murmured as he thrusted deeper. "You feel too good."

His voice was hoarse with satisfaction as he slammed into me, each stroke harder and deeper than the latter.

Sebastian's muscles rippled as he bent his neck down to claim my mouth while his cock throbbed deep inside of me. I moved a finger to the sensitive nub between my thighs and started rubbing, playing with myself while he moved within me.

"As much as I'd love to watch you touch yourself," Sebastian growled as he grabbed my wrists and moved my hands away, pinning them over my head, "I'd prefer to make you come by myself." He pressed his mouth back to mine and dropped one of his hands to take over teasing my clit.

Gods.

I bordered the edge of my climax and didn't know how much longer I could hold off from tunneling into oblivion as his tantalizing strokes claimed me. "Seb, I—" My voice escaped me as the motion of his hips made me cry out louder than I had wanted.

My moaning just encouraged him. He fucked me harder until I was whimpering and breathless, coming undone around him. My orgasm led him to claim his own. He pulled out of me, moaning as he spilled himself all over the space between my thighs.

Breathing heavily, he dropped his neck down, smirking at where he released himself. I bit my lip at the view of him admiring me, then he raised his starry eyes to mine.

We smiled at each other. Satisfied with what we'd done, but also knowing that neither of us was completely satiated.

Sebastian kissed me once more before rolling off of me and lying down next to me on the bed. I curled to my side, placing my head in the crook of his arm. He tugged the covers over us and planted yet another kiss on my forehead.

Neither of us spoke. There was nothing we could possibly say to add to this moment. Instead, we closed our eyes and absorbed the feel of each other's skin, damp and clammy from what we had done.

We soaked in our silence for a while, the moment feeling even more intimate than what we did together just minutes prior.

Soon enough, the tension rose inside of me again as my body

refilled with need for him. He just got home and must be exhausted, so I doubted he would be up for round two.

"Do the others know you're back?" I asked, still out of breath from him ruining me. I desperately needed to distract myself from my growing desire for him.

Sebastian's lips curved up as he shuffled beside me. "No. But they will." He kissed my neck sensually, proving how mistaken I was about his needs as his arousal brushed against my thigh.

"Because what I'm going to do to you next…" He paused, dipping his hand under the covers and trailing it over my navel, down lower and lower. "Will have you screaming my name so loud…" He stopped himself again, this time to position himself on his side behind me. "That the whole kingdom will know what we've done." He took a fistful of my hair and I cried out in pleasure when he pushed himself between my thighs.

My head rested on Sebastian's bare chest. We laid still in the mess of sheets we'd created. I trailed a finger along the scar on his elbow, dismay creeping in as I remembered how he got it. I wondered what he'd been through in the past three months—if there were any new scars cut into his skin.

I refused to take my gaze off of him, in fear that if I did, he'd be gone again. I watched the rise and fall of his chest, reveling in the knowledge that he was truly here, and I sent a thank you up to the gods for bringing him back to me.

Sebastian's eyes fluttered open, and he smirked groggily. "Are you watching me sleep?"

A smile tugged at my own mouth. "I'm just making sure that you're really here, that this isn't a dream."

He reached over and collected me in his arms, guiding me to sit on his lap. "I'm really here."

My smile faded the longer I stared at him. I had so much to tell him. So many questions, too.

His eyebrow raised. "What's wrong?"

I knew better than to say nothing, so I blurted out the first thing on my mind. "Aren't you worried by being with me that I'm just going to die from the sacrifice?"

He huffed a laugh. "Way to kill the mood."

"I'm serious."

"I think I was more worried that you would die during the trials."

"Come on," I groaned.

Sebastian's hand rested on my lower back, preventing me from sliding off of him as he sat up. He shifted us backwards, using the headboard to support him. "Where's this coming from?" he asked, moving his hands to both sides of my hips.

I didn't want to ruin his homecoming, but the visions wouldn't get out of my head, so I told him everything.

I relayed my visions of war, explaining how I believed it was Blythe sending me the messages and how she told me not to fear the sacrifice. I told him how she instructed me to find Stoll's book, and about the fable I read within it. Every little detail came pouring out of me in a sputtered mess of words.

Sebastian was unaware of how tight his grip had become on my hips. "When did these visions start?"

"The first one was the night in the archives. The second one was a month or so after you left."

"Have you told anyone this?" he asked.

"I told Sawyer a bit of it, but not all the details."

Sebastian's eyes widened in discontent.

"I know, I know, but I only told him because he was there when—"

Sebastian shook his head in an interruption. "No, it's not that. Granted, Sawyer can't keep a secret for shit, but it's not that."

"What is it?"

"While I was away, I overheard a Draemornian soldier say something about the same fable. He mentioned the statues. I don't remember every detail of what he said though. Everything becomes a little fuzzy during battle as the days mesh together."

The statues?

The statues.

Blythe's skin looked almost stone-like in my vision.

A crazy thought struck me and I shot out of the bed, wrapping a sheet around myself—not that I needed to. He had just explored every part of my naked body.

I made for my desk, rummaging through it until I found the page from Stoll's book. I reread it to ensure the information was matching up as it had in my brain, then I lunged back onto the bed, waving the parchment in Sebastian's face.

"Read this," I demanded. "It says how the other gods and goddesses took action to stop her. Is it possible they banished her soul within the constellastone statue?"

Sebastian read and looked up at me when he was done, shaking his head. "Those statues have been in our kingdom for centuries. I suppose theoretically it's possible, but it's a stretch. I don't even know how they would perform such an act."

He handed me back the page. "Regardless, if her soul *is* in there, there's nothing we can do to change that." He looked into my eyes sadly. "And it won't change the prophecy."

I closed my mouth. "You're right. I'm screwed."

Sebastian pulled me back onto him. I leaned forwards, letting him wrap his arms around me in an embrace.

"It's just a story, Maeve. There's no proof of it," he said softly.

I sighed into his neck. "I know. I was just hoping that if it were true, maybe I could stop the rest of the prophecy from being fulfilled."

Sebastian put his lips to my forehead. "Well, to answer your question from before, no, I'm not worried about the sacrifice."

My hair tumbled over my face as I looked up at him. "Why not?"

He brushed the strands away. "No veil between life or death could ever keep me from you."

I smiled faintly, my heart swelling. He said he couldn't give me what I wanted or deserved, but he was doing that very thing without even realizing it.

I should have told him right then and there that I loved him, but

I worried it would be too much for him. Could he really handle that added emotion after what he'd been through the past few months? And who's to say he even loved me back? He only admitted his feelings for me right before he left, and even then he wasn't sure if he could give me all of him. Although, when he got home, *I* was the first person he came to see. *I* was the person he'd let his guard down for. *I'm* the one he said not even death would keep him from.

Maybe he was wrong about himself. Maybe he was capable of giving me all of him, even if he thought that he couldn't.

My lips parted to tell him my deepest feelings, but we were rudely interrupted by an obnoxious banging on my door.

"Hey, asshole, open up!" Kohen's voice cascaded through the walls.

"You get back and the first thing you do is fuck Willawood, instead of coming to see us?" Sawyer yelled after him.

"Oh my gods." My cheeks burned red and I buried my face in Sebastian's chest.

"I told you they'd hear us," he said cockily.

CHAPTER
THIRTY-FIVE

Sebastian and I got dressed and made our way to our group's usual hangout spot—Kohen's room.

"Aren't you tired?" I asked him as we sauntered through the hall, my legs still weak from pleasure. I quite honestly didn't know how he was still standing. We slept for an hour or so, but his ride home from Craterra took a few days, and after what we just did, he must be exhausted.

He shrugged, suddenly solemn. "I probably won't be able to sleep much, anyway."

I figured that much. He'd likely lie in bed tonight, gazing at the ceiling while he relived the past few months over and over in his head.

I couldn't even begin to imagine the things he'd seen as a soldier. Someday I'd have to see those things as well. To my knowledge, there was no way to prepare for seeing bodies collapse and bleed out around you, some of them by the knife in your own hand.

The vision made me tremble. I didn't know how I could ever kill someone. I did know however, that someday—likely soon—I'd have no other choice.

No wonder Sebastian was the way he was. I could hardly stomach the thought of killing someone, let alone actually do it.

I took a step back and watched him stroll to his friend's room as if nothing at all happened back in Craterra.

Sebastian caught me studying him. He fell back and put his arm over my shoulder. "I know what you're thinking, and I'm telling you, I'm really fine."

"I know." I let him think that I believed him. There was no way he was okay after all of that. He was the strongest man I'd ever met, but he would break. It was just a matter of time. And when he did, I'd be there to pick up the pieces.

Sebastian dropped his arm to open Kohen's door, where our friends were waiting to welcome him home. Pia's eyes widened when she saw him. She lunged at her cousin, squealing as she wrapped her arms around him in a hug. Kohen had to practically tear her away so that he could greet his friend after months of uncertainty.

Sawyer winked as he approached us. My cheeks flushed as he held his hand up to Sebastian for a high five, which he of course declined with a look of warning, instead pulling his friend into a one-armed hug.

Sawyer's expression softened. "Glad you're back."

Sebastian patted his back. "Me too."

They pulled away from each other when Kohen waved a bottle between them. "Who wants a celebratory drink?"

We all took turns with the bottle and filled Sebastian in on what he missed. Sawyer told him how my training had been going well, and how I *almost* kicked his ass. His words, not mine. I knew that I knocked him down at least a couple times in the past few months. We laughed as we told Sebastian about the sad excuse of a birthday party we threw him, ruined by yours truly. I was glad there were no hard feelings about that night.

It was making for a fun evening, but then Pia raised a question. "Hey, where's Jocelyn? She must be back now, too, right?" She took a slug from the bottle, then passed it to Kohen.

Sawyer tried to act nonchalant, but I knew he was wondering

about Jocelyn's whereabouts, as well. He was just too uptight to ask himself.

All eyes pointed to Sebastian, awaiting his response, but he didn't say a word.

He just…froze.

Complete and utter silence filled the room, and my heart sank with realization.

Pia gasped, throwing a hand up to cover her quivering lips.

Kohen clenched his jaw, his knuckles turning white around the bottle.

And Sawyer fucking screamed.

He yelled so loud that the bottle fell from Kohen's hand, shattering on the floor.

Sawyer stepped through the shards of glass and grabbed Sebastian by the shoulders, shaking him. "Do not tell me that what I'm thinking is true." His eyes were already sparkled with wetness.

"I'm sorry, man. I did everything I could, but there was too much blood. I couldn't stop it. She…I—" Sebastian stuttered through the unwelcome news. "She wasn't alone. I buried her. I—" He stopped himself again. There was no need to say anything more.

Sawyer's arms slumped to his sides. He looked up at the ceiling in disbelief, then hung his head and began to pace through the room.

The silence was deafening. *Horrifying*. But no one dared to break it despite our own grief. We waited for Sawyer to do the honors.

With a tic in his jaw, Sawyer stormed back to where Sebastian stood, jamming an accusatory finger into his chest. "I was here, keeping *your girl* safe, and you couldn't do the same fucking thing for *me*?" he cursed through gritted teeth.

Though I shouldn't have, I pitched in. "Sawyer, you know he has no control over what happens—"

"Don't." Sawyer turned his attention to me. "This is your fucking fault, and you know it." He glowered at me, an expression I hadn't seen from him since we first met. "None of this shit would even be happening if it weren't for you and your rare fucking gemstones."

My jaw clamped shut and I backed away at his accusation. Why was he taking this out on me? I thought we were friends—maybe even best friends.

He stepped towards me again, removing the space I just gave myself.

Sebastian threw his arm between us, using it to push Sawyer away from me. "This is not on her," he hissed, backing his friend into the wall.

"Are you that fucking oblivious?" Sawyer argued. "That whole damn battle was because of her! The war that Draemor's going to start any day now, is because of *her*."

I opened my mouth, but then closed it tightly. I didn't know what to say. The more I thought about it, the more I realized he was right. In a way, this *was* all my fault. The woman he loved was dead. More people would die, and their deaths would be in my name.

"Oh fuck off, Sawyer." Sebastian rolled his eyes. "Maeve didn't cause this. You're just trying to find someone to blame."

Sawyer stood his ground, crossing his arms over his chest as he fought a losing battle with his eyes. "Why didn't you tell me the second you walked into this room?" he demanded an answer. "Better yet, why didn't you tell me the moment you got back?"

"I didn't even know that you and her were serious. You never told anyone anything!" Sebastian shouted back in defense.

There was some truth to that. Sawyer never told anyone except for me about his feelings towards Jocelyn. Even then he didn't say much, but I could tell by the way he looked at her that she was more than just a friend to him—or at least he wanted her to be.

Sawyer's face relaxed for a brief second, panning between Sebastian and myself before settling in a scowl. "You're my best friend…my brother. I shouldn't have had to," he spat. Then, his anger took over and he swiped at Sebastian, knocking him in the side of his face.

Sebastian clutched his crimson jaw, slowly panning his furrowed brows back towards Sawyer. He restrained himself from hitting back—

Never mind.

Sebastian decked Sawyer in the nose. I heard bone crack and my eyes widened as a gush of blood dripped onto the rug.

Sawyer growled animalistically. His body shuddered as he harnessed his magic, blasting Sebastian with a heavy stream of water from his fingers. The pressure of the blast knocked Sebastian backwards, and he hit the ground with a thud. Sawyer attacked him with power, increasing the intensity of his magic and aiming the stream directly at Sebastian's face. Sebastian fought back with his own magic, wielding a frost to freeze Sawyer's water as soon as it came shooting from his hand.

"Stop it, you two!" Pia wailed. Her and I made brief eye contact, and the gleam in her eyes crushed me. Her and Jocelyn had been close.

The water wasn't the only thing turned to ice as Sebastian harnessed his powers. Sawyer's hand froze as well, resulting in his skin turning stiff and white.

Sebastian jumped to his feet while Sawyer agonized over his hand. He released the hold on his magic as he stomped towards Sawyer, shoving him in the chest when he was close enough to reach.

Sawyer fell back and I heard another crack as he caught himself with his icy wrist. Despite the additional broken bone, Sawyer rose to his feet, pulling his other fist back to throw another punch.

Sebastian raised his arm to block the blow, but before Sawyer could even throw the punch, the whole room was shrouded by darkness as a loud boom of thunder shook us.

Kohen positioned himself between them, his hands raised in the air as he wielded a storm in the middle of the room. Wind swirled around us. Thunder crashed and papers flew as onyx magic quite literally put us in the eye of the storm.

Sebastian and Sawyer dropped their arms, and Kohen released his powers when they no longer looked like they were going to kill each other.

Kohen tended to keep to himself, so I was not expecting him to have much to say, however he surprised me. "You two are acting like assholes," he huffed, turning to Sawyer. "It's no one's fault that

Jocelyn is dead, except for the Draemornians. I'm sorry that she's gone, I truly am. But stop being a dick and blaming everyone else because you're hurting."

He then turned to Sebastian. "And what's your problem? A girl your friend cared about is dead, and instead of saying your condolences, you're getting defensive about it. I don't know why you did, but you shouldn't have waited to say something."

Sawyer scoffed. "I know why he waited," he gestured his neck at me. "He was too busy *fucking* his *problem* to say anything."

My mouth dropped in shock at Sawyer's claim, and Sebastian lunged for him, knocking him so hard that it took his breath away when he hit the floor. Sawyer gasped from the ground, clutching his chest with his good hand as he scrunched his face up at Sebastian.

"Don't you *ever* talk about her like that again." Sebastian spat next to him, then turned his back and stormed out of the room. He gave me a sideways glance as he passed, his face pale and showcasing obvious nausea.

I had a feeling that this would be the cause of Sebastian's inevitable breakdown. Delivering the news of death would do that to a person, I imagined.

My feet were cemented to the floor in distress. I wanted to go after him, but needed a moment to process what the fuck just happened.

"So much for a welcome home party," Kohen quipped under his breath. He reached a hand down to Sawyer, helping him to his feet.

I looked at Pia, her eyes wide as she glanced around all of us. "Wait." She pointed to the door where Sebastian just left from, then looked at me. "You two finally had sex?"

I couldn't tell if she was trying to distract everyone from the news we'd just received, or if she was really just shocked.

I shrugged innocently. Now was not the time to delve into the details of my sex life.

Sawyer bumped into my shoulder, shoving me aside as he left the room.

Kohen went after him, leaving Pia and I alone. She came over to me, pulling me into a hug.

"He's wrong," she said. "It's not your fault that Jocelyn died."

"It kind of is," I replied.

"Draemor would have attacked to try and claim the land, anyways."

"Yeah. But word of my gift helped speed up the process." There was no convincing me otherwise.

Pia moved her arms to my shoulders. "Sawyer's angry at the world right now. And sometimes when you're angry, you take it out on the people you care about. Because you know that you can. You know that they'll still be there."

I nodded in acknowledgement. Though maybe I should have been, I wasn't mad at Sawyer. His heart ached so badly that he didn't know what to do with it.

"Now, go deal with Seb." She grinned faintly, even though her eyes were still wet over the death of our friend.

I could hear her sobbing as soon as I left.

When I tried my luck with Sebastian's door, I found that he'd left it unlocked, so I let myself in. The noise of running water came from his washroom. His mattress concaved where I sat, waiting for him to come out.

Sebastian had a tough outer shell, but he harbored so much pain inside. When he finally allowed some of the pain to break free, it was harsh and sharp like the blade of a knife.

The sound of water trickled away. Sebastian stepped out of the washroom, a towel wrapped around his waist. He jumped back when he saw me sitting on his bed. "Gods, you scared me."

My eyes stuck to him as he walked to his wardrobe, pulling some loungewear from it. I turned my head, giving him some pointless privacy as he dropped his towel.

He rustled his hair, drying it slightly before sitting next to me on the bed. "What are you doing here?" His voice was sharp, as if he didn't want me there.

"You need someone to talk to." He would argue with me, but I didn't care.

"No I don't, Maeve," he scoffed.

I glared at him until he gave in with a roll of his neck. "That went pretty horribly, yeah. But it would have gone that way no matter what. There's no good way to announce someone's death."

"That I agree with, but still—"

"Sawyer will get over it and move on to someone else like he does every few months," he sneered, his words announcing his anger.

I took his hand in mine. "I'm not defending Sawyer by any means, but why *did* you wait to say anything? I mean, we were with each other for hours and you didn't say a word." How did he do what he did to me, with all that weight on his mind?

His silence told me that if I wanted him to open I was going to have to work at it a little. He needed to vent, and though I wasn't one to shy away from a challenge, I didn't want to push him.

"Alright, if you don't want to talk it's fine, I understand." Maybe he just needed some alone time. I stood up and started towards the door, but his grave words stopped me.

"I was five when I saw my mother's head severed clean from her body."

My head shot up and I pivoted back to face him.

"I was six when my father made me watch while he murdered the parents of the one who killed her."

I took my place beside him again.

"I was seven when I first executed a person." His knuckles gripped the sheets. "I was eight when I killed someone younger than me."

I had no words. Absolutely *none.*

"Nine when I almost died for the first time. Ten when I was locked in the dungeons for refusing to torture someone whom I believed was innocent. So on and so forth until the present age of twenty-six."

His gaze turned heavy on me. Teary. Heartbroken. "So I just wanted a few hours of normalcy before everything in my life went to shit yet again. And I had to see you first. I had to explain why I left and—" He looked down at his hands, twirling his thumbs around each other. "I just needed to see you."

I stole his fidgeting palms, collapsing my much smaller ones around them.

"I just feel like—" He stopped himself and he threw his back down onto the mattress.

"Feel like what?" I asked, following him down.

He sighed, turning his head towards me. "I pray that you never have to feel the way I do. That you never know what it's like to live a lifestyle such as mine. It's become all too natural to me. The fighting. Killing. Burying." He looked dead into my eyes. "Don't get me wrong, I'd do it all day everyday if it meant keeping you and the kingdom safe. But…" He hesitated to continue, but I laid my hand over his, letting him know that it was okay. "The past few months have made me so numb to it all. None of it fazes me anymore. Stabbing a dagger through someone's chest…watching them cry as they plead for their life, begging for their mother. Stealing the last breath from their lungs—it doesn't affect me like it used to."

My insides clenched at the darkness of his confession, reminding me of the things he's done. They didn't scare me, but I'd be lying if I said that I didn't try hard not to think about them.

"I've spent my life fighting that part of me—the part that was born into battle, forced to do horrific things as a child. Then I rejected the crown and was thrown back into it even harder. Soon there will be no other choice but to accept that's just who I am."

I sat up and rested my hands on my knees, looking straight ahead out the window as I tried to think of something to say. "Someday this will all be over and you'll be able to live again." I told him the thing I'd been reminding myself of daily since the summer.

His lips curved up. "You told me that about yourself months ago."

"It's true. Someday you'll spend your days in the archives. Always needing to wear your glasses because you'll be working as a bookkeeper—the career you truly belong in."

He chuckled, pulling me down and into his chest. "Someday you'll be tanning naked on a beach, soaking in the waves as the sun sets around you every evening," he told me my own fantasy.

I smiled at the thought. I needed this reminder, too.

Someday I'd live again.

"Someday *we'll* live again," we said together.

Sebastian pressed his lips to my forehead. They were soft against my skin—comforting. "Do you want to stay the night?"

I did, but needed to be alone. So much had already happened since he'd been back, and the overwhelm of it all was closing in on me. Plus he needed a chance to *actually* rest.

I shook my head. "That's okay. You need to sleep, and if I stay I doubt you'll get very much."

Sebastian frowned. "I told you earlier that I doubted I'd get much, anyways."

"No. It's okay, really. I think I'll just go back to my room and—" My throat constricted and I choked on my words as brutal realization struck me. Why did I think that Sebastian coming home would just suddenly solve all my problems?

Jocelyn was really dead, and Sawyer blamed me. The kingdom was on the brink of a war that was being expedited because of *me*. Sebastian had become indifferent to killing, which was arguably my fault, too. Just hours ago, I had sex with the man I was in love with, but couldn't bring myself to tell him. I was being hunted by Draemornians for gemstones and powers that I never even wanted, and I had a prophecy hanging over my head that suggested my death.

It was too fucking much.

My breath pulled forcefully into my lungs, quaking under the pressure of my life.

"Goodnight," I said, my voice already unsteady. My eyes started to burn. I could hardly breathe.

Sebastian studied me as I tried my hardest to hide the distress I felt. "Are you—?"

"I'll see you in the morning." I didn't give him a chance to coerce me into staying. I'd thought for sure he'd be the one who broke down tonight—turned out it was me.

CHAPTER THIRTY-SIX

Sawyer was a master of avoidance. He hadn't so much as looked in mine or Sebastian's direction for nearly two weeks. He was in mourning—we all were. But instead of leaning on each other for support, Sawyer was holding a grudge over something not even the gods had control over.

"Let's get this over with," Sebastian groaned, pushing open the door to his father's study. We were a few minutes early, but he seemed to be lacking patience today.

"What the hell?" he murmured as we stepped into the room.

The king was not there, instead, Lucan stood in his place, fumbling through a stack of papers on the desk. He came to an abrupt stop upon our arrival, peering over his glasses at us.

"Oh! Hello, Mr. Hawthorne…Miss Willawood. To what do I owe the pleasure?" Lucan's voice reflected his surprise.

Sebastian gripped the edge of the desk, splintering the wood as he leaned into Lucan's face. He glared at the king's advisor, who fidgeted uncomfortably at the intimidation. "What are you doing in my father's study without him here?" His head cocked as the words slid off of his tongue in accusation.

Lucan looked down, fussing to put the papers back in order. "I…He moved your meeting to the throne room. Mr. Sinclair was supposed to inform all of the head guards to attend."

"Fucking Sawyer," Sebastian scoffed, then glowered back at Lucan. "You didn't answer my question."

"I am gathering some information that the king requested be sent to the duke."

Sebastian crossed his arms over his chest, unintentionally flaunting his muscles under his fitted shirt. "And what information might that be?"

"Just some data from the first year's coursework," Lucan jumbled his words, scurrying to finish his task.

"Interesting," Sebastian sneered, his suspicion obvious. He was being awfully harsh, in my opinion.

Lucan pushed his glasses up on his nose and stepped out from behind the desk, gathering a stack of papers in his arms. "Very well, I must be on my way now. I have to make sure this gets delivered in a timely manner." His voice shook, then he waited for Sebastian to move so he could leave.

I didn't think he would, but Sebastian let him go.

The king's advisor hurried out of the room, picking up speed when he entered the corridor.

I turned to Sebastian, whose knuckles at last unclenched. "First of all, it's hot when you act all intimidating. Second of all, what the hell was that?"

"Fuck if I know." He spun on his toes, heading right back out the way we came. His pockets filled with his hands as he rushed us down the hall, not giving me any indication as to where we were going.

"Why were you being so cold towards him?" Lucan had never done me any wrong. He didn't seem to have a mean bone in his body.

"He knows better than to be in there without the king."

"You don't believe him?" I asked, jogging after him.

"Nope."

"Well then shouldn't we tell someone?"

Silence.

I sneered at his disregard for my question. "Where are we going?"

"Throne room."

Right. We still had a meeting to attend. I glanced around the hall—I really should have known the castle better by now.

Sebastian burst into the throne room, throwing the doors open, loudly announcing our presence.

King Hawthorne sat on his throne, his crown sparkling in the candlelight above him. Duke Sinclair stood beside him, and the head soldiers were in formation—minus Jocelyn.

Lucan's words became more incredulous by the second as he was nowhere to be seen.

"Sorry we're late," Sebastian bellowed as he strutted to his place in formation. "*Someone* failed to inform us of the change of location." He gave Sawyer a sideways glance.

"I couldn't find you," Sawyer huffed.

"You didn't even try." Sebastian rolled his eyes to the veil above.

"I tried your room, but you weren't there. Maybe I should have checked Willawood's." He lowered his voice with his last sentence, so the king wouldn't overhear.

"Watch your mouth," Sebastian cautioned.

"You guys are acting like children." Kohen leaned out of line to intrude on their bickering.

"*Me?* I'm not the one who's been avoiding his friends for two weeks," Sebastian shot back.

Sawyer scoffed in response.

King Hawthorne loudly cleared his throat to grab their attention. "Sebastian, are you done picking arguments with your fellow soldiers?" He glared at his son, the heat of his gaze as hot as the fire that emitted from his ruby.

Sebastian straightened his posture and clasped his hands behind his back, standing in the same position as the other soldiers.

"Now that everyone has joined us, I have an announcement to make that should bring joy to each and every one of you."

I settled myself in a seat at the front of the room, pointing my eyes on Sawyer while the king continued.

"Although Draemor ultimately retreated, and despite the fact that our army had the advantage of time and size, the Draemornian force was still better prepared and stronger than we anticipated. It was a close fight in Craterra. We lost many of our own."

Sawyer was deadpanned as he stared at Aldous Hawthorne, who grasped my attention when I noticed how rundown he looked. His usual clean cut goatee had grown to a full beard, and his under-eyes were dark, hollow bags. I couldn't say that I blamed him. Running a kingdom must be difficult—even if you were doing a shitty job at it.

"Cyprian Beaumont has made his intentions clear for years—that he would one day reclaim land lost." The king rose from his throne, stepping down the burgundy scaffold it sat upon. "Then the stakes were raised when he was presented with an additional incentive." He approached me, placing a hand on my shoulder and I shivered at the touch of his wretched skin. "Beaumont had been consistently threatening Caelestis with war for years now, but all of that ended today." He removed his hand, facing his soldiers to elaborate. "He has withdrawn his threats, knowing that the Caelestian army outnumbers his own, and that his army stands no chance at winning a war against us." Looking down at me, he said, "You are safe, and the eastern territory will remain free."

The blinking of my eyelids was responsible for the only movement coming from my body.

Surely this couldn't be true. Beaumont wouldn't just give up like this. There was too much history between the kingdoms, and he had been pining for me for almost a year.

"Oh bullshit," Sebastian drawled his words and stepped out of formation. "You really believe that?" he questioned his father, striding towards him. "Do you truly think that after everything, Draemor is just going to give up? That Beaumont is just going to forget about the land and let Maeve live freely?" Sebastian held an arm out directed at me.

"Why yes, soldier, I do." King Hawthorne held his ground.

Sebastian scoffed, and to my surprise Sawyer stepped out of formation as well, followed by Kohen.

"With all due respect, Your Highness, I have to agree with your son," Sawyer disclosed. "Beaumont has had his focus on Maeve for months. It doesn't make sense that all of a sudden he just has no desire for her. I don't think we should conclude from this that she's safe."

"I agree as well, sir," Kohen interjected. "Have you considered the possibility that Draemor is using this as a tactic to get us to drop our wards?"

The king scowled at the three of them questioning his authority. "Of course I have considered that, Mr. Sharpe," he snarled.

Duke Sinclair chimed in before any of them could speak any further. "We have calculated the risks that come with accepting these terms, and at this point in time have no reason to believe that King Beaumont is stating anything other than the truth."

These two were bigger idiots than I'd ever realized.

I stepped forward, joining my friends. "If I may, I have something I'd like to say. Seeing as I'm the one who's been used as a pawn between the two kingdoms for months on end, I think I should be entitled to have an opinion in this."

The king nodded his approval.

I cleared my throat, glancing around, all too aware of all the attention directed at me. "We are all aware that there are still *at least* two traitors living among us, likely in this very castle, correct?" I asked, referring to the conversation Sebastian and I overheard in the archives. When the king and duke nodded, I carried on. "That alone has to make you wonder if your soldiers are right. Maybe this really is a tactic to throw us off. To get us to drop our guard. I don't think we should jump to any conclusions—"

"That is enough!" the king bellowed. "From all of you." His eyes darted between the four of us. "I will not tolerate being ridiculed by my own army. Draemor has pulled back, and that is that. Until we have reason to believe otherwise, you will accept these terms and I will not continue this conversation any further." The king's soulless eyes found mine. "I expect to see you at the end of the week for the ceremony. And don't be late again."

Shit. I had forgotten all about the armoring ceremony this weekend. When the year of Caelestis academy concludes, the surviving first years are presented with their first set of armor. The event is followed by a grand gala in the courtyard.

King Hawthorne removed himself from the room, everyone else filing out after him except for Sebastian, Sawyer, Kohen, and I. We waited until the others left, huddling together once they were gone.

"I hate him," Sebastian muttered. "Gods damn fucking moron —" he mumbled a few more curse words, but I could not make them out.

"I have a really bad feeling about this," Kohen exhaled sharply, crossing his arms over his chest.

I nodded in agreement. "Something about this isn't right." Something about Lucan being in the king's study did not feel right either, though I had no idea why.

"So what do we do?" Kohen asked.

Sebastian shrugged, at a loss for words.

I turned towards Sawyer, hoping that his presence meant he was coming around. "Thanks for sticking up for me, I—"

He turned his back to us before I could finish, following the footsteps of the others who had left before him.

I winced at the resentment he still gave me. The weeks had been long without Sawyer's gentle bullying, and I missed my friend. Sometimes I felt like he understood me better than my own sister.

Kohen placed a hand on my shoulder. "He just needs more time."

I sighed. "How is he doing?"

"He's okay all things considered. He's pretty undone about Jocelyn still."

"Were they even ever together?" Sebastian asked, the question having a bite to it. "Like I said before, no one even knew he liked her."

"I knew," I said under my breath.

Kohen shrugged. "I dunno, haven't asked. Honestly I think there's something else bothering him, but he won't tell me."

"I don't know what I can do to make things better between us." I didn't know how much more of this I could stand. I had considered bombarding his room and forcing him to talk to me more than once, but the idea had been shot down by Pia.

"Just give him space. He'll come around. He cares about you both, even if he won't say it," Kohen replied.

"Yeah, I guess." I frowned.

Sebastian took my hand in his. "Come on. I have something that will cheer you up."

"Is that an innuendo for your dick?" Kohen scrunched his face.

Sebastian winked. "No. But I suppose it could be."

The silver blade was about as long as my forearm—the perfect size to conceal under my sleeve if needed. The metal was polished so finely that the edge gleamed without needing any source of light.

My fingers traced over the carvings on the handle. Hundreds of intricate stars and a crescent moon were chiseled within the pale birch wood. The hilt, coated in a pearlescent varnish, created colorful prisms of reflection on the wall as I rotated the weapon in my palms.

"Look at this." Sebastian interrupted my admiration, which was fine because I was at a loss for words from his gift. He took the dagger from me, twisting off a cap that I hadn't even noticed on the end of the grip. He held the end of the handle so that I could see the hollow center that flowed through the blade.

"What's that for?" I asked, pulling my head back.

He twisted the cap back on. "Toxin. Should you ever need it." The already deadly weapon became even more lethal with the addition.

He passed the blade back to me, but I hesitated to take it.

"Sebastian, this is beautiful, but I can't accept this. It's too much." I shook my head gently.

Running his fingers over my palm, the tingle of his touch forced my hand open so he could place the blade in it. "It was supposed to be for your birthday, but with what my father just told us, I figured it'd be good for you to have it early. Just in case."

"My birthday?" I had completely forgotten that the Jewel-Light Festival was soon approaching.

He chuckled. "Yes. Did you forget?"

Passing the blade between my hands, I admired it some more before tucking it safely away in its velvet sheath. "I guess so. I've had a lot on my mind."

I laid the dagger down gently on Sebastian's bed, then stood on the tips of my toes to plant a kiss on his cheek. "Thank you." I smiled softly as I forced my lips away.

Sebastian smirked and wrapped his arms around my waist, pulling me into him. He set his chin on top of my head, then blew out a bubbled breath. "My father is a fucking idiot."

"I know."

He pulled back from our embrace just enough so that he could see my face while still keeping his arms clasped behind me. "We've been slacking with our training. You and Sawyer had a good pattern going, but when I got back it started to slip. We need to get back to it."

"Do we have to?" I groaned, not having missed my training sessions.

"You need to be prepared." He pulled away from me for real now so he could begin pacing around his room. "You need to continue wielding so that you can be as strong as possible. I pray to Caius that my father is right about Draemor's intentions, but he wasn't there in Craterra. He didn't see what I saw. Didn't hear what I heard."

"What did you hear?" I pried, even though he refused to tell me last time I asked.

He looked back at me, his eyes narrow slits. "No."

My nose scrunched, but I dropped the subject.

"This isn't the end. Draemor wouldn't just retreat after all of that. This must be a ploy."

"Can you talk to your father again? Maybe if you get enough soldiers on your side, he'll listen." I tried to help, but knew the idea was useless.

"He'll never listen. You should know that better than anyone."

I had seen Sebastian scared before, but this was different. He seemed really, truly, terrified. And it was making him come off as an ass.

"Well what else is there to do except for at least try?"

"We brace ourselves and draw up a plan in the event the castle is attacked. We can't count on him to do it, and I sure as fuck don't plan on dying. Or letting you die for that matter, in case it wasn't obvious. If Draemor's army does attack, my father is going to turn to the head soldiers for guidance, and I'll make damn sure we have a plan in place for when that happens."

My heart skipped a beat. "*When*?"

He noticed my voice crack. "I meant if."

"You did not." I took a step back. "You really think this is going to happen? There is at least a slim chance that Beaumont is being honest."

He hung his head, rocking it slowly to the side. "I would bet my life on a gamble that he's not."

"Someone's a pessimist," I quipped.

"I'm not being pessimistic, I'm being realistic. Don't act like you weren't just arguing the same point back in the throne room."

"I'm not disagreeing with you. I'm just saying that there's a chance." Because there was. Until we had reason to believe otherwise.

In a heartbeat, Sebastian's hands were cupped around my face, directing my eyes into his. "Do *not* let your guard down." He emphasized each word. "Not for even a single second. And don't trust *anyone* besides the few you know for sure that you can."

I huffed a breath of frustration, but kept my eyes locked onto his. "And who might that be? You and myself?"

"Why are you being so argumentative right now?"

"I'm not," I shot back. "I'm genuinely curious as to who I'm allowed to trust."

A sound somewhere between a growl and a plea released from deep in Sebastian's chest. "Fine then. Yes. You can trust me. Pia and Kohen. Sawyer is still being a dick, but you can count on him, too. Besides that, no one."

"What about—"

"No."

I bobbed my head in comprehension, realizing I didn't get a say here.

Sebastian dropped his hands from my face, and though the moment wasn't right, I found myself craving his touch back.

Pushing those thoughts aside, I focused on the matter at hand. He was entirely right. Even though it was possible Beaumont was being honest, we should still have a plan in place in case Draemor attacked. The king obviously wasn't going to do it, so that left it up to us.

"Maybe it's time to really try and make up with Sawyer," I suggested. "He could really be useful in this situation."

"I know." Sebastian sighed as he moved to his desk and slumped into the chair. "I'll call a meeting with the other head soldiers. I'll keep it on the down low." He pulled his glasses from one of the drawers, sliding the frames onto his face. They made him look so innocent—a trait we both knew he was not. Sebastian had so many sides to him, making it easy to forget that he was one of the most lethal men in our kingdom.

His elbows pressed into the wood and he used a fist to support his chin as he began to write on a piece of parchment.

"You know something is serious when the glasses come out." I chuckled, trying to clear the air, but instead I cleared my throat when he didn't respond.

He was so absorbed in composing a plan that I wouldn't have been surprised if he forgot I was here.

I gave him a few minutes of quiet before pointing out the obvious. "You seem stressed."

"I am."

"Let me help."

After a brief moment's hesitation, Sebastian spun his chair around, his posture casual with his legs splayed apart. He smiled cockily. "How do you plan to do that?"

My cheeks rounded with my grin. "That's not what I meant." Though my entire body flushed at the temptation.

His eyes invited me to indulge in a moment of bliss with him, and my lungs snagged on my ribs in response. All it took to turn me on was for him to look at me like that, and he knew it. I almost gave in, but shoved my desire down. We had more dire matters to worry about.

"What are you writing?" I questioned in an attempt to calm the fire blazing in my veins.

Sebastian spun back around with a shrug of his shoulders. "Offer stands," he mumbled.

I advanced on him, peering over his shoulder at the parchment. "What the hell is that?" I yelled and laughed at the same time.

Sebastian tried to keep a serious face, but failed. "Just a few ideas to keep us safe in the event that war still commences." His voice shook to try and mask his laughter.

"*That's* what you're going to present at your meeting?" I snatched up the paper. "*Lock Maeve and myself in the dungeon where we can spend the entirety of the war pleasuring each other unbothered*," I read the first line out loud then crumpled the paper into a ball and threw it at him. "You should be ashamed, soldier."

"You didn't even read the rest. There were actually some legitimate ideas there," he argued, throwing his quill down on the desk.

I rolled my eyes. "Oh yeah, I'm sure there were."

Our expressions softened as we absorbed one another. Every time we were together, I added a new detail of him to my memory, knowing that things could change in the blink of an eye.

"Come here." Sebastian patted his lap.

"I don't know if I should. I am having a bit of trouble remembering if you are on the list of people I can trust."

Sebastian's lips curved upwards. "Do you need me to write the names down for you?"

Dismissing my joke, I straddled him. Our chests pressed together as I rested my head on his shoulder. His arms held me tightly, and despite the comfort of his scent, my mind still wandered to all of the horrific thoughts that drowned it.

When I released a deep breath, he asked, "What are you agonizing over in that pretty little mind of yours? Reconsidering my offer?"

"Nothing," I muttered into his shoulder, pulling back afterwards to press a kiss into his jawline.

"You're a bad liar," he teased with a smile that I didn't return. He adjusted us in the chair, furrowing his eyebrows. "Tell me."

"I'm scared," I whispered.

He put a firm hand on the back of my head, gently stroking my hair. "I know." His breath warmed my neck. "But you don't need to be. Nothing is going to happen to you. I won't allow it."

Sawyer's blame was embedded in my brain. "I don't even care about myself anymore. I'm worried about you, my family, and our friends. If it weren't for me, none of the people I care about would be in jeopardy. I can't help but think that removing myself from the equation would solve the problem. That if I handed myself over to Beaumont, this would all be over. Well, not the impending death that's coming for me, but at least the war."

Sebastian pulled back, and his expression turned sour. Nothing about him has ever scared me, but the seriousness of his voice did when he said, "Do not *ever* say that again. That will never be an option. Remove that from your list of ideas right now." He glared at me, not releasing me from the sternness of his gaze until I agreed.

"Just hear me out—"

"Absolutely not." His dark brows drew together.

"Maybe I'm just overthinking." My lungs expelled a breath as I stared up at the ceiling.

"I'm going to think of something. I'll talk with the others. Everything is going to be okay."

I wasn't convinced that was true. This year had been non-stop turmoil, and I was exhausted.

"Mhm." Now I was the one who was stressed.

"Find anything interesting up there?"

"Nope." I dropped my head back down. "But if your offer from before still stands, I think I'll take you up on it." I needed a distraction.

Sebastian donned a smile, his eyes sparkling as he shot up from the chair. He carried me with him, crushing his lips into mine as he moved us to his bed.

CHAPTER THIRTY-SEVEN

"You're making me miss training with Sawyer." I threw my elbow backwards, jamming it into Sebastian's ribcage to try and release his hold on me. He grunted at the force and loosened his grip just enough so I could drop down between his arms.

"Am I going too hard on you?"

Rising to my full height, I spun and raised my weapon in defense. "A little bit, yeah," I choked the words out.

"Good."

My eyebrows drew together, then I lunged at him, my dagger angled at his heart. Before he could adjust himself, the clang of metal pierced my ears as my blade collided with his armor.

My arm fell and I smiled at my victory, sheathing the dagger in the wrapping around my thigh.

Sebastian dropped his guard, relaxing his stance. "I thought you said I was going too hard on you. What the fuck was that?" he panted.

I smiled knowingly. "I lied. Sawyer and I worked a lot on battle techniques while you were gone. Not to sound arrogant, but I've become pretty talented when it comes to combat." I was confident that if I were presented with a real opponent, that I'd have a good chance at success.

He wiped the sweat from his forehead with the back of his hand. "You're proving that claim true. Before we finish up, how about one more attempt at wielding your magic?" he panted.

We'd been bouncing back and forth between sparring and harnessing my powers, sometimes putting the two together. Sebastian had been pushing me a little harder than usual, but I knew he just wanted to prepare me.

"Fine," I agreed. "One more, but then I'm done. I can't be late for the armoring ceremony."

"Deal."

"I'm out of ideas though, so you gotta give me something." I brushed the braid off of my shoulder, my fingers sticking to the sweat soaked pieces that had split out of it.

Sebastian tapped a finger to his chin. "Compel me to kiss you."

A laugh released from deep within me. "What are we, teenagers?"

"No, but you *are* much younger than me."

"Oh whatever." I rolled my eyes. "I don't want to use my magic to coerce you into doing anything sexual with me."

"Who said anything about sex?"

I cocked my head, raising a brow. "Kissing always seems to turn into something more between us."

"Well I wouldn't mind trying my hand at being the submissive one."

My eyes rolled back into my skull again. "I don't think I need to press you into kissing me, anyways."

"No, you don't *need* to, but I want you to."

"On the gods." My eyes rolled back into my skull. "Fine, come here."

I had just begun tapping into my powers to fulfill his fantasy when a throat cleared behind us. We both jerked our heads towards the entrance of the arena. Sawyer leaned against the wall, his arms crossed over his chest. "I need to talk to you." He nodded towards Sebastian.

Sebastian's jaw tightened, recognizing that this wasn't something that could wait. It must have been important, because the two of them still weren't on good terms.

He turned to me, placing his hands on my upper arms. "If I let you walk back to the castle alone, do you promise to be careful?"

"Of course."

He raised his eyebrows. "Are you sure?"

"Yes, I'm sure. Go."

Sebastian dropped his hands. "Okay. I'll come get you before the ceremony." He planted a brief and uncoerced kiss on my lips.

My gaze followed him to Sawyer, who dropped his head to avoid eye contact with me. He still refused to talk to me, and I didn't fully understand why. Surely he didn't *actually* blame me for Jocelyn's death? I thought he was just angry and needed to point the blame at someone, but with each passing day, I became more unsure.

"ALRIGHT, *THAT* MIGHT BE MY FAVORITE DRESS I'VE SEEN YOU IN," Pia chimed when I exited my washroom in the gown I chose for this evening.

The dress of luxurious, black silk clung to my curves, flaring out at the bottom with the help of a slit on each side. The top was snug and sleeveless, the plunging neckline edged in gold beading. A cascade of golden leaves adorned the gown, flowing from my waist all the way to the bottom of the skirt which was trimmed with the same beading. The dress twinkled from my reflection in the window. "I might have to agree with you."

"Woah."

My skirt flowed as I spun around at the sound of Sebastian's voice. He approached me, his attention roaming me up and down. "You look…I don't even have the words."

Pia cut in. "I believe the words you're looking for are gorgeous, breathtaking, totally hot, bangable—" She stopped herself when she noticed Kohen in the doorway, waiting to escort her to the ceremony.

"Speaking of breathtaking." He wrapped his arms around the waist of her navy gown, pulling her into his chest.

"I'll see you down there," she addressed me, her cheeks blushed.

Kohen led her down the hall, then Sebastian shut the door behind them. He made himself comfortable, sitting in my armchair by the window, eyeballing me as I collected my comb and started working it through my hair.

"You look quite handsome," I complimented his usual dress suit.

"I'll admit that I do clean up nice."

"I still think I prefer you in your work leathers, though."

Sebastian smirked. "I prefer you in whatever is under that tight dress."

My thighs clenched. "What did Sawyer want to talk to you about?"

He crossed one leg over his knee and released a sound somewhere between a sigh and a groan. "Apparently him and Kohen overheard a conversation between two guards earlier that sparked some concern."

My hands released my hair as panic filled me. "Okay? What did they say?"

He sucked his lips in, then blew out a breath. "One of them said something about a group of stray Draemornian soldiers showing up at the ceremony tonight. Something about them being pissed that Beaumont pulled back his war threats, and how they want justice for what happened in Craterra. We don't even know if there's any truth to it, but we have to act like there is."

"Who were the guards?"

"Two guys who graduated last year, I think. Sawyer wasn't exactly sure."

"Why wouldn't they report it to your father?"

"I dunno. Maybe they hadn't gotten that far yet. Maybe they thought they could handle it on their own."

I moved to sit on the edge of my mattress. "Do you really think any Draemornians would be stupid enough to try something like that? Especially at such a large event?"

"I'd sure hope not. But if we don't prepare for the worst, and then the worst happens, we're screwed." He pulled himself from the chair and came to sit next to me, picking up the comb I'd neglected. "Unfortunately this means I'm going to be on duty tonight." Sebastian sounded disappointed as he started working the comb through my waves.

"Oh," I grimaced. "It's okay. Maybe just try to save time for one dance with me?"

Sebastian smiled, untangling a knot of my hair. "Of course."

When he finished, he laid the comb down to tilt my chin up with his finger. His lips were soft and smooth as they grazed my own gently. Lovingly. The contact gradually deepened, and I parted my mouth, entangling my tongue with his. I savored the taste of him as his hand moved through the slit of my dress and to my thigh.

"Remember what I said earlier about what happens when we kiss?"

"We have a few minutes to spare." His fingers caressed my skin, tracing the inside of my leg. He was dangerously close to where I really wished his hands would go, when he stopped abruptly and broke our mouths apart.

His forehead creased. "Where is your dagger?"

"Did you really stop kissing me to ask me that?"

"I'm serious, Maeve."

"It's over there." I pointed to the drawer of my desk. "Why?"

Sebastian marched to my desk, opening the drawer and taking out the dagger and its sheath before storming back. "Put it on," he demanded, handing the weapon out to me.

I raised an eyebrow. "Seriously? We're just going to the courtyard."

"Put it on," he said again, his tone advising me not to argue.

Still, I hesitated, so he took matters into his own hands, separating the slit of my gown to reveal my thigh. He tied the sheath snuggly around my leg, then slid the blade into it.

"You shouldn't be going anywhere without this anymore." He tightened the wrap to make sure it wasn't going to wriggle loose.

"I think you're forgetting that I have the most powerful magic in the kingdom. At least from what I'm told."

"I think *you're* forgetting that you have a whole army who's pissed at you, and a king who presumably still wants you under his control," he snapped. Though he disguised it by anger, I could sense the fear in his tone.

"Okay, Prince Hawthorne, damn." I gave in to his concern with a hint of an attitude. I stood up, wiggling a bit to test out the fit of the sheath.

"Thank you." Sebastian glanced over at my clock. "Shit, I have to go. Are you almost ready?"

"I need a few minutes. Go ahead. I'll see you down there."

"I don't know about that."

"You let me walk alone earlier. I'll be fine. I'm armed now, remember?" I teased.

"You sure?" He hesitated. "I dunno."

"I'm good, Seb. Go." I guided him to the door, waving my hands to usher him out. "Go or you'll be late."

Sebastian sighed. "Okay, I'll see you after the ceremony then." He leaned into my ear before leaving. "I can't wait to see how hot you look in your armor."

I finished my hair, messily pulling the sides back to keep it out of my face. I put on a pair of low heels, then adjusted my dagger once more before scrambling out the door. I would be late, too, if I didn't hurry, so I broke into a jog down the stairs.

A few steps from the bottom, my foot slipped out from under me and I plummeted down the remainder of the steps. The edge of my elbow collided with the railing and I cried out in agony. I pulled myself upright on the last step, then lifted my arm to get a look at my elbow.

"Fuck."

The skin had completely split, the wound so deep that there was exposed bone. Blood poured from the gash, leaking down my forearm in a consistent flow.

The adrenaline from the fall wore off, and I started to feel how painful the injury was. I put pressure on it with my hand, but the blood seeped through the cracks of my fingers.

I toyed with the idea of going to the infirmary, but King Hawthorne would have a conniption if I didn't show up to the armoring ceremony. Hopefully I could find Pia before it began. She would be able to heal the gash enough to cease the bleeding. I'd deal with the rest of it after.

Using my free arm, I pushed off of the step to stand up straight. I kept my hand tightly against my elbow and started down the hallway towards the door, much slower than before.

"Are you alright?" A man's voice stopped me in my tracks.

I looked over my shoulder at a sturdy, light-haired soldier standing at the bottom of the staircase. Caelestian armor covered his abdomen, and though I didn't recognize his face, his voice sounded familiar.

He pointed at my arm.

I turned fully to face him. "I'm okay. I just tripped."

He cocked his head towards my injury. "It looks pretty bad. There's blood dripping on your dress."

I glanced down at my gown, the black fabric appearing even darker from the blood saturating it. "My friend can heal it."

He nodded slowly, his boots scraping the cement as he took a step towards me. "You're a first year, right? I think I've seen you around."

I briefly glanced back at the door. There wasn't time to chat, but I also didn't want to be rude. "Yes. I'm Maeve."

"Calvin," he introduced himself with a smile.

"It's nice to meet you, Calvin, but I have to go before I miss the ceremony."

I started to turn from him, but he took another hasty step, flashing me the back of his hand. His amethyst stone glistened from the flames that burned in the lanterns on the wall. "I can heal you."

For a fraction of a second, I considered it, but my pulse quickened as he stared at me. He didn't blink—just watched my blood drip into a puddle on the floor.

"Thanks for the offer, but I really should go." I made haste, strutting for the door as fast as possible without making it obvious that I was trying to get away from him. My hand locked around the door handle, but it pulled me in as it was opened for me.

Lucan entered the corridor, a smile splayed on his face. I backed up into the corridor and he pushed the door closed, leaning his back against it.

"Hello, Maeve."

"Hi," I said blandly. *What was he doing in the soldiers' quarters?*

"How are you?"

"I've been better…clearly." I flashed him my elbow, then raised an eyebrow. "Shouldn't you be at the ceremony?"

"Yes, I should be." Lucan raised a hand to his mouth, faking a cough. "Unfortunately I am too ill to attend."

I glanced back to see if Calvin had left, then swallowed down a knot in my throat when I saw that he was still there, guarding the staircase and leaving me with no escape route.

Dread plummeted through me.

I suddenly found myself very grateful that Sebastian convinced me to take my dagger.

Lucan noticed my breathing quicken. "Relax," he said.

"What the hell is this?" I snarled, glaring at the king's advisor.

Lucan pushed his glasses higher on his nose, then in sync with Calvin, closed in on me.

"No need to worry." He raised his hands in surrender, his voice lacking emotion. "I just have a message for you." On his toes, he peered over my shoulders and granted the man behind me a singular nod.

Without warning, hard leather kicked the back of my knee. Somehow I kept my hand pressed on my wound when I collapsed onto my shin, cursing as my bone collided with the cement.

The bruise was already forming—I could tell by the ache that shot up my thigh as I tried to stand.

I didn't get very far.

Calvin's arms shot out from behind me. His hand secured the back of my neck and he pushed me down. He held me on my knees with his full weight, and though I tried to wriggle free, he was too strong.

I stilled my body, quickly realizing that I should reserve every ounce of energy that I could.

Lucan spoke again, "King Beaumont would like to personally extend you an offer."

I stifled a laugh of disbelief. "If he wanted to get a message to me, why is he having you deliver it and not King Hawthorne like he has every other time?"

Lucan stared at me, emotionless as he ignored my question. "The king of Draemor would like to give you one more chance to turn yourself over to him, promising safety for yourself and your loved ones if you accept and cooperate under his reign."

I couldn't help but snicker at the offer. "I thought Beaumont no longer wanted me."

"You thought wrong."

"Does King Hawthorne know you're trying to seduce me into abandoning Caelestis?" I smirked, adding a wink to really tweak him.

Big mistake.

My sarcasm granted me another kick from the solid sole of Calvin's boot, this time in the middle of my back.

"Ow, asshole. What the hell?" I cursed at the soldier behind me.

"King Hawthorne is not aware of this *transaction*," Lucan said.

"Okay, hold on. I don't understand." My head shook as much as was possible with the hand squeezing my neck. "How do you even know all of this then?"

My thoughts jumbled as I thought back to when Sebastian and I found Lucan in the king's study. He seemed like he was lying, but with everything else that was thrown at us that day, I had forgotten all about it.

Wait.

My mouth fell agape as reality dawned on me. I knew Calvin's voice sounded familiar.

"Holy shit," I muttered under my breath, glancing between the two men above me. "You were the two we overheard in the archives?"

"Took you long enough," the soldier sneered. He moved his hand from my neck to grasp a hold of my hair, pulling my head back so that I could see Lucan better.

"You're the one who's been telling Beaumont about me?" I snarled the question, though I didn't need to ask for confirmation. "You've been selling me out for months!"

"I cannot take all of the credit." Lucan shrugged, turning his back to me. "I've had plenty of help along the way. Though many of them were not cunning enough to avoid execution. The Fletcher boy, for example." He paraded around the corridor. "Calvin here, however, has been quite useful. One of the last standing."

I adjusted the grip on my elbow, pain searing up my arm as my palm skimmed my bare bone. "Why?" I snarled.

"Why?" Lucan scoffed. "Cyprian has offered me more than Aldous ever could. When I am successful with my quest, he promises to have me rule beside him."

"As what? Another king's bitch?"

Calvin yanked my neck back by a fistful of my hair. "Watch your mouth," he hissed.

Lucan's jaw ticked, but he continued his explanation. "Cyprian vowed that if I bring you to him before the prophecy is complete, that I can expect a reward of the highest honor."

In the midst of my shock, I bit my tongue. "How does he even know of the prophecy? How do *you* know about it?"

Lucan cleared his throat and crouched in front of me, putting his face in line with mine. "Tell me, Maeve, how do you sleep?"

"What?"

"Are you prone to nightmares?"

I scoffed with a shake of my head.

"You enjoy journaling, is that correct?"

I didn't answer until my scalp burned as my hair was tugged once more. "Fucking hell," I swore in pain. "Yes. Why?"

"I should be thanking you, because all of your pathetically sad admissions and shredded book pages have been quite helpful in this process." Lucan shook his head in false disappointment. "You should know better than to write things on paper that you wish to keep private."

My expression turned dull. He found my journal entries? I had written everything down on those loose pages of parchment. *Everything*. "When I saw you in the soldiers' quarters, before the winter gala, you were going to break into my room?"

"Goodness no. I would never invade a young woman's privacy like that." He glanced up. "Calvin however does not uphold the same moral standards. It was quite easy for someone so charming to convince a house maiden to create him a master key. When you moved to the soldiers' quarters, it got even easier for him. He even helped you pack. How kind."

I was lost for words, remembering the way my papers were crumpled when I first moved rooms—like someone had looked through them.

Lucan rose to his feet. "Prince Hawthorne, huh?" He leaned back against the wall. "Never would have expected that. Does his father know? I can't imagine that would go over well."

Rampant palpitations took over the normal rhythm of my heart.

"What were you doing in the king's study when we found you?" I asked, knowing damn well he wasn't gathering data. "You said you were going to see the duke when you left, but Duke Sinclair was at the meeting in the throne room…you weren't."

"Funny you should ask. That actually had to do with you! What are the odds?" Lucan responded facetiously. "I was planning to leave him some evidence of your failure to wield—glad to see you're gaining some weight back, by the way—in hopes that Aldous would just hand you over. But you and your *boyfriend* interrupted me. I planned to go back at a later time, but decided it was too risky after you two saw me."

"So why would you give me Ridgeroot at the trials if you were just going to try and get King Hawthorne to hand me over?"

"Because you very well would have died at the trials without the Ridgeroot, and then you would have been of no use to anyone."

"Huh. Well, you may be interested to know that I never even took the damn capsule. I'm no cheater," I spat.

"My dear, utilizing your resources is not cheating. But I suppose maybe you aren't as weak as I thought. Although I would have expected someone with power such as yours to have won their first trial. Never mind that now, though."

"What do you want from me?" I asked again, anger coating my tongue like sap.

"I already told you."

The man clearly was no fool. He wouldn't just trust that I would keep this information to myself if I declined his offer. No. If Lucan was telling me all this, then he only planned for one of two things. Either I'd give myself to Draemor or give myself to death.

Despite my best efforts, the gash on my elbow continued to leak thick, crimson blood. If I needed to reach for my dagger—which seemed like a likely possibility—I would have to let the bleeding flow freely.

"And if I decline?" I asked, though I dreaded the answer.

Lucan's features contorted him into someone almost unrecognizable as he bent down in front of me again. This was not the man who had helped ease my nerves in the throne on my very first day here. This man was corrupt. Malicious.

"It would be very unwise of you to decline," he hissed, his breath smelling like smoke when it slithered its way into my nostrils.

Although panic threatened to break my composure, I held on to every bit of it that I could. "I did not ask if declining was wise, I asked what would happen if I did," I spat, causing him to abruptly pull back.

"Let me rephrase," Lucan glowered at me while wiping the moisture off his face. "You *are* coming with me to Draemor. You can come willingly or forcefully. That, I'll leave up to you."

I'd hate myself for it later, but I considered the offer. I'd already been the cause of so much bad in Caelestis, and this could solve the problems of so many.

If I was gone, Sebastian wouldn't have to worry about watching over me. He wouldn't have to *kill* anymore because of me. Sawyer would no longer have to face the person who was vicariously responsible for the death of the woman he loved. If I went, the lives of those I cared for would no longer be in jeopardy.

But there was also the possibility that nothing changed. Beaumont could still declare war and my loved ones could still be hurt even if I went with Lucan. Their best chance at survival was if I stayed.

The risks out-weighed the benefits.

"I'm not going anywhere with you," I hissed at the traitor standing before me.

"Is that your final answer?"

Every cell in my body was soaked in adrenaline. I tried to tap into my magic, the task difficult under this much pressure. It was likely that the two of them had their shields up, but I was hopeful that I could break through at least one of them and get out of this without having to pull my dagger.

"Yes," I grunted.

"Very well." Lucan nodded at Calvin, who forced me to my feet by my neck.

Before I could react to the change of position, Calvin dropped his hand to my side, and my body recoiled at a stabbing pain, piercing between my ribs.

The knife cut deep, its lethal tip teasing my heart. There was a release of pressure as he pulled the blade out and my blood began to spill.

My eyes squeezed shut in agony, but no noise escaped my lips. I would not falter and show them any weakness.

"You may be the strongest in the empire with your gift, but even the power of a constellastone isn't invincible against magic suppressant," Calvin whispered before releasing his hold on me.

The knife dropped to the floor with a clang, and my eyes darted to it, noting the deep green liquid of the toxin that dripped from the blade.

"Fuck," I cursed. Within seconds, burning heat coursed into my blood, the sting sending every nerve in my body into overdrive.

My palms caught me when I fell back to the ground, fresh blood spurting from the hole in my arm as I removed the only thing holding it in.

I moaned in agony as the toxin circulated within me, and swore I could feel my magic disintegrating with each passing moment. Despite Calvin's claim, I held my breath, biting back the pain of the suppressant and trying to summon my power.

It wasn't there. Not a shred of it.

There was no other option—I would have to fight my way out of this.

I released my breath and let the sting of the poison flow back in. I gave myself a moment to adjust to the pain, then used every ounce of my strength to block it out, needing to fight the ache just long enough to get out of here.

I pushed myself to my feet with my weak, paling limb, while using my good arm to reach for my thigh. My fingers locked around the hilt of my dagger, and before anyone could react, I spun on my heel, swinging my blade through the air and slicing through Calvin's shirt. I curved my wrist sharply, gouging a chunk of flesh out of his bicep.

He cursed, and while preoccupied with pain, I swung at him again. This time I tore through his stomach, slicing through his navel deeper than intended. Layers of muscle snapped apart, yellow, fatty flesh peeking through the hole in his shirt.

Calvin growled as he stumbled back, clutching his abdomen. Plasma poured from him in an aggressive eruption, and if it weren't for his healing magic, he would have bled out within a minute.

My hand lubricated with my own blood as I clutched my side, putting pointless pressure on the hole between my ribs. The bleeding was thick and heavy, seeping right through the gaps of my fingers.

I was going to bleed dry either way, so didn't bother continuing to apply pressure. I dropped my hand and, while Calvin worked vigorously to heal the damage I'd done, put my attention on Lucan.

The king's poor excuse of an advisor didn't waste any time. I hadn't even taken a step towards him before he used his emerald magic to send vines twisting around my arms.

The creeping plant squeezed me so tightly that it forced my wrist open, and my dagger fell from my clutch. Lucan kicked it away and my eyes watched in panic as my only shot at saving myself slid across the floor.

Shit. And to think I really thought I was becoming skilled in combat.

Lucan then aimed his earth magic towards my legs, constricting my thighs with leafy green ropes. I tried to take a step forward, but he tightened his reins and I plummeted to the ground.

I narrowly avoided hitting my face, but Calvin—who was quicker at healing himself than I'd expected—came up behind me, slamming my head into the cement.

The bones in my face cracked against the cement as Calvin pressed his knee onto my back, holding me to the ground.

My ribcage was crushed by the force of the impact. The air escaped from my lungs, and the agony from the toxin was replaced by something much worse as I struggled to breathe.

Calvin jerked his leg back and forth, dragging my face across the rough stone. I screamed as my skin ripped, tearing in multiple spots, though I was no longer coherent enough to know where.

The soldier relieved enough of the pressure to allow me to look up into Lucan's slanted eyes. "You are making this much more difficult than it has to be, Maeve." He snickered, a devious smirk pulling his lips up.

I could hardly see him through the redness coating my irises as vital fluid expelled from my skull. I raised a finger to my face, and gagged in response to a piece of hanging flesh on my forehead.

Dizziness overwhelmed me for a few moments, but I blinked through the tunnel of darkness—there was no time to show any weakness.

Lucan crouched down to where I laid under Calvin's hold. "Tell me. These visions you wrote about, has there been any truth to them yet?"

"Wouldn't you like to know," I gargled through a mouthful of blood.

I needed a way out of this, though there weren't many options. My dagger was on the other side of the corridor, my magic inaccessible, and I couldn't move due to the two-hundred and fifty pound man on my back.

Despite my best efforts to stay awake, I bordered on the edge of blacking out. My face swelled rapidly and blood expelled from so many parts of my body that I'd surely be too weak to move any minute now.

I was going to die. Unless Calvin granted me mercy and healed me, but why would he bother? King Beaumont would rather me alive, but he didn't need me to be. As long as he cut my gemstones out before their magic died with my vessel, he could access my power.

I tried one more attempt at fighting my way out of Calvin's hold, but with no luck, I stopped moving, allowing my body to reserve any energy I had left.

Calvin sensed my retreat and moved his body off of mine. He grabbed me by the backs of the shoulders, and picked my limp torso off the ground, holding me upright as Lucan approached me.

"I was planning to keep you alive to use you during the battle, but I can reconsider. Stop fighting and come with me." Lucan held a hand out to me.

Staring at it, I slowly processed what he was telling me to do, and used the last of my energy to clasp my palm around his.

Then I broke his fucking wrist.

My hand squeezed his in a death grip, and I jolted my arm to the right, snapping his in one fluid motion.

"You fucking bitch!" he growled out in anguish, clutching his wrist in his other hand as he gave Calvin permission to destroy me.

The soldier pulled me into his chest, turning me to face him just so he could slam me into the cement even harder than before. The back of my skull hit the ground, and I made out muffled voices as my head bounced.

The two of them stood over me, staring at my borderline lifeless body. I made out the glint of a blade hovering inches from my face. Lucan said something, but my ears rang so loudly that I couldn't make it out. Then, their eyes widened and their bodies vanished.

Shallow, labored breaths were all my lungs could expel as I

choked on the metallic taste of my own blood pooling in the back of my throat.

I turned my head as much as possible towards the door, letting the blood dribble from my lips. My eyes settled on two pairs of dress boots, and I scanned up their owners' legs. The fog in my brain prevented me from putting a name to the faces, but I recognized the two men.

The one with darker hair approached Lucan and Calvin at once, blade extended. The other vanished, only to appear by my side moments later.

His mouth moved, though his words were unrecognizable. He gathered me into his arms, lifting me from the cement that was cooling the pain within me.

I didn't fight him—I couldn't move. I couldn't *feel.* Blood stung my eyes, so I let them close, succumbing to the darkness that had been trailing me.

CHAPTER
THIRTY-EIGHT
SEBASTIAN

I took one look at her, and that was all the motivation I needed to explode on the two assholes standing over her mutilated body.

Her face was almost unrecognizable from the mix of bruising, swelling, and bleeding. She was still awake, but so lifeless that it wouldn't be long before she was completely comatose.

I gestured to Sawyer with my head. "Take her upstairs and send someone to find Pia. I'll take care of these assholes."

It took everything in me to not stay with her, but I needed to ensure these two got what they deserved. And for the sake of my sanity, I needed to be the one to do it.

Sawyer nodded and rushed to Maeve's side. I watched him scoop her safely into his arms, then didn't allow myself to focus any more attention on her—not right now. I had business with the royal advisor to take care of.

I turned towards Lucan and the second year soldier, whose name I believed to be Calvin. They both looked absolutely terrified of me. Smart men. They should be.

"I'll give you ten seconds to explain before I fucking kill you both," I snarled.

Lucan began to stutter, but I interjected. "Actually, I changed my mind. There's no excuse for what you did to her." As soon as the words left my lips, I tapped into the magic from my diamond, shooting pointed blades of ice into the chest of the soldier responsible.

Lucan watched, his mouth agape as the heat from Calvin's blood melted the icicles embedded in his skin. The substances mixed together and dripped into a flood on the floor.

Calvin reached down, palming at the blades, trying to pull them from his skin. They slipped through his fingers and he fell to his knees, crying out in agony.

I approached the soldier, who didn't dare try to fight back as I pulled my dagger from the sheath around my waist.

"Watch closely. If you try to stop me, you'll be next," I threatened the advisor, pointing my blade at him. Little did he know that I wasn't going to spare him, anyways.

I grabbed the top of Calvin's hair, jerking his head back to expose his neck to me. Tears poured from the bastard's eyes. He knew the fate he was about to meet.

"Please," he begged, still grasping at the melting ice in his chest.

I leaned my face into his, putting emphasis on my words as they rolled off my tongue, "May the gods damn you beyond the veil for what you've done."

I lifted my dagger, angling my wrist to slice through the throat of the man on his knees before me. I dragged the blade slowly, taking my time and making sure to nick the artery on the side of his neck.

Calvin gurgled on his own blood as it filled his mouth. His head dropped forward when I released it, and his eyes sank into his skull as he began to bleed out like a creature being slaughtered for meat.

I wiped the blade on my pants, then pivoted and marched to the door, leaning against it with my arms crossed to watch the man in front of me die.

Lucan didn't dare move a muscle. He held his position next to Calvin, letting the soldier's blood soak through the soles of his shoes. The advisor paled as his prodigy ceased to breathe.

Calvin aimlessly clutched his neck, trying to stop his artery from spurting away the remainder of his life. But he failed, and fell forward onto his face. Dead.

I ground my jaw, then casually tilted my head toward Lucan. Granting him a heinous smirk, I kicked off of the door and strode for him. "Get on your knees," I demanded, pointing to the ground with the tip of my dagger.

Lucan put his arms up in submission, but I was not here to take pity on him. The fucker was going to die. That was not up for debate.

"Get. On. Your. Knees," I repeated, this time the advisor doing as I said.

Lucan dropped down, shaking as he cowered before me. "Let me explain, Crown Prince. There is more to this than it seems," his hollow voice wavered.

I crouched in front of him, passing my dagger between my hands. "First of all, don't fucking call me that. And is there now? Because from my point of view, it looks like you were trying to kill my girl." I glared into his eyes, and he looked side to side, trying to avoid my gaze. "Is that true?"

Lucan did not respond with words. His eyes did the talking for him.

"Are you scared?" I taunted, noting how his teeth chattered in his skull. I outstretched my arm, placing one hand on his shoulder. "Don't be scared. I hear death can be quick and painless." His death wouldn't be, though.

I jammed the tip of my dagger into his throat, not yet using enough pressure to break the skin. "Here's what's going to happen." I applied a little more pressure to my blade. "You're going to tell me why you tried to kill Maeve, then I'm going to decide how painful of a death you'll receive."

Lucan scoffed, finally gathering enough courage to meet my gaze. "If you kill me, your father will never believe you."

I snickered at his stupidity. "You think I give a shit if he believes me? I know what I saw—what would have happened had I got here a minute later. Whether or not my father believes me is the least of my concerns." I put more pressure on the dagger, breaking through the skin enough to draw some blood.

Lucan winced, bending his head backwards to avoid the blade. I moved my other hand to the back of his neck, keeping him still.

"What's the point of telling you if you're just going to kill me, anyway?" he countered my request.

"If you tell me what I want to know, I'll make your death a *little* less horrific."

Lucan spit at the ground next to me. "Just ask *your girl* when she wakes up." He paused, smiling deviously at me. "*If* she wakes up, that is."

That comment didn't go over well with me.

I pulled my dagger from his neck, then ripped him by the collar of his shirt to stand up.

He groaned in agony as I shoved him back and his spine collided with the stone. I held him against the wall with my forearm and aimed my blade at his throat with the other hand. He didn't even try to fight back. I had well over two feet on him in height, and muscle mass that he couldn't even challenge.

"Tell me why you hurt her, *now*," I demanded through gritted teeth, while putting enough pressure on his chest that he couldn't take a deep breath.

"I simply offered her one more chance to turn herself over to King Beaumont," Lucan sputtered. "She even considered taking it for a moment, too," he sniped, his voice dry from struggling to inhale.

"Maeve would never consider that." I shook my head.

"But she did."

She wouldn't. Would she? Her and I just talked about this, and I thought we were on the same page.

"I told her if she declined, that there would be consequences." Lucan shrugged, his eyes peering over at the pool of blood Maeve left behind. "Clearly she rejected the offer." He chortled.

That was it. I'd had it with his snide sense of humor. Nothing about this was fucking funny. Time to finish the job so that I could make sure she was okay.

She better fucking be okay.

"You're not going to tell me anything more, are you?" I asked, accepting the defeat that he wasn't going to divulge any information to me.

The king's former advisor shook his head, and as he did, I plunged my dagger straight into his throat. The blade twisted in my hand, the sounds of cartilage cracking as the dagger scraped against his insides.

His blood drained over me, saturating my dress uniform. The tangy smell of metal filled the corridor, the hall now coated in the blood of three.

Lucan exhaled his last breath, and only then did I pull my dagger from his flesh. I backed away, letting his body drop to the floor with a hefty thud. For good measure, I stomped the sole of my boot into his skull.

Crack.

My hands ran through my hair as I stepped back and stood in the wreckage before me, turning in a circle to truly absorb the bloody carnage left behind.

I looked to where she had been lying. Some of her blood had dried black, absorbed into the cement.

She was hardly conscious, but I'm glad Sawyer got Maeve out of here when he did. I didn't want her to see this side of me—the side that I hated, but accepted with a fury of passion when I needed to.

I shouldn't have left her. I'd never forgive myself for what they did to her. And if she died…

I swallowed the nausea that burned my esophagus.

There was no time for emotions right now. I had to get to her.

I picked up her dagger, then took one last look at the mess before starting off in a sprint up the staircase.

I was met by my friends surrounding her when I burst through the door of Maeve's room.

She laid lifeless in her bed. So pale and still that I had to focus to catch the rise and fall of her stomach to know that she was still breathing.

Sawyer crouched on the floor next to her bedside. Kohen watched from afar while Pia worked her healing magic.

"Is she okay?" Panic pulled at my insides as I stared at her lifeless frame. I hadn't moved from the doorway—couldn't bring myself to.

Sawyer approached me, letting out a deep sigh. "She's alive…I wouldn't go as far as to say that she's *okay*."

I peered over his shoulder. Her hair was matted with blood—her face so swollen and purple that I could hardly make out her beautiful features.

My gaze fell and tears pooled in my eyes.

She's going to be fine. She has to be fine.

"Come out here." Sawyer placed a hand on my back and guided me out of the room, leaving the door open a crack so that we could still hear what was going on.

I drew a shuddered breath, all the anger and fear inside of me coming to a head. My teeth bit into my lip as I looked up at the ceiling, trying to hide the wetness in my eyes.

"Deep breaths, man."

I listened, counting my inhales to try and gather myself. I needed to keep my shit together.

When I finally dropped my head, Sawyer stared at me like he was trying to decide if he should tell me everything, but he knew better than to withhold information from me—especially when it came to her.

I took another breath, then nodded to give him the go ahead.

"To start, it's not as bad as it looks. Her elbow is busted open. There's exposed bone and it's a pretty gnarly gash, but Pia closed it up enough so that it stopped bleeding."

Sawyer's expression changed as he continued. "Her breathing is fucked. One of those assholes collapsed her lung. We were going to bring her to the infirmary, but since I didn't know what was really going on down there, we held off. I think that was the right call anyway—Pia worked on that first and her breathing seems more normal now."

I let out a sigh of relief.

"Her face looks worse than it really is, I think. There were pieces of skin hanging but Pia got them to scab up pretty good—she doesn't even think it will leave a scar. She's working on reducing the swelling now. She definitely has a gnarly concussion though, but Pia should be able to help that at least a little bit."

Thank the gods.

"Overall, Maeve should be fine. But Seb, that was close…too close. We shouldn't have left—"

I cut him off. "Don't tell me that we shouldn't have left her," I snarled, emphasizing each word. "Don't you think I fucking know that *I* shouldn't have left her?" I slammed my fist into the stone wall. "FUCK."

I put my back against the wall, sliding down it and supporting my arms on my knees, sinking my head between them. My knuckles bled and ached as I shook my head, scoffing to myself.

This is what I had been worried about. I let myself care too much. I cared about her more than I ever planned to, more than I should.

She didn't believe me, but I was no good for her. The things I just did to those men down there, without showing an ounce of mercy—the things I've done to others before them—if she saw that side of me then she would understand.

Sawyer sat down next to me, ignoring my outburst. "She's gonna be fine, Seb, really."

My fingers tangled into my hair. "I know, I know, I just—"

"What?"

I looked up at Sawyer. "I just brutally executed two men for her, and I don't have an *ounce* of remorse. None at all. That's *never* happened to me before." I always felt a twinge or pain with each life I took, no matter the circumstances. But not this time. If anything, I felt overjoyed knowing the assholes were dead.

"The fuckers had it coming."

"I know they did. They deserved even more for what they did to her. It's just the fact that I did it so easily…So relentlessly."

There was nothing I wouldn't do for her. Absolutely *nothing*.

"I slit their throats and watched them bleed out." I said quietly, staring at Sawyer, who didn't so much as blink. "I crushed Lucan's skull with my boot after he was already dead. Just because."

Sawyer shuffled a little, but still did not respond.

"I would do it time and time again if I had to. The extent I would go to keep her safe is fucking terrifying," I confessed, although I didn't know why I said it out loud, especially to Sawyer who had been a damn ghost lately.

"That's love, man." Kohen's soft spoken voice appeared. "I'd do the same for Pia. And both of you idiots, too, if I had to."

I didn't even hear him join us. How long had he been out here?

My head shook, trying to deny his claim, but he was right. I fucking loved her. I loved her more than anything in our realm or beyond the veil. I just wanted to be able to love her in the way that she deserved. There was too much she didn't know about me. Too much I hadn't told her.

"She'll hate me when she sees who I really am. I've been telling her that for months…I'll ruin her. I can't love her in the way she wants me to. I—" My voice trailed off as I rambled. I was too fired up right now and divulging more than I typically liked to share.

Sawyer put his hand on my shoulder. "Yes, you can. You just won't let yourself."

I raised an eyebrow and glanced between the two of them.

"You won't hurt her," Kohen chimed in. "You may hurt others *for* her, but you won't hurt her. Not intentionally, at least. You're better than that."

Sawyer nodded in agreement as he rose to his feet. "I know you're in love with her, and whether or not you're ready to admit that to yourself is on you. But she almost died tonight, and you should take that as a sign from the gods to tell her."

How were they being so rational about this? Was I just overly emotional right now? "How do you guys act like it doesn't bother you? The way killing has changed you?"

"Now probably isn't the right time to get into this, Seb. You have a lot on your mind and Maeve needs you in there," Sawyer said, angling a thumb towards the door.

"I mean, there's no way it hasn't affected you. Am I just really shitty at hiding it?" I replied, ignoring his suggestion.

"I don't look at it the way that you do, I guess. The way I see it, I'm just protecting the ones I care about and the kingdom. It's just part of the job," Kohen said. "I don't think about it as deeply."

I turned to Sawyer who shrugged. "I don't know, man. Maybe it's easier because I haven't been forced into killing since I was a kid."

Kohen's jaw went slack at the brash remark, but I couldn't help but let out a snort of laughter. That was the Sawyer I'd missed.

He smiled at me, pulling me into a one-armed hug. "You're too hard on yourself, man. Just let yourself be fucking happy. You deserve it, whether you believe that or not. You just killed two men for her—if that's not honorable as fuck, then I don't know what is."

"You and I have very different definitions of honorable."

Kohen replaced Sawyer's embrace, patting my back. "You know, I hate when I have to admit this, but Sawyer is right." He pulled away. "Regardless, you should really be in there with her. She's going to want to see you when she wakes up."

Right. Time to stop my damn pity party. I blew out a breath, then rose and marched into the room to be with the woman I loved.

CHAPTER THIRTY-NINE

"M*aeve."*

"Maeve, can you hear me?"

Everything was dark, but I made out the sound of a familiar voice. A woman's voice.

"We only have a moment, so listen closely."

I couldn't move or see anything. Listening was all I could do.

"The day will soon be here," the breathy voice called out to me, just as a beam of light bisected the darkness encompassing me.

"The prophecy will soon be fulfilled. Prepare yourself. Prepare your loved ones. Merciless bloodshed is just among the horizon."

Reality began to resurface as more light gradually pooled in.

"*Do not fight the sacrifice. Do not fear it."* I recognized the soft voice as Blythe's.

I felt my consciousness returning and realized that I was lying somewhere between the veil. Though hoarse, I found my voice. "I am no longer afraid of death." If the sacrifice was catching up to me, I would let it.

"Nevertheless, it's not death you need to fear."

I didn't get a chance to counter as beams of shimmering light dripped from the walls, replacing the darkness with a nothingness of white.

"I think she's waking up," I heard a male voice from somewhere to my left.

"What did she say?" another person asked.

My senses were returning as I came to. I blinked once, but my eyes were too heavy to hold open. Floating in empty space, the tranquility of the silence washed over me. Nothing mattered in that moment. Not a thing. If this was what death was like, I would welcome it with open arms.

"Maeve?"

"Someone grab a wet cloth," a frantic voice demanded one of the others.

Cool water dampened my skin, forcing my eyelids apart. I held my gaze long enough to make out a blurred figure standing before me and some of my surroundings. I was in my room—I think. Everything within my view spun and wavered, so it was hard to know for sure. My arms left my sides, padding around on the surface I laid upon. My bed.

A groan of pain escaped me as I tried to sit up. My body was in pure agony. Every inch of it. My veins were on fire, granting me a sting of devastating pain with each pump of my heart. My finger quivered as I raised it to my forehead, trying to put pressure on the relentless throbbing.

"I don't know, guys, she's still pretty out of it. I did everything I could, but maybe we should bring her to the infirmary. There could be something else going on internally."

I looked at the girl who was talking, recognizing her face as one of my friends.

"We could get her into the shower. The water might help her wake up."

"Oh yeah, Sawyer, that's a great idea, you idiot. She can barely hold her head up. How is she supposed to stand in the shower?"

"Don't be an ass, Kohen," the girl said.

Sawyer? Kohen? I knew them. And if they were here—

The thought of him motivated me enough to lift my head, holding it as steady as I could.

The blurriness faded away as I rubbed my eyes. My friends came into view, one by one. I focused on them. On *him.* And everything came back to me in a jarring revelation.

Sebastian crouched by my side, putting his head level with mine. "How do you feel?"

I tried to tell him that the pain made me wish I were dead, but without warning, horrific nausea overcame me. My hand found my mouth, and though I was nowhere near ready to be walking, I forced myself out of bed.

I didn't even make it a few feet before I heaved and vomited all over myself and the floor. My sudden burst of movement took all of my energy and I fell to my knees, hanging my head and trying my hardest to stay conscious.

"Oh shit," someone cursed.

My vision dissipated again and the last thing I felt was two strong hands lifting my limp figure from the ground.

✦✧✦✧✦

WATER RUSHED OVER MY INJURED SKIN. IT FELT LIKE RAIN, BUT THAT couldn't be right. The liquid warmed my scalp, though it burned my skin elsewhere. A film of sleep clouded my eyes when I opened them to discover that the shower was what produced the drizzle.

My heart skipped—there was someone here with me. My body was relaxed, limp against theirs, the firmness of their hands around my waist keeping me upright. My breath clenched as I started to panic.

A deep male voice shushed to calm me. He kept one arm wrapped around me for support, while raising the other to stroke my wet hair.

I looked over my shoulder, my panic instantly ceasing to see that Sebastian was the one holding me. Unlike my own bare skin, he was fully clothed, his eyes dark and sunken in.

Despite how my legs wobbled, I turned in his arms, putting us face to face. I had to put a considerable amount of effort into raising my head to meet his gaze. My breasts pressed against the fabric of his shirt, but nothing about this moment was sensual. It was safe.

"I'm sorry, but you weren't waking up and you had gotten sick. I needed to get you clean." His voice was almost silent as he spoke. "I made sure everyone else left before I brought you in here. It's just us," he assured me.

I forced my lips to crack a faint smile, appreciating that he was so concerned about preserving my dignity. "You don't need to apologize," I rasped, attempting to find my voice. The words made my throat ache, as if my insides were dry and scraped.

His top clung to him, the soaked fabric caressing my cheek as I leaned into his chest. He supported most of my weight. If he were to let go, I would collapse.

"How do you feel?" he asked, his voice gruff.

"Not great," I admitted. My veins no longer burned, indicating that the magic suppressant had worked its way out of my system. But my limbs ached and my face felt exactly how I'd expect it to.

Sebastian placed a kiss on the top of my head. I didn't look, but I heard him sniffle. "I thought you were going to die," he breathed into my hair.

Sadness overwhelmed me as I recalled the details of what happened, remembering everything up until him and Sawyer showed up. I hated that Sebastian had to see me like that—bordering life and death. If the shoe were on the other foot, I would have been a complete wreck.

"So did I." The words came out so quietly that I was not sure if he heard them over the trickling water. "But I didn't."

Water dripped off his lips as he blew out a deep breath. "No. You didn't." His hand slid from my hair, down to the middle of my back where he clasped it with his other. I looked up into his face. He looked so somber. Broken.

"I'm okay," I assured him and myself, the statement not feeling true until I said it out loud.

"Thank the gods." Sebastian held onto me tightly, as if he was worried I'd slip from his grasp if he let go.

I welcomed the comfort and stretched my arms out to embrace him back, my heart swollen with love for him.

"What do you remember?" His chin rested on top of my head, water dribbling down the front of his face and on to mine as he waited for an answer.

"Mostly everything until I blacked out. Then I remember waking up in my bed, but only for a moment." I racked my brain, trying to recall all of the details. "I had a strange dream, too, while I was out. I think it may have been another vision."

Sebastian's jaw tightened.

"What?"

His voice lowered. "You were muttering right before you woke up—something about death."

"Yeah…that was it."

Heartbeats passed before either of us spoke again.

Pulling my chest from his, I stared up at him. "Lucan found my journal entries. Calvin had been breaking into my room. He read them all," I blurted out. "When we found him in your father's study, he was planning to plant information on me. He was going to give away how weak my magic makes me in hopes that King Hawthorne would hand me over to Draemor."

Sebastian's jaw ticked, and I could tell that he was fighting his anger in order to keep me calm.

"We should probably get out. Get you dressed and fed. Then we can talk about this." He reached around me to turn the water off, and I shivered with the sudden lack of heat.

He wrapped me in a towel, warm from the humidity of the washroom, then he scooped me in his arms. I caught a glimpse of myself in the mirror when he walked by, and a gasp escaped me. Bruises and scabs covered a good portion of my skin. The pad of my finger grazed my forehead, recalling how it felt to have my face scraped against concrete.

"It looks way better than it was." Sebastian noticed my shock. "Pia healed most of it."

Fuck. I looked *worse*?

Sebastian carried me to my bed, placing me gently down on it. I pulled the towel tightly around myself, using it as a replacement for the warmth of his body.

"Give me two minutes. I'm going to run down to my room and change into some dry clothes, then I'll be right back." His eyes shot me a warning. "Don't try and get up."

My eyes rolled back in my head at his bossiness in a moment like this, but in this situation, he was probably right. I was far too weak to walk.

His clothes left a trail of water as he left, and while I waited for him to return, I took inventory of my injuries. Moving the towel to see my knees, my mouth clamped shut to see black and purple from where Calvin slammed me down onto them.

I palmed my elbow, wincing at the scab that had replaced the exposed bone. I'd no doubt have a scar there—just like Sebastian. I almost smirked at the thought of our matching scar tissue, but the stories behind them were nothing to smile about.

The sun rose over the cliffside outside my window. "How long was I out?" I asked as soon as Sebastian reappeared in dry clothing.

He marched straight for my wardrobe, rummaging through it. "I dunno. Lost track of time. At least half a day," he said, holding out a pair of lounge pants and a shirt. "Would have been longer if it weren't for Pia."

"Yeah. Like, forever," I quipped.

He glared at me.

"Is she okay? Pia? That must have taken a lot out of her."

"She's resting now. We want to keep a close eye on you for a while in case there's anything internally she missed, but she thinks she fixed most of the damage."

I raised my arms, letting him slide a shirt over my head ever so carefully. "Have you slept?"

"No." He pulled my lounge pants over my knees, and I lifted my hips to assist him the rest of the way.

"You look exhausted. I'll be fine if you want to go rest."

"I'm not leaving you." His tone left no room for discussion. He fell onto the mattress beside me, running his hands over his face.

"Is that normal? For a first year to be so talented with their magic?" I returned the conversation to Pia as I rested my head on his shoulder.

"She's definitely gifted if that's what you're asking. I've only seen healing magic that advanced by the infirmary menders. But they've had years of practice. Some of them have been healing since before the war."

At the mention of battle, my mind went back to my most recent vision. Maybe when my head hit the pavement last night it knocked some sense into me, because everything started to add up.

It was all tied together. The visions of war. Beaumont's retreat. Lucan's attack on me. All of it.

"Draemor is going to declare war any day now, despite what Beaumont told your father," I spat out the words as the information clicked into place.

Sebastian raised an eyebrow. "What?"

"Beaumont lied when he pulled back his threats—he never had any intentions of following through, like we predicted. We weren't giving him what he wanted, so he pretended not to care to get your father to drop the wards. He used our naivety to give Draemor more time to prepare their attack." I shook my head. "That's why Lucan came after me—his last chance at taking me to Draemor before they declared war."

Sebastian stared blankly at me, absorbing everything I blurted out. He turned his head slowly towards the window, and nodded. "Can't say I didn't see that coming, but how do you know this?"

"Lucan told me that he wanted me alive to be used during battle." I hadn't asked Sebastian what happened to the king's advisor—I didn't need to. "And the vision I had when waking up—Blythe said to prepare for war *soon*. When word gets back to Beaumont that I refused his offer again, he'll have no reason to hold back."

"Shit." Sebastian rolled off the bed and started pacing. "The conversation Sawyer overheard was just a ploy to get us away from you. Those probably weren't even our soldiers. Lucan wanted to try and persuade you to take the offer in private."

"Draemor was going to attack Caelestis whether they had me or not. The only difference would be that I'd be the one doing the damage," I added.

"It was so simple that I completely overlooked it. Fucking stupid. I know better," Sebastian grumbled and put his back to me. "Did your vision give you any indication of when Draemor may attack?"

"No. She just said soon."

He dropped to a crouch in front of me. "I have to inform my father. He doesn't even know Lucan is dead yet, and it would be quite the shock if Draemornian soldiers come knocking on his door before I get the chance to tell him. We'll get the wards back up and prepare our troops. We don't want to waste a single second."

He leaned forward, brushing his mouth lightly over mine. My split lip stung from his kiss, but I accepted the pain with passion.

"I'll have Sawyer stay with you while I'm gone," he said after he pulled away.

My stomach dropped. Sawyer and I still weren't on good terms. "Oh no, that's okay. I'm just going to sleep, anyway."

"I am not leaving you alone after this. That's not up for negotiation. I'll try to be quick, and I'll bring you something to eat when I get back."

"Can't you stay for a little longer? Can we just lay here and pretend that everything is okay for a moment?" I pleaded, batting my heavy eyes.

Sebastian grinned apologetically, softening his presence. "I wish we could, baby. But I almost just lost you, and I will be damned if I waste a single second that could have been spent protecting you."

I wanted to argue further, but dropped it and curled up in the comfort of my quilt. Sebastian left, then I closed my eyes and tried everything in my power to fall asleep before Sawyer arrived.

CHAPTER FORTY

It didn't work.

Sawyer marched into my room, not even trying to be quiet as he slammed the door shut. His boots stomped heavily across the floor as he approached my bedside, ripping the quilt off that I had strategically put over my face.

"Hey!" I whined.

"Oh good. You're up."

"Like anyone could sleep through the ruckus you're making," I scoffed

"What the hell happened?" he asked sternly, looking pissed.

Though my muscles burned with movement, I sat up on my mattress. "You *saw* what happened. You walked in on them trying to kill me."

Sawyer glared at me, clenching his fists. "I meant the part where you somehow forgot how to use your combat skills. I mean, come on, Maeve! Seb and I have been training you for almost a year, how the hell did you let them beat on you like that?" he shouted at me.

My eyes widened. "Are you serious right now?"

"Dead."

My teeth ground against each other. "Well for starters, *asshole*, it was two against one. One of them was a second year who had a hundred pounds on me, and the other was a damn psycho who knew how to wield tripwire from fucking vines!" I yelled back.

Sawyer huffed, his face turning red from anger. "You're better than that. *I taught you* better than that," he snarled.

I crossed my arms over my chest. "I guess you aren't as good of a teacher as you think."

Sawyer's mouth clamped shut, pressing into a thin line as he glared at me, completely unamused with my comeback.

"I'm the one who almost died, so if you came in here just to be a dick, do me a favor and screw off." I gestured to the door. This was the last thing I needed right now.

Sawyer grasped the footboard, his forehead creased as he leaned into my face. "Yeah, you're the one who almost died. But *I'm* the one who carried your practically lifeless body upstairs, praying to the gods that you were still alive by the time Pia got here. I'm the one who had to lie to his best fucking friend and tell him that his girl just '*looked worse than she really was.*' And I'm the one who still has your blood stained into their skin!" He held his hands up to me, veiny and dyed red.

His face softened into an expression that could have been confused for heartbreak. "You could have died, Maeve. I'm sure Sebastian didn't tell you because he doesn't even know the half of it, but if it weren't for Pia getting here when she did, you *would* be dead right now. You were barely breathing by the time I got you upstairs." His voice lowered and he pulled his face back. "You scared the shit out of me."

Frowning, my eyes dropped to my sheets. "I tried. I really, really tried," I croaked, the bleak sentence the only thing I could come up with at the moment.

Sawyer shoved his hands into his pockets as he moved to take a seat at the foot of my bed. "I know." He sighed, his tone relaxing a bit. His back was to me, leaving only his uniform and the shags of his brown hair visible. His head shook ever so faintly. "I'm sorry. I've been a complete ass to you the past few weeks."

"Yeah, you kind of have."

He looked to the side, angling an eye at me. "Sometimes in my life it just seems like I'm always the one that gets screwed over. And I don't mind because I care about you—you're one of my best friends. But—" He stopped himself.

"But what?"

Sawyer inhaled deeply, blowing the breath out audibly as he continued. "Yeah, I *had* feelings for Jocelyn. But the way I reacted when she died—" He turned to face me head on. "Maybe this makes me even more of a dick, but when I found out that she died, I just kept thinking about you—how it could be you that we'd bury next, and it terrified me."

My insides tangled. "But I was fine. I wasn't the one who went to Craterra. Nothing happened to me."

He shook his head once more. "You aren't understanding."

"What?"

"I can't lose you."

My heart raced. "Oh."

"I wouldn't survive it."

Oh.

Sawyer looked away again, then pushed his hands off his lap to stand. His demeanor completely changed, as if he didn't just spill some of his deepest feelings to me. "Anyways, I'm sorry for how I've been acting. I truly am relieved that you're okay, I know Seb is, too." He moved to my armchair, where he got comfortable to wait until Sebastian returned.

I didn't know what to say—not after what he just admitted to me.

What exactly *did* he admit to me? Sure, I was one of his closest friends and vice versa, but I had a feeling that our friendship was not what he referred to.

I gawked at him for a moment, then fell back down on the mattress. My body was getting weaker by the minute, and I needed to rest, especially knowing that a war could be declared any second.

My eyes fluttered shut as I tried to clear my mind of all the trauma I'd endured. I hadn't fully processed everything yet, and was due for a panic attack over it any minute.

Regardless, I was almost asleep when Sawyer woke me. In fact, from what he said, I think Sawyer thought I *was* asleep.

"Seb is in love with you. He's too much of a wuss to say it, but he is. He has this idea in his head that he can't love you the way you need." He paused to breathe, and his tone was bleak—dejected—when he continued. "I know you're in love with him, too."

I rolled to face him, letting him know that I was awake.

His green eyes met mine dead on. "If you're gonna tell him, don't wait too long. Take it from me."

I couldn't help but grin at Sawyer's blunt honesty. The latter of his confession sent sorrow throughout me, but I clung to the part about Sebastian loving me, and my stomach fluttered as I drifted off to sleep.

"I'd say you're as close to *good as new* as you'll get," Pia chimed, concluding her last go at healing me.

"You're amazing. Truly," I beamed and admired myself in the mirror of my washroom. The only scars I bore from my near death experience was the self-inflicted one on my elbow, and the one between my ribs.

"I've been told." She grinned, pulling me into a quick hug before we abandoned my room and started down the hall.

The academy year was coming to a close, so we had some free time today. With the heat of summer rolling in, we decided to spend some time by the shore while we still could.

King Hawthorne had called an assembly for everyone on the castle grounds a few days ago. He put an immediate hold on classes in preparation for Draemor's attack. Though we didn't know for certain when it would happen, at least he was actually taking the threat seriously. If only he had that sense of logic before I was almost killed.

Sebastian suggested that we send Caelestian soldiers to Draemor first—catch them off guard like we had with Craterra and keep the battle further from our territory. Of course the king shot the idea down, claiming we stood more of a chance fighting on familiar land.

I couldn't stress enough how much of a moron that man was.

It was basically a waiting game now. We were to sit here and twiddle our thumbs until the first sign of interference. First years were not expected to fight. I, of course, was the exception. I didn't mind, though. After everything I'd been through this year—hell, this week alone—I was craving some reprisal.

We stepped outside, Kohen trailing behind us. Sebastian didn't dare leave me without a guard after what happened. He usually did the honors himself, but in the event he couldn't, I had Sawyer or Kohen on my tail.

Sunlight blazed down onto my skin, and I smiled as the warmth embraced me. The sand welcomed my bare toes while I stood at the edge of the water, planting my feet into the ground and letting the ocean crawl over me. I gazed down the coast line, admiring the view of the rocky cliffside that the castle laid upon.

My skin stung from the salt as it soaked into my flesh—the bite of the sea. The horizon faded into hues of orange and pink, the daylight melting away as each second passed. Gods, I'd missed this.

"You look awfully peaceful, maybe I should come back later."

My lips formed an immediate smile.

Sebastian's skin glowed from the golden rays of the sun, his dark hair swirling around his face from the coastal breeze as he stepped through the sand towards me. His biceps tightened around me, strong and firm, holding me close against his chest.

"I still like my beach better," he teased, referring to the one he brought me to on our first night of training. We hadn't been back there yet, but that small piece of paradise would forever hold a special place in my heart.

I smiled, reminiscing on everything that we'd been through since he brought me there. "That night seems so long ago."

"Don't I know it. It's been a hell of a year."

Pia complained from down the beach, yelling at Sawyer who had showed up with Sebastian. He waved a bottle of some spirit above her head, and she desperately tried to reach it. They bickered like siblings while Kohen sat in the sand, a silent observer to their antics.

My smile faded to a frown.

"What's wrong?"

I chewed my lip. "I can't help but feel like this will be one of our last times together as a group where everything is normal. For a while at least."

Sebastian kissed the side of my neck. "Nothing is ever normal. I mean, have you *met* Sawyer?" He huffed a laugh.

I elbowed him, though the fresh skin of my scar was sensitive and twinged at the contact. "You know what I mean."

Sebastian spun me in his arms. With my back towards the ocean, my hair blew wildly in the wind. He tucked the stray pieces behind my ears and gazed into my eyes. I stared back, not breaking the contact as I counted the speckles in his irises.

I traced his jawline with my fingertip, feeling the sharp edge before pressing my lips to it, holding them there for a moment before moving to his lips.

He kissed me back, his lips soft as they grazed mine affectionately. Not caring that our friends were just feet away, his tongue gently slipped between my lips, and we both gave into our greed, the movement of our mouths intensifying.

This kiss was unlike any of our previous ones. Filled with the same desire and passion that we always had, but with a new addition. Something more that I know he sensed, too. The same feeling I'd had for him since we'd met, now swollen with devotion as I had grown to know him. Since we'd learned each other's secrets, explored each other's skin, and chose to trust each other over anyone else.

"Seb," I breathed his name into our kiss and he devoured it.

"Maeve?" he said my name back as a question.

My heart relentlessly battered on my ribs, but I retained my courage, preparing to divulge the words I had waited much too long to say, despite knowing that he may not say it back.

"I'm in love with you."

Relief encased me with my confession. Now, no matter what

happened, whether I lived or died, he'd know that he was loved—something I truly believed he didn't hear often.

He separated his lips from mine, but left them lingering close by.

Then, silence.

Heartbeats passed.

Nothing.

Not a word from him.

No indication that he'd even heard me.

Oh no.

My relief was short lived, replaced with adrenaline coursing through my veins.

Gods.

I knew he might not feel the same, but Sawyer said that he did… he said that he loved me.

I stared at him, trying to figure out what he was thinking, but his expression didn't have any give. My feet backed away from him, and I tried to mentally prepare for the sting of heartbreak that seemed to be coming straight for me.

The inside of my cheek began to bleed from the bite of my angst, and regret fueled my words. "I'm sorry, I shouldn't have said anything. I knew that the feeling could be one-sided, but I said it anyway." I dropped my gaze to the sand. "We had a good thing going and I just ruined it." I kicked a shell around with my toe, trying to ease the turbulence that circulated in my body.

Sebastian shook his head, his gaze hollow. "No, Maeve, please don't apologize. It's not that."

Though I had no right to be angry when I knew his rejection was a possible outcome, irritation greeted me as my eyes darted back to him.

"What is it then? Because if you don't feel the same, if *this*," I gestured between the two of us, "was just a fling for you, it's fine. But I need to hear you say it." I bit back tears while I waited for his response.

He hung his head and his voice lowered. "It's not just a fling to me. Please don't say that."

I threw my arms up towards the heavens. "Am I just not what

you want then? Because I've given you everything I have to offer, and you can't even give me a straight answer."

Sawyer's wandering eyes shone over Sebastian's shoulder. He shot his head to the side when he noticed that I'd caught him. Maybe I should have chosen a better location to do this. Granted, I thought it would go better than this.

"If you don't love me, it's fine. I'll be fine. But at least have the decency to tell me." *Have the decency to shatter my heart and soul into a million pieces.*

Sebastian followed my gaze, also becoming aware that our friends were still present. His jaw ticked as he caught my wrist and led me off of the beach, stopping to pick up my shoes. "Excuse us," he stated blandly, busting by the others and not giving them a second glance.

He guided me all the way back to the castle, not making a sound until we were in his bedroom and the door was closed behind us. He locked and leaned against it, all while staring at me with his arms crossed.

I stared back, nothing left to say. *He* was the one who brought us here, so *he* could speak the hell up.

My eyes drifted to his arms, marveling at the way his shirt clung to the muscles. My attention was drawn towards his abdomen, and I reveled in the nostalgia of the way his skin felt rubbing against mine, and—

Nope. Not going there.

"Did I do something?" I finally broke the silence when he still hadn't spoken. "I thought you felt the same." Despair poured from my voice.

Sebastian exhaled a deep breath. "Gods no, Maeve. You could never." Finally ready to communicate, he kicked off of the door and stormed towards me. "You are *everything* that I want."

My heart jolted. "Then what's the problem?"

He looked up, biting his lip as he shook his head.

I crossed my arms over my own chest, supplying myself some comfort in anticipation of what he could possibly say.

Cerulean eyes locked onto me. "The problem is that I want you so badly—*need you* so badly—that it scares the hell out of me." He didn't yell, but his tone didn't convey calm, either. "I have become so cold because of you. The things I would do for you—the things I *have* done for you—are fucking terrifying. But I have no problem doing them because I'd do absolutely *anything* if it meant keeping you safe. Happy. Alive."

I winced at the reminder of what he did to Lucan and Calvin.

Sebastian moved in on me, closing the gap between us and pressing our bodies together. He dipped his head, his voice light and airy as he spoke. "But I have also gone soft for you, in ways I never thought my mind could allow. In ways I could never even imagine until I met you, because I am in love with you, undoubtedly more than you could ever love me."

The only movement in my body was the hammering beat of my heart as he somehow managed to get even closer to me. So close to me that his breath tickled my neck, making the hair on my arms stand up as I shivered.

Sebastian traced a finger along my collar bone, and his lips brushed against my neck as he spoke softly to me. "I can't even fathom why the gods would place someone like you into my life, because I certainly don't deserve you. I swear you must have been created from stardust because there's no way that someone like you just...*exists*. You are every single thing I've needed to complete my soul. Without you, I am nothing. Without you, I am an empty shell. I love you—yes—but I *need* you. And *that* is what frightens me the most." He pulled his face free from the crook of my neck. "So please don't ever think that I don't want you, because I'll always choose you."

All of my nerves were alleviated at his proclamation. The gemstones in my cheek spasmed, my body trying to create an outlet for my emotions. I used my thumb to wipe away the single tear that left a dewy trail on his cheek, ignoring my own as they fell from my eyes.

My words had escaped me. Nothing I would say could follow that. Instead of using words, I grabbed his face in my hands and crushed my lips to his.

He kissed me back hungrily and our mouths tangled together as we devastated each other, ignoring everything going on outside the walls of this room. All the worries in the world vanished. It was just him and I.

Without breaking our kiss, Sebastian cupped his hands behind my knees and scooped me into his arms. He spun us around, pushing my back against his bookshelf, the moment reminding me of our first night together in the archives all those months ago.

I wrapped my legs around him while he held me against his hips effortlessly. My mouth parted, welcoming his tongue which caressed mine in a familiar way—like we'd been savoring each other for years. I let my body guide my motions and tangled my hands through his dark hair, tugging a little, provoking him to moan quietly.

Kissing him was always extraordinarily devastating, but it was so much better knowing there was a shared love between us.

The bookshelf shook from our conjoined pressure. Grinding my hips, I shuffled myself up higher on his torso, my panties dampening in response to his body against mine. The tension increased as we teased each other with our tongues. He stiffened underneath me, and I wouldn't have been surprised if I soon had no clothing on.

Sebastian broke his lips from mine to gasp out a breathy, "I fucking love you," then he turned me away from the bookshelf, tightening his grip on me as he slid his hands under my ass and carried me to the bed.

He threw me down onto the mattress, ripping his shirt off as he leaned over me to reveal the hard ridges of his abdomen. He lowered himself down to me, reclaiming my aching, swollen lips in a possessive kiss.

"I can't believe you ever thought I didn't want you," he began, clutching my wrist and guiding my hand to the front of his slacks so I could feel how hard he was for me. "Feel that? That's because of you. I want you so badly, this is what happens every time you're anywhere near me."

My breath caught in my lungs at the way he described what I did to him. I massaged the front of his pants, taunting the hard length of him concealed beneath them. "You're not exactly easy to read," I spoke in a whisper, still rubbing my hand over him.

His fingers hooked under the bottom of my shirt, pulling it over my head to allow himself access to more of my skin. Calloused hands rubbed along my back, unclasping my bra to reveal my breasts.

My nipples hardened in response to him admiring me. Sebastian dropped his head to kiss my neck while I moved my fingers to work the buttons of his pants. He groaned as I slipped my hand into them before clasping around his hard length, jerking my wrist up and down. It throbbed in my grasp as I teased the tip with my thumb.

"Fuck, Maeve," he moaned, a bead of wetness releasing from his cock. "I meant it when I said that I don't deserve you, but I'm greedy, and I need you now." His voice was guttural, and I devoured his words in the midst of our kiss.

His touch was a temptation of desire—one that I didn't have the power to fight.

"That's good, because I really fucking need you," I replied, pulling my hand from his slacks so that I could take my own off.

Once bare, he laid back on the bed, grabbing my waist and pulling me on top of him in the process. Our eyes locked as I rolled my hips against his cock before taking it in my hand. I guided it to my entrance then sank myself down onto him.

His mouth fell agape in pleasure as he settled inside of me. I moved down slowly, letting myself adjust to the fit of him. He hardened even more within me as I joined our bodies.

His hands guided my hips at first, teaching me how to move my body in motions that pleased us both. Luckily for him, I was a quick learner. I allowed my eyes to flutter closed and based my movements off of pure sensation as I rode him, grinding my ass against his thighs on the downbeats.

"I will never get enough of this," Sebastian growled. Once I got into a rhythm, he moved a hand to my nipple, pinching and twisting it between his fingers. I leaned back, taking him deeper, but keeping my motions steady as I rocked my hips.

Sitting upright, he wrapped an arm around me while I

continued to bounce on him. He trailed his tongue over my nipple, and I cried out from the added ecstasy. My jewels twitched, my magic threatening its release as lust fortified within me.

"I can't wait to feel you coming around my cock," he moaned breathily, watching as he let me use his body. "Then when you're finished, I'll spill myself inside of you, claiming you as mine."

The filth of his words pushed me close to my climax, and I savored the feel of him moving inside me before he made good on those intentions.

Sebastian wedged his hand down between us, using my wetness as lubrication to massage a single finger over my clit, teasing me.

"Stop," I begged, knowing if he kept doing what he was that I wouldn't last.

"Do you really want me to stop?" he teased, his voice an airy whisper. He halted the movement of his finger, letting it linger over the most sensitive part of me.

"No," I whined, still rocking my hips on the length of him. "I just don't want this to end." I bit my lip, missing the roll of his fingers taunting me.

Sebastian smirked knowingly. "Don't worry, baby. I plan on having you more than once tonight."

I rolled my head into the crook of his neck and tried to hold my orgasm from breaching, but it claimed me explosively, and I screamed out in pleasure as my muscles tightened around him.

Sebastian sucked my lips into another kiss as I rode him through the waves of my climax. His body shook and he moaned into our kiss as he found his own release, doing to me exactly what he said he would.

My hips slowed, and I pulled myself off of him when he finished. I threw myself down on the bed alongside him, both of us panting to catch our breath.

He turned his head towards me, smiling. "Fuck, I love you."

"And I love you."

"SEB! GET UP NOW OR I'M COMING IN." SAWYER'S VOICE BELLOWED as his fist pounded on the door.

Sebastian and I had dozed off in each other's arms after round two. We lay exposed on his bed. There was no point in putting our clothes on just to take them off again.

Our eyes shot open in response to Sawyer's yelling. I wondered if he'd been knocking for a while.

Sebastian sat up and groaned. "Ugh. What do you want, Sawyer?"

Sawyer took his response as an invitation and used his water magic to unlock the door. He didn't give Sebastian or I any time to cover up before he barged into the room, donning his full set of chest armor with a sword sheathed against his black leathers.

"What the fuck, man?" Sebastian cursed, throwing a quilt over me. I scrambled to hide my fully exposed body with the fabric.

Sawyer's voice was droll. "Oh relax, it's nothing I haven't seen before. Well, mostly nothing I haven't seen before." He smirked in my direction.

I rolled my eyes, my cheeks flushing as I pulled the blanket tighter around myself.

Sebastian jumped out of bed, swiping his battle leathers from the floor, tugging them on and then grabbing Sawyer by the shoulders to turn him away from me.

"Get dressed." Sebastian looked back at me as he directed Sawyer out of the room.

I did as he said then sat on the edge of his bed, gazing out the window while I waited for him to return. It was still dark outside. The stars were sprinkled throughout the night sky, sparkling arrogantly, aware that they were responsible for embellishing the twilight. I completely immersed myself in the view—in the philosophy of the cosmos. I imagined the vibrant colors of starlight that formed the galaxies surrounding us. How could such beauty exist without ever being seen by the mortal eye?

I suddenly got excruciatingly jealous of Blythe.

My fantasy was destroyed as Sebastian and Sawyer erupted into the room, both of their faces much too serious for my liking.

"Throne room. Now," Sawyer demanded.

Sebastian dropped to his knees in front of me, tying my boots around my ankles.

I raised an eyebrow. "In the middle of the night?"

Neither of them answered me. Sawyer frantically dug through Sebastian's wardrobe, gathering his armor for him.

"What's going on?"

Sebastian caught my hand, pulling me to my feet. "Draemornian soldiers just attacked a village just a few miles from here—burned it to the ground," he stated, taking his armor from Sawyer as we rushed out of his bedchambers.

We started down the corridor, walking at such a fast pace that we may as well have just ran. Sebastian pulled his chest plate over his head, buckling the sides as we moved.

"A few miles from here?" My forehead creased. There were only a couple of villages in that range of the castle.

Sebastian and Sawyer started down the staircase, reaching the bottom before I'd even stepped foot onto it.

"Which village?" I asked, my voice cold and bleak.

They looked up at me from the bottom of the stairs, neither one speaking as they gave each other a knowing glance.

"Which. Village. Was. Attacked?" I enunciated each word through the tight barrier of my clenched jaw.

"Yours."

CHAPTER FORTY-ONE

"Draemornian troops are closing in on the castle grounds, I would predict that within a few hours—by midday at the latest—we will be in the depths of battle. Prepare yourselves to protect what's ours." King Hawthorne sounded terrified, but I had a hard time focusing on his words.

My family's village was gone. Burned into ash. The place where I was raised, a pile of ruins. The village where my mother and sister *lived*. Destroyed.

There was no chance that they survived. Not if things really happened how Sawyer described them. And by the way the king spoke, I had no reason to doubt his claim.

My nails left indents in my sweating palms. I held back tears as my mind intruded on me, forcing me to vividly imagine their screams as they were suffocated beneath piles of rock and burning wood. I couldn't stop myself from picturing their charred carcasses, surrounded by smoke and lying in the rubble of my childhood home—now their grave.

I wanted to vomit. Cry. Scream. But an outburst wouldn't bring them back. I needed vengeance, and I would have it. King Beaumont and his piece of shit soldiers would soon learn just how powerful a product of Blythe was.

Glancing up, I noticed Sebastian staring at me. His eyebrows furrowed as he watched me intently, waiting for me to snap. But I wouldn't break. Not yet. There was work to do.

My hearing narrowed in on the tail end of King Hawthorne's speech. "The first years are not responsible to fight, but we need all the hands we can get, so if those in your combat groups are willing, please direct them accordingly." He rose from his throne, stepping down the velvet steps to approach me.

"Yeah, yeah. I know. I have no choice but to fight. You don't need to remind me," I snarled at him before he got a chance to speak.

He didn't flinch at my rudeness. "I want you to flee. The Draemornians are going to be coming after you. They want to take over the kingdom, yes, but they want you more. Leave the grounds, and stay hidden."

My neck bounced back at his words. I certainly did not expect him to want me to hide. Shaking my head side to side, I dismissed the order. "No way in hell, *Your Majesty*. Beaumont's soldiers just burned my family's fucking home to the ground, meaning my mother and sister went down with it."

Ignoring my choice of words, Aldous said, "This is an order, soldier. Protecting your gift is more important than you getting revenge."

"What happened to me having to fight no matter the cost? Remember your whole broken arm, fighting even if I am laboring my child speech?"

Gasps emitted from the bystanders in the room, but I ignored them.

"I have changed my mind. Now leave."

I put my hands on my hips, scowling at the king of Caelestis. I'd had more than enough of him controlling every aspect of my life. The worst part is that I'd let him. For almost a year I had let this man dictate my every move. Not anymore.

I was done.

Straightening my posture, I leaned my face close to his. "I'm not a coward. And you don't control me." My words spat through bared teeth.

Turning from him, I stormed out of the throne room, leaving Caelestis' ruler dumbfounded. I smirked to myself, proud of my long-awaited resistance to authority.

Footsteps followed me out, but I didn't look to see who it was.

"Maeve, can we talk about this, please?" Sebastian's voice of concern passed through one ear and out the other.

I kept walking, heading for my room to get my armor.

"Maeve?"

I closed in on the door of the soldier's housing.

"Maeve!" Sebastian cut in front of me, stopping the in entryway where I laid bleeding not long ago.

"Move," I warned, my fists clenching by my sides.

He shook his head. "I know you're upset about your family, and you have every right to be, but you're not fighting this battle."

His words came out as a demand, but I would not tolerate being bossed around by *anyone* right now—not even him.

"Upset?" I scoffed. "I'm not *upset*." Jutting my shoulder into his chest, I pushed by him and started up the stairs. "I'm shattered. I'm devastated. I'm fucking pissed!" I yelled down the steps.

I barged into my room, immediately stripping my clothes off to change into something more combat appropriate. I pulled on a pair of leather pants that matched my boots and a long sleeved top. After tying my hair into a quick, messy braid, I moved to my desk, hunching over it and shuffling through the drawers trying to find my dagger.

Sebastian watched as I scrambled frantically around my room, collecting everything I needed to go destroy some Draemornian assholes. He came up behind me and tried to wrap his arms around me, but I turned out of his hold.

"Don't," I cautioned, knowing if he tried to talk some sense into me that I may just listen.

His shoulders drooped in defeat. "I will get on my knees and beg you if I have to. Please just let me bring you somewhere safe."

I glared at him, chewing on the inside of my cheek as my anger boiled over.

I should have listened. Should have done as he advised. But there was no retribution if there was no pain, and I'd be damned if I let him avenge my family for me.

"No." My hand secured around the dagger he gifted me and I sidestepped away from him, moving to sit on my bed so that I could tie my sheath.

"Gods, Maeve, come on!" Sebastian threw his arms in the air. "You almost died like, a week ago for fuck's sake!"

"Yeah, but I didn't. Pia healed me and I'm fine," I growled at him.

"But you almost did!"

I jumped back to my feet. "BUT I DIDN'T!" I screamed in his face.

My yelling didn't faze him. "*Please.* Just let me keep you safe—"

"Sebastian Aldous freakin' Hawthorne!" I shouted, interjecting his plea.

His eyes widened at the use of his full name.

"You can either stand there and argue with me over something that I'm going to do anyway, or you can help me buckle this damn chest plate." I rose to my feet and shuffled the armor that matched his over my head.

A muscle in his jaw ticked as he considered his options, neither of which he was thrilled with—his face gave that much away. He grunted in disapproval, but caved and stepped behind me to tighten the sides of my armor.

"I'll be fine," I assured him, my tone relaxing as I met the mask of fear he wore.

"You better be, because I meant what I said—no veil or life or death will keep me from you."

Amidst all the chaos, the prophecy had been tucked neatly away in the back of my mind. Though Blythe told me not to fear, adrenaline coursed through me at the idea that I might actually *not be fine.*

When he finished, I brushed my lips against Sebastian's, possibly our last kiss for the unforeseeable future—or forever if the prophecy ended with my demise. Then I packed a few things into my rucksack and tossed it over my shoulder.

"Just promise me you'll stay by my side?" he asked.

"I promise," I said dryly, unsure if that was a promise possible to truly keep.

Sighing in defeat, he offered me a soft smile as he backed away. "Let's go fuck up some Draemornians then."

Smiling back at the man I loved, I prayed to the gods that this moment together wouldn't be our last.

"EVERYONE SPLIT INTO THEIR TRAINING GROUPS, THEN FOLLOW THE orders your instructors have put in place for you." Sebastian's voice boomed throughout the great hall, addressing all of the first years who were willing to fight. Good thing he had more sense than his father and came up with a plan in case this happened. Otherwise we would have been screwed. He stepped off of the pedestal, maneuvering his way through the crowd to my group.

Kohen followed him, glowering at Pia as he approached. He tried to talk her out of fighting, as well, but she wouldn't give in.

"Here's how this is going to go." Kohen took charge, clasping his hands together behind his back. "The Draemornian army is expected to attack by midday. Most of the more experienced soldiers have really advanced mental shields, so don't bother using your powers as your first line of defense. A swift stab of a blade will do the trick. Many of you are going to die, so if anyone wants to change their mind, there's the door." Kohen gestured to the exit. "There's a group in the throne room waiting to go to the dungeons. There's a tunnel down there that travels about a mile underground. It will take you to a concealed exit chamber—where? I can't disclose that because I don't know. But that's your best bet at staying alive through all of this."

"Did you know about that?" I bent to the side to whisper to Pia, figuring that she'd lived in the castle long enough to know its hidden passages.

She shook her head.

A few first years made a run for it, but most of us stayed. We knew what we signed up for.

"Our group is going to man the wards that surround the castle. We will be on the front lines, stopping the Draemornians from the second they step foot onto the grounds." Sebastian's eyes rolled over me, and I could sense his apprehension from even this distance.

"If you don't have a weapon already, get your ass to the armory and get one, then make your way to the main gate," Kohen ordered.

"NOW!" Sebastian yelled for added dramatization.

Our group separated, and Pia and I gathered in the front of the room with Sebastian and Kohen.

Sebastian ran a finger over my thigh, stopping at my sheath to remove my dagger. I raised an eyebrow as he pulled a small vile from his back pocket.

"What's that?" I watched as he wrenched the cap off my dagger and emptied the contents of the vile into the hollowed out center, careful not to spill any on himself.

"Poison."

"What kind?"

"The kind that kills someone within minutes of simply touching their skin. Seconds if it enters the bloodstream."

I winced, uncomfortable that I would have something so deadly strapped to me.

Sebastian twisted the cap back on, then resheathed the blade against my leg. "To put it lightly, don't screw up," he warned when he met my distressed gaze.

"Very reassuring. Thanks."

Sawyer joined us when he was done briefing his soldiers. "Those idiots are going to die." He angled a thumb back at his group. "One of them just asked me how long I think this will take."

"What you tell 'em?" Kohen snorted.

"Few hours at most."

"That's cruel," Pia sneered. "You know damn well no war had ever finished in a few hours."

"Maybe it will motivate them to try and make history," Sawyer replied, then turned his gaze to me. "You need more than just a dagger, Maeve."

I glanced at Pia, noticing that she had a few blades strapped to her. "Shit, yeah. Okay, I'll run to the armory and then I'll meet you guys outside."

All four of them shot me down.

"You're not leaving my side, remember?" Sebastian argued, receiving an eye roll from me in response.

"I'll go," Sawyer offered. "What's your preference?"

Unsure, I looked to Sebastian for guidance. "I dunno. I've mostly only worked with a dagger." I'd only used a sword a few times in practice and during the trials. I was much more confident with a dagger, but options were good.

"You should have a sword in a situation like this." He turned to Sawyer. "Something light. A thin blade but sturdy hilt. Bring a sheath to go with it."

Sawyer nodded, then took off in a jog.

"It's not too late, I can still bring you to the dungeons. You can get out of here," Sebastian suggested as he turned back to me.

"No. I need to do this." My family deserved retribution, and I would make damn sure they got it. Only then would I allow myself to grieve.

He puffed his cheeks out, nodding as his hand settled on the back of my armor and guided me out of the hall.

CHAPTER FORTY-TWO

Absolute chaos surrounded me.

Within minutes of Sawyer meeting us in the courtyard with my sword, the dormitories were attacked. I had barely attached the sheath around my waist before needing to draw the weapon, as the first Draemornian soldier reached the cobblestone path leading straight to us.

Now—just hours later—there were bodies piled up around my feet. They were yet to be anyone I knew, but my fear intensified with the rattle of each cadaver. The continuous clang of metal caused my ears to ring, and it was difficult to hear anything over the bloodcurdling screams of mortals as they killed or *were* killed.

Sebastian had his back against mine. Because of him, I hadn't made a kill yet, but it was only a matter of time before someone's death was on my name. Though I should have felt remorseful about that, I didn't. I felt *vengeful*. These people were the reason that I'd been left without a family, and I would make them beg for my mercy.

The thought smacked me in my soul, cascading into an unbearable ache in my heart with the realization that I had no blood left alive. It was just me.

The brutal truth made me want to crumble to the ground, but I had to resist. I'd pretend it wasn't real—pretend that this horrific reality was simply a nightmare.

I held onto my courage, using it as motivation to pivot my torso and swing my sword through the bicep of a Draemornian who tried to sneak up behind me. The soldier cried out, the force of my swing jolting his body back. Blood dripped from the slice in his arm as he moved in on me with his teeth jarred.

Before he could retaliate, Sebastian peeled himself from my back, swinging around me and slashing his sword through the air. The blade slid through the gap between the soldier's helmet and chest armor, cutting his head clean off. It dropped to the ground with a thud. Blood splashed over the fronts of my legs as the skull tumbled, stopping when it hit my foot.

I looked down at it, motionless.

Adrenaline stole my disgust.

Shit.

This was really happening.

My gaze rolled slowly to Sebastian, who stared, silently judging my reaction. "You okay?" His eyes peered at me through the steel helmet that covered his beautiful skin.

He killed that man with such ease, such poise, that I now understood why he had been so worried that I wouldn't love the real him. *That* was the real Sebastian. Charming, but celestially lethal when he needed to be. A prince. A soldier—a head soldier, at that—and a damn good one. He thought that side of him would scare me, but I welcomed it. I'd take him in every form, the good or the bad.

He was too immersed in making sure I was okay to notice that another Draemornian was running at him, sword raised.

My heart pounded sporadically as I ripped my dagger from its sheath. My eyes narrowed in on my target, planning for the best course of action and noticing how the Draemornian lacked a helmet.

Pulling my arm back, I chucked my dagger as powerfully as my muscles could manage. The blade hit the soldier in between the eyes, embedding itself deep enough into his skull that it no doubt hit brain matter. He dropped forward onto his knees before face planting in the dirt.

Sebastian's eyes widened as he spun around just in time to see the Draemornian's corpse drop. "Holy shit," he marveled under his breath.

I stepped around him and bent down in front of the dead soldier, where I ripped my blade from his skull, wiping the blood and dripping turquoise toxin on the grass next to me before sheathing it back in the strap on my thigh.

"Yeah. I'm okay." My response was nonchalant as I rose, choosing to ignore the fact that I just made my first kill.

While we had a brief moment of peace, Sebastian closed in on me, pulling my helmet off so he could brush his hand over my cheek. His fingers grazed over my jewels. "That shouldn't turn me on, but fucking hell, that was badass." He pulled his own helmet up enough to crush his lips to mine in a *thank you for saving my life* kind of kiss.

The moment of tranquility was short lived. Sawyer showed up out of nowhere, gesturing for us to come with him. "Let's move!" he yelled through his helmet, his eyes darting around frantically.

We followed him along the border of the castle, clinging to the walls as we crept our way to the back end of the tower. Sunlight broke through the murkiness of dust, scorching my skin as I leaned against the stone. Shockingly, no Draemornians were over here, which allowed us a moment to catch our breath.

"Where's Pia and Kohen?" I asked Sawyer, my voice shaking from adrenaline.

"Haven't seen them in over an hour. Last I knew they were helping to barricade the castle's entrance. It didn't look like it was going well, though. I wouldn't be surprised if the Draemornians break in soon."

I dropped my helmet into the dirt to drink from my canteen, rehydrating my cells so they could help me continue on. The past few hours of battle had been relentless, and it wouldn't be letting up anytime soon.

"So much for making history," I teased, out of breath.

"Ha-ha," Sawyer snarked.

"There's way more of them than I'd expected," Sebastian panted, hunched over on his knees.

I had to agree. The Draemornians greatly outnumbered us, which came as a shock. We were all under the impression that Caelestis had the bigger army.

"Was there this many of them back in Craterra?" Sawyer asked.

Sebastian shook his head. "No. They must have been holding back like we were. I know it's only just begun, but I honestly have no idea how we are going to win this if it keeps up like this."

My heart sank. "Please don't say that," I pleaded. "We can't lose this battle. My family is dead and it's my fault. This is all my fault and if we lose, I—"

Sawyer put a gloved hand on my metal shoulder. "It's not your fault. I should have never said that. We're going to do everything we can, Maevey baby."

Sebastian raised an eyebrow. "Maevey baby?"

I was about to explain the nickname when a fiery beam flew through the fucking air. The ball of fire skimmed my upper arm on its course to hit the tower behind me. It absorbed into the brick, leaving only a black ring of soot.

I cried out in pain, forcing my eyes down at the hole in my sleeve. Blackened flesh painted my arm. The wound, though mostly cauterized, still smoked and steamed as fresh blood leaked out. "Fucking hell," I cursed through a clenched jaw, poking the charred skin. Of course, my armor stopped right after my shoulders.

Without even hesitating, Sebastian ripped my canteen from my hands, pouring the cool water on the burn. The liquid relieved some of the burning, but when he tore a piece of his undershirt off to tie around the wound, a whole new kind of pain overcame me.

I screamed and tried to bite my lip to suppress the noise, but he slapped his free hand over my mouth to silence me. "I know it hurts, but try to keep quiet. We don't want to give away our—"

"King Beaumont is going to be thrilled when I deliver you to him." A Draemornian soldier flashed us his blazing hands, his eyes focused on my gemstones.

Sawyer raised his sword, ready to lunge while I stood back in shock.

"We all figured you would be hidden away. Quite interesting that Aldous Hawthorne let his most prized possession fight his battles for him."

Sebastian tapped into his power, freezing the Draemornian's flaming hands before he could throw another bomb of fire at us.

Sawyer then charged, stabbing his sword into the gap in the side of the soldier's armor. He twisted the blade, ensuring it mangled the muscles of his heart before pulling it out with force. Blood spurted from the hole, hitting me in the face.

Another man, dead.

"Are you okay?" both men asked me in sync.

I raised my injured arm to wipe the splattered blood off my face. The skin was tight and hurt like a bitch when I moved it. "It's not that bad."

"Don't lie. It looks like shit," Sawyer commented as he took my canteen to refill it with his water magic.

I scrunched my nose. "Gee, thanks."

"Let me look at it again." Sebastian reached out for me.

I shuffled away from him. "It's fine. Really. We have bigger things to worry—" My words stuck to my tongue as a voice carried through the wind.

"*My star. Come to me.*"

I glanced between Sawyer and Sebastian, both looking utterly defeated from the hours of combat they'd endured.

"Did one of you just say something?" There were so many noises filling my ears that I wasn't sure what exactly I'd heard.

They shook their heads.

"*My star.*"

This time, I was able to make out the nickname that only two people had ever called me. My mother—who was dead—and Blythe.

A powerful gust of wind blew by, likely crafted by an onyx gifted soldier. The smokey smell of burnt brick mixed with death surrounded us, filling my nostrils on my inhales. My mouth fell agape as I glanced around in realization.

I stood motionless.

My visions…

I was currently living them.

The explanation pieced itself together in my brain like a puzzle. The rumors Sebastian heard in Craterra—he had shot down the idea, but I was right. I *knew* in my soul that I was right.

The fable was not a fable at all. Blythe's soul *was* trapped in her statue, and I had to grant her freedom. That's how I'd stop this. That's how we'd win, and that's how the prophecy would fulfill itself.

"Maybe it's time to get out of here, Maeve. This is way more intense than we'd expected," Sebastian begged again.

"No."

He glared at me, his fists clenched by his side.

Sawyer groaned, his voice interrupting my epiphany as he cleaned his blade on his pants. "You heard what that dick said. They assumed you were hiding. Maybe you should be."

"They are going to start realizing who you are. You could even just go rest for a while in the tunnel, replenish your energy—" Sebastian chimed in again.

"For the love of the gods, both of you, please stop trying," I snarled at the two of them.

"What are you trying to prove?" Sawyer argued, sudden anger coating his tongue.

"I'm not trying to prove anything." Neither of them had any idea of what was about to happen.

Sawyer stormed up to me, his fists clenched "Do you want to die?"

"Of course not." *But I'm going to.*

"Then just let Seb bring you to the tunnel."

"No."

Sawyer threw his arms up in dismissal. "Fine. But I'm not going to stay here and watch you die."

What the hell is with the men in my life using anger to mask their fear?

Sawyer started to turn away, but I grabbed his hand and pulled him into a hug. "Be safe," I told him.

He grunted but hugged me back briefly before storming off to destroy some more Draemornians.

At least his absence would make this next part easier.

I turned to Sebastian, his fear stricken face sending chills throughout me. I didn't want to leave this world without him—we'd only just started our story. But if I was going to die in this battle, he didn't need to be there to see it.

"Kiss me," I demanded, and he did without hesitation.

He would want to kill me for what I was about to do, but I'd already be dead by the next time he saw me.

I still tasted him on my lips when I broke our kiss. "You know how much I love you, right?" I asked, my heart shattering with the question.

Sebastian raised an eyebrow. "Yes. And you know how much I love you, right?"

"Of course." My voice shook.

"Why are you asking me this?"

My lip quivered. "Do you trust me?"

Sebastian stepped towards me, reaching a hand out to my upper arm. "Maeve…What—"

I used his touch to my advantage while I tapped into my magic. Though it would take up a good portion of my strength, I powered through, cracking the solid shell of his mental shield.

"Leave my side. Fight this war without me. Find me when it's all over." I left out the part about finding my corpse. That would be too distracting, and he needed to have his full attention on winning this battle.

Sebastian's eyes sank instantly when he realized what I'd done.

"I'm sorry…" My voice quaked in a whisper. "My time spent loving you has been the greatest chapter of my life. My only regret is that our story was too short." I bit my lip, fighting back tears.

His own eyes flooded over in tears of betrayal, but he couldn't fight my compulsion. He followed my orders without another word, pulling his helmet on and turning to follow the path that Sawyer led.

He didn't know that this was the last time he'd see me alive. The ache from that truth was the worst thing I had ever felt—and I had just lost my family.

It's for the best.

My lungs burned as I watched him leave. "I love you," I said one last time, though he was already too far away to hear me.

With a sniffle, I pulled myself together and revealed my sword from its bounds, then marched in the opposite direction of the man I'd been blessed to love.

CHAPTER FORTY-THREE

SEBASTIAN

How could she do this?

How could I *let her* do this? I had my shields up, and they were pretty damn strong in preparation for combat—at least I thought they were. I knew she could break through them when she really wanted to, but I never expected her to use her magic on me like this.

I tried everything in my being to not leave her, but as soon as she broke through my barriers, I had no other choice. My legs started moving without my telling them to, and before I knew it, she was gone.

She thought I was oblivious, but as soon as she said her command, I knew why she did it.

She told me about her visions, described them to me in detail. This war we were fighting—she'd seen it before. She'd *lived* it before in her dreams. She had walked this same field filled of death and torture.

For months, she'd been agonizing over the sacrifice, and I'd fought my own mind's concerns about it to keep her off the ledge. Inside though, I'd been battling unnerving fear over her safety and her life.

Now, all of a sudden she wasn't worried about dying. *Why?*

There must be something she hadn't told me. What? Beats the fuck out of me. But I knew that it was the reason for her compelling me.

I forced my way through crowds of soldiers, swiping and slicing through their bodies as they came at me. My magic assisted me when needed. In fact, I had just summoned a solid brick of ice, which I dropped on the head of a Draemornian. The woman's skull cracked and burst open from the pressure, splattering my boots with skull fragments.

I was always surprised during battle that soldiers did not use more of their magic, but then again, stabbing someone to death was just faster.

I stepped around her body, picking my pace up to a run as I made for the main gate to find Kohen and Sawyer, hopefully Pia, too. As far as I knew, Maeve hadn't used her magic on them. I could send one of them after her. She was capable of protecting herself, especially armed, but for my own sanity, I needed someone with her.

There were things she didn't know—things I *wished* that I didn't know. I'd kept them from her, not wanting to add to the piles of worries she kept harbored inside. It was wrong of me, but I really planned to tell her when the time was right. The moment just never came.

Aside from that, I overheard things in Craterra that to this day made my skin crawl. Beaumont's plans for Maeve were far worse than just using her for her powers. I should have told her that as well—almost did when I got home, but she'd already been through so much. I didn't want to scare her even more over something that I was sure I could protect her from. But she wouldn't let me, and now she was alone out there. I shuddered at the thought of what could happen to her.

I didn't allow myself to panic often, but right now, it was a feeling that couldn't be fought no matter how hard I tried. I had to find Kohen or Sawyer. Soon. Before one of those Draemornian fucks got their hands on her.

I barreled through the patio, my sword still clutched tightly in my fist. The main gate of the castle came into view, encased in insane fucking turmoil. There must have been at least fifty soldiers —a mix of Caelestians and Draemornians—battling each other on the balcony, fighting to break through the wards to gain entry to the castle.

I stopped briefly to scan my eyes over the crowd, searching for one of my friends, but it was just an array of clanging metal and spraying blood.

My legs carried me up the steps towards the chaos where I was immediately met by a blast of blazing white light. My enemy's magic shot past me, blinding me for a few seconds. My eyes didn't have time to fully adjust before there was another soldier on the step above me, his dagger raised and pointed at my chest.

The soldier jammed the tip of his dagger into my sternum before I could block him, but the weapon was no match for the steel of my chest plate.

Idiot.

Everyone knew you aimed for the throat when using a dagger against armor.

I caught his wrist before he could pull it back. My grip was firm as I twisted his arm so hard that I felt his bone snap underneath my glove.

The soldier shouted out in agony and I raised my leg, kicking him in the stomach with the sole of my boot. He fell backward, his head ricocheting off of the cement while the rest of his body went limp on the steps.

My body cast a shadow as I leaned over his bleeding head. I thought for sure he was dead, but he lay paralyzed on the stone, gasping for the air I kicked out of his lungs.

"Should have worn a helmet," I taunted, tilting my head as I raised my sword and stabbed it through his open mouth.

I didn't give the Draemornian another glance as I stepped onto the curved stone platform, looking around desperately for a sign of anyone familiar. I raised my sword to block an attack from another asshole's weapon as it swung at my face. It fell from his hand, and I bent down to pick it up before he could. Then I used the two blades together to do something brutally lethal to the man before me. His body separated into halves, and I would be lying if I said that the sight of his organs spilling out in a flood didn't make me want to vomit at least a little.

I stared for a heartbeat, in total awe that I was capable of doing something so horrific to a man. My stomach lurched.

Get it together.

There was no time to show weakness. I had to find—

"Holy shit, Seb, that was harsh."

Pia.

Relief washed over me.

She looked exactly how I'd expect—covered in dirt and ash, blood crusted over a cut on her neck.

I dropped the extra sword and she grabbed my hand, dragging me out of the chaos of combat and to a side door on the castle.

"Open up, Kohen, it's me." She banged a gloved fist on the door, and it swung open to allow us entry.

I knocked one soldier back with the blunt force of my elbow as he tried to follow us in. Pia finished the job with her dagger, not killing the man but injuring him enough to back off.

Kohen pulled her inside, and I followed after her, pushing my back against the barricades to keep the door from bursting open.

I glanced around the space, bloody and reeking from the corpses scattered about. There were a few other soldiers guarding various entrances, but Kohen sent them down the hall once we arrived.

"Why are they trying so hard to get in?" Pia gasped.

Kohen shrugged. "Dunno. Probably looking for your father to persuade him to surrender." He gestured at me with his head.

"I don't even think they care about gaining territory anymore. They want Maeve. Speaking of which—"

"Wait, where is she?" Pia's expression sank as she crossed her arms.

I knew what she was thinking. I wished I could tell her for certain that Maeve was still alive, but couldn't. "I don't know," I admitted. “She used her powers on me, forcing me to stay away from her.”

Pia’s arms pulled at her disheveled hair, before crossing over her armor. “What in the gods names? Why would she do that?”

“I don't know,” I fabricated my answer.

“Why did you let her do that?”

I furrowed my brows. “Let her? I didn't *let* her.”

Pia uncrossed her arms to slap me upside the head.

“What the hell, Pia!”

“Why didn't you have your shields up, dumbass?”

“I did! We are in the middle of a battle—of course I had them up! She broke through them.”

“Pretty crappy shields you have then, cousin,” she countered.

“Coming from someone who can hardly even use hers,” I spat back.

Pia rolled her eyes and Kohen interjected our banter. “You two are ridiculous. Shut up.” He turned to me. “Tell me what you need me to do.”

“I obviously can't be with her, so I need you to find and stay with her. Make sure none of the Draemornians get close enough to her to…” I let my voice trail off. I didn't need to disclose what would happen if they got a hold of her.

Kohen nodded in understanding. “Okay. I’ll go. Can you stick with Pia?”

“I don't need him to stay with me,” she argued, and Kohen glared back at her, rolling his eyes.

“Okay, yeah. Sure,” he scoffed sarcastically and turned to me. “Don't you dare leave her.” His voice was stern as he directed his warning to me.

“I won't.”

Pia glowered at him, but accepted a peck on the cheek before he let himself out of the barricades. She didn't take her eyes off of him as he went.

“If he gets hurt, I'll kill you,” she threatened, pointing her dagger at my chest once he was gone.

"Fine by me." I understood her fear—I'd tear my own heart from my chest if it meant keeping *her* safe.

CHAPTER FORTY-FOUR

There were more pressing matters, but I needed to feel at peace once more before I left this world.

"My star…"

I ignored the voice of Blythe, as I had been for about an hour now. I sat on the water's edge, admiring the sunset. My last one.

"Come to me…"

It was pathetic—me sitting here. Secluded and arguably safe while the ones I cared about battled to the death over our kingdom. Battling over a piece of land and *me.*

"My star?"

The voice that encompassed my mind was relentless, not giving me a moment of peace. I knew where she wanted me to go, but despite her orders, I sat here, putting it off.

My vision roamed the orange horizon for any sign of my mother. Searching through the faded, pink clouds for a glimpse of my sister's soul. I prayed for a sign that they were okay beyond the veil.

"I am not ready to die yet, but soon I will join you," I cried out to the heavens as the last glowing beam of sun sank away into the depths of the ocean.

"Come to me. The stars will soon light up the sky."

"No." Staying crouched in the sand, I rubbed the singed skin on my arm.

I couldn't stop thinking about the look of betrayal on Sebastian's face. If I somehow survived this, I didn't know if he'd ever look at me the same.

"Do not fight the sacrifice."

"Maybe if you told me the purpose of this damn sacrifice then I wouldn't be so reluctant," I replied to the nothingness.

"You can stop this."

Palms opened to the heavens, I shouted in disbelief, "Stop this? I'm the reason for all of this!"

"You can put it off no longer. Doing so risks too much."

I pondered the goddess' words, knowing that she was right, but not wanting to admit it. If I didn't fulfill the prophecy, more people I cared about may die, and I'd never forgive myself if I lived and they didn't. I'd already done enough damage in this deranged world of ache and betrayal.

The sun had dissipated and the sky had turned navy. I'd been sitting here too long. Soon enough, someone was bound to find me. Maybe they'd kill me before the prophecy did, which somehow frightened me even more than the alternative.

Everyone was counting on my death, though they didn't know it. All those who gave me the cold shoulder when they learned of my gift, would soon be thanking my memory for saving their lives. All the horrible, twisted comments people said about me, would soon be replaced with words of praise.

Although she said it was not my death I needed to fear, maybe Blythe meant that as a reminder that I will be remembered when I am beyond the veil. Or maybe she meant that it would be quick and painless. Who knew.

I picked at some dried blood on my wrist, wondering which of my rivals it belonged to.

"Stop wasting time, Maeve."

"Get up."

"Move."

I took my helmet from beside me and shook the sand off before securing it over my head. My feet reluctantly pulled me to a stand, my nerves for what was about to come making my bones shake. Forcing my legs to work, I left the safety of the shore and made my way back up the cliffside, climbing and clawing at the stones to pull my body weight up the ledge.

"Good. Come to me. You can stop this."

"So I've been told," I panted sardonically as I threw myself over the edge and onto grass.

The castle came back into view when I stood up, and *holy shit.*

Blazing flames and their corresponding smoke created a haze for as far as I could see. The castle was only a wavering shadow, masked by destruction. Red clouds coated the sky, and the air smelled exactly how it had in my vision, making me gag.

My pulse quickened as I continued on, submerging myself in the fate I'd been in denial of for so long. As I got closer to the castle itself, shrieks of the tortured became audible. I swallowed the fear over who those victims may be, assuring myself that those I cared for were safe.

"They are. For now. Come to me, my star."

Though my breathing was shallow, I marched on. With the haze of smoke clouding my field of vision, I relied on my other senses to take me where I was needed.

Apparently, my other senses were shit.

I didn't get far before I was met with a glinting, silver blade directed at my throat. I jumped back, pulling my dagger instinctively, as it was easier to unsheathe than my sword.

A male soldier came into view—a Draemornian, based on his armor. Their protective gear was much like ours, but black instead of the deep silver metal we wore. The only reason I was able to see him was thanks to a crack of light that flashed every few seconds—the result of another soldier's magic.

The man chuckled at my dagger as he inched his sword closer to me, the tip of it skimming the side of my forehead. I don't know why, but I froze in place, unable to counter his threat with one of my own.

His head tilted as he noticed the jewels on my cheekbone. Smiling deviously, he placed pressure on his weapon, drawing some blood. "I should cut these little beauties right out of your skin. Then finish the job and leave you for dead," he snarled, his voice gruff and cruel.

Was this it? Was this the sacrifice I'd been waiting on? Was this how I died? Was this why I couldn't bring myself to fight back?

"You know that it's not. Kill him. Get away. Come to me." The goddess' voice rang in my ears—a grave warning.

My reluctance was the curse of panic—my body trying to protect myself from the torments of the past. I couldn't function, though I really fucking needed to. My mind wouldn't quiet. My brain wouldn't untangle itself to allow me free will.

"My king would prefer you alive though, he has great intentions of creating more of you—that would be impossible to do without the woman alive to breed," the soldier grumbled, his breath wreaking of malice.

My lungs ceased to expand in response to that cruel truth.

Beaumont wanted to *breed* me? That's not how this even worked. The gods chose who they gave their powers to. You couldn't just create more of us on demand. *Could you?*

I didn't want to find out.

My dagger shook in my quivering hand. I tried to summon my body into allowing me more motion, but my mind wouldn't allow it.

The soldier's blade twisted into my skin and my blood leaked faster, dripping down my cheek. He grabbed a hold of my arm before I could react, dragging me towards him. I ground myself into the dirt, fighting his strength.

"You have a gift, use it."

Gods. She was absolutely right. What in the hell was I doing?

The soldier most likely had his shields up, but if I could get through Sebastian's, then I could get through his.

I allowed my eyes to close, needing more peace than the war

amongst us would grant me. My gemstones pricked at my skin as I summoned my magic, feeling it flood through every organ inside of me as it painted over my soul.

"Remove your weapon from my skin…"

I opened my eyes and watched the soldier pout in confusion as he did what I said.

"Now stab yourself in the heart."

The Draemornian tried to fight my magic, but such a thing was not possible when I held onto it so tightly it could shatter stone. He angled his sword towards himself, then jammed it so hard that it pierced through the walls of his chest plate. His gaze went hollow as he stopped his own heart. Deep, red liquid pooled from the hole in his armor as he fell backwards, his sword sticking straight up in his chest.

I gazed blankly at him as I side stepped around his corpse, continuing on into the fog. My legs wobbled a bit, but I ignored the lingering ache the best I could. If there were ever a time to push through the pain of my weakness, it was now.

The sky started to clear the closer I got to the castle. Most of the battle has been centralized near the main gate. I could see the mass of Draemornians trying to break inside the wards, and it looked as though they were close to being successful.

"Hurry."

I started off running, bolting through the damaged terrain and heading towards the courtyard. The smoke and fog made it difficult to see, but I put my head down to pick up speed. My boots kicked up crimson dirt as I ran, my pace continuous until my helmet met metal. My headgear rebounded off of my skull as my body crossed into something—or rather, someone.

The bleeding from my forehead seeped into my eyes, creating a red film over the world as I fell back on my ass. Anxiety placed its cruel hold on me as I recalled this moment, recognizing this same situation as one of my visions.

I'm on the right path.

I jumped to my feet, drawing my sword in preparation to kill whoever was in my way. Not even really looking, I aimed my weapon.

"Maeve, stop. It's me."

I blinked out some of my blood, allowing the person to come into view, arms up in a sign of peace.

Kohen.

I sighed—in relief or dread, I was not quite sure.

"Are you okay?" he asked, not giving me a chance to answer before asking a follow up question. "What the fuck were you thinking? Using your powers on Seb like that." He grabbed the front of my armor, holding me in his face as he demanded a reason.

I tried to wriggle out of his hold, but he had no problem making me aware of his strength.

"Answer me. We are in the middle of a war here. And in case you didn't know, you're not exactly what I would consider to be an experienced soldier. You shouldn't be alone out here."

I contemplated using my magic on him as well, but the more I thought about it, I might actually need his help. I was sure that setting Blythe free was the key in all of this, but how was that possible without using a force of magic that I had no ability of? How did one release a goddess from constraints put on her by other deities?

My brain replayed the visions to myself. Something I'd neglected in all of this was Blythe's appearance when she reached out for me. Her hand resembled her statue, stone-like and cracking as if it were breaking into rubble. Pieces had crumbled off of her skin as I touched her.

"Maeve?" Kohen's purely irritated expression turned to one of concern. "Can you hear me?"

I looked over his shoulder as a break in the haze cleared, a crystalline statue peeking through the musk in the courtyard, illuminated by the starlight that had surfaced in the heavens.

"You're so close to stopping this. Come to me."

I looked up at Kohen, finally responding to his concerns with a nod. "I don't have time to explain, but if you don't want to die, I need your help."

His brows raised as he loosened his grip a bit, but not fully letting me free.

"Kohen. Please," I begged.

He glared at me like I was deranged, then to my surprise, swallowed audibly and released my shoulders. "What do you need me to do?"

CHAPTER FORTY-FIVE

SEBASTIAN

Pia and I manned the wards inside the castle. Well, she did. I paced back and forth through the corridor, torturing myself with every possible outcome if Kohen couldn't find Maeve in time.

Fuck! I should have told her everything. She never would have done this if she had known the full story. If she had known all the facts. I stomped my boot on a shard of broken glass, crushing it under my weight and shattering it into microscopic shards.

Pia cleared her throat. "Seb?"

"What?" I huffed, grumbling under my breath and peering out a crack in the barricaded window as I paced. The sky was dark aside from various shades of lights exploding across the sky as the battle continued.

I should have been out there fighting for my kingdom instead of cowering away inside. But in all honesty, I didn't give a shit about any of that anymore. All I cared about was her and making sure she was safe. Though she completely screwed me out of being able to do that. So instead, I'd continued to roam, trusting I'd hear good news from Kohen soon.

Pia advanced on me, placing her hand on my back to cease my

marching. "Seb, she's okay. Maeve's smart, and I'm sure Kohen's found her by now."

I shook my head, the shags of my dark hair brushing against my forehead. "No. You don't even know. You have no idea. You…you—" I couldn't finish what I was trying to say. The words caught on my tongue as if it were being cut from my mouth.

Pia's eyebrows lowered. "What are you not telling me?"

I looked up at the ceiling as my eyes started to sting. I wouldn't cry. I was a soldier. And soldiers didn't fucking cry—not during battle.

As horrible as it was that I'd been hiding so much from Maeve, I'd been hiding the same information from Pia. And Sawyer. Kohen. Everyone.

I turned from Pia, tearing her arm off of me, though she knew me too well. She wouldn't let this go. And she shouldn't. She had a right to know. They all did.

Outside, explosions and death chanted, the violence shaking the room. Everything was falling apart right before my very eyes. "FUCK," I blurted out, needing to release *something*.

Pia's eyes widened as she watched me lose control. I ignored her, pretending she wasn't there, even as her voice wavered. "Sebastian…tell me what's going on. *Now*."

I drew a deep breath into my lungs. "Pull yourself together," I mumbled to myself on the exhale, but it was no use. I had to tell someone. Needed to get it off my chest. If I died in this war and this information got lost…

Every muscle in my body clenched as I turned back to Pia. I released a hefty breath of stress, preparing to tell her as much as possible with the very limited time we had. "My mother was a seer. And I only know this because I found her journal hidden in her closet a few years back. She wrote down her visions, the things she saw before they happened. She predicted this war—I've known it's been coming for years. She also predicted Maeve—she didn't give a name, but she described her. I knew the minute I laid eyes on her at Jewel-Light that she was the one my mother wrote about." My fingers ran through my hair before I continued. "Most of her visions were loosely described, but some things she saw so clearly that when I read them, it was like I could see them, too. I don't know if she just didn't see it all, or if she didn't want to write too much in the fear her journal got into the wrong hands." I dipped my eyes from Pia's gaze as I pulled the journal from my pocket. I never went anywhere without it. Passing it to her, I tried to avoid the judgment in her eyes as she reluctantly took it and started to flip through the pages.

"She wrote a lot about this battle—said there were two possible outcomes, but didn't write many details about what they were. She just said that one outcome involved someone crucial dying. With the prophecy and sacrifice lingering in the air, I'm terrified that person is going to be Maeve. This whole time I've been trying to protect her from the truth and ensure that this is not the outcome that occurs, just in case it *is* her. But now she's alone out there and I…I don't know what to do. I feel completely fucking useless," I finished, out of breath from the sputtering confession.

Pia glanced at me, then pretty much ignored everything I said and immersed herself in the journal, her mouth going slack as she read. "Did Aunt Cicily predict Jocelyn's death?" she asked, not moving her eyes from the journal. "It says something about her son —you—having a feud with a friend over a loss?"

I nodded. "Yeah. There's that, too."

Pia's eyes were small, narrow slits when she lifted her gaze from the journal. I fully expected her to yell, but to my shock, she did the opposite. "Seb…How have you kept this in for so long?" Her voice was so calm, that I almost preferred her to yell.

"Fuck if I know. And there's more. Maeve's power—"

I didn't get any further. We were interrupted by the sound of shattering glass as a projectile was thrown through the window, conveniently through the small barrier gap I had been utilizing earlier. Whatever was thrown, struck Pia in the side of her face, knocking her to the floor with a thud. She clutched the broken skin, but before either of us could react further, the cartridge exploded, releasing a powerful force of smoke and flame.

The whole room was ablaze within seconds.

Before I could reach her, Pia vanished from my view. I coughed and choked on the smoke while glittering flames danced around me, the contents of the room going up in smoke.

I called upon my magic, trying to counter the heat with ice, but there was too much fire, and too little of me. "Pia?" I barked, each breath I took causing my lungs to constrict and fill with black smoke.

While waiting for her response, I prayed to the gods that she was at least conscious. I was good at a lot of things. But I wasn't confident that I could find her amongst all the smoke.

"Pia?" My voice croaked, trying to be loud enough to overpower the crackling of burning wood. I scanned the room for any sign of her as I stumbled around, trying to devise a plan to save us.

"I'm okay."

Thank fuck. Relief encased me as I made her voice out. I wouldn't be able to live with myself if my cousin and another one of my friends' mates died on my watch. "Where are you?" I called back, wafting away a cloud of black smoke while pushing towards her voice.

"I'm heading towards your voice. Keep talking!"

"We have to get out of here!" I shouted back through the soot as I searched for any sign of an exit, landing on the broken window as our best option. Fuck. That was gonna hurt like a bitch. "The window!" I yelled to her as I fought my way through scorching furniture.

"Okay," she gagged out as she approached me, her hand reaching for mine amidst the flame.

I guided us blindly through the havoc. My eyes burned from the heavy darkness of smoke, but I led us to our only chance at survival. "Draw your weapon," I instructed. "We have no idea what's waiting for us out there."

She dropped my hand to follow orders and I waited until her palm was in mine again to continue.

Broken glass crunched under our boots as we walked blindly towards the window, using the minuscule amount of starlight that shone through it despite the smoke. With each second we stayed in this room, the more my eyes and throat burned. It was too fucking hot.

I dropped Pia's hand. "Drop to your knees. Crawl," I called out, though my words were barely more than a gasp as my lungs begged for fresh air.

Head down, I made for the window, checking in with Pia every few seconds to make sure she was okay. When fresh air began to break through the smoke, I rose and used the sole of my boot to kick the window's rough edges off, in hopes we could crawl through without shredding our skin.

I went first, peering outside to make sure no Draemornians were around before I lowered Pia out. My hip stung as it brushed against the jagged glass remains, tearing a hole in my pants. "Motherfucker," I cursed, but disregarded the pain as I'd done plenty of times before, and carried on.

I tossed myself out of the window, reaching a hand up to grab Pia's as she threw her own body over the ledge and onto the balcony. The smoke was so heavy that all of our enemies had cleared the area, which gave us the briefest of moments to center ourselves.

We both coughed and gasped for any ounce of fresh air, but smoke still pooled from the window, inching closer to us with each gust of wind. My gut churned. "We need to move." My throat scratched out the warning, and as soon as we started our descent down the balcony stairs, I was proven right.

"Run!" I shrieked, dragging Pia down the steps with me, trying to avoid the chunks of stone that fell from the castle walls.

We dove onto the grassy area at the bottom of the staircase. I scrambled to pull myself up to sit, watching as the room we narrowly escaped collapsed into itself. The entirety of the space shot up in flames. Anything that could be destroyed by fire, was.

"Holy shit," Pia retched, tucking her singed hair behind her ears.

My throat bobbed. At this rate, if we didn't stop them, it wouldn't be long before the Draemornians burned the entirety of the castle to the ground. "Holy shit is right."

She nodded as she rose to her knees and hunched over. Smoke came from her lungs as she wheezed, trying to catch her breath. “That was too close.”

“Those fuckers must have gotten inside through one of the towers,” I gasped to her, still struggling to breathe.

She nodded as she rose to her knees and hunched over. Smoke came from her lungs as she wheezed, trying to catch her breath. Her face was already swollen and purple from the hit she took. “Which group was stationed at the east tower?”

There was no time to get my response out before her wild eyes darted to me, gesturing to my leg. She rose up instantly. “Seb, you're bleeding. Like…a lot.”

I glanced down, my jaw tightening at the gash on my outer thigh. It was deeper than I realized. The bleeding was heavy, almost black as it seeped into my pants. I gulped as my adrenaline faded and I started to feel the burn of the wound. “Yeah. I guess I am.” I shrugged the injury off. There was no time to waste on flesh wounds.

She moved forward, hand extended and ready to heal me, but I stepped back.

“It's fine,” I lied, pressing a hand to the gouge. I winced as I felt the indescribable feel of busted muscle. “Don't bother. Preserve your energy. Better yet, use it on your own face.”

“It’s not fucking fine, Seb, you’re turning the grass red.”

Blood seeped between my fingers, but I cocked an eyebrow up. “Who cares about the damn grass, Pia?”

“I don't care about the grass. I just meant that you're bleeding a lot and it's not going to just stop on its own.”

I ripped another piece of my undershirt off and tied it around my leg. The makeshift bandage held for a moment, but soon enough the material started to drip red. “Gods dammit,” I muttered.

“Oh for fuck’s sake, Sebastian. Can you not be stubborn for once in your life?”

My palm pressed harder on the wound. “I'm not being stubborn.” I really was—though I didn't know why.

She glared at me so intently, that I actually felt some fear from the girl.

"Pia. I'm fine. Let's go, we have to move." I started to limp off, but she didn't follow.

"Here you go. Lying to me *yet again*," she snarled.

I froze in place, my back towards her. There it was. It was only a matter of time. Her acting fine about the journal had been a fluke, and why wouldn't she be angry about it? If she'd been hiding things from me for years, I'd be pissed, too. I slowly rotated, facing her where she stood tapping her foot, arms crossed.

"I know it's not the time to get into this, but now that some of the shock is wearing off, I can feel how absolutely pissed I am at you for not telling me about this!" she yelled, chucking the journal to me.

Thank gods she kept it safe through all of that.

My teeth clenched as I bent down to pick it up, fresh blood spurting from my thigh. My body recoiled as I rose and stuffed it into my back pocket, and though I wanted to defend myself, I really couldn't, so I didn't bother trying.

"We have always told each other everything. Do you not trust me?" Pia asked, her tone reflecting her betrayal.

I shook my head. "Of course I do. I just…I don't know. The journal just felt like something special between just my mother and me. Like a secret her and I had together even though she's gone. For a while none of her predictions were coming true anyway, at least none that I saw. But then Maeve showed up, and it all started piecing together."

"Does she know?" Pia asked, her face softening at my confession.

I frowned, dropping my neck down in shame. "No. I didn't plan on telling her when we first met. She hated me and I didn't see the point anyways, because so far the only prediction that had come true was her even existing. But then things started happening—little pieces of my mother's writing coming to life. And *then* I fell for Maeve…hard. At that point though I was so deep into the mess that I felt like telling her would ruin everything." Saying the words aloud made me realize how much I really fucked up. *I'm sorry*, I mouthed the two words that I found myself telling the women in my life all too often.

Pia sighed as she approached to pull me into a hug. "That may just be one of the most pitiful stories I've ever heard." She chuckled. "I forgive you. Of course I do. But you are going to tell Maeve…or I will," she threatened. "But I think it would be best coming from you, seeing as you two are *in love* now."

"I know. I just hope I even get the chance to tell her." Even if she hated me for it—getting to tell Maeve would mean that she was alive, and that's what mattered the most. "I'll tell Sawyer and Kohen, too. But Pia, there's one more thing from the journal that I really need to tell you." There was a key piece to my mother's predictions that she really should know.

She pulled away from me. "Not now. My brain has had enough for the hour. Just let me heal your damn leg," she demanded.

I blew out a breath. This really shouldn't wait any longer, but I'd already ticked her off enough, so I nodded in agreement and gave her access to my wound.

CHAPTER FORTY-SIX

"Where are we going?" Kohen followed behind me, keeping up with my footing as I directed us to my impending funeral.

"Courtyard," I muttered, my mind on one track.

I scanned our surroundings, keeping a constant eye out for enemy soldiers. Where did they all go? Beats me. They certainly had not retreated, but we'd only encountered one since Kohen found me. He took care of the Draemornian before I had even noticed the threat.

"What's in the courtyard?"

"The statues," I said.

"Oh really? I had no idea."

When I did not respond to his sarcasm, Kohen picked up his pace to walk by my side. "And why does that matter? Fancy doing a little tourism while we are in the middle of a war?"

I rolled my eyes. "That was such a Sawyer thing to say. Speaking of Sawyer, have you seen him?" I hoped he had caught up with the others.

Kohen shook his head. "No. Pia and I were guarding the wards at the main gate. I haven't seen him for a few hours."

"I hope he's okay." Worry fueled my voice cracks.

"I'm sure he is. Sawyer is one of the most powerful soldiers we have. You could argue he is the same, if not stronger than Seb."

He wasn't wrong. Sawyer showed me that side of him plenty of times in combat training. Stronger than Sebastian, though?

"It's quiet," I said, pausing in my tracks. "Weirdly quiet for a battle. Isn't it?"

Kohen nodded, his head darting side to side.

As if on cue, a horrendous crash came from somewhere near the main gate—where Pia and Sebastian were, according to Kohen.

Eyes rising towards the sound, we stood silent viewers as a portion of the castle crumbled in on itself, pieces of the tower and the entryway collapsing. The whole area blew up in smoke as flame encapsulated it.

As I watched the destruction, my pulse quickened to a speed that threatened to make my veins burst. *They made it out. They made it out. They have to have made it out.*

A good portion of the Draemornian army ran along the other side of the castle, making for the back entrance.

"They're trying to destroy the castle," Kohen said under his breath.

"They're going to leave us without a kingdom to even rule," I replied under mine, and picked up my speed.

I knew it killed Kohen not to turn back for Pia, but he stayed with me. If he was anything, Kohen was loyal.

We trudged along through the grass, wet with dew and blood. The haze was still heavy, but cleared up the closer we inched to the courtyard. We were almost there, just a few more yards.

I stepped onto the cobblestone patio and took a quick inventory of my surroundings, making sure there was no one waiting for us. There were plenty of bodies around, but the dead were not a threat.

"Come to me."

I marched straight for the statue of Blythe, stopping in front of her and taking my rucksack off, tossing it to the side. The blue and opalescent hues of her statue glistened despite the smoke dancing around it. I took in the beauty of her figure one last time before Kohen and I broke her into smithereens.

I sucked in a few deep breaths—very well the last few I'd ever take. Once we did this, there was no going back. But by the scene we just witnessed at the castle, it seemed that Caelestis was losing this battle. It was my life or theirs, and I chose them…I chose *him.*

Finalizing my decision, I accepted my fate and turned to Kohen. "We need to break this statue."

He raised an eyebrow, crossing his steel-coated arms as he glared at me. "What?"

"You heard me."

"You're joking, right? People are dying, Maeve."

"Yeah, and more will die if we don't break the statue of Blythe."

He scoffed. "Alright. I've always thought you were a little crazy, but now I'm sure of it."

I stared at him, my gaze unfaltering as I waited for him to break.

"Fine. But you need to tell me why."

"There's no time, my star. Soon the castle will fall. You can stop this."

"I'll tell you after, now please!" I pleaded, reaching out for the statue. I used all of my strength to try and push it down, but it was too heavy. Constellastone was not a light mineral.

"King Hawthorne is going to kill me," Kohen groaned, stepping forward. "Back up."

He closed his eyes, tapping into his power and forcing the wind surrounding us to increase. Granted to him by the God of Weather, Zenith, Kohen's onyx jewel flashed as he created a damn tornado right before him. The force of the gust threatened to knock me down. I backed up further to avoid toppling over as his power built the windstorm up higher and higher, until it was taller than the statue itself.

Kohen looked back at me, his arms shaking from the extent of the power he held onto. "Are you sure about this?"

I nodded, brushing my hair out of my eyes.

Kohen clenched his jaw, then turned from me and released the full magnitude of his power.

The tornado collided with the statue, knocking it to the ground, where it shattered into a million glittering pieces of crystal. I had doubted the statue's integrity, but as the shards spread out over the courtyard, it was clear that the sparkling pieces were in fact the most sought after jewel in the world.

The final blow of wind shoved us both to the ground. We stayed down, watching the timeless figurine be destroyed right in front of us, and for the first time in hours, the voice that'd been filling my mind, quieted.

Once the dust had settled, Kohen rose to his feet. "Sooo...What was the purpose of that?"

Ignoring him, I stayed down, waiting for something to happen. Shouldn't *something* have happened? My hand found my neck, checking my pulse just to be sure. It was still there, pounding away.

"What the fuck?"

Kohen looked down at me, his eyes tired and heavy. "Care to explain why I just put myself on Hawthorne's shit list?"

My lips turned down and I gave him a half shrug as I attempted to pull myself to my feet. "I thought for sure that was the answer—" My knees broke down from the pressure, and I collapsed, my head throbbing with the familiar ache granted to me when I overused my power.

"Woah," I hummed, holding a hand to my head and trying to recenter my sense of gravity.

Kohen crouched down before me. "What's wrong? You good?"

"Yeah. I don't know what happened."

He grabbed my arm, pulling me to my feet. He held me steady for a moment, but when he let go, the same thing happened. My vision faltered and my knees hit the ground with such force that it sent a shock through my nervous system. I rolled back, sitting on my behind and blinking my vision back.

I hardly used my magic, so why did I feel like I just compelled an entire army?

"My star..."

My head snapped up. I looked in every direction, searching for the goddess who should have no longer been able to contact me.

My eyes caught on Kohen, whose face clearly conveyed his concern.

"Did you hear that?" he asked, and I nodded a yes.

The wind picked back up, and this time it was not Kohen's doing. As the speed intensified, the shards of crystal covering the courtyard danced along the ground. They shimmered in the glare of the starlight and pulled to each other like magnets, sticking together and building up off of the patio into a mass.

My mouth went slack as a body manifested from the grains of scattered gemstones. They glued themselves together with magic, first creating two legs, then a torso, continuing until the courtyard was cleared of debris, and a glimmering goddess stood tall before us.

We were so small and fragile compared to her magnificent figure. Her skin twinkled with light, so bright and sparkling that she looked as though she had pure starlight emitting from her skin. Her hair was the color of ice and swirled down past her waist, ending in a soft curl. She looked just as her statue did, except *real.* Exquisite.

Blythe's silver eyes locked onto me. "So nice to finally meet you in the flesh." Her voice hummed as she addressed me and offered me a dazzling grin.

I couldn't speak.

The goddess turned to Kohen, whose blank expression proved him to be just as dumbfounded as me. "Thank you for your help in freeing me. Go collect your loved ones—anyone who you don't wish death upon—then return here with them."

Kohen's mouth snapped shut. He gave me a quick glance before making his exit to follow orders.

Anxiety swelled within my core, mixing with my shock and creating an undeniable sense of trepidation as Blythe crouched in front of where I sat.

"Am I about to die?" I felt so weak right now that I must have been edging the veil of life and death.

She blessed me with a comforting smile. Her glass arm reached out to me, brushing the tangles of my hair over my shoulder. "No, my star."

My head rocked side to side. "But…the sacrifice. The prophecy…I thought if I set you free, that it would be fulfilled. I don't understand."

"I told you not to fear the sacrifice, did I not?"

"Well, yes, but—"

"You let your mistrust of yourself and others get in the way of your excellence. I hope that with what's to come, you are able to relieve yourself of that agony." Her voice strummed something in my brain, creating a sense of tranquility within the layers of my soul.

"The fable I guided you to is correct, but you already knew that. I was banished centuries ago by my siblings—locked into that figurine for being too powerful. There is some truth to that claim, but they were destroying everything. I had no choice but to undo the horror they were creating. They had gotten lazy. With each mortal they gifted to work for them, more havoc overtook the beauty of the world we had worked so hard at building. The balance of nature was unwinding beneath our very feet." She paused to place a finger under my chin, tipping my gaze to meet hers. "I could not allow that."

Blythe rose to her full height, which would tower over me if I had the strength to stand. "I knew my siblings' intentions for me, so I had an enchanter help me devise the prophecy. I needed a plan to ensure that when unbalance caused the world to cave in on itself, there would be a fix. Before my siblings fated me to my tomb of stone, I gifted one last soul a fragment of my power in order to keep my line of magic alive." Her head shot towards me. "*You.*"

Her words didn't surprise me, as everything she told me I more or less had pieced together through the manuscripts and my visions.

"I knew you would be created before generations of your ancestors even existed. I was waiting for the right moment to give the world my last gift. Things needed to get worse before you could make them better."

"How has the balance of nature unwound?" I asked, confused by her claim.

She spun in a circle, her palms opened flat towards the stars.

"Don't you see it? The very chaos we are standing in the midst of, flows throughout the entity of our world."

"Sure, things in Caelestis are pretty catastrophic, but surely that's not the case over the entire planet?"

"Horrific things are underway. You may not see it now, but you will."

"But you're free now. You've been saved, can't you stop it?" Using all of my strength, I tried to push myself up from the ground.

The goddess came back for me, assisting my efforts by pulling me to my feet. Her touch was light and feathery on my skin. "There is no hope for saving me, my star. There never was."

I stared at her blankly, studying her bittersweet expression. I had been following what she was telling me, but now I honestly had no clue what she was even talking about. "You mean I just destroyed a priceless statue for no reason?" Kohen was right. The king would definitely have a shit fit about this.

She caught onto my confusion, and breathed out a breath of starlight, though ignoring my accusatory question. "You will not be the one who dies tonight."

A sigh of relief-coated air poured from my throat. My posture laxed where I stood, somehow steadier than I was a few moments prior.

Blythe dropped her hand from me. "The sacrifice is in regard to myself. When I am gone, you will take my place."

My relief was short-lived.

Though it was a struggle, I formed a singular word of shock. "Wh…what?"

I shivered as Blythe made contact with my jewels, trailing a single crystalline finger over my cheekbone. "I could not have chosen a better soul to give these to." A connection sparked between us as she touched me—magic flickering between our souls.

She'd been waltzing around a clear explanation, leaving too much up to my imagination. "Please, tell me what is going on," I prompted the goddess.

Blythe's eyes drooped with sorrow and a single drop of silvery liquid streamed down her skin. "I wish we had more time, but the clock runs short. We must be quick with completing the transition."

"Transition?"

"Take my hands." Blythe reached her palms out to me.

I glanced down at them, shaking my head.

"My star, you are capable of so much more than you realize. Take my hands, and allow me to show you." Her voice flowed into my ears, a calming whisper that soothed my soul. "You believe that you *only* have power over the mind of mortal souls…" she hummed, her voice dragging my gaze to her irises that twinkled like the cosmos.

As if I had no control over my own being—and maybe I didn't—I placed my hands in hers, allowing the cool touch of her crystallized flesh to wash over me.

The goddess beamed. "My dear, you will soon be able to manipulate *the stars*."

"The stars?" The sentence was simple, but I scrambled for the words all the same. I briefly recalled something I'd read about the possibility of Blythe having more power than we realized.

"Why do you think I chose to give you the constellastones? The jewel was the closest thing I could give to the cosmos." Her lips quirked up. "Until now."

Light exploded out of the woman before me.

Her eyes closed and her face emitted deep focus as she pointed her head towards the heavens. I fought to maintain my balance as the ground quaked beneath us, but she held onto my hands, keeping me upright and durable.

My eyes were forced to squint as the glow from her skin intensified, illuminating so brightly that I was sure the creatures in the ocean would be blinded by her power. Starlight dripped off of her. The luminosity crept its way from her fingertips and slithered up mine. I stood a silent observer to the glimmering, white substance that felt slick as it masked my skin, and as her physical excretion of magic covered my flesh, pieces of hers vanished.

"You need to stop this war," she whispered, her voice beginning to sound frail as she evaporated before me.

"How?" My throat shivered as her magic consumed me, filling my veins with the power of the constellations.

"I am granting you the power of the cosmos. Use it. Save who you can, then leave through the tunnel under the castle. If things play out correctly, you will find safety at the end of it."

"And if they don't?"

"There is more than one outcome," she answered.

My body tingled at the continuous absorption of power. Sparkling beads of constellastone sank their way into me, making my skin crawl. Like water, I soaked the magic in, allowing it to consume me.

The goddess' legs had dissipated and her torso was now only half visible. She floated before me, her hair blowing in the cosmic wind of magic spilling out of her.

I scanned my eyes over my own body. My clothing and armor had been melted away by the heat of the starlight, allowing me to see the trail of crystals that embedded themselves into me. They covered my skin, gleaming and twinkling for a few seconds before absorbing and leaving my flesh with a glowy hue.

My hands went slack as hers vanished, only her neck and face left for me to see. She smiled faintly, but did not say another word before the rest of her faded away into nothingness.

I fell victim to another excruciatingly bright beam of light that flashed as soon as she had dissipated. The force knocked my bare body to the ground, where I sank into the cobblestone, the aftershock of whatever the fuck that was leaving me completely jarred.

My hands quivered in front of my face. White swirls of stars circulated around my fingers, coating my palms and trailing up the backs of my hands. The delicate design faded halfway up my forearms, leaving a permanent reminder of the goddess marked into my skin.

The beating of my heart as it tried to escape my ribcage let me know that I was very much alive.

I pulled my knees to my chest, hugging my arms around myself and erupting into tears. Relieved to be alive but also in complete shock, my emotions needed an outlet. I sat for an incomprehensible amount of time, rocking back and forth like a child, only flinching when I felt a rough hand on my spine as someone knelt behind me.

CHAPTER FORTY-SEVEN

Arms pulled me backwards, and despite not knowing who they belonged to, I let my body sink into their owners.

My breathing was harsh, every inhale tearing me further apart. I was physically fine. Mentally, I wasn't sure.

"Sebastian?"

The figure who held me shuffled, releasing one arm to pull off their helmet. It hit the patio with a harsh chime.

"No."

Sawyer.

He tightened his grip on me, careful to avoid any parts of my body that he shouldn't be touching. "Are you okay? What happened?"

"I…I—" I tried, but couldn't speak about it. I didn't even know how to explain what the fuck just happened.

"Never mind that. Are you hurt?"

Still not facing him, I shook my head just enough to give him an answer, then I allowed my eyes to close and ignored the rest of the world.

"Thank the gods." He sighed in pure relief. "The others are on their way. Kohen found me first. Sent me back here while he went to find Seb and Pia."

I sniffled, more tears pooling from me. I didn't know why I was so upset. I was alive.

Sawyer held me while I sobbed. "You're okay. I promise you. Everything is okay," he whispered, pulling my hair back in a way that almost felt too intimate coming from a friend.

I shook my head. "It's not okay." I didn't know why I felt that way, but something was off. I couldn't quite place what, but I just didn't feel like *me*.

"You are safe for right now. Try to relax."

"I…I…Can't. I—" My words broke through the midst of my hyperventilation, the shallow breaths not allowing for my vocal cords to function.

Sawyer's armored biceps tightened around me, the pressure helping to ease the other feelings that swirled in my veins. "Deep breaths. Inhale for me. Come on, Maeve. You can do this."

I was panicking—a feeling not new to me, but very much unappreciated at this time. There was still a battle going on just steps away from where we sat, huddled together in the center of the courtyard.

"Look at me."

I scanned my eyes to find Sawyer's deep green ones, my shoulders following my neck.

"Follow my lead. Breathe in." Sawyer drew a deep breath, and I tried to do the same.

The dusty air pulled into my lungs, crackling when it met the walls of my chest.

"Good. Now out."

It blew out completely broken and shuddered, but it was air nonetheless.

"Again."

When I no longer gasped like a fish out of water, I turned back towards the statues.

Still shaking in his arms, Sawyer asked, "Is there anything I need to know?"

We both fell silent while he waited for my answer. He didn't move a muscle until we heard heavy, panicked footsteps rushing towards us, and I hardly flinched when I felt his body be replaced by one more familiar.

Pinewood and frost.

"How are you here?" My words were no more than a broken whisper.

Sebastian's breath tickled my neck as he settled himself behind me, cradling me in his arms. His armor felt cool on my skin, and helped ease the flames of starlight that raged within me. "I don't know."

I went out on a limb and assumed that when Blythe transferred her magic to me, it undid any commands I had in place. It was okay though—I was glad he was here. I needed him.

His hair was matted with sweat and his eyebrows were pulled together as I looked back at him. My eyes were drawn to his battle leathers, sopping wet with someone's blood.

"Yours?" I asked, now noticing his lower hip.

"Yes." Sebastian nodded. "I'm fine." He sat on the ground behind me, pulling me back between his legs. His arms cradled around me, holding me tightly against his chest as I continued to cry.

Another glimpse of my hands made me realize that the markings sparkled. Shimmering pieces of starlight permanently emulating from my flesh. The sight caused my breath to lock in my lungs, initiating more hyperventilation.

Sebastian brushed my hair to the side. "You're okay," he said as a statement. "You're alive."

My body shook as I used him for support. I pretended there was not a war going on around us and took a moment to collect myself. The knowledge that we were both alive was almost enough to calm me completely, despite the intensity of the aftershock.

I breathed out one last shuddered breath, but that was all the panic I allowed myself to have. There was still work to be done.

"What happened?" Sebastian asked in a whisper when I got a hold of myself.

"You wouldn't believe me if I told you."

Sebastian leaned into my ear. "Maeve, you have brand new markings on your hands. Kohen only left you for maybe a half hour, and I know from experience that ink that intricate would take longer than that to complete—and that's if you aren't in the middle of a war. Not to mention, you're completely naked in the center of the courtyard."

Shit. I forgot my clothes were burned away.

I cringed when I turned my attention, noticing the rest of my friends standing a few yards back, staring at me like they had no idea who I was. Good thing Sebastian's frame was large enough to cover most of mine, although I'd try to forget that Sawyer had his arms around my bare body only minutes ago.

I turned my whole torso so I could look at him without straining my neck, ignoring the eyes of my friends as I revealed more skin with my movements. "Everything in the manuscripts and my visions were true."

Sebastian gave me his full attention while I debriefed him as quickly as I could. There was still a threat waiting for us just beyond the courtyard.

"It wasn't me who the sacrifice was referring to," I finished, quiet enough so only he could hear me. "It was her. She transferred her magic to me before she died, and I think…I think I can control the stars," I stuttered.

Sebastian shuffled uncomfortably. He didn't look as shocked as I'd expected. "I know," he said, though I didn't fully absorb his words.

"She told me to finish this war. End it. Then to go to the passageway in the dungeon. She said if we can reach the end of the tunnel we will be safe. Wait—" My head cocked to the side as I gathered what he had said. "Know what?"

He exhaled deeply through his clenched jaw. His lips parted and his face looked pained, as if what he was about to say would cut deep. "There's some things I really need to tell you. Now isn't the best time, but I found—"

Our attention was directed to the tower closest to us as its peak came crashing down in chunks of stone. The impact made the whole patio shake, and I jumped up instinctively, forgetting about my lack of clothing.

Sebastian moved his body to block me from the eyes of our friends. "Clothes. *Please*!" he yelled over to them, and backed us away from the tumbling rock.

Pia stepped forward with my rucksack in hand. I always had an extra pair of pants and a shirt packed for emergencies. My instincts must have kicked before I even knew what would happen.

She flashed Sebastian a sideways glance while handing me the clothes. He put his head down, disregarding her presence.

I pulled the top over my head, then worked on the pants. They were an old pair, so they were a bit snug. I had to wiggle them over my hips, but it beat fighting in the nude.

Sawyer took a pair of boots from a deceased female soldier, setting them down in front of me once I was fully clothed. I stepped into them and he bent down on one knee, tying the laces tightly around my shins.

Another boom of destruction echoed through my eardrums.

Our heads turned towards the castle. Flames rose throughout the building, peeking out from the windows on the higher levels. Voices screamed in distress. I had tuned them out before, but was sure they had never ceased.

We didn't have a lot of time before our escape route was destroyed.

I looked around desperately for my dagger, praying it was intact. The glint of the hilt caught my gaze near the statue of Sloane. The burst of energy from Blythe's final use of power must have caused it to slide over there.

I moved for it—the one thing that didn't melt off of me. The starlight had even melted my Caelestian armor, and I couldn't help but wonder if the goddess had something to do with the preservation of my blade.

When I crouched down to pick it up, something crunched under my foot. I raised my boot and saw the pendant from my mother lying in a seam of the cobblestone. My hand automatically snapped to my chest, feeling to make sure it really had fallen off.

I picked the necklace up with a sigh—the last reminder of my family. I jostled it in my hand, admiring it briefly then stuffing it in my pocket. Make that *two* things that didn't melt. I glanced up towards the veil and whispered an airy, "Thank you."

With my dagger firmly in my palm, I joined my friends. They were huddled together, their weapons drawn and ready to combat anyone who may strike. Their wide eyes were all the confirmation I needed to know that Sebastian had filled them in on what happened to me.

Pia pulled me into a constricting hug. "Are you okay?"

"I think so. I feel weird, though."

"I'd imagine so. What's up with this?" She pulled back and took one of my forearms in her hands, examining the swirling design that trailed up from my fingertips.

"I have no idea, but now isn't the best time to try and figure it out." I turned to the rest of the group.

"What's the plan?" Kohen asked, and they all looked at me.

"Blythe said to use my power and told me how to make a clean exit if needed. Other than that, I have no idea."

They still stared at me like I had died and come back to life—aside from Sebastian, who seemed pretty unfazed by all of this.

"Well, by the looks of it, if our army doesn't get a grip, the rest of the castle is going down," Sawyer said.

I peered over the shrubs surrounding the patio. Spouts of water from sapphire gifted soldiers shot down the flames that raged inside the castle. I thought back to my visions and tried to remember if I saw the outcome of this, but all I could remember was the castle burning, not if it met its demise.

"How many of our troops do you think are left in the castle?" I asked, mostly to Sebastian.

"Uh, I don't know. Likely more Draemornians than our men. Those fuckers are searching high and low for you."

I nodded. Good. The less of our kind I had to kill, the better.

"How about your father?" I asked next.

Sawyer scoffed, answering before Sebastian could. "That coward fled through the tunnels as soon as we all left the throne room. He's long gone by now."

Okay—also good. Although he was a complete ass, I wasn't too keen on killing the father of the man I loved.

"By the way things are going, it looks like we are going to lose the castle anyway." I paused to glance between the four of them. "I think we should lure as many Draemornians inside as we can. Then I'll burn the castle and whoever is inside to the ground. If what Blythe said about me having the power to manipulate the stars is true, I should have no problem conducting enough power to finish the job." My eyes bounced between my friends. "We can rebuild a castle, but we can't rebuild lives."

"Absolutely no fucking way we are doing that!" Sebastian shouted, grabbing me by the shoulders. "You don't even know for certain what your new powers are. And just because you have the power doesn't mean you should use it. It could kill you!" His eyes drifted to Pia and they gave each other a look that said that they knew something the rest of us didn't.

"What was that?" I raised an eyebrow in suspicion, acknowledging that I saw their shared glance.

Pia bit her lip and Sebastian dropped his arms from me, shaking his head in denial. "Nothing."

I crossed my arms and pointed a finger at Pia. "The look on your face says enough." Then I directed my finger at him. "And you're a horrible liar."

Sawyer interjected before either of them had a chance to defend themselves. "Maeve, I gotta agree with them. No offense, but you don't have a great history with using your magic, and now is really not a good time to test fate."

My eyes shot to him, then I flipped him the finger for not defending me. He scrunched his nose, but backed down.

Kohen took his turn arguing with me. "Sorry, Maeve, but they're right. You've never used this side of your magic before. You don't know what you're capable of or how to control it."

I tapped my foot in annoyance. "You do realize I could compel every single one of you to screw off, right?"

I swear I could see Sebastian tightening his shields as he flashed me a look of warning. "Don't you dare," he snarled.

I was taken aback at his tone and prepared to counter when Pia jumped in. "Okay, everyone *calm down*. The more I think about this, Maeve may actually be right in some sense."

"Pia, stop." Sebastian's eyes begged for her to listen.

What was he not telling me?

She ignored him. "I'm sorry, Seb, but we have to look at the big picture here. The castle is almost a pile of ruins, anyway—there's no chance Caelestis is winning this war. If you can even call it a war, I mean, it's been a day. But anyways, the best case scenario is that we destroy as many of Beaumont's soldiers as we can before we get out of here."

Sebastian's nostrils flared and he clenched his fists. They were turning white when he looked back to me, his face softening as he pleaded for me to listen. "Let's just all make for the dungeon. We can get out of here." He put his face close to mine. "*Please.*"

Gods, he was beautiful. I loved him. More than I had ever loved anyone or anything. But I couldn't falter on this. I had to do this for myself. For my mother and Delani. My head hung as I shook it. I couldn't bear to see the betrayal on his face another time today.

His feet backed away from me slowly, and the sight hurt my heart—just as it did before. I would make it up to him later, right now I had some Draemornians to fuck up.

Sawyer piped in. "Fine. I'm in. But if we are doing this, I want a say in how it's executed."

I offered him a grin as a thank you, then turned my attention to Kohen, waiting for his approval as well.

He caved with a hearty sigh. "Okay, I'm in, too. But I think we should attack from inside the dungeon, that way we can start right through the passageway when you're finished. Can you work from the ground up?"

"Guess we'll find out," I replied, rolling the sleeves of my shirt up to my elbows.

I turned to Sebastian, who looked completely devastated. I took his hand in mine, pulling him off to the side to give us a little privacy. His eyes refused to meet mine.

"What's going on?" I asked.

"I thought we were in the clear now that the sacrifice has been taken care of."

"What are you talking about?" We couldn't just be *in the clear*. We were in the midst of a battle for the gods' sakes.

He raised his gaze, giving me the eye contact I'd been waiting for. An anguish filled breath poured from his mouth. "There's things I haven't told you…things I swore I was going to, but never did. I know there's no time to explain it all right now, but I really need you to trust me." He shook his head. "I can't lose you." His lip quivered.

"You aren't going to lose me," I assured him, but he was persistent.

"No, Maeve, you're not listening. I know things about this war and its potential outcomes that you don't—"

"A goddess just gave me her damn magic, Seb! I can do this, I know I can. Why are you so insistent on fighting me on this? "

"I'm not trying to fight with you, I'm trying to make you understand!"

We were interrupted by Sawyer calling back to us. "Hey. Uh, sorry to interrupt what sounds like a very *endearing* moment between the two of you, but there's been a change of plans."

Sebastian and I shot our heads towards our friends, who were face to face with King Beaumont and a hefty group of his soldiers.

CHAPTER FORTY-EIGHT

The king of Draemor looked different than I had expected. He was much younger than King Hawthorne, and was almost, dare I say, handsome.

He was tall. Very tall—more than Sebastian's six and a half foot frame.

His hair was short, cut only an inch or so from his scalp and was auburn in color. He wore armor that matched his soldiers, but there was no mistaking him for a king.

Sebastian pulled me behind him, though trying to hide was pointless.

"Ah, Sebastian Hawthorne, Crown Prince of Caelestis. How lovely it is to see you again," Cyprian hummed as he stepped towards us, a devious smirk splayed across the sharp edges of his cheeks.

Sebastian drew his sword, still holding me behind him.

The king of Draemor tapped a finger to his chin. "Last time I saw you…Hmm, let me think. Oh right. The last time I saw you was when I sliced your mother's skull from her body." He smirked at the release of his twisted comment.

Sebastian's grip tightened at the reminder of the worst day of his life, but he stood his ground, not giving in to the king's attempt at breaking him.

Beaumont took another few steps for us, the muscles of his arms flaring as he moved. He walked right by Sawyer, Kohen, and Pia, then stopped in front of Sebastian.

The dark king angled the tip of his sword into his neck. "Step aside," he demanded.

Sebastian tilted his head back, giving him even more access.

"Do not test me, boy. I will not hesitate to deliver you the same fate as your bitch mother."

"Don't you *dare* speak about her in that manner," Sebastian growled, teeth bared.

My heart thumped in my chest. I knew how this would play out. Sebastian would do anything to protect me, even if it meant giving his life. I couldn't handle losing another person I loved.

I ripped my arm from his hold and stepped out from behind him, putting myself on display.

Beaumont beamed, though it was not a welcoming smile. He lowered his sword from Sebastian's throat and directed his posture towards me. His gaze immediately dropped to the pearlescent markings on my arms and he followed them up until he met my face.

"Those must be new. Lucan never mentioned that you had such power."

My eyebrow quirked. "You know what these are?" I asked, saying my first ever words to the powerhouse of a man before me.

"Of course I do. The mark of a god—" He cut himself off to correct himself, "Actually, by the design, I can only assume it's the mark of a *goddess*. Only those truly blessed will ever receive such a gift. Blythe must really cherish you, granting you such a rare jewel along with that mark."

I noticed the tense of the word 'cherish' when he spoke of Blythe. He had no idea that the prophecy had already played out.

"What does it mean?" I asked—genuinely curious, but also trying to buy us some time.

"According to ancient history, those with a mark have even greater powers than those with just a jewel. In your case, though, I think it means more than that." He inched closer to me, bending down into my neck. "I would love to find out more about you, if you'll allow me," he purred, trailing a finger along my earlobe.

It was a risky move, but I jammed my elbow into the space between his armor, hitting him hard in the ribcage.

He jumped back and winked at me. "Feisty—just as I predicted."

Beaumont took an additional few steps back to address my friends. "We have already gained control of most of the castle grounds. Soon the fortress in its entirety will be nothing more than a pile of wreckage, so I present you all with an opportunity that I'm sure you will not want to pass up."

I glanced over at Sebastian. He shook his head in a subtle reminder to deny anything that the king of Draemor offered.

Beaumont cleared his throat, then directed his words at me. "I know you have denied my offers in the past, but I'm feeling…generous. So let's raise the stakes, shall we?" He peered over at Sebastian, smiling coldly before turning his gaze back to me. "You come with me and become my wife, and in return I will allow you to bring your *friends* along. I will keep you all safe and fed. In the meantime, you and I will work together to discover the extent of your gift."

"That's it? I thought you wanted to *breed* me?" I quoted one of his soldiers.

I heard Sebastian's gulp from behind me, confirming that the claim was one of the many he heard in Craterra.

"You are quite stunning I shall say, so yes, intimacy would be part of the arrangement. I would love to test the limits of the gods' gifts."

I pretended to gag, eliciting a scowl from Cyprian.

"Should you deny again, I will execute your friends while you watch. Then, I will cut a slab of skin off of your face, thus removing your jewels before leaving you for my soldiers to do with whatever they please before they kill you. And I should remind you that many of them haven't been near a woman in quite some time."

His words were so harsh. So cruel, that they made me *actually* gag.

Cyprian noticed my weak stomach, and huffed a laugh. "I know what you're thinking, *Cyprian, that's absolutely horrific. How could you do such a thing*?" he mocked, imitating a female voice. His eyes narrowed as he stormed towards me, blade angled in my direction. "Here's the thing, I've asked politely for what I want, and it has gotten me nowhere. I am done asking. Those are your options, choose wisely."

"And how could I be sure that you would be honorable with your offer?"

"I suppose you just have to take my word for it."

"Well you seem to have a history of being a liar, so your word doesn't mean much," I shot back.

Cyprian chuckled. "Feisty *and* sarcastic. I like it." He leaned in closer to me, his breath warming my neck. "I don't have all day, and neither do you. Make up your mind."

My gaze flickered between my friends. If I said yes to the king's plea, I knew it would not turn out how he claimed it would. The king of Draemor was such a sadistic fuck that he made Aldous Hawthorne look like a saint.

I caught Sebastian's gaze, giving him the slightest nod, which he repeated back to me in understanding.

Looking up at the king, I met his dark, soulless expression with my own empty gaze. Leaning closer to him, I pointed my lips at his ear. "Such a considerate offer," I whispered breathily into him, matching the flirtatious tone he used with me. "But *for the last fucking time*, I'm not going with you." As soon as the words rolled off my tongue, I flicked my wrist, stabbing my dagger into his thigh.

The toxin had been cleaned out on my last opponent, but Beaumont still jumped back in pain, cursing as blood spurted from the gash in his leg. He growled at me, his eyebrows sinking into his forehead. Then, all hell broke loose.

The Draemornian soldiers drew their weapons and lunged at us. I jumped backwards a few feet, putting enough distance between the king and I so that he couldn't reach me as he drew his own sword.

Sebastian met me where I stood, putting his back to me as the Draemornians swarmed in. Sawyer took up residence by my front, their bodies blocking the soldiers from reaching me.

Sawyer made the first kill, slicing the arm of a Draemornian clean off. He pierced the man's neck while he grasped for his missing limb, crying out in agony.

I peered over at Kohen, who was responsible for the next execution. As an enemy took a swing at Pia, he kneed the soldier in the chest, knocking them back. Before they could rebound, Kohen put his blade through the top of their skull.

For each kill we made, three more Draemornians showed up to take the place of the deceased.

The sounds of metal meeting flesh circulated throughout the courtyard as we battled with an army that significantly outnumbered us.

King Beaumont stepped back from the chaos, still clutching his sword, but just a silent observer to the bodies falling.

A soldier lunged for me, and my skin prickled as I was met with a gush of cold air. Sebastian used his magic on the man, freezing him into a block of ice mid-step. I kicked the sole of my boot into his chest. His skin and bones shattered as they hit the concrete, breaking into frozen, meaty shards of human remains.

The Draemornians kept pouring in, and it was no question that it was going to take more of us to finish them off.

"Where the hell are the rest of our soldiers?" Sebastian shouted over my back to Sawyer.

"Wish the fuck I knew."

Kohen and Pia inched their way towards us until we finally collided. Our weapons continued to swing as we discussed the best course of action.

"There's no chance of us stopping all of them, they just keep coming. You heard what Beaumont said—the castle is done for, anyways. Let's just try and get out of here," Pia gasped, raising her sword to counter a swing from an incoming soldier. Metal clanged as she blocked a death kill.

"We can't give up now," I countered as Kohen finished the deed for Pia. My plans had changed when this asshole showed up.

Kohen turned his back towards the battle to shout out a few

quick words. "She's right, let's make a break for the tunnel. We can—"

As if Sebastian had used his magic on me as well, my heart froze at the sound of hollow gasping.

The tip of a blade poked clean through Kohen's stomach, just a little to the left of his naval. Without a sound, he sank to his knees, eyes wide with adrenaline as the Draemornian yanked his sword back, twisting and pulling it from Kohen's abdomen.

Pia screamed the most heart wrenching wail I'd ever heard. She fell to her own knees, dropping her sword so that she could hold her hands over Kohen's wound. "You're okay. You're going to be okay, Kohen, I promise," she cried and tried to heal the hole, but there was too much emotion and chaos surrounding us for her to relax enough to focus on it.

Time seemed to stop with Sawyer's guttural growl as he took charge and brutalized the soldier responsible.

"Get him out of here. Go to the tunnel. I'll finish this and meet you there," I urged Sebastian, whose skin had lightened to the color of snow.

He started to shake his head, but I interjected with another plea. "Sebastian, I'm begging you. Please just trust me."

His eyes stayed on mine as he put his sword in one hand—surprisingly steady for only having one arm for support—and stabbed it into an incoming Draemornian.

Sebastian pulled it free, then moved his eyes from me, truly taking in our surroundings. His gaze dipped to Kohen, who was hanging on, but hardly. Blood pooled on the stone beneath him, and his eyes had fallen dark. Sawyer fought off any soldiers who tried to get at Pia while she attempted to heal him, but soon enough they would exceed his capabilities. When Sebastian looked back at me, his expression had changed, and I knew he'd realized that I was right.

"There's no way we can win this. There's too many of them, and now only four of us are able to fight. I'm the only chance we have at making it out of here alive, and Kohen needs help or he is going to die," I said, my voice hushed. For a moment it felt like it was just him and I.

He chewed the inside of his cheek. "Maeve, if you die, I—"

"I won't," I promised. "Besides, you said it yourself, that no veil of life or death will keep us apart. So even if I do…" I forced a smile, which he did not reciprocate.

Another excruciating wail came from Pia. Her body draped over Kohen, blocking anyone from reaching him. I could still see the rise and fall of his chest, but if Pia couldn't heal him in time—

My soul ached at the thought.

"Go. *Please*. I'll be there soon," I instructed Sebastian to leave me, and though I knew it absolutely killed him to do so, he rose, pulling Pia off of Kohen's limp body, keeping his sword drawn as she fought him, still screaming.

Sawyer lifted Kohen off the ground, throwing him over his shoulder, and the four of them started to back out of the courtyard, fighting off the enemies that tried to stop them.

I turned, unable to give them another second of attention. There were more pressing matters in front of me.

"Call your soldiers off so we can talk," I shouted my demand to Beaumont, who stood all too casual, unfazed by the bloodbath unfolding in front of him.

His eyes glossed over mine, and a smirk enveloped his face. "Stand down," he demanded of his army.

They obeyed, retreating to take up residence behind their ruler.

I took a moment before approaching him to solidify my course of action and catch my breath.

My vision scanned over the patio covered in dead Draemornians. I had to admit, their army may have outnumbered ours, but my friends were some kickass soldiers.

I blew out a heavy breath, then forced my legs to move, striding towards the man who had no clue that I was about to destroy him.

"Fine," I panted. "I will go with you, but only if you stop all of this." I gestured vaguely to the turmoil of the war amongst us.

Cyprian chuckled, shaking his head. "That was not part of the deal." He stepped towards me, putting only a few feet between us.

"I never said I would retreat. I still have every intention of claiming the eastern and Caelestis' territory," he sneered.

"Screw it then. Take over Caelestis," I huffed. He pretty much already had, anyway. "Just give my friends a few minutes to get out safely, then I will go with you." I tried to bargain with the man, simply to gain some time for them to reach the dungeon.

"Do you not remember, Maeve?" The king cocked his head to the side, tapping a finger to his chin. "I do recall saying something about executing your loved ones if you denied me for a final time. Did I not?" He circled me, trying to be intimidating as he threatened my friends.

I clenched my jaw. "You did. But—"

He waved a finger. "No buts. You already denied my last offer."

"Well I have an offer of my own for you to consider." I approached him, gripping my dagger tightly in my palm.

"If you let my friends go, then I will go with you. If you don't, I will kill myself before you get a chance to cut my jewels from my skin. They will be useless if they are removed after I'm dead."

"You don't have the guts," Beaumont snarled.

I put the tip of my dagger into my flesh, right under my chin, angled up. "I didn't want this life. Removing myself from it would be a blessing." The peak of the blade entered my flesh, cutting my throat just enough for blood to dribble down my blade.

"Maeve, stop it!" Sebastian screamed, his voice sounding completely horrified. I turned my head over so slightly to see Sawyer holding him back—he must have caught on to my plan.

Beaumont cocked his head in consideration. "I don't believe you."

Digging the blade in deeper, I winced at the sting. "Is that a gamble you're willing to take?" I gargled.

Beaumont briefly looked over his shoulder at his army before turning back to me, an insidious grin painted his face. "Very well." He gestured to Sebastian and the others. "Go, before I change my mind."

I pulled my dagger from my flesh and didn't watch as they left me.

At the release of his command, Beaumont's soldiers moved out from behind him. They advanced on me, and I let them, needing them close to do what I had planned.

My skin pulled as two Draemornians gripped my arms, holding me tightly in place. My muscles burned from the strength of their grip, but I displaced the pain, putting the energy elsewhere.

A few soldiers took their position behind me in case I tried to escape. The rest stayed behind Cyprian. No matter which direction I looked, there was a soldier waiting.

I tilted my head up towards the twilight sky. Despite the haze of smoke creating a film over the air, the stars were vibrant. My cheek twitched at the sight of them, the markings on my arm doing the same as I reveled in the power of the cosmos that now circulated within my soul.

For once in my life, I was free of fear.

My gaze fell, locking my eyes with the king. I bared my teeth as his soldiers held me down. I didn't struggle to get out of their grasp. I let them think they had me in their control.

And then I fucking exploded.

CHAPTER FORTY-NINE

Starlight flew out of me in all directions, soaring from every pore in my skin. The glimmering substance was much like the one that covered me during my transition, only this was much more potent. Much more powerful.

The brightest of lights beamed from within me, blinding those near and singeing the skin of those too close to the blast. I collected the starlight from the heavens, soaking it into my soul and displaying it in a rare, raw form of magic.

The hands that held me down went slack, melted away into piles of ash and starlight. Men went aerial as my eruption of cosmic energy was too much for their bodies to withstand. I heard their corpses crack as they hit the ground, but I still aimed my magic at them just to make sure they were truly done for. I burned every single one of those motherfuckers with the galaxies that flooded me. They completely dissipated, melting away into nothing, and I didn't stop until I destroyed every last one of them.

I expected myself to feel weak, but I didn't falter. Maybe it was the adrenaline, but my body stayed steady as I strode towards Beaumont, who looked utterly horrified. I came to a halt in front of him, staring mercilessly for a second as I tried to comprehend what the hell I just did to those men.

Blythe was not joking about the power she granted me. Even the gods' damn stars were at my mercy.

I was *unstoppable*.

Cyprian's teeth visibly chattered. I held a twinkling finger to my mouth, shushing him. Then, I told him the same sentence that I told King Hawthorne not even one day prior. "You. Don't. Control. Me," I spat in his face, throwing a small taste of my power at him with each word, leaving small, white burns on his skin.

He shook aggressively in response.

"Scared?" I taunted.

"More like *in awe* of the pure power you carry within you. Power that will soon be mine, so I am far from scared, Maeve," he snarled back.

"A shame." I grinned and stepped back, preparing to summon more of my magic. "Because you should be."

I would ruin him.

My hands splayed out before me, starlight dripping from my fingertips into piles of heated, luminous light on the cobblestone. I made sure to keep my eyes wide—I wanted to watch as he ceased to exist.

For some unknown reason, I hesitated. And he noticed, his frown reconfiguring into a smirk. "Having second thoughts?" he mocked, pointing his sword at me in defense. "You can still come with me willingly. I'll allow it even though you lied to me about your intentions."

"No. Just trying to figure out the most painful way to kill you," I lied, because that was not it. I didn't know what was holding me back—maybe the shock setting in over the new use of my gift.

I needed to hurry up and finish this so that I could get to the tunnel. My mind flashed to Sebastian and my friends...*Kohen*. I sent a quick prayer to the gods for him, then directed my attention back on Beaumont, whose body had relaxed in response to my hesitation.

I tapped back into my powers, feeling the crackling of my magic coursing through my veins. With the force of the cosmos in my clutch, I was about to relinquish my power when I was stopped by a deafening noise.

My head turned towards the castle just in time to see the rest of it cracking and crumbling as it collapsed. The ground quaked as bricks and stones fell with such force that it threatened to take me down with it.

My feet failed me as the pressure of the falling fortress knocked me down. I was bombarded by piles of rubble and a fierce cloud of dust which clogged my airway with each breath I took.

The remaining seven statues fell with the wreckage that cascaded into the courtyard, making its way towards me in a rock and dust avalanche. I glanced around desperately for an exit route, but noticed instead that Beaumont was gone.

After every near death experience I'd survived, this was how I would die—by blunt force trauma. I chuckled in despair. What were the odds?

"What happened to 'you will not be the one who dies today'?" I yelled up at the goddess who no longer existed.

I jumped away from broken rocks that landed in front of my feet, then everything else happened so fast. Before I could run from the tumbling turmoil, my surroundings faded to black and the air in my lungs was entirely replaced with dust.

My lethargic shell of a body was pulled from the rubble, twisted and mangled. My eyes wouldn't open to see, but the pain made it obvious that I was covered in bruises, scrapes, and gashes. Probably internal injuries that were even worse.

My abdomen throbbed an unbearable ache that made me want to shriek, but I couldn't cry out. My mouth was stuffed with dirt and dust, like a taxidermy pet.

I coughed out an esophagus of rubble, my throat hoarse and dry as the darkness surrounding me peeled away and bright light sank in through my eyelids.

My body dangled limply in someone's arms. Their heavy footsteps crunched the stone beneath us as they carried me off. I hoped it was Sebastian that held me, but the odds were slim. He should have been in the passageway under the castle by now with the others. I prayed that they made it in time.

It could be Beaumont who held me, but I lost sight of him before the castle finished falling. He either made it out, or the wreckage had swallowed him as well.

A muffled, gruff voice rumbled through my ears. I was unable to make out the words, and feared that the pressure from the stone that crushed me had busted my eardrums.

Coughing a few more breaths of dirt and dust, I cleared my airway. Upon another attempt at opening my eyes, I found a layer of filth affecting my vision. Blinking them slowly, my eyes watered to wash it away with each open and close, then stayed open to adjust to the obnoxious daylight.

My surroundings were unrecognizable. Vibrant and green—a large shift from what I saw last time my eyes were open. We were in the forest. How we got there so quickly, I did not understand.

Lingering weakness had a death grip on every part of my body. Taking in as many details as I could before fading away again, I turned my head up to see a burly, middle aged man—

CHAPTER
FIFTY

I gasped when my body flew upright, putting me into a sitting position on a bed that was not mine. Instant panic consumed me as I glanced around, not recognizing the room in the slightest. I tried to kickstart my brain into remembering the space, wondering if it was somewhere I'd been before that I couldn't recall.

The room was small and tidy, its sage curtains drawn to a close, preventing me from getting a hint at my whereabouts. The wood walls almost reminded me of home, before I remembered that my home no longer existed.

I sat up a bit straighter. My entire body ached, as if it were crushed. Wait—

I *was* crushed.

Recollection swarmed me as I recalled the details of what happened. Last I knew, I was face to face with Beaumont, preparing to destroy him before the castle caved in on me.

I took inventory of my injuries. There were a few scrapes and bruises on my arms and legs, but other than that and a general soreness, I felt fine. Someone must have healed me because the odds of surviving what I did were slim. So incredibly slim.

My eyes peeked at the iridescent constellations on my arms and more memories came rushing back to me. I shuffled back towards the headboard, pulling my hand to my mouth, and chewing the tips of my fingers as more unease filled me.

Was I in Draemor?

Did Beaumont make it out? Did he bring me here?

Was Sebastian okay? Sawyer? Pia?

Was Kohen even *alive*?

I rocked back and forth, hugging my knees to my chest like an infant. Tears poured from my eyes in response to the fear building up inside of me.

"Hey, hey, Maeve. It's okay. It's me."

My head skipped to my right when something familiar finally appeared, Sebastian's voice calming me instantly as he stepped into the room.

"Oh thank the gods," I whispered as he rushed for me and threw himself down beside me on the bed.

He cupped his hands around my cheeks, then sucked my lips into a long, deep kiss. When he pulled away, he dipped his forehead against mine, releasing a throaty sigh.

"You're okay," he assured me again, and though nothing *felt* okay, I trusted him. "How much do you remember?"

I looked down with focus. "I remember everything until the castle fell. I think Beaumont got away, or was crushed. I'm not sure. After that, nothing." I raised my head, reality sinking in. "What the hell happened? Are you okay? Is Kohen okay?" I sputtered out question after question as I scanned my eyes over his body, looking for any injuries. "How did we get here? Where even *is here*?"

Sebastian chuckled a little. "First of all, yes. Kohen is okay. We made it to the tunnel just before the castle caved in, and Pia was able to heal him enough to keep him alive until we made it out. Sawyer is fine, too."

Alleviated, I nodded, waiting eagerly for him to tell me more.

"*What happened* is that you kicked fucking ass. You mutilated the Draemornians with starlight just before the castle fell."

"I remember all of that—" I glanced up at Sebastian as confusion toppled over me. "How do you know what my new magic is? Weren't you in the tunnel when I did that?" I asked, raising an eyebrow.

He bit his inner cheek, nodding slowly. Stray strands of his dark hair wavering with the motion. "Yes."

"So how do you know what I did?"

Sebastian shifted uncomfortably. "I tried to tell you. Wanted to tell you so many times, but I—" He looked down, avoiding my eyes.

I flipped through my memories, recalling what he said just before Beaumont showed up—something about *things he hadn't told me.*

"Tell me," I demanded.

His gaze collided with mine, his eyes filled to the brim with sorrow. "I'm sorry," he apologized.

"For what?"

Sebastian sucked in a sharp breath as he rose to his feet, angling his back to me. "I've known more about this war and about you than I've let on."

My heart suddenly had to work extra hard to beat. "Care to elaborate?"

"You're going to hate me." He hung his head.

I didn't think it was possible for me to hate him, but then again, I had no idea what he was about to tell me.

Sebastian turned back to look at me and his posture sank as he blurted out the words that caused my heart to break. "My mother was a seer, which I know sounds crazy, but it happens. Once in a while there's an anomaly, and she was it. I found her journal a few years back. She wrote visions that she had, a lot of them having to do with the war we are in and you."

I interrupted him with an eye roll. "You realize that sounds like a load of crap, right?"

Sebastian huffed a laugh. "I know, but I swear on everything I love that it's true."

"Was that what you were reading in the archives the night we overheard Lucan? That's what you stuffed away and wouldn't let me see?"

He nodded softly and cleared his throat before continuing to wreck me with his confession. "As soon as I saw you last summer, I knew who you were. She predicted you—described you in detail. She also *saw* two outcomes of this war, though she didn't give many details about them, only that one outcome involved someone important dying. At first I thought it was you. I was relieved beyond measure to learn that it was Blythe."

That's why he didn't want me to fight. That's why he pushed so hard to bring me to the tunnel. He was trying to change an uncertain fate.

Sebastian took a deep breath, spilling the rest of his confession in a mess of stutters and shambles, as if he'd been holding the words in for so long that they'd forgotten how to piece themselves together. "She also wrote about your power. How it was more than just mind compulsion, but she didn't elaborate too much on what. I pieced two and two together the more I got to know you, and the more I learned about Blythe and the prophecy. I didn't know for certain that you would be able to control the cosmos, but it was in the back of my mind for a while."

He sat back on the bed and I leaned away from him, absolutely appalled. "How did you just 'piece that together'?"

"She wrote a small entry about the cosmos. How a god was responsible for them, but did not name who. I thought at first that maybe it was Zenith." His voice lowered. "When I found you after the sacrifice and saw the markings on your arms, I knew my assumptions were right—"

I held my hand up to stop him. I'd heard enough.

He'd been lying to me for the better portion of a year. Well, not so much *lying* as he was withholding information. Regardless, the betrayal hurt the same. "You knew about me from the very moment we'd met, and didn't say anything?" I asked, my shock reflecting in my voice.

He'd kissed me—*slept with me*—all while hiding that he had information about the prophecy. About what was going to happen to me. He could have cured so much of my fears had he just told me. Looking back, it made sense. There were clues along the way.

The way he stared at me when we first saw each other at Jewel-Light last summer as if he already knew me.

My eyes burned as they filled with scalding hot tears. No longer caring that I had no idea where we were, I stood up and pointed to the door. "Get out."

Sebastian shook his head. "No. Maeve, there's really more I should tell you. And *please* let me explain," he begged, his own eyes turning wet.

"Get. Out," I repeated icily, needing him gone.

Sebastian rose to a stand, ignoring my plea for him to leave. "I love you, Maeve. I never meant to hurt you. I was going to tell you everything, the time was just never right—"

I scoffed and rolled my eyes. "Oh bullshit. I have a few ideas of when the 'right time' may have been, *Sebastian*." His name rolled off my tongue like a curse. "Maybe, oh, I don't know, when we first met? Or when I was so weak and sick from using my power that I couldn't eat—a little heads up that things would change would have been nice." I began pacing, tapping a finger on my chin as I roamed. "Maybe when I saw you reading the journal in the archives that night. Or maybe before you *fucked me*." I turned to face him, showing the anger displayed on my face. My shoulders drooped, and my voice broke and cracked under the weight of my sorrow. "Before you told me you loved me?"

My gaze fell to my feet to watch my tears splash on the floor. Sebastian reached out for me, but I rolled my shoulder back and away from him.

"I trusted you," I squeaked out.

"Maeve…" he whispered my name apologetically.

"For the last time, Sebastian, just get the fuck out!" I screamed and cried at the same time.

The harshness of my words visibly shattered him. But I was too broken, too devastated to care.

"I know you're mad, but please try to understand. And just let me finish. Your father—"

"No! Don't you dare mention my family. They are all dead, and I bet you knew about that, too, right?"

"I—"

My anger came to a head and I shoved him hard in the chest, the moment all too reminiscent of when he returned from Craterra. My heart ached at the memory of what we shared the night of his homecoming. That evening held some of my best memories with him, even though it began much like this.

I swallowed the nostalgia and pushed him towards the door. My shaking fingers twisted the knob and tried to guide him out, but he got caught on his exit, slamming into another body.

My eyes rose to meet a set that looked quite similar to mine. I knew by the resemblance who the man was before he could even tell me. Which either meant that none of this was real and I was actually dead…

Or *he* never was.

AN EXCERPT OF DEFINITIONS FROM THE ROYAL ARCHIVES OF CAELESTIS

Kingdoms, Cities, and Villages Within the Empire

City of Craterra: The largest city in the Kingdom of Caelestis, that is also closest to the borders of Draemor

Kingdom of Caelestis (Say-less-tis) - The northernmost kingdom in the Prilarean Empire

Kingdom of Draemor (Dray-more) - The southernmost kingdom in the Prilarean Empire

Kingdom of Mealioria (Meal-ee-or-ee-ah) - The kingdom south-east of Caelestis

Prilarean Empire (Pre-lar-ee-an) - The empire that holds the Kingdoms of Caelestis, Draemer, and Mealioria, along with a vast range of unclaimed land

Village of Elscara (Ell-scar-ah) - A village in the Kingdom of Caelestis

Village of Ferolla (Fur-oh-la) - A village in the Kingdom of Caelestis

Village of Vierallo (Vi-er-all-oh) - The village in the Kingdom of Caelestis that is closest to the castle grounds

Gods and Goddesses

Blythe, The Goddess of the Mind - The goddess has never gifted a mortal before, but if she were to, the chosen would be granted a constellastone, accompanied by unknown power

Cauis, The God of Ice and Snow (Kay-us) - Those gifted by Caius are granted a diamond jewel and the ability to manipulate all aspects of ice and snow, along with crafting the substances on demand

Eloise, The Goddess of Health and Healing (El-oh-leese) - Those gifted by Eloise are granted an amethyst gemstone and the ability to increase the healing time of those injured. In addition, some may mend injuries that have been considered life threatening

Emrys, The God of Fire (Em-ris) - Those gifted by Emrys are granted a ruby gemstone and the ability to manipulate all aspects of flame and summon fire on demand

Jesper, The God of Light and Darkness - Those gifted by Jesper are granted an topaz jewel and the ability to manipulate light and shadows

Sloane, The Goddess of Plants and Nature - Those gifted by Sloane are granted an emerald jewel and the ability to manipulate various forms of plants and nature

Thea, The Goddess of Water - Those gifted by Thea are granted a sapphire gemstone and the ability to manipulate all aspects of water, or summon water on demand

Zenith, The God of the Sky and Weather (Zen-ith) - Those gifted by Zenith are granted an onyx gemstone and the ability to manipulate the sky and various forms of weather conditions

Miscellaneous

Constellastone (Con-stell-ah-stone) - A jewel that is found at the crash site of fallen Jewel-Light meteors, originating from a dying star only when conditions are pristine

Jewel-Light Meteor Shower - A meteor shower occurring at the midway point of each calendar year in which colored cosmos that resemble the precious gemstones of the gods fall from the sky. During this meteor shower, all those who had been gifted that year will gain access to their powers

ABOUT THE AUTHOR

Liv Webster is a romance and fantasy author from a small town in Massachusetts. She has been writing ever since she was young, her first story being written at seven years old. This story was a Cinderella remake, in which the princess was a fish. As you can imagine, it did not end up on the bestseller list.

When she is not writing, Liv enjoys reading, baking, spending time at the beach, and all things science. She lives and breathes for her two sons, who are her greatest motivations to be the best version of herself. In addition, Liv is an avid mental health advocate, and showcases that in her writing with various themes of mental illness.

Website - www.authorlivwebster.com

Instagram - @authorlivwebster

www.ingramcontent.com/pod-product-compliance
Lightning Source LLC
Chambersburg PA
CBHW020931310726
48980CB00007B/724/J

* 9 7 9 8 9 9 9 8 8 8 9 2 1 *